JENN ASHWORTH

A Kind of Intimacy

Arcadia Books Ltd
15–16 Nassau Street
London W1W 7AB

www.arcadiabooks.co.uk

First published in the United Kingdom by Bliss Books, an imprint of Arcadia Books 2009
Copyright © Jenn Ashworth 2009

Jenn Ashworth has asserted her moral right to be identified as the author of this work in accordance with the Copyright, Designs and Patents Act, 1988.

A catalogue record for this book is available from the British Library.

ISBN 978-1-906413-06-4

Typeset in Minion by MacGuru Ltd
Printed in Finland by WS Bookwell

Epigraph from *The Sea* by John Banville is taken from the edition published by Picador, 2005; and epigraph from *Aspects of the Novel* by E.M. Forster is taken from the edition published by Penguin Books Ltd, 2000

Arcadia Books supports English PEN, the fellowship of writers who work together to promote literature and its understanding. English PEN upholds writers' freedoms in Britain and around the world, challenging political and cultural limits on free expression. To find out more, visit www.englishpen.org or contact English PEN, 6–8 Amwell Street, London EC1R 1UQ

Arcadia Books distributors are as follows:

in the UK and elsewhere in Europe:
Turnaround Publishers Services
Unit 3, Olympia Trading Estate
Coburg Road
London N22 6TZ

in the US and Canada:
Independent Publishers Group
814 N. Franklin Street
Chicago, IL 60610

in Australia:
Tower Books
PO Box 213
Brookvale, NSW 2100

in New Zealand:
Addenda
PO Box 78224
Grey Lynn
Auckland

in South Africa:
Quartet Sales and Marketing
PO Box 1218
Northcliffe
Johannesburg 2115

Arcadia Books is the *Sunday Times* Small Publisher of the Year

In daily life we never really understand each other, neither complete clairvoyance nor complete confessional exists. We know each other approximately, by external signs, and these serve well enough as a basis for society and even for intimacy.

E. M. Forster, *Aspects of the Novel*

The past beats inside me like a second heart.

John Banville, *The Sea*

Part One

1

After the van had been loaded and sent on its way I took off all my clothes and kicked the sofa I was about to abandon. Not just a little kick either. I really belted it.

That bloody sofa! Hairy, brownly uncomfortable, smelling of damp: the pile on the armrests was clogged flat, shiny with filth. Naked, my twenties nearly gone, and all I could think to do with myself was kick the settee. I threw my old clothes away as if they were dirty, giggling at the swishing sound my jumper made as it sailed through the room and made the lampshade swing. The air hit my skin and I stretched out my arms. I filled the room: as large and white as the removal van that had just left me. My thighs wobbled, dimpled with fat and puckered with stretch marks, and I saw myself kick again, hopping from one foot to another, breasts bouncing, arms shaking, getting out of breath.

What had a bit of furniture done to offend me? You might well ask. I'd been sitting on it when I'd been proposed to as a fat seventeen-year-old. I must have smelled the thing, must have realised that if he was going to get something nicer he would have done it already. If he'd had half a thought in his head he'd have done it before asking me to be his wife. I should have known but I was hopeful and grateful and I'd said yes. And I'd been sitting on it ever since. Almost every memory I have of Will, our marriage and my time in that house features that settee, and I've always bloody hated it.

You might be wondering how I put up with it for so long. I know I did. I can only explain it in terms of living near a farm, which I've done, or sleeping in a bedsit with walls so thin you can feel the trams shudder by, which I've done too. What starts off as intolerable, whether it's the smell of slurry or the rattle and creak of trams rocking on their tracks, eventually becomes merely irritating and in time, in a matter of months or years, you become immune to it. You've got to, haven't you? Some things you've got to stop thinking about, or you'd never survive.

Nine years, I spent, not thinking about it. You might get less for murder and it wasn't that I didn't ask him if we could get a new one. I remember bringing up the subject at least four or five times and each time he'd claw at the upholstery and thump the seat so hard the springs creaked. 'There's life in this yet, Annie. Consume less, share more! Reduce! Reuse! Recycle!'

At the sound of his voice in my head, I kicked it again – mainly to make some noise in the silent room, something to drown him out. I suppose I got carried away. My little episode went on some time; could have gone on longer but I stubbed my toe and had to stop, gasping, eyes watering, laughing in spite of the pain. The couch had spun back on its creaking castors to expose the one bit of the carpet that was still fluffy. Flowers and leaves curled around each other like snakes and for a while I couldn't stop laughing.

Mr Tips poked his nose between the bars of his cat-carrier, swished his tail and regarded me curiously with soft, clever eyes. Not green, but the colour of pond water. I bit my lip hard to make myself stop because I could see that I was upsetting him, then when I remembered that the taxi was coming for me I took a few deep breaths, wiped my eyes and started to dress.

The new clothes were folded neatly on the floor and I bit off the tags and slipped into them. Nothing fancy: I knew I'd have a long day. I'd bought fawn-coloured leggings and a long T-shirt the colour of a Christmas tree. Soft, cottony white underwear and brown sandals so my wide feet could splay in comfort. They smelled like the carrier bag they'd come in, which was good: I didn't want to smell like this house, or even like the fabric conditioner Will and I used. Had used.

When I left, I poked my head around the living-room door to give the sofa one final contemptuous glance, then picked up Mr Tips and went, banging the door shut behind me and only looking back to post my key through the letter box.

Out on the grey street, dark shapes hovered behind net curtains, looking. I placed the cat-carrier gently onto the pavement and hummed cheerfully as I waited, looking back evenly at the narrow cladded terraces and wondering if I would miss being stared at and feeling like a celebrity. I could sense eyes touching me: some hostile, some curious, some, I like to imagine, wishing me well. Then the taxi was at the kerb, I stepped into it and disappeared from the street forever.

There's black and white television footage of Jackie Kennedy getting out of an aeroplane. She's tiptoeing down the steps, her hair like sculpted soap, waving gently with white-gloved hands to the people waiting for her and looking smiley and sophisticated and the tiniest bit puzzled at all the fuss. I felt a bit like that. My sandals slapped the pavement as I got out of the taxi and I only noticed the sound because I was in the suburbs and rare quiet descended like the curtain between first class and the rest of the plane. I could hear children and a dog barking, but the sounds were far away on the main road, emphasising the relative quietness of the street.

Even the air was different, like I was in a new country. It smelled less like the sea, less like discarded chip papers and candyfloss. It was clean, full of the alive, warm smell of wet gardens and flower beds beginning their April bloom.

'That's eight pounds.'

The tone of the taxi driver suggested he'd had to repeat himself, and I turned to pay him quickly, fumbling in my handbag for my purse. I was light-hearted enough to pass him a ten-pound note and let him keep the change. He nodded his thanks, waited until I unloaded the cat-carrier, and then drove on. I watched the taxi turn at the bottom of the cul-de-sac and rumble away. That the cab was the last link between my future and what I used to be, and it was gone. I wasn't scared, I was euphoric.

Along the road closed doors and windows made shinily opaque with reflections lined up around me like a dream. I was eager to make a start with meeting people and part of me had expected a welcome from one of the neighbours but nothing interrupted the quiet except me. Well, it stood to reason. It was a Wednesday, mid-morning: anyone worth talking to would be busy at work. I clutched my handbag against my body, found the new keys in my coat pocket and pushed open the gate.

I could have rushed in, I felt like it, but I forced myself to wait. I knew I'd be in and out of that door thousands of times in the years that lay ahead of me, and I'd already been through it twice when I was viewing the house. But this time I wouldn't have to knock: I had my own key in my hand fresh from the solicitor's brown envelope, and I'd only get to do this once. I'd never been carried over a threshold before, but the feeling I had was probably something like the one a bride experiences on first entering her marital home. I looked at the windows and twirled the key around between my fingers. I still miss the place, even now.

The previous occupants had only left that morning, and the smell of air freshener hit me as soon as I walked in. A bulb upstairs had been left on and yellow light trickled down the carpet from the top step to the hall. Mr Tips was yowling in his carrier wanting to be let out, so I put him in one of the upstairs bedrooms and locked him in, then started looking around, feeling silly for wanting to knock on the doors and tiptoe across the landing. I walked softly, slowly, but then again I never run. When I do, I tend to lift and subside under my clothes; people stare at me rippling and sometimes they laugh. Moving gently has become a habit I keep even when I'm alone. I went through the house testing the door handles and pulling open the windows. I coughed, and startled myself by making an echo on the landing.

There were light patches on the wallpaper where pictures had been taken down, depressions in the carpet: the ghostly traces of where someone else's bed and wardrobe had been. A family used to live here: I met the woman and her little boy when I came to see the place. The window in the smallest bedroom was decorated with stickers of robots and spaceships, a mottled splotch of old bubblegum still ground into the carpet. I ran my fingers over the edge of the bath, the banister, the light switches and door frames, and my tour complete, went back downstairs to take a meter reading and wait.

The van arrived a few minutes later, and as I went down the path to greet it, my neighbour's door opened and a man came out.

'You've picked a good day for it,' he said, with a familiarity that pleased me. He glanced up at the sky, blue and cloudless. 'And a good time too – half an hour earlier and you'd have run into the last lot coming out! Surprised you didn't see their van. I'm Neil, by the way.'

'Annie,' I said.

'One of your vans, was it? Same company? You coordinate the times and that?' He nodded, as if I'd answered him. 'Makes sense.'

'Excuse me?' I said. I was smiling: he was being so friendly and it was just what I'd imagined, but I had the feeling I was missing something.

'The family not arrived yet? I've a spare key if you're stuck. Might as well get going – you might be able to knock off early if that's all there is.'

'We're all here,' I said doubtfully, 'and I've got my own key.' It was still in my hand and I showed it to him. I was like that, those first few days: carrying it about with me just to get the thrill every time I looked at it.

Neil frowned, rubbed the back of his head, and then smiled, 'I am sorry,' he said, much more formally, and grimacing. 'I thought you were with the... well, never mind. Welcome to the street!'

I realised, too late, what he'd thought, and became aware I was hardly dressed for meeting new people. I'd been so caught up in the practicalities I hadn't considered the other aspects to the day, and would have been pickier about my apparel if I had. Knowing I was going to be busy, I'd opted for comfort rather than style. I laughed uncomfortably, plucked at my T-shirt and dropped my key on the path.

'These are just old clothes,' I said, 'just something for moving the boxes about. I've got much nicer things to wear than this!'

'Do you need a hand with anything?' he asked, nodding towards the van.

'Oh no, they'll bring it all in for me,' I said. 'I don't have much.' We moved away from my side of the path to let them pass and were standing on the grass in front of his house. There were a few moments of silence as we watched the man open the back of the van and heave boxes out onto the pavement.

Neil moved his head and looked over my shoulder into the house. 'Have you left the little girl with someone else? I suppose she'd be better off out of it today, until you get sorted.'

'Excuse me?' I said, smiling. He was casually dressed and stood several inches shorter than me. There was nothing striking about his appearance, he had one of those average faces framed by messy dark hair. He was probably mistaken a lot for someone else. In actual fact I had the odd sensation that I had met him somewhere before.

'Your daughter?' he said, and when I shook my head, he looked confused.

'Charlotte, the woman who's just moved out – I'm sure she said you had a daughter. Mikey was making her promise you weren't going to paint his room pink!' He laughed, and I shook my head again, feeling sick.

'It's only me,' I said slowly, 'and my cat. Just the two of us. Perhaps Charlotte got me mixed up with someone else?'

What had I told her that for? Honestly, you can sit me down with a cup of tea and a packet of biscuits and ten minutes later you've got my whole life story. I clamped my lips together to stop any more noise coming out until I'd decided how I was going to approach things. There was no point making a fresh start if you were going to bring all of the old junk along with you and I certainly didn't want new friends to become unnecessarily embroiled in my history.

'She must have got the wrong end of the stick. Never mind.' He shrugged agreeably and the motion seemed to clear the air. The van started reversing, making a beeping noise, and we stood back from the pavement and watched it make its slow progress.

'I'll let you have that spare key,' he said, 'while we're here.'

'I've got a key,' I said again, fumbling on the path for it.

The man shook his head and spoke more slowly, 'No, a spare one. Charlotte used to leave it with me in case Mikey came back early from school and needed to get in. She didn't trust him with his own. It's in the house.'

'Oh, I see!' I laughed. 'My head's spaghetti with all this,' I gestured towards the van, 'I've been up since the crack of dawn.'

'I'll bring it out for you,' he said, 'or just post it through the letter box if you're busy, shall I?' he said, and started to move towards his house.

'No need for that,' I said, 'why don't you keep it? Just in case of emergencies. I don't know what you all do around here but I'm perfectly happy to take one of yours if it's the done thing. I'm very trustworthy!' I smiled reassuringly but the men were already getting down from the front of the van and looking at me for instructions. I had to turn away and direct them into the house so I missed his reply.

'Shall I give you a hand until your husband gets here?' he asked, nodding towards the van, 'I'm hardly Mr Muscle, but Lucy, that's my girlfriend, you'll meet her – she gets a bit tense sometimes. The noise of the other lot this morning put her off her yoga practice, or something.' He leaned forward confidentially, 'Actually, she sent me out to help so the van would be away faster. Better look busy, hadn't I?'

'Oh no,' I said, 'they'll bring it all in for me. I don't have much. And there isn't a husband. Just me.'

I didn't like having to repeat myself like that. It made me want to lean over to his ear and shout what I'd much rather whisper. He opened his mouth – 'I know,' I said, slightly irritably, 'Charlotte must have been mistaken.'

There was a long pause, and we stood behind the front gate and watched the men open the back of the van. They started heaving the boxes onto the pavement. I was pointing at the labels and telling them what to put where when I heard a door close and realised Neil had slipped away back inside his own house.

I wasn't trying to be polite when I told Neil that I didn't have much: it was true. The van was a small one, and in half an hour it was empty, the movers were gone and I was alone again. It wasn't as if I didn't have any nice things of my own, but once I knew for sure I'd be getting away, I wanted to hurry, and leave all the reminders of my old life behind me. It made the packing easier: I just handpicked what I wanted to take, and abandoned everything else. Because of that, I was low on furniture, and my first night in the new house was a restless one. I spent it huddled on a neon-pink airbed meant for floating about in the sea. Around midnight, Mr Tips came up and decided to play on it, striding up and down until he finally snagged the plastic with his claws. The air hissed out, and for the rest of the night I had to be content with the floor.

Awake before dawn, I went downstairs, feeling unsettled and disoriented. I didn't have a television yet, and my radio was still packed, so I was considering hunting for a book or a magazine when I heard the quiet hum of a vehicle in front of my house. A peek through the closed curtains and the sound of glass clinking told me what I already knew: the milkman was doing his rounds. That's when I made my first mistake.

'You're up early, aren't you?' In my defence, he did speak to me first. I'd been waiting for him on the step in my dressing gown and I'd given him a little wave as he stopped the float and pulled a crate out of the back. He had a friendly voice and he spoke loudly, as if he didn't care what time in the morning it was. He checked something on a clipboard and bent to deposit a milk bottle at Neil's door.

'I can't sleep, never could,' I said. 'Always been a bad sleeper. I was lying there in bed listening to the birds and then I heard you coming, so I thought I might as well get up and make myself a cup of tea.'

I knew there was a trick to it: I wonder sometimes if I'd still be able to do it, given the opportunity. Raise my voice a notch or two; twiddle with my hair. It had worked in the past and I saw no reason to assume that it wouldn't work again.

'Well, that's one thing you can't do without, milk.' He winked, and started to walk away.

'You must be used to it, though, being up early,' I called after him.

He turned back. I couldn't tell, at first, if he was the kind of man that might appreciate a larger woman. It was worth a try.

'I'm up with the birds every day except Sunday,' he said cheerfully, 'even God gets a lie in on Sunday. Unlike him though, I also get the bank holidays, so I reckon my job's a bit better than his.'

I laughed quietly, and looked at my feet. Men like it when you laugh at their jokes. I didn't say anything for a few seconds to give him a chance to see the rosy cheeks, the dimples and the upturned nose, the extra layers of flesh under my chin and the huge swaying shelf of my chest.

'Well, seeing as it's still only Thursday and one way or another, both of us are up and about, how about a tea break? I've got the kettle on already; teabags are in the pot.'

He looked closely at me, and I made sure he could see a fold of pale, damp-seeming cleavage as I modestly tucked in the gown. He gave me another wink and tucked his clipboard under his arm.

'That's the best offer I've had in about two days,' he said, 'but I've got three more streets to do before I'm due home and if the wife doesn't get her cup of tea in bed in,' he made a show of looking at his watch, 'ooh, an hour and a half's time, my life's not worth living.'

I nodded, and tucked my hair behind my ears, not bothering about the gown flapping open now. Nothing ventured, and all that. I'd learned not to take it personally. I'm not to everybody's taste. A friend of mine, Boris, told me I was a minority interest, like collecting Stilton jars or learning to fold paper birds.

'Well, just remember the insomniac at number forty-seven if you ever fancy a chat. We're all very friendly round here,' I said, thinking of Neil, 'even if it doesn't seem it first thing in the morning!'

He touched the brim of an imaginary hat with his finger, and walked away. I went back into the house, humming deliberately cheerfully because I was already dreading the blank sound the door made as it clicked shut emptily behind me.

When I'd made the tea and sat at the window watching the street get light that morning, I reflected on my actions and far from feeling rejected, breathed a sigh of relief that my plans for the milkman had been frustrated. Sometimes, I've realised, life is kind and saves you from yourself. It would take time to get used to a new house, and a brief period of solitude in the interim was to be expected. In fact, it would probably do me good. I'd been, despite all my hopes and plans, perilously close to returning to my old ways and scuppering the programme of self development and personal progress I had mentally set in place.

There were noises from next door as Neil and his yoga-loving girlfriend got up and started their day. I sipped my tea, wondered what they were having for breakfast, and now I had peace and time to think, tried to remember where I'd seen him before.

2

The next incident of note in those early days occurred during Neil's barbecue – it was on that evening that I was confronted with the unpleasant reality of the woman I had the misfortune to call my neighbour. It was early June – I remember because I'd only been in the house three weeks – and the weather was bright and warm, for once, and just right for a barbecue.

I smiled as I heard his friends arrive. My windows were open and I heard laughter, cheeks being kissed, wine unwrapped from crinkling paper. A barbecue with my neighbours would be a perfect start to a friendship, and I'd been on my own in the house for long enough. They probably assumed a last-minute knock on the door would suffice, as I was so near to them an official invitation was unnecessary – it goes without saying.

When I smelled the meat cooking I brushed my hair and hesitated behind my front door for their knock. It wasn't forthcoming so I slipped off my shoes and went into the kitchen to wait in a spot where I could hear them in the back. It was warm enough to leave the kitchen door ajar: all the smoke and cooking smells were drifting right in over their garden fence. It made me hungry and I put the cooker on to grill some sausages for myself. Perhaps they'd decided on a more formal meal, and I'd be invited round for drinks afterwards. It would be better to eat now, I thought, rather than go hungry and demolish a plate of nibbles on my own. Mr Tips coiled around my legs as I cooked, and, indulgently, I dropped one of the sausages into his bowl and listened to him purr as I stood at the cooker.

I took my plate and glass out into the garden and sat on the back step to eat. The sounds of people chatting came over the high fence and I tapped my foot gently to the music. I'd burned the sausages a little, and didn't have anything like salad in the fridge, so I'd put a dollop of mayonnaise on the side, a couple of slices of buttered bread, and, because I like to be healthy, some broccoli I had in the freezer. It was lovely. Something told me Neil wouldn't mind me sharing the music and I was pleased the afternoon had presented me with an opportunity to get to know him a little better. For a while I sat like that, listening to the music and losing myself in my thoughts, tracing my finger around and around the Greek key pattern that circled the edge of my plate.

After the incident with the milkman I'd given serious thought to my goals in life and so had renewed my membership at the library. I availed myself fully of the facilities on offer, using the Internet, borrowing inspirational DVDs and in particular, had started reading certain books on the subject of personal development. I'd grown in confidence and was certain that my behaviour where the milkman was concerned was an isolated mishap. From my books I'd learned that the best way to form new friendships was to develop an attitude of willingness, to fit in and be flexible; in other words, to try things you ordinarily wouldn't. I remember thinking, as I finished my own food and put the plate down beside me on the step, what a good idea a barbecue was. Maybe the idea of throwing my own party was forming in my mind that afternoon. I sat admiring the clink of the wine bottle against the glasses as drink was generously poured, imagining how nice it would be if I had a house full of people too.

At first I couldn't hear much of what was said, but as the guests drank more they started to get louder and I felt more confident getting nearer to the fence, knowing that I wouldn't disturb them. I hovered there for quite some time, feeling happy hearing them laugh and imagining myself as a kind of guardian angel to ward off accidents while they could relax and have fun. They talked about their jobs a lot, and people they knew. It sounds silly, but even though I wasn't joining in, I liked the company. It wasn't that I'd been lonely: apart from the milkman I'd had two or three chats with library assistants and a woman who worked behind the counter in the cream-cake shop.

When it got cooler I realised evening was coming and I probably wasn't going to be asked for drinks. Dejected, I fetched a cardigan and went back to my lookout post. It was better than nothing. Eventually I heard them talking about me.

'Have you met your new neighbour yet?' someone asked.

'No. Neil has, but she's only been here a couple of weeks,' replied a female voice, high-pitched and happy sounding. I'd heard Lucy's voice before; out shrieking at spiders in the garden or yelling commands up the stairs to Neil.

'We should go round, really, and take her something for the house,' Neil said.

Someone else asked a question, but the words were indistinct.

'No, I don't know what she does. I thought she was coming with a family too, but she says Charlotte must have had her wires crossed. You don't like to ask too much, do you? She hangs around the place a lot during the week. Doesn't work, by the looks of it,' Neil said, and I was touched that he'd been feeling the connection growing, assisted by nothing more than proximity. I was looking forward to us becoming friends and I wracked my brains. Where had I heard his voice before? If he'd played some part in my past I wanted to know about it and be prepared before I got any friendlier with him.

I put my glass down on the step and stood up. It seemed like a good idea to get closer to the fence, and I tried to move silently. If I bent my head at a certain angle I could see in to Neil's garden through a gap between two warped boards. There were four of them sitting around the plastic table. The two guests were sitting with their backs to me but between them I could get a fairly good view of Neil. I was surprised to see that the girl with the laugh, Lucy, was sitting on his lap. He had a hand on her bare calf, and was stroking it possessively.

I looked at her as closely as my limited point of view would allow, noticed her short white dress, flip-flops, and a crocheted navy cardigan that didn't match thrown casually over the top. It was too big for her, and every time she brought her glass to her lips she had to move the cuff out of the way of her mouth. She lifted her head from Neil's shoulder and started playing with the hair on the back of his neck. She was young, very young, but the skin around her eyes and mouth had already started to fray and I wondered if she was a smoker.

'I've never met her,' she said, 'heard her thumping about all hours, though.' She sniffed, 'Even in the night. Still, I suppose she'll be unpacking.'

The woman with her back to me said, 'Well, why don't you invite her? There's food left, isn't there? Get her to bring a bottle and come over for a while.'

I held my breath and quickly checked my appearance. There was a spot of grease on my sleeve from the sausage, but I could have quickly changed my blouse. Yes, why not? I could have gone over. It's only fair: I didn't get to go to parties very often.

Lucy shook her head and said something, I didn't quite catch it, and the other woman spoke again. 'What's wrong with her? It's nice to get to know your neighbours. You're sat in front of your computer all day, Neil – stuck in the house. If you'd invited her round for a meal when she first moved in you'd be inseparable by now!' Someone laughed, and tried to interrupt her, but she carried on. 'You're anti-social buggers, you two. It won't always be like this, you know – wrapped up in each other.'

I saw her turn towards the man she was with and start gesturing at him drunkenly with an unlit cigarette. 'Do you remember when we were like that? Quite happy to lock ourselves in all weekend so we could stay in bed and eat pizza? Where does it all go to, eh?' she laughed bitterly and looked at Lucy, who wasn't listening, as far as I could tell. 'You've only been together a year. You wait and see. It'll get to the point where you don't even like each other anymore.'

The man with her, I assumed he was her husband, touched her arm gently as if to warn her but she recoiled. 'What?' she said, incredulous, 'it's true!'

There was a pause when no one spoke, and then she shook her honey-coloured high-lighted hair out of her face and said, 'She'll know you're having a party anyway, all the noise we're making,' and I knew she was talking about me again.

'You make it sound like *The Good Life*,' her husband said abruptly. 'There's a good reason people don't duck into each other's houses these days.'

'And what's that?'

'They're always nuts!' he laughed, and leaned back in his chair. 'Nuts, or single mothers with kids that are going to trash the garden, or asylum seekers, or squatters, or drug dealers, or paedos...'

'You're being ridiculous,' she said, 'if she was a terrorist they'd have known about it by now.' She turned to Lucy, 'Go on, invite her over. It'll be nice. You got on with the last lot, didn't you?'

The glasses clinked, and I saw Lucy put a finger to her lips and point at the fence. She was wearing pink nail varnish, but no engagement or wedding ring. I felt exposed, and stood up straight, thinking that if I made a move to go into the house, I'd be heard, and it would be obvious. I wasn't sure what to do. I kept still, standing there and looking at my reflection in the glass of the kitchen door, and decided that if I was asked, I'd say I was merely checking the fence for safety against burglars. Lucy was whispering something about me. Because she was drunk it wasn't much of a whisper, I could hear everything, every wet hiccup and throaty giggle.

'She hangs about and *listens*,' she said, putting her hand over her mouth, and spluttering between her fingers.

There was a muffled laugh from the other girl. I was disappointed with her, because I'd decided that Neil's female guest seemed like a decent enough person and someone to whom I could chat quite easily, should they decide to invite me over.

'Maybe she fancies you, Neil. Doesn't everybody?' she laughed again, asked for a light and more wine. 'Or maybe, Lucy, it's you she's after!' This set everyone off, and there was a period of time, I'm not sure how long, when all I could hear was hard, retching laughter. They settled, and Lucy went on.

'No, I mean it, it's really creepy. When I'm in the kitchen I can hear her sometimes, doing her washing-up, and it makes me feel as if she's following me about the house. I was taking a shit the other day and I was convinced she was standing in her bathroom with her ear to the wall!'

What can I say? There wasn't the opportunity to defend myself, but if there had been, I would have pointed out that first, I didn't much care for her language, tipsy or not, and secondly, our bathrooms *were* next door to each other and where else was I supposed to go? They laughed drunkenly, and it hurts me to say so but there's no point in covering up the truth: Neil's rumbling, friendly laugh was the loudest. Still, Neil was obviously one of those people who are apt to laugh at anything once they've had a couple of drinks inside them. I've behaved the same way myself.

The man with them stood up, and tapped on the fence with a finger. The panels vibrated and I had a terrible feeling that some part of it would fall away and I would be left standing there for them all to see.

'Do you think she's there now?' he said, in an exaggerated whisper. 'Maybe she's waiting until we go so she can throw her knickers over at the pair of you. You should ask her back for a threesome!'

'Have you seen the size of her?' said Lucy, and laughed again. 'She's massive!'

'Come on, don't be cruel,' Neil said mildly, and I was grateful.

'Throw her knickers over?' Lucy giggled. 'I've seen them on the line: like bloody parachutes. Tents! Duvet covers! She must get them specially made!' There was another bout of laughter but Lucy, perhaps realising she had gone too far and was only embarrassing herself, stood up to change the music.

It's true, I am a large woman, although I'm very happy with my size, thank you very much, and true beauty, as we all know, comes from within. Still, when I heard those words I tiptoed inside and closed the door gently behind me. It must have clicked too loudly because even with it shut and a chair against it I could hear them banging on the table, laughing their guts up.

In the dim, sausage-smelling quiet of my kitchen, I held on to the edge of the draining board so tightly it left white ridges on my palms. I looked at the taps, at the plug hole, and the chrome top of the new pedal bin caught my eye. I lifted the lid, eyeing a bruised banana skin and some chicken bones. My head started to throb: feeling as hot and swollen as an over-filled hot-water bottle. I bit my lip and tried to think about water and aspirin.

I was angry, to tell you the truth. To have to stand there in the sanctuary of my own garden, doing nothing more sinister than enjoying a warm evening, and then suffer the verbal assault of a woman I'd never even met, well, it was more than I could take.

My hands started to hurt again and I looked at them, surprised at the grazes on my knuckles. I'd been hitting the wall above the pedal bin with my fists, over and over without realising it. I can't tell you how long had passed, me standing looking into the bin and thumping the wall like that. It couldn't have been more than a matter of minutes: when I held my breath I could hear, above the sound of my own blood booming in my ears, the continuing music and laughter from outside.

I took a few deep breaths in an attempt to get myself back on an even keel. There was a dark, sweetly tempting smell inside the bin, like the sour air between my body and the duvet in the morning, or the dead space in the back of airing cupboards. It reminded me of my mum emptying the bin every night when I was a child. She was a fastidious woman and lived by many rules, one of them being that rubbish would not sit in the house overnight. All the bins were emptied last thing, and I don't think she could get herself to bed and rest until it was done. Even when it was snowing, or she was ill, she'd do it all the same, and I stood there inhaling the stink from my own waste and remembering my mother struggling to lift out the bags, wincing at the pain in her side as the carrot tops and potato peelings spilled onto the floor. More deep breaths, and then the memory and the smell together made me want to get the rubbish out of my house as quickly as I could.

I scooped out the contents softly, filled both fists and went out the front of the house to push the whole lot through Lucy's letter box. They were making so much noise out there in the garden she wouldn't even notice, and by the time they did there'd be a filthy mess to clean up on the hall carpet. I went back into my house, and returned to the pedal bin, making silent trips back and forth until it was empty.

'Annie reacts with appropriate anger when her human rights are infringed,' I recited, which was an assertiveness affirmation I'd picked up from one of the new books. You were supposed to write them on slips of paper and stick them to all the mirrors in the house, but there were too many, the scraps of paper kept falling off and drifting to the carpet like oblong snowflakes, and so I just spent some time learning them instead. I said it ten times as I washed my bloody and dirtied hands with lily of the valley liquid soap then I went to my bedroom for a lie down. I stayed up there for a couple of hours, only coming down to get a tub of ice cream and a tin of condensed milk because I hadn't eaten anything since the sausages, and I was hungry again.

You don't need to tell me: I know I demeaned only myself that evening. When I got up the next morning I knew it, and pushed my new couch over to the window so I could look out of it while I nursed my sugar hangover. I saw Lucy leave the house, and return a few hours later laden with shopping bags. I didn't dare to go out myself in case Neil approached me and asked me what I was playing at. I decided that Lucy herself deserved putting straight on a thing or two, but my actions, the incident with the rubbish, affected Neil as well as her and so was manifestly unfair.

Now that I think about it again, it is also possible that I may have misunderstood the snatches of conversation that I heard, or my memory was playing tricks on me. It is likely that, not sleeping well in my new house, surrounded by items of flat-packed furniture I hadn't yet been able to assemble, I was slightly unsettled and more emotionally sensitive than is usual for me.

As I reflected on my behaviour and realised how out-of-character and unreasonable it was I grew more and more embarrassed about how volatile I had been, and began to feel guilty. I probably blew what I'd done out of all proportion; it was just a slip, a minor one, like the incident with the milkman, but I started to wonder how I could make it up to them, and thought about knocking on their door, confessing, and asking for their understanding and compassion. I probably would have done too, but out on an errand two days later, I met Lucy on the street, swinging her hair about and wearing a clingy white vest, which left the protrusions of her nipples highly visible.

'You're Annie, aren't you?' she said, smiling brightly. She didn't seem to notice my nervousness and welcomed me to the neighbourhood. She even introduced herself to me as if we were about to embark on some great friendship. We chatted for a few minutes, and then she told me to watch out for the boys who hung about at the bus stop, got drunk on bottles of cider, and were apt to play pranks.

'Little beggars,' she said, 'I was on my hands and knees soaping the hall carpet for half an hour. I was never allowed out at that time when I was their age, were you?'

'It does sound worrying,' I said, uncomfortably. 'Did anyone see anything?'

She was much taller than me, as tall as a model, perhaps, and I felt squat and clumsy standing in front of her, all too aware of her previous comments. I pulled my cardigan around my chest and knotted the cord tightly.

'We had people round, so we were out in the garden. You should have been there, we had a right laugh. Come over sometime,' she said, 'once you get yourself sorted out.'

'I'm almost there,' I lied, 'just a few more boxes to go.' I was carrying a bag of empty food tins, which I was planning to take down to the recycling bins that were outside the shop on the main road. The smell of ripe cat food and fermenting tomato juice wafted up between us and made me feel nauseous. I took a step backwards, worried that she might think the odour was coming from me, but not wanting to explain. She didn't seem to notice.

'I know, it takes ages, doesn't it!' she said. 'Let us know if you need a hand with any lifting or carrying.'

I smiled and went on my way, but her hypocrisy had jolted me out of my guilt, and I knew that from then on I'd have to watch out for her.

The very next day, I spoke to Neil again and finally remembered where I'd come across him. I was getting ready for a bath when the light bulb in the bathroom blew, and try as I might, I simply could not reach up to replace it. This discouraged me more than I liked to admit, and I was forced to acknowledge how dependent I'd become on a man's help in the previous years. I considered leaving the bathroom door open and bathing in the light from the bulb in the landing, but I didn't like the idea of that and so, reluctantly, put on my dressing gown and went next door to ask for Neil's help.

He came with me into the house. I led him up the stairs and gave him the bulb. I was feeling a little silly, standing there in my dressing gown with a man I hardly knew balancing on the edge of the bath, but he did it cheerfully enough. Becoming too independent, as I tried to remind myself, wasn't in my best interests. *Alone But Not Lonely: Starting Again*, had advised that however painful it was in the short term to have an empty space at the table, to struggle with the shopping bags and fill the long evenings when it seemed everyone else was surrounded with loved ones, it was better that than filling the gap left so completely that there would never be room for anyone else.

Neil jumped down from the bath, slid on the bathmat and bumped his elbow on the radiator. He swore, and I flinched, thinking he was angry with me.

'Sorry, sorry about that,' he said, noticing me shrink away. 'My elbow. Got me right on the funny bone. My own fault: gymnastics in a room this small! I only just got it in, Lucy does this kind of thing normally – she's loads taller than me.'

'I didn't think to stand on the bath,' I said, feeling sheepish.

'Don't worry about it,' he replied, smiling, 'we wouldn't want you falling and getting stuck, would we?'

He had a nice, deep, friendly voice, with a vaguely southern accent, and he spoke slowly, which I liked. It was as if he wanted to think very carefully about everything he was going to say before he spoke and he didn't mind taking a bit of time doing it. More than that, he didn't mind me taking up a bit of his time; he wasn't in a rush to leave or anything like that. I thought about offering him a cup of tea, but the water in the bath was cooling.

'You've got a lot of books in here,' he said. I coughed gently, embarrassed about the stacks of thin romance novels piled up on the toilet cistern. Their pink and purple spines screamed in the white tiled blandness of the room, and I resisted the urge to throw a flannel in their direction in order to hide the cover of one of the more lurid ones. It wasn't that I was ashamed: those who aren't experiencing relationships in real life might as well read about them in order to keep their hands in; it was just that some people make judgements about others based on the smallest things and I wanted to make a good impression on Neil.

'They're not real books,' I said, 'not clever or anything. Just a bit of escapism. I like having a soak every now and again and reading something while I'm in there.' I laughed for some reason, I don't know why.

'Nothing wrong with that,' he said, and moved towards the door. 'I'll let you get on with your bath. Don't worry about seeing me out.' He was on the landing with his hand on the banister and something about the expression on his face had made me remember, all of a sudden, where I'd seen him before.

Back when I was still living on the other side of Fleetwood, in the house of the brown sofa, I'd got into a bit of trouble one afternoon. It wasn't my fault, just one of those things, and I needed to get myself on a bus as soon as possible. I'd broken one of my own rules and actually ran to the bus stop, everything I had jiggling about – much to the amusement of the teenagers who crammed the pavement queuing for chips. To add insult to injury, when I'd got to the stop and managed, through blurred vision, to consult the timetable, I realised I'd just missed the bus I wanted and had another twenty minutes to wait.

I was sitting there, trying to appear inconspicuous but actually feeling very shaken and distressed, when a man walked past me, obviously on his way to somewhere else. I looked up, and when our eyes met he drew his breath in quickly and stopped.

'Do you need any help, love?' he'd asked, and come right up close to me. I wiped my hand across my nostrils and patted the hot skin over my eye gently. Blood was trickling from my lips between my teeth and because I was in public, I was resisting the almost over-whelming urge to spit, instead letting the greasy, metallic liquid slip down my throat. I was having trouble sitting on the bench in the shelter because of my ribs, and had propped myself against it, unable, because of the pain, to even bend and tie my shoelaces or rearrange my clothing. It would be an understatement to say I was quite dishevelled and in no fit state to meet new people. I moved my hand gingerly and tried to wave him away, but he frowned and came closer.

'Look at the state of you,' he'd said, and, when I didn't answer, raised his voice. 'Can you hear me all right?'

I'm afraid that given my state, I was probably quite rude to him, because I remember him frowning, and saying, 'I'm not trying to interfere in your business. But you can't walk about like that: you should be on your way to hospital!' He was right: I was bleeding quite heavily and he took a tissue from his back pocket and gave it to me.

'I've got a phone in my bag; let me call someone for you. Is there someone I can get, someone to pick you up?' I'd taken the tissue, held it against my nose, and shook my head.

'I'll be fine very soon,' I said thickly, through swollen lips, 'it's not as bad as it looks.'

'Are you waiting for the bus?' he said, and I nodded, my head jangling. He dipped his hand back into his pocket and pressed some folded money into my fist.

'Do yourself a favour and get a taxi,' he'd said. 'If you aren't going to let me call someone, at least do that for me, eh?'

A few people had passed me by while I'd been sitting there, avoiding my eye and walking more quickly as if the sight of me offended them. Once Neil had started to talk to me, it seemed to open the floodgates and soon three others were standing in a neat semi-circle behind him, carrier bags resting on the pavement, faces stretched with curiosity. I turned my head away, clung to the popped buttons of my blouse and started to cry. The wailing hurt, and the blood and saliva leaking out of my mouth embarrassed me, so I started to cry more and it was a few minutes before I could get myself under control or was aware of anything except what I was feeling.

Neil had turned to the others and waved them away.

'She's all right,' he said loudly, 'she's going to get a taxi to the hospital.' When a persistent straggler remained, he stepped towards her and shook his head.

'What this lady does not need is an audience. Now,' he turned back towards me and helped me stand, 'are you going to let me walk you to the taxi rank?'

I shook my head and after a few minutes of protest, the money going back and forth between us and him searching his rucksack for another tissue, he sighed, and left me standing at the bus stop with his paper money getting sticky in my hand.

I'm certain that man was Neil: I'd spent minutes watching him walk along the street and saw him look over his shoulder at me once or twice until he turned a corner and disappeared. And there he was, standing in my house with an empty light-bulb box in his hand and he'd just helped me again. I didn't know what to make of it but I knew I didn't need to worry about him recognising me: my face was so swollen that afternoon my own mother would have had trouble knowing who I was.

'I've decided to have a house-warming party,' I said abruptly as he started to go down the stairs. 'You and Lucy are invited, of course.'

'That sounds nice. Get all your old friends around to see the new pad?'

'I'll put an official invitation through your door,' I tried not to think about the barbecue, 'but just so you know.'

'I'll tell Lucy,' he said, 'she likes an excuse to buy earrings.'

I nodded and closed the bathroom door behind me, hearing him slam the front door a couple of seconds later.

My decision to throw a house-warming party wasn't as impulsive as it sounds, although it was only after Neil had left that I started to think about the matter seriously. Like I say, his barbecue had given me the idea, and the fact that I'd been established in the new house almost a month by then and had yet to receive any visitors spurred me on. It was time, I thought, to become proactive, and create the kind of life I wanted for myself. Having a party would be the first step on the path to achieving this, and would also, I realised, be a good way to keep an eye on Lucy, if, as I already suspected, she sensed the power of that chance connection between Neil and I, and was planning to do something to spoil it.

3

I made thirty invitations for my party from three sheets of pink cardboard, and wrote the time and the date on them with a silver glitter pen. After agonising for a whole afternoon over whether writing 'bring a bottle' on the invitation was rude or not, I finally compromised by writing the words in tiny letters in the corner of the card, where they could easily be overlooked or ignored. I posted an invitation through each letter box on the street one evening after tea, giving three days' notice which I thought would be sufficient for a casual gathering. I expected maybe ten or twenty people to attend, and catered accordingly.

On the day, I pushed my new coffee table against the wall and put six bottles of wine, a cheese and pickled onion hedgehog, a bowl of Twiglets and a plate of fairy cakes on it. There were plenty more cakes in the kitchen and a tray of sausage rolls warming in the oven. I hoovered the curtains and the lampshade, and thought about making a mad dash into town and getting scented candles on sticks for the garden. They sell them in Woolworth's and as well as providing a party atmosphere, they also keep the midges away. I decided against it in the end: I hadn't managed to lay my hands on a patio set so there seemed little point.

When I thought everything was ready for the guests I went to the bathroom to shower and dress, and then in the half hour before the party was due to start, worried about being under-catered, and opened two packets of ready salted crisps into a cereal bowl, which I placed on the mantelpiece. The crisps were a little soft, and the bowl wasn't a real serving bowl, but people didn't notice these things at parties, not when the wine was flowing, and there would be enough wine, I was sure of it. I'd gone without any treats for a week so I could afford the bottles, and people would bring their own too, it was only polite.

Although I was nervous, I smiled as I waited, flitting about the house making sure everything was straight and wishing my old neighbours could see me. I wasn't that traumatised naked woman hysterically kicking at a sofa anymore: I was the hostess of a house-warming party, wearing a fancy party dress and patiently awaiting her guests.

There was a knock at the door. It thought it would be Neil; it would make sense for him to arrive first because he was only next door, but it still surprised me: I'd popped upstairs to use the lavatory a couple of times and I hadn't heard him have a shower yet. I adjusted the straps on my dress, wiped a smudge of lipstick from my teeth and hurried to the hallway.

A pale, chubby man wearing a white jacket and a pair of blue jeans stood on the doorstep expectantly. The smell of his aftershave, something soapy and alcoholic, wafted into my house as he stepped forward. In one hand he was carrying four cans of lager by the plastic loops, and a jumbo packet of crisps in the other. My heart sank, but because I'd vowed to make a success of the evening, I smiled and tried to shake hands with him. I'd forgotten that both of his hands were full and instead he gave me the bag of crisps.

'Hello,' I said, 'you're just on time.'

He nodded at me, I handed him his crisps back awkwardly and he came past me into the house. I could see my fat hands twiddling with my wedding ring and fluttering nervously, I waited for him to introduce himself.

'I'm the first here?' he said, as he entered the empty living room. He looked surprised; a little disappointed, and put his cans and crisps down on the floor. He shrugged himself out of his jacket, threw it over the back of the sofa, and sat down.

'Raymond,' he said, 'your house, I take it?' He opened one of his cans of lager and slurped noisily. I studied him. He was probably in his late twenties, like myself, and wasn't wearing a wedding ring. His trainers were spotlessly white, even the soles.

'Hello Raymond.' I smoothed out my skirt and perched on the edge of the armchair. 'Can I offer you something to eat?' He shook his head and opened the mammoth packet of crisps.

'I always bring my own, thanks.' For a minute or two he didn't say anything, but occupied himself in finishing the first can of lager and making an impression on the crisps. He tipped his head back to drain the last drops from the tin, and I noticed he had a piece of toilet paper sticking to a cut on his Adam's apple. I didn't know if it would be polite to mention it or not. He pulled a packet of cigarettes out of the pocket of his jeans, lit one without asking, and flicked the ash into his empty can.

'Would you like an ashtray? I could get you a saucer, if you'd prefer?' I said. It did look untidy, him sitting there with the can in his hand, and Neil would be arriving any minute so obviously I wanted everything to be neat for that.

'I'm all right,' he said, and flicked the cigarette into the empty can again. I tried to think of something else to say while he leaned over, dropped ash on the carpet, and opened another beer. It clicked down his throat noisily and I realised I'd forgotten about music, forgotten even to buy a cassette player, and it was too late now.

'You've been here a bit though, haven't you?' Raymond said abruptly, blowing smoke at the ceiling as he looked around the room. 'I mean, you've got it all sorted out nice enough.'

I looked around at the patterned carpet and woodchip wallpaper, thinking of all the cleaning I had done and how bare it had looked when I first moved in. At first, when I'd come downstairs in the night and saw bits and pieces from the old house, it had unsettled me; made me wonder, especially if I was still half asleep or upset, whether I'd really moved house at all, and why all the things were in the wrong places. The two pictures of pigs I'd nailed up over the fireplace used to hang in our kitchen and Will had built a set of shelves in an alcove at home for the various ornaments I'd collected over the years. There was nothing like that here, and I'd dotted the ornaments about on the windowsills to try and make it seem a little more homely.

'A month last Wednesday,' I said, 'but I've worked really hard getting it the way I like it.'

'You haven't changed much,' he said. 'Carpet, wallpaper. Just the same. Didn't feel like giving it a lick of paint?'

'You've been in here before?' I was surprised. It hadn't been long, but with enough careful hoovering those impressions in the carpet had faded and I had trouble imagining anyone else had ever lived in my house.

He winked at me, and threw out a smile that revealed his gappy teeth.

'Charlotte and me …' he tailed off vaguely and raised an eyebrow. 'Lets just say I was invited round a couple of times and leave it at that.' He laughed. 'That's not why she moved though, and,' he pointed at me, 'don't you go around saying that it is.'

'I wouldn't,' I said, aghast at the thought that this man had been in my bedroom, and shaking my head eagerly before I realised he'd been joking.

'Had you there!' he said. 'Nah, we were friends. I came round a few times. She could never afford to do the place up properly. You got some plans for it?'

I'd want someone to mention it, I really would, if I had a bloody piece of tissue sticking to my throat, but perhaps he was the kind of person who didn't mind about things like that, and me mentioning it would just betray me for the kind of person who did mind, and so make things awkward. It happens at the parties they have on the television all the time.

'I thought about some yellow, for the walls,' I said at last, and he nodded approvingly, 'but I don't think I'd be very good at painting. I'll have to wait until there's a man around to give me a hand!' I giggled gently, seeing as he was the sort of person who liked a bit of banter in his conversation, but he looked away and didn't respond.

'I live in the one over there,' he gestured vaguely with his cigarette. 'Bit of a state since the wife left, but you can't put a price on peace, eh?' I looked at my watch discreetly and then back at his piece of tissue. Perhaps he really didn't care. I decided to leave it.

'You live alone then?' I enquired politely. The new books I'd been reading said that asking questions of people at parties made them think *you* were interesting but that didn't really make sense, and the book also said not to make the questions too personal, but they didn't tell you what too personal was. Nevertheless, I ploughed on.

'So do I,' I added.

Raymond looked at me strangely. 'Yes, for the past few months,' he said. 'My lad's round every weekend though. I take him into Blackpool for a go on the slot machines, to McDonald's, sometimes the pictures. He's a good lad.'

I nodded, and smiled encouragingly, which was supposed to make him continue, feel at home, comfortable, and in the mood for giving me more information about himself. He scratched his neck, inadvertently dislodging the scrap of paper, and drank from the can again.

'You have any children?' he said, at last. I nodded without thinking about it, shook my head, and then nodded again. I felt like opening one of the bottles and pouring myself a glass of wine, but decided it would be more polite to wait until the others arrived. The paper had fluttered downwards and was perching on one of his shirt-buttons. Whenever he moved or spoke it fell further downwards. Eventually it was going to end up on his lap where everyone could see it and he'd be embarrassed and would go home thinking we'd been staring at him all along.

'A girl,' I said, and imagined myself smiling wistfully, looking serene and somehow motherly. I could have kicked myself in the teeth as soon as I opened my mouth, and I clenched my fists so hard with frustration that my knuckles hurt. Luckily, Raymond didn't seem that interested and was looking around the room again, as if he'd lost something.

Time to keep it together, I said to myself. Keep smiling, make sure everyone has something to drink, and he'll forget about it. Say he must have been hearing things, or drunk, if anyone asks about her. I gulped a few deep breaths and unclenched my fists.

'A bit quiet for a party, this, isn't it? Haven't you got a stereo or something?'

I turned my damp palms to the ceiling casually, shrugged, and laughed. My dress was starting to stick to the backs of my legs; it was made out of a shiny, stiff material that rustled every time I moved, made me feel sweaty, and worse than that, was a lot tighter on me than it had been the last time I'd worn it. I wanted to stand up and pull the skirt away from my thighs, but resisted the impulse.

'Well, it's only just after half-past seven. I'm sure Neil will be along in a moment or two.' I hesitated. How much to tell without being boring, without hogging more than your fair share of conversation?

'That's the man who lives next door to me. We get on really well – and it's good luck we do, with us living right next door to each other.'

'Yes, we're good mates, he's a decent bloke, is Neil. He's lived here for a good five years or so now. He jump-started my car once, when I was late for work.'

'Oh yes, I know, he mentioned it,' I said. 'He's like that though, isn't he?' I bit my lip to stop myself from smiling because I found the thought of Neil going out of his way to help someone he obviously had so little in common with very endearing. Helping a woman in distress was one thing, but to come to the assistance of this man: he was clearly one of those good Samaritan types, and liked looking after people.

'You expecting him then?'

'Of course,' I said, 'he'll be along any minute.'

'Thank God for that!'

Things were getting going now, they really were, and just as I was thinking about passing the plate of fairy cakes the doorbell rang. It made me jump and I sprang from the chair.

'That'll be him now. I'll just go and answer that door. You make yourself at home, Raymond.' He nodded and spread himself out on the sofa: the cushions flexed under his weight and sagged between his knees, and I caught myself wishing he'd sat on one of the hard chairs so Neil could have the couch.

It wasn't Neil. It was more people I hadn't met before: an Indian couple. The man was wearing a pale suit with a brightly coloured tie, and the woman with him was wearing a green sari and carrying an African violet in her hands. The man shook my hand expertly (I'm never quite sure whether to take the hand or not, because sometimes when they've got hold of your hand they lean in for the kiss, and then you've only got a second, if that, to decide whether to present the cheek or mouth). He pumped my hand three times, dropped it and then presented the pink invitation I'd put through his door the week before. They both smiled at me, flashing rows of perfect, straight teeth. Will would have loved them.

'Baravesh Choudhry,' his hand was dry and cool, like a dentist's hand. I imagined if he'd brought it near to my face, it would smell of antiseptic hand soap and TCP. I still didn't know whether to lean over and kiss his cheek, or not. *Find Your Inner Goddess* advised it, said it showed warmth and confidence, but it could be against his religion. I smiled doubtfully, and remembered that *Come Out Of Your Shell* had recommended shy people behave authentically and not try to over-compensate because it could come across as drunkenness or instability.

'You can call me Barry, most of my English friends do,' he said.

'I will,' I said, 'and you must call me Annie.' I looked at the woman, who was very short. She smiled again, and proffered the African violet.

'You said to bring a bottle, on the invitation,' they both nodded sincerely, apologetically, 'but we don't drink alcohol. So we thought, a gift. In lieu of a bottle.'

I felt the clay pot pressed into my hands, the warm dampness of the soil and the fleshy leaves under my thumbs stung like a reproach.

'Thank you,' I said, quietly ashamed. I found myself unable to look at them and with my face flushing and sweating I turned and led them through the hallway with my head bowed to the hairy petals of my new African violet like a bride making the long trip back down the aisle alone. Baravesh and his wife followed me, politely admiring the cleanliness of the carpet and skirting boards in the hall. I noted their confidence, how well it came across. I've always wondered whether complimenting people on cleanness could be construed as an insult, as if you expected them to be filthy.

'Raymond, can I introduce you to our neighbours, Barak… Barry Choudhry, and his wife, er…'

'My name is Sangita,' she laughed delicately, 'but Raymond and I have already met.' She nodded at Raymond and turned back to me, 'My husband and I are quite active in the local community. I run the Neighbourhood Watch – you should get involved, when you're more settled.'

Raymond grunted, and nodded at them. I deposited the potted plant on the mantelpiece next to the bowl of crisps, turned, and noticed the Choudhrys were still standing.

'Please,' I gestured towards the armchairs, but remained standing myself. They shuffled into their seats and there was a moment of silence. Raymond had lit another cigarette and was staring at the blank television screen as if he wished someone would turn it on.

'Doesn't it look nice up there? What a lovely colour. I hope it's not too difficult to take care of, I always manage to kill things that need looking after,' I said.

Sangita shook her head, 'I have six of them on my kitchen windowsill, all grown from cuttings. Just remember to water it every now and again and you'll be fine.'

'Thank you,' I said, 'it's much nicer than wine, anyway. Can I get you something to drink? Coffee perhaps?'

'We'd like some tea, I think, if that's convenient.' Baravesh stretched his legs out into the room. 'Well.' He sounded pleased, and rubbed his dry hands together gently, 'Well, Annie.'

Sangita tucked her sari between her knees, flicked her thick plait over her shoulder and tittered, as if he'd made a joke. 'You've certainly made yourself at home here. The decoration is lovely,' she said.

I paced across the room and picked up the plate with the hedgehog on it. I was quite proud of this and so far no one had commented on what I thought would be a conversational piece. What I'd done was covered the grapefruit half with tin foil, and spent a long time doing it so that it wouldn't look cheap and creased. The eyes were the smallest pickled onions in the jar impaled with a cocktail stick into the side of the grapefruit. I'd had a stroke of genius late on into it and stuck raisins on the end of the sticks holding the eyes on, for the irises. It had a slightly bug-eyed, shocked look, as if it had a neck and someone had their hands around it and was slowly squeezing.

'That's very kind. I sewed the curtains myself. I have a machine, just an old one, but it does. The hems are a little crooked, but not so you'd notice,' I was babbling. I remembered my exercise, took a deep breath and imagined a pleasant scene from my childhood.

'Help yourself,' I gave the hedgehog to Barry, who said 'well' again, and held it in front of him like it was a bomb. 'I'll just go and make the tea.' I gestured towards the hedgehog, 'Dig in, all of you. There's plenty to go around!'

'Can I give you a hand?' Sangita started to rise out of the chair, and I shook my head.

'No, no, I'm fine. You stay here and mingle.'

I hadn't drank a drop and all the laughing and nodding and shaking my head was making the blood in my skull slosh about like fluid in a brandy glass. My face felt hot and I planned to kneel in front of the fridge for a couple of seconds to collect myself.

In the kitchen, the floors and walls started to sway suddenly, as if I was in a soap opera and the whole house was just a cheap cardboard set. I put my hands on the wall over the sink to brace myself and let my head hang between my arms. I waited for the kettle to boil. Sometimes when I ate too much and needed to vomit I stood like that, and the association was making me feel queasy. Tea, I hadn't thought anyone would want tea. There might not be enough milk. I opened the fridge and predictably enough, there was only a green-looking chicken breast on a saucer, a rind of cheese and a bottle with two inches of lumpy-looking milk in it.

I only stopped panicking long enough to despair: if I wasn't going to make the effort to take care of myself and make this work out, who would? Who would ever come into this house and help me with the shopping list, unload the bags onto the kitchen counter, notice when the food was going bad? I remembered meeting the milkman that first morning and wondered why I hadn't thought to ask him to start making regular deliveries. A notebook, that's what I needed, somewhere safe I could write all my new resolutions down so I wouldn't forget them.

The kettle clicked and I poured the water into the pot.

'Well, the job isn't what it used to be. Less contact with people, paperwork – paperwork all the time. These people think all I have to do all day is sign my name and stamp forms! I'm my own secretary really – what I need is a wife at work, as well as in the home, so I could get back to the real business of working with *people.*'

Barry was in full flow, Sangita nodding, nodding like a pretty china doll, and Raymond, resting his head on the back of the couch as if he was asleep. He was exposing his throat; it was livid with shaving rash. I glanced at his lap for the tissue paper but I couldn't find it. He opened his eyes and noticed me staring at his crotch. I pretended to be looking casually at the crocheted protectors on the arms of the sofa so as not to embarrass him.

'You work in the shop?' I said, trying to chip gently into the conversation. There was a shop at the top of the cul-de-sac on the main road, where I got milk and magazines. I was considering making the walk up the street in my party dress to buy a bottle of milk when I had a brainwave: I'd pop next door and ask Neil. That idea changed my mood and instead of panicking I was glad someone had asked for tea: a trip next door to borrow milk while he was getting ready for the party would give me a chance to say a few words to Neil alone, in his own territory.

'It's such a handy little shop,' I said, but Sangita laughed.

'No, my husband is an oncologist at the hospital. People are always asking him that though, if he works at the shop, mixing him up with that dreadful little man.' She put her head on one side and thickened her accent so she became nasal, masculine, Indian: 'Ten Marlboro Lights and a packet of extra large Rizlas? Very good sir, certainly sir.'

Barry laughed loudly, and Raymond coughed. I didn't know what an oncologist was, but I laughed too, in case it was a joke.

'How interesting. I just need to go next door for a moment – would you believe I've run out of milk?' I headed out of the room, 'Just make yourselves at home, help yourselves to the food. I'll only be a moment.'

Trembling, I fled the scene.

4

Neil didn't answer the door, Lucy did. She was wearing a man's shirt and a pair of woolly-looking grey socks. And nothing else. The white shirt was open to the sternum and barely grazed the tops of her thighs. Her legs were the artificial colour of tights, as if she'd spent too long on a sunbed. She looked more like a model than ever: all eyebrows and cheekbones and tendrils of artfully teased brown hair. While I'd been keeping an eye on her throughout the previous week, I'd managed to find out she'd been shopping for new clothes at least twice. You couldn't tell though, if this was how she saw fit to answer the door.

'I was just wondering if I could borrow some milk. It's for the party. I can bring over a bottle tomorrow morning to replace it, if it's a problem.'

I spoke stiffly, wondering what would possess a decent woman to answer the door in that state, and this early in the evening. She nodded and smiled weakly and murmured something or other and then I was in the front room, and I took a good look around while I was waiting. It was the first time I'd been invited in and I wanted to get an idea of their tastes in case I ever decided to buy Neil a present.

It was bare: all wooden floors and white walls, chairs made from tubes of chrome and wicker. They'd drawn the red curtains even though it wasn't quite dark yet and the room seemed cosy, lit by gentle orange light coming from a couple of lamps near Neil. The television was playing silently and there were white mugs on the table. I could smell coffee.

Neil was sitting at a table in front of a laptop computer, frowning at something on the screen and tugging at the hair on the back of his neck. I stood in the doorway, feeling out of place in my coral party dress. I pulled one of the straps away from my shoulder for a second to give my skin a rest, and felt the ridge it had tracked through my flesh.

Lucy looked over her shoulder at Neil, 'Annie says she wants some milk. Shall I give her the skimmed?' she said.

Neil raised his head from the computer, and frowned slightly. He didn't like being interrupted, that's what it was. He was hurrying to get his work finished so he could come next door to my party, and she was getting in the way. The atmosphere in the room was thickening. I wondered if I'd interrupted an argument. It would explain their lateness.

'Just half a pint really, I'm making tea for the Choudhrys – they don't drink wine.'

'You're having a party?' Neil said, standing up and moving his head from side to side as if his neck was hurting him. He'd been working hard on something important, I could tell, and concentrating on that had wiped everything else from his mind. 'Oh, yes. You did mention something.'

'When was this?' Lucy asked, bending her knee and catching hold of her ankle behind her back. She leaned against the door frame and stretched. She was always doing things like that, yoga in the back garden, a pilates video and a mat in front of the living-room window, various ways of waving her limbs about in order to draw attention to herself. I didn't find it tasteful.

'Last week,' Neil began.

'He was good enough to pop over and help me with a bit of DIY,' I said, smiling, 'didn't he tell you?'

Lucy frowned. Aha! I thought. So she was jealous, that's what it was.

'We're not making too much noise and disturbing your work, are we?' I asked Neil. There was music playing in the room, something quiet and repetitive, without any words. I noticed him glance at Lucy warily, as if he was embarrassed that she'd made no move to get properly dressed. She pursed her lips at him and widened her eyes. Another argument was coming – I'd heard one or two through the walls already.

'Haven't heard a peep all day,' he said, 'milk's no problem. Lucy, get her the bottle from the fridge.'

Lucy stalked into the kitchen. I watched her through the open door and saw the tendons in the backs of her knees flex as she bent down to open the fridge. I'd noticed she'd shaved her legs, but not recently. I bet sleeping next to her was like lying in bed with a clothes brush.

'I sent you an invitation. It was on a pink card, about this big.' I put my hands in the air and made a rectangle with my fingers. My nails still smelled of the fresh varnish I'd put on that afternoon, to match the coral outfit. Three attempts and half a packet of cotton wool and there were still flakes of it on my cuticles. 'Maybe it got stuck under the doormat, or caught up with some junk mail?' I said.

Neil looked away from me and into the kitchen. 'Well, don't worry about the milk. You don't need to come around tomorrow with another bottle. It's only milk,' he said.

I smiled. That was just the sort of man Neil was: neighbourly, community-minded. I was about to ask him a question but then Lucy was back, and I had the milk bottle in my hands, cold from the fridge. I wanted to rub it against the veins in my throat and neck to take out some of the heat from my face, the way pastry chefs hold ice against their wrists before getting near the dough. They were both smiling at me sympathetically, as if someone had made a joke about me and I hadn't heard it. I had the creepy feeling that I'd fallen asleep for a few moments or become distracted and had missed out on something that had happened. I couldn't remember what I had said last, or whose turn it was to talk.

'It's a house-warming party,' I explained. The bottle was slippery in my hands, and I clutched at it desperately. All that hard floor: if I dropped it, it would shatter and someone would get cut because you could never get up every single piece of glass.

'You could come over for a drink anyway. There's lots of wine, and some food. We're having a lovely time. It would be a shame for you to miss out just because the invitation got mislaid.'

'That's a dress and a half,' Lucy said, looking me up and down, 'very kitsch. I wouldn't have the nerve, myself. Good on you.' I didn't reply, there was nothing about her clothing I could have decently commented upon in return.

Neil looked at his watch, and stretched again, yawning. 'I was thinking of getting an early night, actually.'

'Oh come on, Neil,' Lucy was crinkling up her nose and turning up the corners of her mouth and I knew she was planning some-thing. 'I'll throw some jeans on and we'll go over to Annie's for a glass. It'll give us a chance *to have a chat.*'

Neil rolled his eyes and as she went out of the room, he stood up, waited a little, looked at me and then followed her out. They talked for a moment in the kitchen, I heard her say '... need to talk to her anyway,' but before I could move closer so that I could hear better Neil reappeared through the kitchen door, shaking his head and saying, 'We can come over for a few minutes. Lucy's just going to chuck some clothes on.'

Neil didn't say anything else to me while Lucy was away, but that was all right. He was busy turning his computer off and putting it back into its case, and knowing him, he probably felt a little uncomfortable, perhaps embarrassed. A lot of men didn't like being alone with women they weren't married to. It was a true sign of a gentleman. And if he did feel a bit shy with me it was only to be expected: I had the advantage over him, being able to clearly remember the circumstances of our first accidental meeting and understand why we were drawn towards each other. Not recognising me in an uninjured state, yet being aware he already felt that he knew me and not being able to understand why: it was bound to be disconcerting for him. I could reveal all that to him later, when the time was right.

He looked up from what he was doing just the once, and caught me staring at him. He smiled, and nodded towards the ceiling.

'She'll be up there all night if I don't shout on her,' he said. 'She loves dressing up.' He went over to the kitchen door and bellowed upwards. 'Lucy! Get a move on, will you, we're only going next door!'

When Lucy came back she'd put on a pair of tight, faded jeans and smeared her lips with Vaseline. She bent over to put her shoes on and I noticed her name was written on the back pocket of her jeans in shiny red buttons. She was still wearing Neil's shirt though. She'd pulled her hair back with an elastic band, hadn't even put a hairbrush through it. That's why Neil was quiet and embarrassed; he was wearing jeans too, but with black shoes and a clean white T-shirt, something casual and appropriate for a house-warming party – no wonder he didn't speak as he scooped up his keys from a bowl on the mantelpiece and followed me back into my house.

Raymond had turned the television on and was crouching in front of it, flicking through the channels. The air was heavy with cigarette smoke; I noticed grey ash on the arm of the sofa and finally, that blood-stained piece of tissue paper had made its appearance on the seat of the couch he had just vacated. The Choudhrys were talking to each other about another party they had been to; a wedding where the bride and groom had both been so drunk that they'd slipped on the dance floor, fallen down, and not been able to get back up again without help from the bridesmaids.

'Ah, Annie, we were just telling young Raymond here about the evils of drink.' Barry nodded towards the bottles of wine lined up on the coffee table, and the cans of beer stacked up between Raymond's feet.

Raymond stood up and turned the television off, shrugging. 'Nothing on anyway.'

'Raymond, Sangita, Barry – I'd like to introduce my next-door neighbour Neil to you, and this is his friend Lucy.'

I think the introductions went off all right. The Choudhrys stood up and shook hands awkwardly. Lucy kissed Sangita on the cheek and complimented her on the colour of her sari. She was talking nineteen to the dozen, probably nervous now she was in my territory and embarrassed about what she was wearing. I hardly remember what she said, just the noise of her voice cantering away in the background.

'It's so exotic, really, what's the word, ethnic. I'd love to be able to carry something like that off.' She laughed loudly, a little tinkling sound. 'I haven't the figure for it, no hips,' she turned to me briefly, 'no offence, Annie,' and then back to Sangita, 'I'm all skin and bone really, look at me.' She put her hands on her hips and wiggled a little. 'No, I could never wear something like that.'

Sangita smiled indulgently, and Barry slung an arm around her shoulders.

'I have the prettiest wife in this street, in the whole county, probably.' He paused, and winked at Neil, 'But I haven't made a thorough enough survey of the ladies to speak any further – not yet anyway! Ha! Ha! Ha!'

I slipped into the kitchen and poured the milk into a jug. The jug was shaped like a cow sitting with its back legs splayed open and holding its front hooves over its eyes. The handle was made with a curve of its tail and when you tipped it, the milk came out of various holes in its udders. I picked it up at a car-boot sale a good few years ago now and I'd always liked it. The tea was stewed but I put everything on a tray anyway and carried it into the front room.

Lucy was sitting next to Sangita on the settee, still twittering. How did she grow her hair so long; was it all her own, or extensions? Had she ever thought of cutting it all off and selling it, or couldn't she, for religious reasons? She'd make a lot of money. Raymond crushed a can between his hands and shrugged himself back into his jacket.

'I reckon I'll be getting off now, Annie. I've got something on tonight that I forgot about.'

'So soon?' I was still holding the tray, and the Choudhrys helped themselves to a cup each from it while I stood there like a waitress. I didn't see if they liked my milk jug because Raymond was distracting me. I noticed this, and decided to write it down in my File when they all left: I need to work on the ability to multitask. I'm always forgetting things, starting to do something and wandering off in the middle.

'We haven't even opened the wine yet,' I said, trying to sound warm and relaxed. 'And there's the fairy cakes. Would you like one of those before you go?'

'Nah, it's all right.' Raymond turned to Neil, who was standing leaning against the wall with a can of lager in his hand. 'I'll come round in the next few days about that disk drive, see if you can have a look at it and sort something out for me?'

'Not a problem. Just pop round and I'll see what I can do,' Neil said, and lifted the can to his mouth to drink from it deeply, as if he didn't like the taste. Like medicine, he was trying to finish it as quickly as possible. Raymond must have offered one to him, and he'd taken it, just to be polite.

'Or what about a little party bag? You can choose what you like from the buffet and take it back with you. A few of those cakes for your boy? If you wait ten minutes the sausage rolls will be ready.'

Raymond didn't answer, and Neil was still knocking back the beer. So polite. I would have offered him a glass if I'd had a minute to think straight, or even opened one of the bottles of wine. They were still lying there on the table, untouched. All that money. I walked

Raymond out into the hall. There was an awkward moment caused by the narrowness of the space, my size and the added bulk of Raymond's jacket.

'Steady on,' he said, his breath wet and hot and alcoholic in my face. He put his hands on my shoulders and pushed me back gently. My back hit the wall and although I caught my toe in the doormat both of us managed to remain upright. I looked up from the carpet at him and saw quite clearly he was doing his best not to burst out laughing. I trembled a little, not expecting to be practically assaulted in my own house. He'd mentioned his wife had left, but I hadn't realised that he was trying to make an advance on me. Probably, as a newly single woman, this was something I was going to have to get used to, and learn to handle with grace. Still, I was shocked, and more than a touch embarrassed for him. I moved forward without saying anything in order to unlatch the door, wobbled again and banged into his shoulder.

'Careful,' he said, smirking, extracted himself, and went out through the front door.

'It's been lovely to meet you, Raymond,' I said, following him out and trying to recover things a little before he reached the gate. There was no point making him feel embarrassed or hurt because of the rejection. In many senses, we were both in the same boat and while he wasn't quite the person I was looking for, he could at least become a friend in the future.

'Please feel free to pop around for a cup the next time you're in the vicinity. I think you'll find it's more or less an open house here. Any time!'

'Thanks. Thanks,' he said, and made his exit. I waved exhaustedly and went back inside to the heat and smoke of the house. There wasn't time to reflect any more on the incident, as people were chatting to each other and I had to think on my feet, leap in right away and resume my duties as hostess.

'Annie, are we going to get this wine opened then, or not?' Lucy was saying, and I leapt towards the kitchen – hunting for a corkscrew, but by the time I'd come back Neil had uncorked one of the bottles, a red, with something on his key ring. The cork had broken into pieces and he'd put it on the coffee table. I hoped it wasn't a sign that the wine was bad; that I hadn't paid enough for it. Will had always dealt with that side of things; I was starting from scratch.

'Should have had this opened half an hour ago, Annie. It lets it breathe,' Lucy said, as Neil poured the wine into her glass.

Breathe?

'Don't be such a snob, it's not going to suffocate in the bottle, is it?' Neil said gently, and I smiled. Just like him, to leap to my defence like that. Lucy glared at him, and Neil seemed about to say something to her when I opened my mouth and said: 'Well, we've put it out of its misery now, at least,' which in retrospect I realise doesn't make a great deal of sense, but the main thing was they both laughed. Even the Choudhrys, sitting sipping their tea and, I noticed with relief, nibbling politely on cheese and pickled onions on sticks, tittered delicately. There was a silence, perhaps it only spanned a minute, but I wracked my brains for something to say and tried to remember something from one of the magazines I'd read that afternoon that had struck me at the time as interesting.

'I read today about a man who'd had an operation to turn him into a woman, only then he, I mean she, I suppose, met a man who he wanted to get married to,' I took a breath and realised I had the full attention of everyone in the room. 'That man didn't like girls, he was like that, and they weren't allowed to get married anyway. They went on a television programme and the viewers all sent in money so she could get an operation to get her pecker put back on again!' I laughed, 'Imagine that!'

I felt particularly proud of myself then, it was something I was good at: commenting on current affairs and the world's goings on. A slightly risqué article like that had struck me as appropriate, something light-hearted and amusing a roomful of adults could giggle over before moving on to more serious topics. Sometimes, when I'm nervous, I forget the things I'd planned to say, but I'd read through this article a couple of times and even kept it handy in the magazine rack in case anyone wanted to look at the pictures. Lucy started to choke, drinking so fast it had gone down the wrong way, and Barry looked up sharply from his teacup.

'Poor soul,' he said, 'makes you realise how lucky we are,' he looked tenderly at Sangita and she squeezed his hand. 'Too many lonely people in the world,' he said quietly, and shook his head. Sangita and he seemed to be sharing one of the special moments that I've seen other couples have sometimes, so I thought it best not to say anything. With Raymond gone, all of a sudden I felt like the odd one out, the only spare in this room of couples, people paired off not only for the evening, but for night time and breakfast time and all the afternoons as well.

Spare was the right word. I was going spare. My mum used to say it when the mashed potatoes cooked down into pulpy water, or my dad came back from the pub much later than expected and in one of his strange moods. She was with me then, the sweet vanilla smell of her hair coiling around my throat and her voice, quiet and worried.

'Do you think your dad'll be much longer, love?'

She'd always been 'going spare' over something or other, but now I thought of it and myself in its other meaning, a spare one, not needed, surplus to requirements. Spare things were only useful once the original ones were broken. I glanced at Lucy, who was reading the label on the bottle of wine. Not the kind of woman who was useful for anything at all, not that I could see anyway. The room was silent again, apart from the sound of people quietly sipping.

'Would anyone like a fairy cake? The ones with the yellow icing are lemon, the rest are just plain ones. They're very nice though. Have as many as you like.' I stood up to get the plate.

'Do you have a jar of olives, Annie? Some Greek ones, I think? This wine really needs some olives with it,' Lucy said, holding the bottle up and reading the label, which was just faking for a start because I'd read all the labels and not one of them had said anything about olives.

'No, no olives. If you're patient I'll have the sausage rolls with you in a few minutes. Pigs in blankets, that's what my mum called them.' She didn't smile.

'There's the onions.' I gestured towards the pickled onion hedge-hog, looking slightly bare and humiliated on the floor where Barry had left him.

'I don't think they'd go,' Lucy said.

'Are you sure you don't have a little jar nestling away at the back of a cupboard? I'm sure you do.'

Even though on balance I would have been justified in calling the party a success, I was worried because I didn't know what 'kitsch' meant and I was feeling ashamed. I'd never had olives before and I hadn't known there was a whole set of people who had jars of olives just lying around in their kitchens. Forgotten in the back of cupboards!

Lucy giggled again, and then I could feel myself starting to get annoyed, wanting to ask her what it was about every sentence that escaped from her perfectly bowed lips that was so blinking hilarious? I'd sat down properly for the first time in the evening, and was holding a tin opener in my hands, rubbing the metal with my thumb. I'd brought it in with me when I couldn't find the corkscrew, thinking that maybe we could open the wine with it, but then Neil had done it and it wasn't needed, and I didn't want to get up again and put it in the kitchen. I gripped it tightly.

'It doesn't matter, Lucy, we'll be going in a minute anyway,' Neil said. Lucy opened her mouth as if to say something else and Neil rolled his eyes at her as if they were the only ones in the room, 'Don't make a fuss.'

I wondered, slightly hopefully, if what he said would make her go off into a sulk, and then maybe, just maybe, she'd go back next door, but she didn't, she sipped at the wine and started looking around the room again, like Sangita had done when she first arrived. It was what people talked about at house-warming parties: it was the number one ice-breaker; the decoration and layout of the house.

'It's pretty much the way it was when I moved in, really,' I said. 'The house was in a very good state. One of the rooms upstairs, a little boy's room, I think, even had a bed left in it, which was nice of them. One of those high beds, the built-in kind.'

'What? Oh, we knew that boy,' Lucy said. 'Mikey, was that his name?' She lowered her voice, 'He was such a bloody nuisance with that ball – chucking it over the fence at the back at least a million times a week. Oh, he looked perfectly adorable, I know, but he was a little brute sometimes, really,' she paused, and looked like she was staring at a corner of the ceiling because that's what people's brains make them do when they're trying to remember something. 'And your little girl, does she live with her father somewhere else now?'

'Lucy,' Neil said in a low voice, looking scandalised. 'Maybe Annie doesn't want to talk about it, hmm?' Neil rubbed his palm along the side of his jeans and looked away from her.

'We were expecting you with a little girl,' she tinkled on, oblivious, 'Charlotte was very particular about it, we remember because of the fuss Mikey was making about his room. Thought you would go and paint it pink!'

There was an awkward silence. Sangita looked into her teacup and Barry found something interesting on the carpet to poke at with his shoe. I stepped in, feeling hot in the face, sweat condensing between my breasts but thankfully, on the ball for once.

'My daughter goes to school during the week. She comes back here at weekends, and when my husband's up from London he'll be staying here with me too,' I said, all in a rush. Lucy and Neil looked at each other and Sangita smiled. It was as if someone had been blowing up a balloon in the centre of the room and I'd just stepped in and popped it. Lucy was swilling the wine about in her glass so it sloshed up the sides, and then sniffing it. Did she think I was going to poison her or something?

Neil raised an eyebrow and put his head on one side, 'London, eh? I've often thought about moving down there myself. It's where the jobs are, although I'd have to sell a kidney to be able to afford a house good enough for this one,' he pointed towards Lucy with his thumb. Even with her nose buried in the wine glass like a dog, she still smiled.

'So what does your husband do then?' she said, once she'd finished sipping. 'Must be a posh job, if he's living in London during the week?'

'Oh, he works in a hospital,' I said airily, and waved my free hand in the air. 'A very rare branch of medicine. I never want to go into it, most people don't have a clue what I'm talking about.' I laughed and felt a bubble of pleasure pop in my chest. That told her! But Barry was turning to me, pouring himself another cup of tea and leaning forward interestedly.

'Well, I'm all ears, Annie. In fact, I'd be interested to meet a fellow physician. He isn't in oncology too, by any chance?'

Lucy didn't wait for me to answer, but leaned forward too, until I felt they were pressing in at me on all sides.

'What did you say your daughter's name was? How old is she? Is there a photograph of her around here somewhere?'

Sangita tapped a finger on my arm. 'Ours are away at school too,' she said sympathetically. Her hair smelled like flowers. 'It's terrible, isn't it – you never stop missing them, even though you know they're having a fantastic time!'

'So you'll be seeing them both this weekend then? I bet you're looking forward to that. Mustn't be nice, being here on your own during the week,' Lucy said.

'Perhaps not this weekend, exactly,' I started, 'it's all a bit up in the air at the moment.'

To tell you the truth, I hadn't prepared myself for these kinds of personal questions at all and had started talking, elaborating a little on my past, to distract attention from myself. I pressed something cold against my thumb and it bit, and hot blood trickled between my fingers. I looked down and it was running over my hands and spotting my skirt, feeling as slick as oil.

5

'Oh, Annie, what have you done to yourself?' Lucy squeaked.

That's right, make it out to be all my fault, I thought. I'd just rubbed my thumb over the wheel on the tin opener that cuts the metal and it had made a fairly deep gash in the fleshy pad of my thumb. Anyone could have done it.

Sangita touched Barry's arm, 'Annie's hurt herself,' and he stood up to take a look but Lucy shook her head.

'You're not at work now,' she said, in a cheerful, bossy tone of voice. She crossed the room to where I was sitting, still twiddling the tin opener. 'Even a shop-girl like me can take care of a little cut!'

Barry laughed and held his hands up in the air, 'I'm not going to insist,' he said, 'I'm quite fond of this suit, actually.'

'Put that down and let me have a look,' she eased the tin opener out of my hand. I felt limp and so I let her take it and toss it casually onto the chair I'd just vacated. As if I was a bank robber and she'd just persuaded me to relinquish a loaded gun. Blood trickled over my hand and I couldn't see the cut but I could feel it starting to burn and throb.

'Oh dear, you're really bleeding. Let's get you into the kitchen before you spoil your nice dress.' She lowered her voice and leaned towards me, 'I wanted to have a bit of a chat with you anyway. All girls together, you know?'

She took my arm like I was an invalid and guided me into the kitchen.

'The guests,' I said weakly, but the sight of the red over my fingers and blooming into roses on the fabric of my skirt was making me feel dizzy. She overruled me easily.

'They'll be fine in there on their own for five minutes, can't let you bleed to death just so you can hand that daft hedgehog about another few times!'

We were through the door and Barry shouted, 'Let me know if anything needs sewing back on and I'll get my bag!' and Sangita laughed, the door swung closed and the sounds grew muffled.

Lucy turned the kitchen tap on and held my hand under the stream until the water dripping from under my thumb was such a different colour to what was coming out of the tap it looked like I was performing a magic trick – water into wine. Looking at the watery splashes of blood on the coffee-coloured tiles behind the kitchen taps I started to shake, and for the first time in a while I felt the stinging along the rims of my eyelids that was a sure warning: embarrassment was going to be making an appearance very soon.

'Annie, don't worry! Look, it's stopped now.' She pulled my thumb out from under the tap and showed it to me, the little semi-circular gash looking like a crescent moon and pursing like an open mouth. She was right. I pulled a tea towel from the drawer and held it over the cut. I noticed there was a spot of blood on her cuff, but seeing as I wasn't prepared to do anything about it, didn't bother pointing it out.

'That's right. Just apply a bit of pressure to make sure,' she said, 'you won't need stitches or anything. It always looks worse than it is. I hate the sight of blood too,' she said, conspiratorially, 'God knows what I'd be like in childbirth. I'm going to ask for an epidural,' she laughed, 'or failing that, crack!'

My chest closed in and I glanced involuntarily at her stomach, hidden beneath the white folds of the shirt. 'So you and Neil are... expecting?'

She paused to pull back the tea towel, inspect the wound, and wrap it back around my thumb again. From next door, I could hear laughing and the low rumble of easy conversation. Through the ridged pane of glass at the top I made out Neil, recognising him by the mottled blotch of his white T-shirt, still leaning against the wall and bobbing his head up and down. I looked back to the front of her shirt, the fabric billowing out. If she were getting bigger it would make sense for her to wear Neil's clothes, wouldn't it? She just pulled a face at me and laughed incredulously.

'God, no! I didn't mean *that*. I just meant, you know, when the time comes. If it comes. I don't like the idea of it much anyway. Sounds a hell of a lot like hard work.' She smiled, 'We women, we always get the shitty end of the stick when it comes to things like that, don't we?'

My insides settled down again and I was so relieved I didn't flinch at her language.

'I suppose you're right,' I replied mildly.

'But I bet you love being a mother. Shame you don't have a photograph up. Does it make it worse – you must miss her a lot?' she said.

'You get used to it, in the end.' I turned away from her. She thought, I believe, that I was experiencing a bout of overwhelming emotion, but I'd noticed, sitting near the kettle, a book called *The Idiot's Guide to Cooking* that I'd accidentally picked up in the library and I wanted to move it so she didn't get the wrong idea about me.

'Don't get worked up about it, here,' she tore off a sheet of kitchen paper from the roll mounted near the window and handed it to me, 'your mascara'll run,' she warned gently. 'Still bleeding? No, I think you're all right now.'

'It's stopped,' I agreed, inspecting the little mouth again. When I flexed my thumb the cut gaped open, a little doorway for infection, a wide gateway to let everything out of me. Crying in front of her? What had possessed me? There were plasters in a little green box in the mug cupboard and I retrieved one and stuck it clumsily around my thumb. Oh well, at least the colour of it matched my dress and nail varnish. I glanced at the stains on my skirt and realised I had nothing better to change into.

'Annie?' she asked, slowly moving between the door and me, and picking up a little egg cup in the shape of a chicken from the top of the microwave. 'While we're in here, on our own, I wanted to mention something to you.'

'Yes?' I said. My tongue stuck to the roof of my mouth and my throat emptied of saliva so suddenly I croaked. Here it was, and she'd caught me off guard when I'd vowed to myself that she wouldn't.

The thing about Lucy, really, was the way she looked. It revealed a lot about who she was on the inside, to my mind. All that female flapping and concern didn't wash with me. She really did have the most feline features: wide square nails polished like claws, that stretched skin over her face, and no, I'm not embellishing, curious, clever eyes so green it didn't matter that they weren't almond-shaped at all. Her irises were contracted small in the bright light from the fluorescent strip on the ceiling and she blinked once before pouncing. I like cats, I do, but I know what they're capable of and I wasn't about to let Lucy paw me about like an injured bird while she was a guest in my house.

'What's on your mind?' I prompted, because she seemed unwilling to begin.

'I'm not sure how to broach this, really. I mean I don't want us to be on bad terms. I really don't.' She smiled at me, meant, perhaps, to be reassuring, but it was too brief, too calculated. All I saw was a short-lived thinning of her lips and a flash of teeth. In slow motion and with the sound turned off, it would have looked like a snarl. I remembered the barbecue again, and realised she didn't care about my thumb, the party, or what terms we were on at all. I was going to have to play this carefully, and find out exactly what she was planning.

'Please,' I said, and then I coughed and turned to get a tumbler from the cupboard behind me for some water. I felt her eyes on my back, the uneven lines of my dress clinging to the bumps of flesh, let's say it, of fat, that protruded from the tight template of my underwear. I sipped, and she waited.

'Please, feel free. We are neighbours, aren't we?'

'Okay then, Annie. Just as long as you know I don't mean anything by it, I just want to clear any bad feeling between us, anything I might have done, inadvertently perhaps? You know?'

I put my head on one side and made a noise in my throat, a little buzzing noise to encourage her to continue.

'There have been a few incidents,' she said carefully, and although she spoke lightly and kept flashing that sharp, concise little smile at me, I caught the lack of a contraction, the studied informality that fell flat on its face. She'd practised this speech, maybe in her head while she was washing the blood off me at the kitchen sink, maybe with Neil one night before bed.

'Incidents?' I echoed. She'd brought her wine glass in with her, and she swirled and sniffed again, and then took a sip.

'Just little things, nothing I'd want to mention. But obviously, cumulatively, it's a little distressing.' She stopped playing with the egg cup and put it back on the microwave.

'Yes,' I said blandly, trying to coax her out. 'I imagine it would be.'

She smiled broadly and sighed.

'Oh, good!' she said, smiling again. '*Good*! I was so nervous about bringing this up, you know.' She started talking quickly, waving her hands about and not stopping for breath, smiling all the time, not at me, but at the straps of my dress. And that was the clue: no matter how kind and confident she might seem, she wasn't making eye contact with me, and we all know what *that* means.

'I even asked Neil to have a word because at least you've met him before and it might make you feel more comfortable, but then he wouldn't, he said I shouldn't interfere and if I felt it needed bringing up, I should do it, because I'm a woman and you might not want to talk about being depressed with a man – especially if it was hormonal – is it?' she stopped to get her breath. 'You can talk to me,' she slowed, and went on, 'woman to woman. Instead of messing about with all the, all the other stuff.'

Depressed? I could talk to her? I couldn't fit a word in sideways.

'And what with the rubbish, peeping about through the windows, the cat-droppings, the primroses – you know, we really felt like it could be a cry for help, rather than anything else. You see what I mean? With your family being away, and things being ... difficult, in that department.' She waved her hands in the air. 'I'm sorry, I can tell this is embarrassing for you.'

I emptied my tumbler and, awkwardly, so as not to wet my plaster, rinsed it a few times under the tap before upending it on the empty draining board. There was blood sitting in the creases of my knuckles, as if I'd been in a fight. I resisted the urge to lick it off and rubbed at my hand with the tea towel, pretending to be so absorbed in what I was doing that I couldn't speak right away. It didn't matter: Lucy only paused a second so I didn't need to say anything at all.

'I'm not very good at this. Hate confrontation, that kind of thing. Really, we're just a bit worried, and not sure what to do because obviously we don't really know you, you haven't been living here for that long. Just those little things, the garden, the rubbish – you can see what I mean? We did think it was those boys, you know, but then, well, I was shutting the curtains in the study and saw you out on our front lawn the other night. With the bin bags. No, don't look like that; I'm not going to shout at you or anything, honestly.

It's obvious you're not coping that well and we'd like to help. That's the main thing. So I thought perhaps you could ask your husband to take some time off work to help you? It's hard moving into a new place, and if you aren't getting to see your little girl much, you know, it's no wonder things have been getting on top of you. Maybe he could take a month off and come back for a while, your daughter take a bit of time off school, have your family around you for a bit, just until you get more settled in?'

She put her glass down abruptly on the draining board and I thought she was finished, but then she clapped her hands over her mouth as if someone had just dropped ice down the back of her shirt.

'I've just thought of the most amazing thing, Annie. A brilliant idea!'

Just thought of it, my foot.

'I think it's great you've tried to throw a little party – really making an effort. No one does things like that, and it's not your fault people didn't turn up. They'll remember being invited, won't they?'

And how old was she anyway – nineteen? Neil must be a good five years older than me, in his early thirties at least. If you let yourself think about it for any length of time, it becomes quite disgusting.

'You just need to work on making yourself a bit more approachable – you know what I'm saying?' She worked up to speed again, smiling a lot and nodding her head as if she was listening to music.

'Update your look,' she glanced at my dress quickly, as if she hadn't meant to, and started counting off on her fingers, 'some new shoes, maybe join the gym or Weight Watchers or something – get the doctor to check your glands, have you thought of that? You could have a word with Barry about it, he's very discreet. And make-up – why don't you come round one night and I'll do you a make-over – get rid of this frosted stuff and...'

I let her voice fade into the background. It's an easy trick; you just concentrate on something else and let it trigger associations that will carry you away like cars.

Let's look at you, I thought, let's have a long hard look at you, then, if you're so clever: skinny nineteen-year-old with no breasts turning up at an evening event wearing your boyfriend's clothes, all crumpled like you've pulled them out of the laundry basket. Her mouth was still moving, and she was showing me her fingernails, recommending a manicurist, telling me to steer clear of Cloud Nine's because the wax was too hot and took the skin off your shins, or worse, depending on which bit of your body your man had decided he wanted hairless. Silly little girl. I nodded at her fingernails.

'There's a great hairdresser off Queen's Terrace, tucked in behind the market, you probably haven't seen it before. I go into Blackpool for mine though.' She took a step closer to me and then she wasn't looking at my face any longer, or raking her gaze over my clothes, my fingernails, my shoes. She reached out a hand to touch my hair and in the seconds before her fingers made contact with it she said, 'You'd look so much better generally if you got rid of these split ends, Annie, you really would. I know it's a bit of a faff making an appointment every six weeks, but they've got reminder cards now and –' her fingers touched my hair and I felt her nails press lightly into my shoulder. 'It's all about effort,' she said gently, still fingering my terrible, dirty, neglected, split-ended hair between her thumb and forefinger, 'you just need to make a little bit more effort with yourself, Annie, then things will come together for you, you'll see. Get your husband to come back, and if you tell him to leave it a fortnight, you can get yourself together a bit and he won't recognise you!'

I stepped back to get her fingers off my head, but I moved too quickly and slipped in my all-wrong shoes. I toppled, fell back against the draining board. My outstretched un-manicured hand knocked against my pound-shop glass tumbler and knocked it into the sink. It smashed instantly.

'I am doing my best! I am making the effort!'

I'd said it louder than I meant to, but it was true all the same. A new house, a party. Spent forty pounds on bottles of wine and cleaned the house for most of the afternoon. Cleaned everywhere. I'd been maintaining my personal development, working on my File and conducting some research into self-esteem and my particular situation. What else was I supposed to be doing?

Neil was still in the living room talking with the Choudhrys. I couldn't hear exactly what he was saying but the tone of it sounded like, 'Women, eh, nattering in the kitchen all evening, what are they like?' Lucy and I must have been standing there for a quarter of an hour. She stopped talking and held a hand against her chin, her index and middle finger lay lightly over her lips.

This was a mannerism of hers I had seen before: when Neil was getting into his car one morning the previous week, and she came out of the house in her dressing gown, running barefoot down the path after him. They'd had an argument, and he'd turned and hissed something to her. I couldn't hear what it was he said, I was standing on the upstairs landing cleaning the inside of the window, but whatever it was, she'd closed her mouth so quickly her teeth must have clicked, and put her fingers against it like that. It was the 'Ouch! That wasn't nice!' expression and the fingers were the 'I'm going to cry now, you've been so horrible to me,' part of it.

She blinked, sniffed, and moved her hand to pick up her wine glass.

'Okay then,' she said, 'be like that. I was just trying to help. A lot of other people wouldn't have been so understanding, you know. I was only saying, that's all.'

The handle turned and Neil poked his head around the door.

'Evening, ladies,' he said. He must have heard the last thing I said, it was loud enough, but if he did he gave no indication of it. He nodded his head back towards the living room.

'Party's dried up a bit, Annie. Your finger all right now?' I nodded and turned to pick up the pieces of glass from the sink. Water from the dripping tap was pooling in the curved pieces and the whole thing sparkling against the shiny stainless steel of the bowl looked like a Habitat Christmas tree: all metal and white fairy lights.

'Lucy?' I suppose he must have raised an eyebrow to her, by way of asking how our little conversation went, because when I tore my eyes away from the lights and the glass, Lucy was shrugging and shaking her head.

'I think we'll get off now,' Neil said. Lucy pushed past him and went into the front room.

'Thanks for the wine, Annie.' Her words, just as she headed for the front door, were in a stiff, scared little voice I could almost have compared to my own. 'We're trying to be nice to you here. We don't want any trouble.'

Neil moved to let her pass and then looked at me for a moment.

'Lovely evening though – should hook up with Ray more often.' He looked awkwardly around the kitchen, nodded at me and then left. I didn't move, and let them see themselves out.

After I heard the front door slam I boiled the kettle again for more tea and took as long as I could over making it. I could hear Barry and Sangita chatting quietly to each other, but neither of them came into the kitchen to see what was taking me so long. I didn't dare go back into the front room, and had a wild moment when I considered escaping out of the back door and running away.

I wrapped my hands around the scalding teapot and imagined it, me haring down the street with my skirt crinkling between my legs. Blowing up around my ears in a high wind. Slipping in my court shoes, no purse, no keys, nowhere to go, and the Choudhrys sitting in my front room chatting about decking and eating all the fairy cakes. I wondered how long it would take before they'd notice I wasn't there anymore, before they'd come into the kitchen to check, and find the glass in the sink, the back door open? They'd call the police, they'd send out people to look for me, and I'd have to hang about under the pier with the tramps until the June night turned dark. And then what would I do? Slink home to an empty house, a hungry cat, and a street full of worried neighbours dotted about in their nightgowns. I wouldn't have any choice but to come back: all my eggs were in this basket.

I forced myself back into the front room.

'Everything present and correct?' Barry asked, and I held up my hand and showed him the plaster.

'Silly me,' I said brightly, 'don't know how I've lasted as long as I have, I really don't.' I sat down next to Sangita and leaned into the couch. I was pretending to look at a picture on the wall behind me, but moved a cushion surreptitiously over the stains on my skirt. Neither of them gave any sign that they had noticed, and feeling braver, I helped myself to a fairy cake and became determined to make a success of what remained of the evening.

'And which part of London is it that your husband lives in just now?' Barry asked. He was standing at the window twitching the curtains and uncovered Mr Tips lying on the sill. He blinked at Barry sleepily and then continued unmoving. The front room looked horribly empty now. Raymond's cans and crisp packet lying abandoned on the floor didn't exactly give the impression I'd been aiming for. I sighed, and looked up at Barry.

'He's just moved, same as me,' I said. 'He'd done so well for himself last year that we both decided to upgrade our living arrangements, and send the little one to a better school. Everything is so hectic right now I'm afraid I couldn't tell you exactly where. There's a photograph of his flat in one of the boxes upstairs and I do have the address but do you know, I can't think of it off the top of my head!' I tried to be cheerful but my words came out flat and without enthusiasm.

Sangita tilted her head and I felt her pat my knee, 'You must be very attached to the area to want to stay up here so far away from them despite everything. I don't know if I could do it unless there were,' she let the pitch of her voice slide up inquisitively, 'special circumstances?'

'It is hard,' I said, ignoring her curious look, 'but we've considered all the options and we think this is best. His job is so demanding on his time we'd never see each other much anyway! People really depend on him, life and death sometimes. Sometimes a wife has to come second to that, and I accept it.' I looked at Barry stoically, but he was scratching Mr Tips's ears and seemed quite oblivious to the conversation.

'It must make the holidays something to look forward to,' Sangita said, 'it's half term soon, and I know it'll be bedlam at our house when that comes around!' She rolled her eyes and then nodded decisively, 'We'll look forward to meeting your little girl then.'

I laughed when she said 'bedlam' and Barry put his cup down on the coffee table. When she finished speaking, Sangita stood up and I realised, not without relief, they were getting ready to leave.

'That was a lovely evening,' Sangita said, and we all shook hands again like friends before they went.

It may appear odd now, the way I was speaking to Sangita and Barry before they left. I was under a considerable amount of stress, remember, and even ignoring that, I think I can be justified in the way I stretched the truth a little during the last part of the party.

These were people I didn't know, and I didn't want to reveal details of my personal life to total strangers. You could even argue it wasn't that polite of them to ask. It was my job as a hostess to keep the conversation going and to make my guests feel comfortable. Allowing Sangita and Barry to think we had more in common than we actually did was one of the ways I tried to do that. And anyway, what I said wasn't a world away from the truth.

Will was a dentist, and had a thriving practice. We could have afforded a car and a nice house in a place like this very easily, I know we could, but he was so concerned about the future, pension plans and university funds, so worried about a drop in house prices or a rise in the cost of equipment needed for his work, that we lived very frugally and he spent money only rarely. We never lived the life we could have done, or the life that I had been led to expect we would live, and apart from the occasional dinner dance with other dentists and their wives, Will might as well have been a dustman or a street cleaner. The most important thing though, was that he didn't do anything like that for a living at all. He was a medical professional, and so whatever elaborations I was forced to make on my past that evening, I like to think I kept to the spirit of the truth, and captured the essentials. That is what counts.

6

If I was asked, I'd say the main reason why I was so skilled at handling the trickier parts of my house-warming party was my early experience with my friend Boris. I realised, even at the time, that he and his family were the sort of people I'd never normally have the opportunity to interact with. The sort of people who would forget about jars of olives in the back of cupboards, I suppose. Luckily for me, our mutual isolation in the rural Cumbria of our childhoods had thrown us together. My mother had at one time worked informally for his mother doing bits of ironing and mending. While she worked Boris and I would be left to our own devices. We used to make tents under the tablecloth or go out into his wild back garden to find toads. In time, we'd become good friends and after my own mother died, Boris's family had almost adopted me.

While my father worked at night and I was too young to be at home on my own, I stayed at their house, sleeping in one of his sisters' rooms or, at the weekends, camping in their back field. Even when I was older and didn't need to be babysat anymore, going to their house after school had become a habit and because they never told me that I couldn't, I ate my evening meal there most nights. I kept my eyes and ears open so I could learn as much as I could about the ways to be sociable, both one on one and in group occasions. I like to think it prepared me well for the demands of my adult life, and I'll always be grateful to them for it.

One particular occasion I remember illustrates my point perfectly. Boris and I had been into his dad's study, where we, or rather he, had been searching the desk drawers for packets of cigarettes. I was his anxious lookout and the sound of the car outside had brought us out into the kitchen: letting us know his parents and remaining sisters had returned. They'd just dropped off one of the older ones at university in Lancaster. We'd sat down at the table and Boris had groaned when they all came in through the door. I'd started to get ready to go home and leave them to it, but his mum saw me stand up and shook her head.

'Don't get up, Annie, stay for a cup of tea and tell us what you've been up to.'

I liked his mother, I really did. Her name is Caroline and she is one of the warmest people I've ever met.

His dad, Adrian, pulled up a chair next to Boris and elbowed him in the ribs, a gesture that I believe was supposed to refer to one possibility of what we'd been 'up to'. I pretended not to notice. The whole family had taken their places at the table and were clutching at the teapot and passing mugs around. Karina, who was the youngest up from Boris, filled the kettle.

'We haven't been doing anything really, just watching some telly,' I answered, to be polite, because Boris didn't look as if he was about to.

Fly had come up under the table and put her head on my knee. I pulled her ears gently. She smelled like tripe and outside. There were burrs caught in her coat and she sat warming my feet while I got them out for her. Dogs were the thing: loyal, gentle creatures, and useful too. I was too sentimental over them, crying whenever my dad had to shoot a dog that he was finished with. Boris's parents had rescued theirs; old farm dogs that were too blind and arthritic to work. When they died they were buried under odd-shaped mounds in the garden and Caroline planted geraniums and daffodil bulbs on the top.

'Annie! It's your play tonight, isn't it?' Adrian said dramatically, and put both his hands on top of his head.

I lowered my face and stared at my chipped and bitten fingernails but Boris slapped the table with his open hand and looked at me, surprised.

'Why didn't you say?' he said. 'Shouldn't you have been practising or something? The school's been doing rehearsals all week!'

I murmured something or other but the family were talking all around me, passing the teapot to each other. If Natasha had still been at home there wouldn't have been room for me to sit down with them. I wondered what they did when they had guests for tea but then I remembered that they had a dining room with family portraits on the walls and they only ate breakfast and casual lunches in the kitchen. It was a more intimate setting, and I felt pleased to have been included in it.

'She's been going on about this play for weeks,' Boris turned back to me, 'all the lines you've had to learn! I can't believe you didn't mention it – weren't you supposed to go early for a last rehearsal?' He looked at his watch. 'And you've missed it? Bloody hell, Annie!'

'Is your dad going?' Karina let her pale hair fall into her eyes as she spoke. The other members of the family fell silent as the conversations they had been having amongst themselves dried up. They looked at her, as if she had made some kind of error in asking.

'It's your first part, isn't it? And you got the lead? It's a big deal. Did he manage to get a ticket?' she said.

'Annie's dad works a lot in the evenings,' Caroline said, 'not everyone's as lucky as we are. Or as lazy!' she laughed. 'We'll come though, shall we, Annie?'

'I think the tickets have all been sold,' I said, 'my dad did ask about it, but I think he just got there too late.'

Caroline and Adrian exchanged a look I couldn't interpret. Adrian pushed back his chair. There were a few toast crumbs perched on a fold in his tie that rolled onto the floor as he stood up.

'I'll telephone the Head, get him to make a bit more room for us. It's all right, Annie, don't look so mortified. I know him; we were at college together. I'll tell him we'll need a set of tickets for us two and Boris, and one for your father. Just in case.'

Boris was looking pleased, 'We'll wait for you afterwards and give you and your dad a lift back with us, won't we?'

'Oh yes,' Caroline nodded at Boris and it was decided, 'be silly not to, we're so close. And it'll be a treat for you, Annie, to arrive in style. Better than crammed into the front of that mucky Land Rover?' She was referring to the vehicle my father used for work, and I couldn't help but agree with her. Arriving in her sleek black car would be a treat indeed.

Adrian went into the hallway to use the telephone. One of the sisters was shaking a set of scrabble tiles out onto the table but I shook my head when they asked me if I wanted to play and tried to keep quiet and listen to what he was saying. What I did hear didn't seem to make sense until I realised he wasn't talking to the head-master at all, but to my father.

'I quite understand your predicament, sir,' he was saying.

'She's just a teenage girl though, it doesn't seem right.'

'Family support and all that. Could make the difference between success and failure to her.'

'Quite so. No, of course not.'

'You bring her up admirably, we can all see that.'

'We can pick you both up together. It would be no trouble. Yes.'

'Right then. Goodbye.'

When he came back into the kitchen he rubbed his hands together and smiled.

'All sorted, Annie. Should be quite a night. You know I'm actually looking forward to it. It's been years since I've seen any Shakespeare, uncultured philistine that I am.' He looked at his watch and walked around the kitchen table. 'Eight o'clock, is it? We've got plenty of time to eat and get ready.'

Adrian touched his wife's shoulder lightly for a moment as he passed her and this seemed to be a kind of private signal between them because she immediately stood up and beckoned me towards her.

'Shall I give your hair a trim, sweetheart? Just an inch or so off the bottom to get rid of your split ends? You want to be looking your best, don't you? Tell me about the costume they've sorted out for you. What's it like?'

I sat on one of the kitchen chairs in the utility room while she snipped with her kitchen scissors. I looked at the varnished floor-boards and saw the wet spikes of my hair fall between them as she cut. She often did things like this for me, knowing from Boris that I didn't have my own mother to rely on. On more than one occasion she'd noticed when a new skirt or top didn't fit right and had taken me upstairs to her own bedroom so she could unpick the seams and let the material out. Her cutting my hair was just one more of the little things she did to look after me and include me in her family, and I must admit she made a very good job of it. I felt more well turned out than I had done in a long time when a few hours later their car pulled up outside my house and my father and I stepped into the back of it to be taken to my school for the play.

The journey home was an entirely different matter. Boris's parents sat together in the front, not speaking, although every few moments his mother would turn around in her seat and smile kindly at me. Boris sat on one side of me with his forehead resting against the window, deliberately making his breath come in gasps so he could create clouds of fog on the glass that he would then write his initials in with a finger. My father, still in the muddy moleskins and body warmer he wore for his work at the farm, sat on the other side awkwardly playing with his cuffs and picking at the toughened skin on his knuckles.

The journey lasted twenty minutes. I passed the time by looking out into the dark and counting the black shapes of the pylons that punctured the fields either side of the road. My dad's silent presence in the back of the car seemed to stifle any attempt Caroline made to initiate some light topic of conversation and eventually she gave up and left the silence uninterrupted.

The way Caroline's earrings moved and swung caught my eye as the car turned around the corner and slowed down as we went into the village. I probably wouldn't have noticed them at any other time but she had put her hair up in a fancy curl on the back of her head for the occasion and so her neck and ears were exposed. Her perfume filled the car with the smell of peaches and the dress she'd selected for the evening was made out of a shiny material that caught the green light from the dials on the dashboard and shimmered slightly in the dark.

My father finally broke the silence himself.

'Well you played a blinder tonight, Annie,' he said, looking at no one, 'had us all on the edge of our seats. Don't know about the rest of you,' he kept his gaze fixed to the knees as he spoke in that quiet, contemptuous voice of his, 'but you certainly had my attention for the full *thirty seconds* you were on stage.'

I paused, hoping someone else would speak first, and Caroline stepped in and saved me.

'I thought it was a fantastic production. I had a wonderful time! Didn't all the children do well!' she said enthusiastically.

'Hear! Hear!' Adrian added, then abruptly turned on the radio, which eliminated the possibility of any further conversation. The programme was about the solo career of John Lennon and we all listened to it intently for the rest of the journey.

When the car drew up outside my house Caroline turned around in her seat and smiled again.

'It's been a lovely evening. Thanks so much for inviting us, Annie. We had a really nice time, didn't we, Boris?' Boris merely shifted in his seat and grunted almost inaudibly. My father, without saying anything, had opened the car door as soon as the vehicle came to a halt and had quickly stepped outside. Adrian got out too and followed him to the back of the car. I thought it best to stay where I was for the time being.

'She's a sixteen-year-old girl, that's all,' I heard him say. I kept my face turned to the front of the car and looked at the drops of rain hitting the windscreen and dripping steadily down the glass. I didn't see my father's reaction or catch anything of what was said next. After a moment or two I unfastened my seat belt and put my hand on the door handle but Caroline leaned between the two front seats and put her hand on my knee.

'You come and see us again soon, Annie, won't you? We love having you around, whenever you like.' I nodded politely and smiled but continued opening the door and moving along the back seat to get out of the car.

'No, I mean it. We're one short now, anyway, with Natasha away, so you must come round for a meal and eat up the extra for us.' She smiled at me but Boris had started at her words and for some inexplicable reason was rolling his eyes at her and shaking his head.

'Oh, don't be silly, Boris. Annie knows what I meant, don't you, sweetie?' I nodded again politely, thanked her for driving my dad and me home, and then got out of the car. I passed Adrian on the garden path as I went towards the house and he put a hand on my shoulder and nodded kindly before letting go of me and getting back into the car. I waved from the doorstep as they pulled away. My father had already gone indoors.

As far as I could tell, everyone should have had a lovely evening. We'd arrived on time and the four of them had good seats, all together on a row of plastic chairs in the sports hall, which had been turned into a theatre for the night. From my vantage point behind the curtain I could see my dad sticking out a little in the aisle seat in order to stretch out his legs and click the heels of his boots together impatiently. Even when the lights went out the green glow from the bulbs above the fire doors illuminated their expressions very clearly.

Caroline, like me, seemed particularly touched when the senior boy and girl playing Romeo and Juliet started dancing at the party, and I stood in the wings, counting the steps and hoping that everything would go right. I'm pleased to say that it did, and my own line went off without a hitch. Because everything had gone so well, I had been quite at a loss as to the origin of the tension and silence in the car on the way home. It is possible that they might have assumed, for some reason, I had been asked to play the lead role in the play. That small misunderstanding had probably been the source of a little surprise and disappointment to Boris and his parents but as to how that misapprehension transpired, I am still none the wiser.

There was a gap of two weeks or so between the night of the play and when I next saw Boris outside of school. That was unusual, but not so much that either of us felt the need to pass comment on it when we were reunited. As I remember, I just turned up at his house one evening, and we carried on as usual without speaking about the last time we'd been in each other's company. We'd sat in his bedroom listening to music and I, lost in my own thoughts, was startled when he'd turned his cassette player off abruptly and said to me:

'My family's so weird, y'know. It's like we're all wearing rubber gloves all the time, no one wanting to touch each other, get their hands dirty with *real* interacting, y'know? We never argue. Really. I bet you don't believe it.'

It was the usual adolescent irritations he was in the habit of spouting. I think he liked me because I was even quieter than him: it looked like I was a good listener.

'Hmm.'

We were sitting on the bed in his attic room. Because he was smoking the skylight was wide open, even though it was raining outside. The rain came in through the window and dropped onto his glasses; made dark spots on his duvet cover. It was navy blue: everything in his room was blue of one shade or another, and because there was only the one window in the slope of the eaves the room was permanently dim, as if we were underwater.

'You're very lucky. A lot of people would love to have your problem to complain about,' I said. I'd say we were close, but I just never understood the way he seemed to be constantly embarrassed by his family.

'It's all an act. It's not real, and being real is the most important thing, isn't it?' he said, and snorted irritably.

'If you say so.'

'It's like they all really do like each other. They get on, my mum and dad. My sisters would probably pick each other for friends even if they weren't related. That's what I mean. It's fake, it must be.'

He leaned back and made an expansive gesture with his cigarette. I think he'd picked it up from something he'd seen on the television because the gesture had appeared suddenly in his repertoire and he seemed particularly pleased with it.

'What are the odds,' he said, still waving the cigarette about and dropping ash on his jeans, 'that people thrown together totally by chance are really going to get on as well as that lot seem to? It's just… weird. You wouldn't put seven total strangers in a room and expect them to take bullets for each other.' He sighed, and looked at me.

'You and your dad aren't like that, are you? You don't get on and you don't make any bones about it. It's just us. Freaks!'

I probably laughed a little and didn't reply: I've never much liked talking about myself.

'I don't know what's wrong with this house anyway. They're such snobs it makes me… I don't know, *cringe*, or something.'

He was angry because his dad had been promoted again and they were moving to Keswick. He felt he should have been consulted rather than just taken along like another piece of luggage.

'Keswick, for Christ's sake!'

I was still finding it difficult to imagine that in a matter of weeks someone else would be living in the house, someone else sleeping in Boris's bedroom. In fact, the news had come as a bit of a blow to me, dropped like a stone one morning at the bus stop.

'Perhaps you'll end up liking it there better than here,' I said. He was always saying how boring it was, how there were only three buses a day and he could never go out in the evenings because his dad would have to pick him up and it would be too humiliating. It wouldn't be like that after the move, that's for certain. He looked at me intensely for a second.

'Of course, you're right. Direct. You're always very direct.' He made *direct* sound like something bad, a criticism, and I mouthed the word silently to myself. Direct. It sounded like a footfall, or the noise a compact mirror makes when it is clicked closed between index finger and thumb.

'That's what I really like about me and you, it's really real, no rubber gloves – not pretending to be sincere or anything. Things are what they are. Someone said that somewhere. I read it. Things are what they are.'

I had, by this point, no idea what he was talking about, but he seemed to be trying to come to something.

'Just going with the flow – no big scenes, right?'

I nodded, because he seemed to want me to, and satisfied, he stood up to throw his cigarette end out of the skylight. The gutter was full of them.

'Maybe I could come too.'

'What?' He looked confused, and I spoke quickly, trying to explain myself.

'Not to live. I mean for visits and things. Your mum wouldn't mind.'

'Maybe. They're always going on about how we should get it together.'

I still remember him moistening his lips as if he was nervous, and as I looked at him I realised he was staring quite obviously at the front of my shirt.

'There won't be many more chances,' he said, and looked at his bedroom door, 'they're all watching telly. They never come up here. Not without knocking anyway.'

I moved my hands to the buttons on my shirt. I suppose I had some idea that I could avert what was going to happen, that by making myself a little more indispensable to the family they would be forced to stay. He seemed taken aback but it was too late to cover up what I had started to do. My shirt was already undone.

'I think you're right,' I said, 'we're adults, aren't we? I think we should do this before you go.'

My fingers stumbled on the zips of my boots while he stood on the bed and closed the skylight, making the room dark. He laughed but it was a forced laugh, almost under his breath.

'Everyone thinks we're doing it anyway. My dad, Natasha. I never hear the end of it. And all the lads at school – I get so much stick for it, believe me.'

While I undressed he put the chair from his desk against the door and lit a candle. He was like that. He carried on talking, a quiet mon-otone that had the effect of soothing my nerves.

'If I'm going to do the time, I might as well do the crime, that's what I think. Stupid not to really, you know, get the practice with each other for when the real thing comes along. Then we won't humiliate ourselves on opening night, will we?'

I'll admit it; he wasn't much of a romantic, but he kept glancing at me in that hungry way that I'd noticed before, had almost become used to the sensation of his eyes on my breasts, on my hips, on the parts of me that swelled and sometimes spilled out of my clothes. There was so much of me to look at, and there's a sort of person who likes that kind of thing – I know that now, but I didn't then, and more than half believed his quiet monologue convincing himself of the sensible practicality of what we were about to do.

When I had undressed down to my underwear I lay down on his bed. I probably was more than a little nervous: it was to be the pin-nacle and the end of our time together, and a new life experience for both of us.

'Don't you want to go under the covers?'

I had to scramble up on my hands and knees and felt self-con-scious about the dimpled slabs of my thighs as he pulled the duvet up around us. He was still fully clothed, and turned away from me before shrugging off his shirt. I was fat, and he had acne on his shoulders. I giggled as he tried to wrestle open his belt and button flies without exposing any of his own flesh to the air.

'Come on, if you're not going to take this seriously...' He looked sulkily at me. 'I didn't laugh at you.' He took off his glasses, folded them closed and placed them prissily on the bed by his pillow.

Without them, his eyes looked smaller and more ordinary. 'Just don't laugh, okay? I won't do it if you're going to laugh at me.'

I apologised, he helped me remove my bra, and rolled on top of me. He was skinny, and the bones of his hips jutted and hurt the insides of my legs.

'Am I too heavy?'

'No, you're fine.' We kissed for a while then he moved his hips away, put his hand between my legs and poked around the side of my knickers. He pushed, and swirled his fingers painfully inside.

'Where are you in your cycle, An?'

'What?'

'I don't have anything, any, well, protection. But it's hard to have a baby if it's the wrong time.'

Then, he knew more about these things than I did; he had a blonde flock of talkative and outgoing sisters, and I only had my father, who was taciturn at the best of times, but silent on the subject of blood and babies.

'When did you last have your period?'

'*Boris.*' I turned my face onto the pillow. He carried on nudging me with his hips, leaning up on his arms so he could inspect my chest, which seemed to help things along because the nudgings became more insistent.

Finally I said, 'I finished a few days ago.'

'It should be okay then. Shall I, or do you want to?'

'No, I will.' He looked relieved. I suppose there are some things that are impossible to learn from your sisters. I took him in my hands and guided him in down the side of my knickers, which was a bit uncomfortable. Going inside itself didn't hurt as much as I expected it might, although I remember feeling surprised by how hot and hard his privates felt. It didn't feel like a part of a human being at all, not when it was like that.

He rocked into me five or six times until our stomachs were touching, I closed my eyes, he yelped, shuddered, and then I felt a spreading wetness between my legs. He rolled away again and the dampness his chest had imprinted on my breasts started to cool.

There were a few moments of silence. I'd imagined it would be more tiring, but neither of us was particularly out of breath. I wondered if I should say something but decided to wait for him to speak first. Some endearment or declaration of affection was, as far as I'd gathered, customary at this point and I didn't want to interrupt anything he had planned to say to me.

'I didn't last very long, did I?' He was gloomy. 'We can do it again if you like.' He coughed and reached for his glasses. 'We could have a cup of tea and then… well, I want you to like it too.'

He spoke formally, as if he'd consulted a book on the matter before my arrival. 'I know what to do, some other things you might like?'

I didn't answer. The line of light around the outside of the skylight where the blind didn't fit properly had caught my eye and I was busily staring at the white outline. It had been worth it, I was thinking, the embarrassment and the messiness of it, worth it to become part of his family and fill in the gap that Natasha's leaving had created for them.

Of course I'd been mistaken. The move went ahead as planned and I never saw Caroline again, nor Boris until much later, after I was married.

7

But I digress.

The morning after the house-warming party I was up early and quite unwell. The thing about vomiting is that no matter how many times you do it, you never get used to it. I closed my eyes as my stomach contracted for the fifth time, hurling the remains of the previous night's indulgences out of my mouth. After a few more minutes of dry heaving, I was satisfied that it had stopped, and recovered enough to stand and wipe my lips.

It was my own fault: after the Choudhrys had left I'd spent an hour or so finishing the leftover food and opened bottle of wine. Barry had made an impression on the hedgehog, but there was plenty of cheese left and I'm afraid that, and the plate of fairy cakes which my guests had left untouched, worked together in my digestive system to produce a very unpleasant bout of indigestion. Instead of tucking myself up in bed with a plate of scrambled egg and a Disney video, I foolishly tottered downstairs, helped myself to the tray of untouched sausage rolls and uncorked two of the remaining bottles of wine.

My memories of the next few days are hazy. Someone called me on the telephone about an unpaid credit card, and I remember sitting at the bottom of the stairs in my nightdress singing all the verses to 'Found a Peanut'. In my mind's eye I can see myself very clearly, stamping my bare feet on the carpet and conducting myself through the chorus with an unlit cigarette. I can only presume I attempted to take up smoking, a habit, I'm pleased to confirm, that didn't stick longer than my celebrations of those few days. I made frequent trips to the corner shop for tins of condensed milk, more wine and cat food, and managed to spend a frightening amount of money there. I also remember a brief conversation with Lucy about local by-laws regarding noise levels in residential areas between the hours of eleven at night and seven in the morning.

I can only explain my behaviour as an adolescent outpouring of exuberance; a long postponed eruption of youthful enthusiasm that had been cut short by my early marriage. When it was over, I awoke from it dazed and exhausted, nauseous and somewhat shamefaced. At twenty-eight, most people would expect me to have grown out of such things, but, as I said, most people were not aware of the special circumstances attached to my case.

Once was enough, I vowed, showering and preparing to catch up on neglected laundry and washing-up. At the sink, I had to prop myself against the fridge during a dizzy spell, and left the water to grow cold as I stumbled back to the sofa. I felt wretched for several days, and could only stir from the sofa to feed Mr Tips and answer my calls of nature. When I was more recovered, I set about scrubbing the bathroom, stained from my days of excess, and immediately started to think about visiting Neil.

A hand with the washing-up and a bunch of carnations bought at the corner shop might have been good enough for Will's friends, but this sort of person was altogether more formal and would welcome, would probably *expect*, a follow-up visit after a party. From the day that I noticed the bags Neil put out for the dustman contained, among other things, one empty jar of organic mayonnaise, the wooden box for a kind of round cheese I couldn't say the name of, and paper bags printed with the name of the local bakery, I knew I should count Neil along with Boris and his family. Evidently, they were the same kind of people.

No doubt Neil would be wondering how my injury was healing, and perhaps waiting politely for me to give him the opportunity to return the invitation. These assumptions were, I admit, tentative, but as I said, I'd had dealings with this kind of person before and so I felt confident that I could still move ahead with my plans to befriend him.

I decided my best approach in terms of developing our friendship would be to buy a bottle of milk for him and take it round to replace the one I'd borrowed for the party. He'd no doubt be pleased I'd remembered, notice my politeness, we'd have a chat and things would crack along nicely from there.

'Annie?'

Neil had swung the door open wide and looked over his shoulder back into the house. There was no noise from within, and I knew for a fact Lucy was out. I took the movement of his head as an invitation to come in further, and brandished the bottle in front of me so he was immediately made aware of the reason for my visit.

'I've brought the milk back – well, not the same milk, obviously, but some new milk, which I've just been to buy to make up for the milk I borrowed for my party.'

I held it out and he took it from me warily. 'Thanks. You shouldn't have gone to any trouble.' He looked puzzled. 'It was a week ago, more than that. You really didn't need to bother.'

A week? I made a mental note to myself to check the batteries in my alarm clock and purchase a calendar.

'As long as that?' I said, laughing a little. 'I've really let the time get away from me this week, haven't I? You were very kind. Call it a... peace offering?'

Neil sighed and smiled, holding the milk in both hands and looking at it as if he didn't know what it was.

'Lucy's not here,' he said, 'but I'll tell her you said that. She'll be pleased.'

I nodded, and waited for him to beckon me in out of the hallway.

'Are you all right?' he asked. 'You look a bit pale?'

I fumbled for my voice. It seemed like only a day or two had passed since the two of us were sharing a neighbourly drink in my front room, but the grass had grown shaggy in my front garden. I rubbed my index finger over my thumb, the way people do when they are talking about money. I could still feel the scar from the tin opener, but there was nothing more to show for it than a tiny white slice that even I wouldn't have noticed unless I'd been looking for it.

'I've been a little unwell,' I said, my stomach still churning, 'I just didn't want you to think I'd forgotten,' I pointed at the milk again, 'you were very kind.'

'You'd have got me out of bed if you'd come any earlier,' he said, 'you aren't the only one with a hangover!' he rolled his eyes and chuckled gently.

'I'm certainly not suffering from a hangover!' I said, pulling myself upright despite the pain in my head. 'I'm not a big drinker, actually. You'll have noticed that at the party.'

He was still holding the milk and I stepped into the house in the hope it would remind him of his manners and prompt him into offering me a seat.

'Just a cold, although I'm still feeling a little unsteady on my feet.' I laughed gently and tasted lipstick.

'I'll just pop this in the fridge.' He disappeared and I heard his voice float in hollowly from the kitchen. 'It was very considerate of you to bring it around. Lucy was a little concerned that, we may have, um …' I heard the fridge close.

'Just a little off-colour, that's all,' I said quickly. I held up my hand and stuck my thumb out, 'Look, all better now. I don't even need a plaster.'

'So I see,' Neil said, peering past the kitchen door. I'd sat down and he leaned against the door frame looking at me. I resisted the urge to put a hand to my face and check my hair: it makes people ill at ease when you fidget.

'I don't suppose you could bring me a glass of water while you're in there?'

I listened to the tap run and looked around again at his front room. Because the houses were semi-detached the doors and windows and light switches were located in a strange mirror image of the way they were in my own house. I found myself thinking of *Alice Through the Looking Glass* and feeling queasy again. My mouth filled with saliva and for one moment I was certain I was going to be sick. I swallowed hard, shuffling across the couch so I would be near to the front door in case I was caught short.

Neil's place was just like my own house: a slightly upgraded, more expensively furnished version, maybe, but the layout and the structure were the same and it was a little reminder to me: my living room could be as nice as this too. Neil was demonstrating what potential my surroundings had, what love and hard work could do to a place. All the books and newspapers lying around, souvenirs from holidays abroad and framed black-and-white photographs of places he'd been to on the walls: they all served to create an atmosphere which reminded me very strongly of Boris and his family. Looking at it all renewed my enthusiasm for the plans I'd made for my own home and I started to feel better.

Neil came back into the front room as I raised my hand to touch a knot of varnished driftwood sitting in the middle of the coffee table. I dropped my hand guiltily and smiled.

'Don't blame me for that,' he said, 'Lucy collects all that kind of trash. She's a magpie. We can't go anywhere without her bringing half the place back! That's from the beach. Brave of her to pull anything out of that water: I bet it glows in the dark when no one's looking.' He smiled and handed me the glass, 'Here's your water.'

I took the glass from him and as I did so my thumb touched his. There was a bead of water from the tap perched on his nail and it ran onto my hand. I sipped slowly, not feeling the pressure to stop or to talk until the glass was nearly empty and the nausea had completely gone.

'So you're feeling better then?' Neil repeated. He was so concerned about my health, and it touched me. 'We, Lucy and me, we were really concerned we'd managed to get off on the wrong foot,' he said awkwardly, 'at your gathering. And this week. She's sensitive to noise, gets a bit ratty. It doesn't bother me if you fancy having a bit of a sing-song, I do it in the shower myself, but she's prone to migraines. Women's things. I'm sure she didn't mean to offend.'

'Of course not. We're neighbours. That's got to mean something, don't you think?' I said. 'And like you say, if she's sensitive to noise it might be better for her to stay at home the next time I have a party. Lively social occasions aren't for everyone, and no one would take offence if, for the sake of her health, she had to stay at home.'

Neil shuffled, took his hands out of his pockets, and sat down next to me on the couch. Our knees pointed at each other, which I knew from my reading about non-verbal communication was a good sign.

'I'm not sure it will come to that,' he said, 'but at the end of the day, this is where we all live, we might as well be pleasant to each other.'

There was a little pause in the conversation and I sipped again from the glass of water. I had been hoping he would offer me a cup of tea and a few biscuits, maybe a slice of cake, but some men don't think of that kind of thing, and it isn't really their fault, just one of those little differences, like women not being very good at driving cars or reading maps. Men and women tend to balance each other out: that's why they need each other.

'Have you managed to get in touch with your daughter yet?' he asked. 'You seemed to be having a bit of trouble with that, as I remember?'

'These things tend to take time,' I said vaguely, distracted by all the nice vases and books and things he had arranged on sets of shelves built in either side of the chimney breast. He'd even fitted some kind of light under the shelves so his possessions were softly illuminated from below. It was small touches like this that made the home so welcoming; I could tell he'd taken a lot of effort to create exactly the right impression of himself by ordering his surroundings. People who came to visit, like me, could not fail to be impressed by his taste and education.

'It must put you under a lot of stress,' he said, sounding sympathetic and looking at me gently for a moment.

I felt the glass start to wobble in my hand.

'It's no way to live, you know. We do have a lot of sympathy for your situation.'

I nodded and put the glass down on the floor, clasping my trembling hands together on my knee.

'And your husband? Lucy told me you were going to get him to come back for a bit and help you out in the house. We haven't seen him yet, is he still working away during the week?'

'Yes, still in London.' I thought in the circumstances it would be best to be discreet. 'The thing is, Neil, he won't be coming at the weekend. Him coming back for a visit, like Lucy suggested, it isn't going to be possible. I don't expect to be seeing him again.'

Neil sighed between his teeth.

'Lucy said she thought there was something like that, you moving to a new house all on your own, so far away from them. It's a shame, it really is.'

I took a sip of water and nodded as I swallowed.

'So you don't see him at all anymore. The relationship is...?' he let his words tail off, embarrassed.

I felt a flutter trill its way up the insides of my ribs when I realised what he was asking me, trying to make sure, in that masculine, clumsy way of his, that I really was unattached.

'Yes. It's all done with now, thank goodness. I won't be seeing him again!' I giggled but because of the way my throat felt it came out very shrilly and sounded embarrassing: like a child who's been let out with the adults to go to a party but can't quite cope with all the bright lights and loud music. An incipient temper tantrum, even though that's not the way I felt at all.

'There's no need for sympathy,' I said. 'I try not to think about it, and keep myself nice and busy. There are,' I looked at him as sadly as I could, 'plenty of things I'd like to forget about from that part of my life. My husband, let's just say he isn't someone I'd want to introduce to the people round here. He had quite a strong personality.'

'Ah,' Neil said, and sighed. 'You don't need to say anything else. There's nothing worse than a man who throws his, ah, his weight about. You wouldn't think it, would you, not from a doctor.'

'No, I suppose you wouldn't,' I agreed, not quite grasping his point.

'And I bet he walks about like butter wouldn't melt. It's disgusting. Lucy's step-dad was a bit like that,' he said, 'that's why she left home so young. It's shocking. I could have swung for him myself, some of the things she told me. They never pick on people their own size, do they?' He shrugged, 'It's just not me though. Never thrown a punch in my life.'

'I can believe that,' I said warmly.

'London's the best place for the toerag. I won't say another word about it.'

'Yes,' I said quietly.

'No need to be embarrassed,' he said quickly, 'none at all. You've just got to think about your daughter now, that's the main thing. Should she really be away at school?'

'Well...'

Neil shook his head, 'It's nothing to do with me. Sorry, sorry, Annie. You should tell me to keep my nose out.'

'It's nice to have someone showing an interest,' I said quietly. There was a pause, and I began to wonder if it was time to go.

'Things will sort themselves out soon,' he said, 'you're better off without him, aren't you, and you've just got to keep that in mind.'

He must have heard something outside on the path because he

looked towards the door and at that moment there was a key scraping the lock. Lucy came in wearing a shiny white raincoat and a red silk scarf wrapped around her hair. I put my glass down on the table hastily and sat up properly. The atmosphere was ruined, and rather irritably I decided to let Neil handle the situation in his own way. He'd already given me quite a clear signal, to say anything else would have been, I realised, very indelicate, especially with Lucy in the room.

'Ah, Lucy!' He sounded immensely relieved, 'You were ages! Annie just came round to return the bottle of milk.'

Lucy looked puzzled and I saw Neil pulse a look at her, raising his eyebrows and opening his eyes wide.

'She's not been very well, but she's feeling much better now.'

'That's nice,' Lucy said slowly, still frowning at me.

'She just wanted to let you know how grateful she was about the milk, how kind it was of you to lend it to her,' Neil said. Lucy seemed to relax, before looking pointedly at the clock attached to the television.

'Well, I've got visitors this afternoon,' I began, and stood up.

They smiled knowingly at each other and I felt left out for a moment, before I realised how sensitive he was being to her needs and feelings. He'd been so tentative with me, asking about Will and making sure I was single, showing his sympathy and concern without doing anything that would have hurt Lucy. He needed to let her down gently in his own time.

'Time waits for no man, as they say!' I said, being very cheerful. I made my way over to the door. Neil opened it for me and just before I left I turned back into the house.

'It was nice to see you again, Lucy. That's a lovely scarf,' I hesitated, trying to remember the right word, 'very kitsch! Feel free to pop around for a cup of tea whenever you like, it would be lovely to get to know each other better.'

I spoke seemingly to them both but of course I was looking at Neil, trying to give him a verbal signal that I had understood the sentiment behind his questions about my marital status and was tentatively returning it.

'Oh yes, and you too, Annie.' He spoke distractedly, looking at

Lucy as if to gauge her reaction. Of course he had to be careful. She was busy taking off her coat and unwrapping the scarf from her head. There was rain on her nose, and the backs of her bare legs were spattered with mud.

I didn't stop smiling for the rest of the day.

8

Perhaps because I'd remembered again how nice it felt to have Caroline sit me in the kitchen and cut my hair, or maybe even because the motivation to look my best had been exacerbated, so to speak, by Neil's attention, I decided that I would go to the hairdresser after all and treat myself to a new style. I remember feeling quite excited about it; it had been a good while since I'd had my hair seen to by a professional because for a long time I had done the job myself in the bathroom mirror and been quite happy with it. I'd realised however, that small indulgences were no great crime, and looking back, Lucy's comments about my appearance had probably stung me more than I allowed myself to admit.

I'd lived in Fleetwood for some years, since the year before I was married, in fact, and although my new house was in a different neighbourhood, I was still familiar with the immediate area and I knew exactly where I wanted to go. Cloud Nine's was a beauty salon I often passed on my way to the supermarket and I'd always looked in through the big windows at the gleaming white sinks, sparkling mirrors and rows of brightly coloured bottles with a kind of envy. I'd often caught myself counting the money Will saw fit to give me for my own use, and wishing I could be the sort of woman to lie back and enjoy the attentions of, from what I could tell, cheerful and experienced staff. And now I could!

Finances were already becoming worrisome, but I decided I could put off one or two of the less urgent bills and update my hairstyle to something more fashionable.

The door tinkled open and I hesitantly walked in to a salon filled with the noise of chatter and hairdryers, smelling pleasantly of expensive shampoo and disinfectant. The girl at the counter took my cagoule from me and hung it up, reappearing moments later as if by magic with a cup of tea. The tea was in a glass cup with a metal handle: I'd never seen anything like it before, and she instructed me to drink it up while I looked at pictures of hairstyles in magazines. I did as she said, sipping quietly and leafing through the glossy pages as I waited for my own, personal stylist to become available. In what seemed like no time at all, one of the junior members of staff led me to the sinks, washed my hair and sat me down in front of a mirror. I was passing the time by looking around me and enjoying the sights and smells of the environment when my stylist's face appeared in the mirror above mine.

'Oh, hello!' she said, and while I didn't recognise her at first, her voice did seem familiar.

'It's Mrs Fairhurst, isn't it? You remember me, don't you?'

She was a young woman, perhaps five or six years younger than myself, dressed in the same black tunic and trousers as the others. I felt panicked, and began to grope around for a name, or at least a plausible excuse when, with a deep sigh, I remembered. Will had employed her for a year or so as a receptionist at his dental practice, and she'd eaten her evening meal with us on several occasions.

'Jessica,' I said, wishing I could do some kind of magic trick that would absent me from the place in a matter of seconds, 'of course I remember. How are you?'

'Good!' she said enthusiastically, and started darting about behind me, arranging combs and scissors and clips on a trolley that was parked next to my chair. She moved easily, almost gliding across the floor like she was on wheels.

She spent a few minutes running her fingers through my hair, telling me about the college course she had done after she left the practice, and how much she was enjoying her new job.

'See people in here that I know all the time, it's like being out at the pub only I get paid as well,' she said, and picked up her scissors, 'no paperwork either.' She giggled, 'I bet you remember how crap I always was at that!'

'Not at all,' I said politely, 'Will was always very pleased with your work. He was sad to see you go, we both were.'

'You've got to follow your dreams, though, haven't you?' she said. 'I know I'm just a hairdresser, it's not like being a dentist, but, well,' she shrugged, and waved her scissors about, 'you've got to do what your heart tells you, you only get one life, don't you?'

Jessica, perhaps inadvertently, had hit upon one of the great realisations of my adulthood. These epiphanies had struck me at various times during my married life, and towards the end of my time with Will I had been in the same position as Jessica when she had been employed by him: secure, perhaps, and receiving adequate remuneration, but nevertheless, unfulfilled. I nodded at her warmly.

'You're exactly right,' I said, 'there's no point making yourself unhappy for the sake of someone else. You've got to go out and make it happen, there's no point staying where you are and hoping that things will change when they won't.'

Jessica looked at my reflection carefully, perhaps touched at the strength of my passionate agreement.

'Better stop gassing before the boss gets on my back about not turning the clients around quick enough,' she said. She put down the scissors and ran her fingers through my wet hair, her pink and white acrylic fingernails scraping my scalp.

'And what are we doing for you today?'

I'd forgotten to bring the magazine with the picture of the hairstyle I'd selected with me and there were a few moments of awkwardness while I heaved myself out of the chair and made my way through the salon. The cape billowed out around me and my hair dripped water onto my shoulders as I trundled back to the waiting area to retrieve it. She looked at the picture and back at me doubtfully.

'It's a bit drastic, isn't it? You could definitely do with a good trim, a conditioning treatment, and maybe we could give you a few highlights, but this – it's an afternoon's work. You'd have to make a special appointment.'

'I see,' I said, feeling disappointed, and then laughing to cover it up, 'well a trim it will have to be then. I don't mind really, I've more important things to think about these days than my hair!'

'Yes, course you do,' Jessica said, and bowed her head towards mine confidentially, 'I heard about it all, you know. I always meant to come back and visit, after your little one was born, that is, to see how you were getting on. I bought a card and everything. But then I heard about, what happened, and I didn't know what to say,' she stared out of the salon window sadly, 'she was young, wasn't she? Did they ever find out why?'

When I didn't answer she looked back into the mirror at me and shook her head. 'Sorry, sorry, Mrs Fairhurst. I'm being –' I shook my head, 'no, it's none of my business. Raking it all up. Open my mouth and put my foot in it, just when you're doing so well, coming into town and treating yourself to a hairdo.' She put her hands in my hair and went back to her work,

'You can see why I didn't want to come around. I wouldn't have known what to say. What can you say, eh? It stinks, it just stinks.' She paused respectfully, and then leaned in again.

'It wasn't long after I heard about your little one that I read about your husband in the paper... when it all came out about what Mr Fairhurst was like with you,' she coughed uncomfortably and I shifted in my seat, feeling the chrome arms dig into my padded sides. 'I told my mum about it, she was flabbergasted – asked me if he'd ever used his temper on me!' She shook her head. 'Lucky escape, she said. Still. Terrible.'

She arranged her face to look serious and started combing my hair and sectioning it off in small clips on the top of my head. I watched the way her hands moved in the mirror and tried to plan what I was going to say next.

'You know he was always so decent to me while I was working for him. A really good boss,' she added, 'just goes to show you never can tell. Didn't think you'd still be living round here. I'd want to get away from the whole place, if I'd been through what you had.'

'Well,' I said, trying to keep very still because she had started to snip at the hair growing at the nape of my neck. It was tickling me but I didn't want to move and cause her to make a mistake. 'I've been here so long I feel like it's my home now, and I don't think I could start again in a totally new town.'

'I know what you mean,' Jessica tilted my head forward and for the next part of her conversation I couldn't see her, or my own face in the mirror, but kept my eyes fixed on my hands and the hem of the black cape I was wearing. The wet ends of my hair dropped into my lap in small crescents which grew fluffy and fell apart as they dried.

'It is a bit of a dump, but it grows on you, once you get settled,' she said.

'You need a familiar environment and good nurturing friends

around you when times get hard,' I agreed, and then, in an attempt to change the subject to something more cheerful, started telling her about Neil and Raymond and the Choudhrys and the house-warming party I'd had.

'One of my neighbours is in charge of the Neighbourhood Watch,' I said, 'and she personally asked me to get involved and perhaps even help run the meetings.'

'Oh yes?' she said, looking at my scalp. 'Meeting new people?' I must have blushed because she gave my shoulder a poke with her comb. 'Look at you! What's the totty like?' I must have looked puzzled, because she went on, 'The blokes? Have you met anyone else yet?' Her face seemed to waver between curiosity and sympathy, 'Or is it still too soon?'

'I'm not really interested in having a fling,' I said carefully, think-ing about my colourful past, 'my time is far too precious for that. But I'm not ruling out the idea of something more serious again either. I am only twenty-eight. I can't be on my own for the rest of my life, can I?' I laughed, but Jessica leaned over and squeezed my shoulders and I realised by her reaction it must have come out all wrong.

'Of course you won't be!' she said, squeezing and patting again before returning to my hair. 'Of course you won't! You've got lovely eyes, Mrs Fairhurst, and such a great sense of humour. You're a very witty woman and there's going to be plenty of men wanting to get to know you.'

'Well, there was someone who seemed quite interested,' I said, not liking the impression I'd inadvertently given her. I tried to imagine the picture in her head she had of me, of someone pining away for male company. 'He's not really my cup of tea, but, well, his name's Raymond and he came round to my house last week. He seemed very eager! I'm going to have to keep an eye on him,' I joked.

'Not your type then?' she said. I thought of the beer cans and that jumbo packet of crisps, him pretending to collide with me in the hallway in order to get closer to me. I shook my head.

'He's not quite what I'm looking for, no,' I said, and laughed, 'but I have a feeling he's going to be quite persistent!'

Jessica nodded and smiled encouragingly and we talked a little more until she'd finished, and then knowing I wouldn't be heard above the buzz of the hairdryer, I fell silent and watched her work in the mirror, marvelling as she dried my hair and arranged it gently with her comb. The way we were sitting reminded me of the times I had sat with my mother and the little talks we had in her bedroom when I came home from school.

I'd first noticed that my mother was getting ill when I was about twelve years old, and by the start of my second year at 'the big school', she wasn't getting out of bed at all. Instead of our usual quiet snacks together in the kitchen, I'd make her and myself something to eat and take it upstairs. We'd have a kind of picnic together spread out on her mustard-coloured candlewick bedspread while we waited for my father to return home from the farm where he worked. After we'd eaten, I'd often sit in front of her, cross-legged on the bed in my school uniform, and she would brush my hair and I'd be able to see her in the mirror in the wardrobe at the bottom of the bed while I chatted to her, often about little difficulties I was having at school. One time, I'd had a particularly bad time of it on the bus journey home, and had rushed right upstairs to her without stopping to make us anything to eat.

'You've got to remember, Annie,' she said, and I can still remember the gentle, soothing quality of her voice as she ran her tortoise-shell comb through my hair, 'they're only like that to you because they're jealous of you. I know it sounds strange but when you grow up you'll understand it for yourself, and in the meantime you're just going to have to trust me.' She had grey eyes and hard skin on her thumb from all the sewing she did, and I believed her.

'That's not going to make things any better for me on the bus though, is it?' I said. 'He's already gone mad this week because of the blazer. I can't tell Him again.'

'He' was how we both referred to my father when he wasn't there, although we tried not to speak about him unless we couldn't really avoid it.

'Sponge it off at the bathroom sink,' she said, 'and when you've done, bring it in here for me and I'll sew it up. You don't need to tell Him this time, not when He's so tired.'

She did favours like that for me quite a lot during the time she was confined to her room. It was her way of keeping close to me: we had our little secrets even though she couldn't get out of bed and because she was helping me out here and there as best she could she still felt like my mother even though everything else was different.

It must have been quite close to the end, because I remember her wedding ring rattling on her shrunken finger as she combed, and the way her nightdress had grown much too big for her and gaped open so much at the armpits I could see, even in the mirror, the scar on her chest from the first operation she had had.

'They'll grow out of it in time, they're just jealous of you,' she insisted again, and would have went on to say more but we both heard the front door open downstairs. She sighed and lay back on the pillows.

'Make sure you don't have your feet up on the bed when He comes in,' she whispered, and I nodded, patted her knee through the candlewick and went into my own room to play.

'All done now, what do you think?' Jessica stood away from me a little and held up a mirror so I could see the back of my own head. To be honest, it didn't look a great deal different from how it had been when I walked in there, but I didn't want to hurt her feelings so I smiled and moved about in my chair so I could see everything.

'It's absolutely lovely, thank you,' I said, and she looked pleased, so that was all right. I wouldn't want to be misunderstood, it wasn't bad, and in fact the products she had used had made it very shiny and it swished gently around my shoulders when I moved instead of lying limply against my neck and that was an improvement. Nevertheless, I had hoped for more of a transformation and couldn't help feeling a little disappointed when I looked back into the big mirror and saw a slightly better groomed version of the same old person looking back at me.

She took me back to the counter and I panicked for a second when she told me the price. Fifty-five pounds – and I'd only brought twenty! I went into my handbag, wrote a cheque and hoped for the best. They had a big black book on the counter, with gold writing and the logo of the salon embossed on the front.

'I'll write down what you had done,' she said, 'and the date, so we know what you like when you come back for your trim. Six weeks,' she said, pointing at me with the pen, 'so we can keep on top of those split ends! And you put your name and address in here, right in that box. Then we can write to you when it's time.'

I took the pen and wrote my new details in with a flourish, feeling the same kind of pride as I'd felt during those first days whenever I looked at my house key. There was no need for it, none at all. I knew I couldn't afford another appointment at a place like this. I was just showing off. But I put my address in anyway, and even underlined my name, never thinking that I would live to regret it.

Part Two

9

Sometimes I liked to imagine that Neil's bed was pushed up against the wall like mine, so near that I could almost hear him breathing. There was nothing inappropriate about my imaginings, far from it. Just the thought of having someone nearby helped me to sleep.

I'd been having trouble sleeping for the previous couple of months, since I'd moved really. Before I'd come to the new house, I was somewhere else, and living there had meant I'd got used to routine, to a degree of rigidity where evening meals and lights out were concerned. I certainly didn't like the constraint, but having people around me all the time, hearing distorted voices echoing through most of the night, had become normal for me and in the silence and comfort of my own suburban haven, I was beset with insomnia. There were many occasions when I lay awake in the dark, too tired to read and too awake to sleep.

That night I watched the streetlamps outside make yellow and black patterns on my bedroom ceiling, and counted the cars as they went by on the main road. I don't have a radio in my bedroom, and I never watch television late at night because it tends to be unsavoury, so, unavoidably, I heard movements from next door.

It wasn't that I was lying awake listening out for them, of course not, but in the dark quiet of my own bedroom things tended to echo across through the plaster. I heard Lucy, crying out or laughing about something. She started to talk animatedly, I heard a bang, and after a few minutes, the silence returned. She'd probably had a bad dream and woken Neil to tell him about it. I envied her, and remained sleepless.

Someone flushed the toilet in the small hours. After that there was nothing until the front door slammed first thing when Lucy went out to work, a little later than usual. It was shortly after breakfast, the washing-up done and me wondering what to do with myself, that there was a knock at the door. My heart leapt into my mouth. I'd seen Neil outside taking in the laundry only minutes before: perhaps he'd decided, now that Lucy was out of the way, to come and see me?

I didn't recognise the woman at first and smiled awkwardly for a few seconds before I put a name to the face and invited Sangita in. We chatted for a while about inconsequential things and then she shifted in her seat to lean closer to me and said:

'And how are you getting on, Annie? You managed to get the house straight yet?' I noticed she was holding a sheaf of brightly coloured leaflets and papers with a big purple paperclip fastening them all together.

'Oh yes,' I said, gesturing at the ornaments I'd placed around the room. 'It seems much more homely with all my own things around me. Quite bare at first, really, and the unpacking is a bit of a chore, but once I forced myself into making a start...' I cut myself off, because I didn't want her to think I was complaining. 'It's wonderful to be living here. Such nice people, such a quiet street.'

'We do our best,' she said, and handed me the leaflets. 'I brought these for you. I should have brought them to your get-together, but I left in a rush and totally forgot.'

They were crisp and glossy and had that shiny new-paper smell that is something between warm glue and fish.

'Don't look at them now,' she said, 'it's just some information about the local recycling scheme and flyers for the Neighbourhood Watch. We've all got stickers in our windows – it acts as a real deterrent to any would-be criminals. There's one in there for you, and a phone number you can call to get them to send you a free personal alarm if you're ever out and about on your own at night. I have one myself, Barry insists.'

I'd made tea and brought out the biscuit tin even though I didn't remember doing it, and she sipped and crunched and kept flicking her plait over her shoulder as she chatted to me about the latest meeting and invited me to come to the next one, which would be at her house in a month's time. Things around here would be very different in a month's time, I remember thinking that, and wanting to hurry her along so I could get on with my preparations, but when she said, 'Barry insists,' so comfortably, as if it pleased and irritated her simultaneously, I felt a great wave of something like sadness wash over me. I picked up the biscuit tin and held it on my knee like a baby.

'Oh, he's such a fusspot, a real worry wart. These men are all old-fashioned though, aren't they? I bet your husband is just the same. And we say it irritates us, but we like it really – it makes us feel cherished. They can't win, can they?' she laughed, and held out her cup for a refill. When I leaned over to pick up the pot from the coffee table the tin slid from my lap onto the floor, the lid popped off and the jammy dodgers and custard creams spilled all over the carpet. I knelt to pick them up.

'Oh dear, have I said something to upset you? I really hope not. Annie? Are you all right?'

I looked back up at her from the floor. 'Quite all right,' I said. 'I'm just going to put these back in the tin. Don't eat them if you don't like though. I have another packet in the kitchen.' I sat back down, shaking, and she moved over to me and put her hand on my arm.

'Annie, what's the matter? Have I said something wrong? I haven't offended you, have I?' she frowned and pouted and rubbed at my arm. 'Oh, what's the matter, Annie? Tell me what's wrong and we can sort it out, can't we?'

Something in my face or my demeanour had obviously led Sangita to believe I was very upset. She had seemingly mistaken my irritation about dropping the biscuits onto the carpet for a genuine emotional crisis of some kind.

'It's my husband,' I said, swallowing hard and not quite sure of what I was going to say until I said it, 'he isn't here anymore. A bit of an accident last year. I don't want to go into it, not really.' I didn't look at her as I spoke. I can still remember staring at a greasy spot on the arm of the sofa while I talked and wondering how it had got there. Probably when I was busy letting it 'all hang out' in the days after my house-warming party. I sighed, and scraped at it with my fingernail. That, I thought, is what comes from letting your hair down.

'I'm all right,' I said quietly. 'Just getting used to things, that's all. It takes a while. Longer than you'd think. Can't just leap into a new life, can you?'

'Oh Annie!' she said, pulling her eyebrows together so that I could see her eyes were shiny with empathy. 'Oh,' she said again, and poured herself and me more tea. It was from the bottom of the pot and I knew it wasn't right at all, that it would be lukewarm and taste metallic and filmy on the teeth. She added milk and I watched her as she sipped again, but she didn't seem to mind.

'I did wonder. I thought you might have been divorced, an affair, something like that. You seemed so sad, and all that about being a doctor, working in London. I did wonder. But not this. I didn't think it would be something like this.'

I ducked my head to hide my face from her. I had gone horribly red at the idea that the elaborations I'd been cornered into making hadn't fooled her for a minute. Some people are naturally honest and can't stretch the facts to save their life. I realised, too late, that I am one of them.

'Didn't want to go into it at the party,' I muttered, 'everyone was supposed to be having a nice time.'

'Of course you didn't! I can understand, of course I can.' She gasped, and put her hand over her mouth. 'And your little one too?' I nodded, and she was back feeling my arm, 'How tragic. How utterly, utterly tragic for you.'

I nodded again and slid the tin of biscuits onto the table. The floor near my feet was covered with crumbs and I thought about dropping one of the scatter cushions from the couch onto the dirty patch.

'How long were you married for, do you mind my asking? Perhaps it will help to talk a bit.' She had on some jingly earrings, nice ones, and they reminded me a bit of the ones Caroline used to wear. I had an urge to stretch out my index finger and poke them just to see them move. I resisted it, of course.

'Eight years married, together for nine,' I said to her. 'I was very young when we met. You know, I don't even remember the wedding at all. Isn't that funny?'

She smiled and shook her head. 'It's the nerves, the excitement. The day went in a blur for me too – that's why us women like looking at the photographs so much. How did you meet him?'

I frowned, wondering if the cushion lying haphazardly on the floor between my feet and the coffee table would make a worse or a better impression than the biscuit crumbs on the carpet.

'A graduation party. I'd just finished this little correspondence course in typing, shorthand, that kind of thing. The college threw a party for us at the end, and he was there.' I knocked the cushion onto the floor with my elbow.

'He did the course too?'

'Oh no, it was all young girls,' I said.

The party was held in a school in Grange-over-Sands. Right in one of the classrooms. They'd laid out sandwiches and cheese on sticks on silver platters on top of the tables the pupils sat at to work.

It had made me think of myself at school, scribbling notes to pass under the table to Boris, sticking pellets of paper up the nozzle of the gas taps in the science labs. School for me had only finished a year ago, and I was having trouble adjusting. The course hadn't really kept me busy, and now it was over and it was time to find a job of some kind. I could have been walking towards the very end of a high diving board: that's what I felt like. People kept asking me what my plans were, and I didn't like it.

The classroom had been filled with talking, some of it coming from my father.

'Shall I just get rid of this? Food's bloody awful. Still, not long till the photo then we can get off.'

'Did you see my certificate? They've printed it out nice, haven't they?'

'I mean, Christ, what is it with buffets and sausages on sticks? Look at that, have you tasted it? Cheese? It's more like plastic.'

Place me in that situation now and I'd be distracted with all kinds of internal deliberations and calculations. I can imagine myself hovering around the jugs of orange juice and bottles of Perrier, eating nothing and trying to decide if it was better to take several lightly laden helpings from the loaded serving platters, or one conspicuous trip with my plate heaped high. I would be so absorbed with the deliberation that any observances of the other guests wouldn't extend further than the relative topography of their plates.

'Go easy, eh, Annie? Don't make a pig out of yourself. It's these people here who'll be writing you your references for the next few years. Have you thought of that?' My father really wanted me to get a job. He was all right for money, because even though he earned hardly anything, the house and the Land Rover came with the job. I think he just wanted me to spread my wings and get a place to live so that he could be on his own a bit more.

'Have you asked for any application forms yet? Enquired after vacancies? Those who don't ask, don't get, and you can't expect me to feed you for the rest of your life.'

Most of the time I dealt with my father by pretending to be deaf. I was standing in front of a window rubbing my tongue over the roof of my mouth and enjoying the tickly paste of egg mayonnaise and fronds of cress. Part of me would want to avoid that now; would be more aware of the way the light coming through the window would be eclipsed by my all too obvious bulk. My father put his plate down and said he was going outside for a smoke. Will was just a lanky man with mousy hair fussing over one of the girls who'd received her certificate on the same day as me. Not his girlfriend, not even his sister or a friend.

'I'm here with Leanne,' he said, after he'd caught my eye and nodded a greeting. He pointed to her with the rim of his glass. Red fluid sloshed inside. She was dressed like the rest of us, in a sensible black skirt, flat shoes and a white blouse. They'd asked us to dress like that for the photograph. In fact, it was good practice to start dressing like the secretaries and receptionists, administrative assist-ants and data-entry clerks we were all about to become.

'That your dad?' he nodded to the black-headed man crossing the car park.

'Hmm,' I swallowed the egg quickly and then had to stop to clear my throat. 'It's not his kind of thing.'

'Looks like a young D.H. Lawrence,' Will said, and then grinned at me. 'Was that a bit rude? Sorry.' He'd introduced himself, juggled plate and glass in his hands so we could shake, and then gave up.

'What will he do, just wait out there?' We got a good view of him out of the window, making his hands into fists and jamming them into the pockets of his formal trousers, then pulling one out again to loosen his tie jerkily. He was always irritated about something, as if his whole skin had been peeled off and his body was one huge weeping graze that chafed and itched with any contact from the world. His other fist appeared and there was a silver flash of keys as he headed towards the freshly washed Land Rover, his mouth working under his facial hair as he ranted to himself.

'I suppose so,' I said. Will smiled gently at me and tilted his head as if he was going to tell me a secret. 'Not my sort of thing really, either. To be honest, this is the third one I've been to. Leanne over there,' I heard her voice coil over to me then, she was saying something about carbon paper and electric typewriters, talking to one of the tutors quite impressively, and I nodded, 'she works for me. Receptionist. I hire them right out of school, bit younger than you, I suppose, then send them on this course so they know what they're doing.' He smiled again and shook his head, perhaps chiding himself at his own foolishness.

'Then they leave,' I said, sucking the last of the egg from the roof of my mouth and laughing a little, 'get a better job with their new qualification?' He nodded, took a sip from his glass and winced a little.

'You'd think I'd know better, you know. But where I come from, it's a bit,' he pulled a face, 'I want to give them a chance, you know, to do something a bit better. If they're going on to something better, well, it's not too bad, is it?'

'You should put it in the contract,' I said. He tried another sip, screwed up his face as if he was drinking cough medicine, and set his glass down lightly on the windowsill behind us. The movement meant he'd turned around, and I turned with him so we were both facing the window again, me looking at my dad sitting nodding his head as if to music in the Land Rover, and Will, when I peeked at him, stroking flecks of sandy stubble on his jaw and looking at him too.

'Say they can't leave if I've paid for their training?' he said, looking at me seriously. He was older than me, not old enough to be my father, but old enough perhaps, to be surprised that I'd said something sensible.

'But if you were applying for a job and, well, wouldn't you think it was a bit funny?' He'd set his plate down on the windowsill too, and was gesturing in the air, a vague circular hand-flapping that struck me then as endearing. I didn't know, of course, that it was a kind of trademark of his. Anyone trying to do an impression of Will would have to perfect that loose hand-flap first of all, capture the slightly camp limp-wristedness of it along with the good-natured exasperation at being unable to find the word that he wanted. But once they'd got the hand-flap, then they'd have to work on his posture, a kind of lanky awkwardness that managed to be conspicuous and retiring at the same time, as if he knew he'd always be the tallest man in the room, didn't like it, and scrunched himself up into an attention-drawing stoop.

'Aw, bollocks,' I said, enjoying the rounded taste of the word in my mouth. That one was from Boris.

'Christ! Fucking tit-wank! Bollocks!' he'd say, when he ran out of cigarette papers or dropped his bus fare in the gutter, even, if he felt like it, in front of his parents. He knew his father would just smile blandly and say 'Charming,' and Caroline, if she reacted at all, would merely roll her eyes and say something sarcastic about how intelligent he sounded with a vocabulary like a bin man. They'd gone, moved, and it had been a few months and I was waiting for the letter from Boris passing on his new address and the invitation for tea that I was still certain would be coming soon. I got the same kind of feeling from Will; I could try out a word like that with him and he wouldn't mind at all.

I could only see Will's profile, those flecks on his jaw glittering like grains of sand, because he was leaning with his hands on the windowsill catching the light and looking out, obviously not seeing what I was seeing, or if he was, not registering the importance of it.

'Bollocks!' I said again, picking up my certificate from between my feet and putting the plate down so hard on the windowsill a mini prawn quiche bounced from it onto the floor.

'Look,' I said, pointing out of the window. My dad was turning the Land Rover around in the car park, gesturing jerkily to me with the hand that wasn't grasping the wheel. 'I'm going to have to go,' I said.

'What about the photograph? You can't not be in that.'

'I don't plan on walking back either, we're miles away. Middle of nowhere.'

'Wait a minute,' he said, 'honestly.' He went out into the car park and I saw him tap on the driver's side window and smile apologetically. The window was lowered, there was a minute or so of mouth-flapping and pointing, some conciliatory smiling and then my dad abruptly threw both his hands up into the air as if he was releasing a bird into the smelly interior of his vehicle.

I can imagine what he said, something about the dogs needing to be fed, him not being a paid chauffeur, enough for Will to pass it off as a normal father and daughter spat. My father nodded at me through the window and then drove away without looking back. I grabbed my coat from a pile on another cloth-covered table by the door and met Will in the car park. In fact, I nearly ran into him because he grabbed my elbows gently. I was out of breath – not able to talk – but opening and closing my mouth anyway, and it made him laugh.

'Less of the panicking – it's sorted. He had some jobs to do at home or something, I didn't exactly catch what. Anyway,' he said, 'I'm going to give you a lift home.'

'I'm miles away,' I said, still panting slightly despite the short distance I had come. 'Miles. It took us an hour to get here.'

Will shrugged, 'Doesn't matter. I've nowhere to be this afternoon.'

I looked up at him, and because he was quite a bit taller than me I ended up squinting against the watery sunshine coming down through the clouds.

'Thanks,' I said, 'if you're really sure.' I tried to make it sound like I'd only reluctantly accepted, but I think both of us knew that I didn't have any other option.

After the over-enthusiastic photographer had done his stuff and a formulaic speech had been made by the course director, the party was over and, feeling slightly tired and embarrassed by all the posing and smiling I'd been asked to do that afternoon, I got into the front of Will's car. It was one of those that had three wheels, and the front wobbled slightly like a wheelbarrow whenever we were going fast or around a corner. It made me want to laugh when I first saw it: light blue and slightly rusty and like a toy. He made it clear he could have afforded better when he told me he was a dentist, and although I wondered, it wasn't until a few weeks later that I learned he refused to replace it for something better for 'environmental reasons'. Story of my life!

Still, once I was inside it I couldn't see what other people were seeing. The view from inside his odd little car was exactly the same as it would have been from a limousine. It wasn't long before we were driving past the neat gardens and promenade that overlooked the strange, grassy little beach that gave Grange-over-Sands its name.

'Have a look out of that window, Annie,' he said. 'Over there, over the water. Can you see that?'

'What?'

'That's where I live, down there.' I squinted over the misty water, which at that moment had the colour and texture of a stainless steel draining board. Far away I could just make out the grey shapes of buildings on the other side of Morecambe Bay.

'Fleetwood,' he said. 'Seaside, like here, but not as nice. Ever heard of it?'

I shook my head for no but something else was bothering me.

'It's going to take you hours to get back to your own place, it really is. I thought you lived here.'

'Shush, you. It doesn't matter. I live on my own now anyway, so no one's going to be putting my dinner in the dog if I'm late back.'

I caught that, the little hint of something in the way he let me know he was living on his own, but of course told myself I was being stupid. Still, there was something about him: something naïve and self-pitying, as if he didn't mind making it clear to me that I was doing him as much of a favour as he was doing me. We joined the motorway and headed north, following the blue signs overhead to 'The Lakes'.

'No, I've never been there. Is it nice?'

He screwed up his mouth and made a little noise with his tongue. 'Hmm, it's a little, well, dismal, I suppose, but I quite like it. You can get a tram into Blackpool quite easily if you want to go shopping.'

'I've been to Blackpool,' I said hopefully, remembering the last holiday the three of us had before my mother got too ill to go anymore.

She'd sat on the sand picking chips out of a polystyrene cone while I was further down the beach where the sand was wetter, busy trying to dig a hole big enough to bury my dad in. She'd shouted, her voice floating over to me then the same way it would continue to do after she was dead, 'Dig a nice deep hole, Annie!' and laughing, as if she wasn't ill at all.

'Well, it's not like Blackpool. There's really hardly anything there,' Will said.

'Really?' I was just being polite, minding my manners because it was his car and his petrol and I was anticipating the embarrassment of not even being able to offer him money when he dropped me off at my house. What a place to live if you were on your own and didn't want to be, that's what I thought.

By the time we'd got off the motorway and were rolling along the country roads getting nearer to where I lived I'd got quite a good idea about what kind of person Will was and what he thought of me. He was always careful to add lots of qualifiers to his sentences, so 'politically correct' sometimes that I couldn't follow his meaning, or understand if he really meant anything at all. He was nervous, and he didn't want to offend me, whatever my opinions on things were. A people-pleaser, some would have said.

So when he said, 'Well, I'm not sure if you've thought about this, not to imply that you haven't, of course, but some women receptionists, and not, mind you, that I'm trying to imply all receptionists are women, or that they should be...' and then tailed away, getting lost in his own vague inoffensiveness, it pleased me to be sharp and specific and tell him what it was he was trying to say.

'Some of the girls you've had working for you have been a bit stupid?' I said, not really asking at all because it was obvious, well, it was to me at least, that he was stabbing at that from the beginning.

And as well as that, he thought I was a little dim. I could tell that by the way he kept explaining the meanings of quite simple words to me, and giving me little plot summaries of books he referred to that he thought I might not have read. I could have put him straight easily enough – pointed out to him that with no cinema, no nightclub and only Boris and his collection of slasher films for entertainment, I was bound to have got through a good whack of the books he presumed I knew nothing about. But I didn't put him right on that one. I liked him underestimating me: it made me feel as if I had something in reserve, something secret he didn't know about. And of course, I realised later, that was part of what he liked about me: being young, someone he could educate and be unthreatened by. I suppose you could say I have a gift for reading people.

'You know, you try to be kind to these young women you've employed, get them through their training and so on. Some even want to go on to be dental nurses in the end,' he lectured solemnly against the steady swish and beat of the windscreen wipers.

There was something in that too, I thought, him going on about dental nurses and receptionists and pondering the mystery of his staff turnover. I was wondering myself, not about his nurses and receptionists and secretaries ('six months, at most, that's all they stay for') which I almost believed he was using as a metaphor for his love life, but about his aloneness when he obviously had a decent job and a far from repellent personality.

No, perhaps I'm adding in nuances that just weren't there at the time, adding in the colour from the facts that I learned later about a wife he'd had before, a Hungarian dental nurse he'd had a daughter with and who had left him and taken the baby back to her own country after they'd only been together a year and a half. Still, there was a musty smell of sadness that hung about him, which I might have picked up on even as early as that.

'I haven't been to the dentist in years,' I said cheerfully, 'there's something about it that makes my blood run cold.'

'A lot of people are scared,' Will said, switching back into professional mode again, 'but it's very different now to how it used to be. I'm looking into contracting a hypnotist, and I've been doing a bit of research into acupuncture as well – just a bit of a sideline, you know, another string to my bow.'

I laughed again then, I couldn't help it – he didn't seem to see what was staring me in the face.

'So you think telling people not to be scared of the drill because you're going to stick them full of pins is going to help, then?' I said, and he inclined his head to me again, conceding a point, and the motion became a kind of private joke between us from then onwards.

'My mum was the same,' I went on, 'had all kinds of operations, used to drink this herbal stuff, black, it was, and smelled like slurry. Not that it did her any good. She went through all that without complaining, but the dentist,' I smiled, I hadn't talked about my mother in years, 'she'd cry all the way there, couldn't even drive herself, she'd be shaking that much. I probably get it off her.'

'Your mother, she's passed away?' he asked, delicately.

'A while ago now,' I said. 'It's just me and my dad.' There was an awkward silence. Will stepped in and changed the subject, and I was grateful to him.

'You're obviously not keen on dentistry,' he took his hand off the wheel for a second to offer me a Mint Imperial ('don't worry, they're sugar free,') from a packet he kept in the glove compartment, 'so what *do* you like, Annie?' he asked, probably laughing at the idea that we'd ever have something in common.

I giggled a bit too. He was thirty-two, fifteen years older than me, but I felt like he was taking me seriously, and other than Boris's parents and various teachers, he was the first real adult I'd ever spoken to.

'I don't like anything,' I said, shrugging. 'I don't have a job, and there isn't anyone who lives near me. There's no school any more, my dad's working all the time, or he's sleeping so I have to be quiet. There are never any buses and even when there are, I'm not allowed to get on them.' Will looked away from the road for a second, probably to check if I was joking. I smiled, 'There is a mobile library though. The van comes once a week. The woman who drives it is called Helen and she gave me a cigarette once. She saves things she thinks I'd like under the counter. So I read a lot, and rent videos.'

'What kind of videos?' he asked, like he was really interested.

'Romances,' I said, 'anything with a happy ending. I don't like thrillers or ones that are too violent.'

Will laughed, 'Proper girly films?' I thought he was making fun of me for a second, but he waved his hand in the air, 'No, no, I like those kinds of films too. I often get a tear in my eye at the end. Hey, have you ever seen *Pretty Woman*? I know it's a bit racy, but –' he stopped when he noticed me nodding enthusiastically,

'I rented it from the library, but someone else requested it and I had to give it back. Helen bought me a copy for my birthday last year! I have to hide it under my mattress so my dad won't see it, but it's one of my favourite films.'

Will laughed again, just because he was pleased, I think, and started humming the song from the film. I thought about the ending, where Richard Gere climbs up on the balcony to rescue Julia Roberts from her flat.

'I thought of something else,' I said, feeling more comfortable talking about myself the longer the car journey went on.

'Go on,' he encouraged me.

'Well, I like watching *You've Been Framed* with the sound turned down and laughing at all the drunk idiots cracking their heads open on the pavement,' I said. 'I like watching the kids fall off their bikes or pull Christmas trees down on their heads or ruin their own birthday cakes and wonder what their parents were thinking when they sent in the tape to humiliate them on the telly.'

Will looked at me with his eyebrows raised as if he wasn't quite sure whether to believe me or not.

'Last week there was a bride walking around her own wedding reception with her dress tucked into her knickers. Everyone was laughing at her, the guy with the camcorder following her around, and she just kept turning and smiling because she didn't get what was going on.'

Grey flicked past outside the windows and I took a mint but kept it in the palm of my hand for a second. Will had returned his hands to the ten to two position and was staring straight ahead, but still smiling.

'She kept posing with people and waving at the camera,' I said.

He cringed: 'And it was stuck…'

'In the back of her knickers the whole time. People were falling about laughing. The groom was there, getting her to twirl around for the camera and show off her dress.'

'No one told her?'

I shook my head, 'Not even her mother.'

He looked at me again and then burst out laughing, 'That's sick, it really is.'

I laughed myself, 'Well, you asked me what I liked doing.'

'You've got a dark side hidden away in there somewhere, haven't you?' He was still laughing. I could tell I'd surprised him and I liked that. People assume such a lot about other people, don't they, but it's hard to genuinely make an impression on someone, just by telling the truth the way you see it.

'Your teeth look fine to me, anyway,' he said, turning the steering wheel. We were there now, and I plucked at the seat belt that was cutting between my breasts and thought of Caroline, that handbag strap and the wrong sort of attention. Will had given no signal that he'd noticed, none at all.

'Some people pay a lot to get them as straight as yours.' He looked at me again then, ignoring the breasts totally, and focusing a trained eye on my mouth.

'They're very, um, pretty, if that doesn't sound a bit funny,' he said, and seeing as he liked them, I smiled again.

'You going to be all right then? Your dad won't be too annoyed, will he?'

'Oh no,' I said lightly. He didn't move and I kept still, my fingers hooked around the plastic handle on the inside of the car door.

'Right.'

'Thanks ever so much.' The car was hot and I pulled the blouse away from my throat a little and fanned my damp flesh with it. He still didn't look at me anywhere except my mouth.

'I suppose you'll be applying for jobs soon,' he said, 'now you've finished the course.'

'Yes, I suppose,' I said. I hadn't thought about it, not much anyway.

'You could give me your phone number, if you liked,' his face looked red, and it was getting redder, the blotch spreading onto his throat and edging beneath his collar. 'I mean, I have contacts, friends with surgeries, that kind of thing – they're always looking for girls with that kind of qualification.'

'All right then,' I said, and wrote the number down on the back of an organ donor card he pulled from his wallet.

'Don't ask for me if my dad answers, just say that you've got a wrong number or something.'

He looked concerned. 'I don't want to cause any trouble for you,' he said. 'He did seem a little, well, how to put it,' he chewed the insides of his cheeks, 'erratic?'

'You could say that,' I said, trying to make a joke of it and dreading going back into the house. I'd almost forgotten about it all on the way home, because of the easy conversation and the strange but enjoyable experience of meeting someone new and getting to talk about myself a bit. He didn't laugh.

'Shall I come in with you?' he said. 'I know it's hardly up to me to interfere, but if you're having problems...'

'No, don't worry. He was just tired, that's all. He'll be crashed out in front of the telly when I get in, waiting for me to get him his tea and wake him up for work. If you're going to call, call after seven o'clock because he's out then.'

'All right, I will do,' Will said. 'Get you a little job before you know it, and if you need some help in finding a flat, I'm your man.'

I got out of the car and waved, and he waved back as he reversed, the blue and red of the card I'd written my number on moving in front of his face like a semaphore flag.

Will had to wait a long time for his divorce because the girl he'd married was in Hungary again and didn't want to be found. When it came though, he proposed to me. I'd kind of been hoping that he would. He'd invited me for tea at his house a few times, we got on, and I had given up hope of hearing from Caroline and Boris by that time. I'd been living in a damp bedsit in Fleetwood paid for with the earnings from the job Will had helped me to get.

As he pointed out, over coffee on his brown, hairy settee, it was the right time for me to move away from there because the six-month lease I'd signed was about to run out and the landlady was making noises about raising the rent. He was right; and of course I didn't want to go back to Cumbria and my father. Will even had a ring ready: a little gold thing with a speck of an emerald in it which I couldn't wear on my finger until we had it resized. Anyway, without much convincing I agreed and let him fasten it around my neck on a chain.

So we got married. But, like I told Sangita, I don't remember anything about the wedding at all, just that after it I didn't need to go to work again and all of a sudden he didn't find the little things I said funny any more.

10

'What a lovely story,' Sangita said, 'and you know you'll always have those happy memories to look back on, no matter what happens.'

I took another biscuit and nodded. There was a hair on the biscuit from the floor and I tried to get it out of my mouth without Sangita noticing. I finally managed to get it onto the tip of my tongue. I waited until Sangita was looking at something else, then licked it off onto the back of my hand.

'I suppose I will,' I said wearily, and leaned back into the sofa. I wiped my hand on the cushion.

Happy memories indeed! I could have told her a few things that would amply demonstrate that that car journey and the promise of being somewhere different constituted the peak emotional point of my relationship with Will. After that, it all went steeply downhill and was characterised by nothing short of sheer misery!

'Yes, of course you will,' she said. Sangita couldn't have been that much older than me, but she always wrinkled her nose and raised her shoulders when she smiled, put her head on one side and talked to me more loudly than was really necessary. It made me feel like a child, sullen and petulant and in the mood for disagreeing.

'It wasn't always like that though,' I said tentatively.

'Well no, the romance never lasts forever, does it?' she said. 'Barry used to bring me roses, big bunches of them, and jewellery for every special occasion!' She played an imaginary piano in the air, showing me her rings. 'These days, all his money goes on the boys! Last year for my birthday...'

'He was always on at me about my weight,' I said quietly, running a hand over the folds of tummy that rested on the waistband of my jeans. I let my voice drop until I was almost whispering. 'I don't think he thought I was very pretty.'

'Oh, nonsense,' she cried out, 'they just forget to say! I'm sure that's what it was.' She shook her head emphatically. 'They just get used to you being there, that's all.'

'Yes, and you become invisible,' I replied and realised she might think I was trying to start an argument. I pressed my lips together stubbornly and decided that that would be the last thing I would say on the matter.

'No,' she said, rubbing my knee like I had cramp, 'no, not invisible. Barry says...'

'Things are different with you and Barry,' I said hastily, 'I can tell. I've got a nose for these things. It was never quite right with me and Will. I realised it very soon after we were married. You want to know what I think?' she didn't nod, but I carried on anyway, 'I think if you meet the right person, it doesn't wear off. I think it does stay like that forever!'

Sangita leaned towards me and I thought she was going to hug me. I stiffened and pulled the biscuit tin towards me protectively until she drew back.

'Maybe so, Annie, maybe so. You never know what life has in store for you, do you?' She paused, then put her hand on my arm again. I was getting quite irritated with all this touching.

'Anyway, you must have guessed I'm not just dropping in to leave you these leaflets and sign you up for the Neighbourhood Watch.' She put her cup down on the table and started twisting her rings around on her fingers. They clicked between her knuckles and the red and white stones flashed. They were very nice rings.

'Oh?' I said, mystified. I wasn't aware of how much time had passed until I looked at my lap and noticed the tin of biscuits was empty. All that talk of Will and my dad and Cumbria had taken me somewhere very different in my mind and Sangita had changed the subject so abruptly I felt sure I'd been talking too long. I couldn't recall exactly what I'd said to her, and it made me nervous. I stood up to refill the kettle but Sangita put her hand over the top of her cup and carried on speaking. I thought it was best to sit back down again, and did so.

'Lucy's got some idea in her head,' she shrugged, 'something about cat-droppings, primroses, bin bags being moved. I'm pretty sure it's that gang of lads who hang about outside the paper shop – and I'm probably going to have a word with their parents about it. But because it all started to happen around the same time as you moved here, when was that...?'

'Two and a half months ago now.'

'Yes, about two months ago, she's convinced you've got something to do with it,' Sangita laughed. 'I've got to take her seriously, part of my job, if I'm the person she chooses to come to, but the idea of it, you on your hands and knees in the middle of the night ripping open their bin bags – it's preposterous. I did tell her that. I'm sure you know what she's like, though.'

'Yes,' I said, trying to sound expressionless and unconcerned, 'I know what she's like.'

'A very immature woman, I'd say – and going to the shop in her dressing gown first thing in the morning with legs up to here, well of course those boys are going to notice, and there's going to be pranks. She just can't understand it. You can see she's got a kind heart, she really worries about things, but a bit dim too, don't you think – she can't see she just might have brought some of this on herself, and she's making you, poor thing, the scapegoat for it.'

'Perhaps there are problems with her job? Or, maybe, things aren't going so well between her and Neil? Something affecting her judgement?'

Sangita nodded, 'You might well be right, and it's very generous of you to say so.' She put her head on one side and smiled mischievously, 'This is very unprofessional of me, I know, but between you and me, don't you think the whole thing with her and Neil is bizarre? She's barely out of her school uniform and he must be thirty at least, maybe more. It's obvious what he's getting out of it, and she's fallen on her feet too – the house is all paid for and he's got a very good job. His parents aren't short of money, or so I've heard.'

I giggled slightly, and put my hand over my mouth to stop it.

'Well, Lucy's silliness, and,' she nodded her head respectfully, 'the sad news you confided in me just now,' she looked like she was going to touch me again so I choked back the chuckle that was threatening to become a full-blown giggling fit and tried to listen attentively.

'The whole thing's got me thinking,' she said. 'How about you come around to my house for a dinner party next weekend? It won't do you any good to be in the house all the time. You need to start getting out, you know you do. And after your party, well, we owe you a meal, at least. I can get Lucy to come over and we'll have a nice evening in and get to know each other better. Then she'll see how ridiculous she's being. Bin bags! It's ludicrous! I'll make pasta and everything will blow over before you can say parmesan! What do you think?'

'Are you going to invite Neil?' I asked.

'I can if you like,' she said, nodding. 'Why not? I'll get the nice crockery out and get everyone round, shall I?'

Then it was me who felt like hugging her, and I was so excited I was afraid of saying something stupid: all I could do was nod eagerly, which seemed to please her.

'A dinner party will be just the thing,' she said. 'I'll find out when Barry's free and let you all know. Hopefully it will be enough to smooth things over and you won't need to worry about it. It's not what you need, is it?'

I shook my head. 'Certainly not,' I agreed soberly. 'Absolutely. You couldn't be more correct.' Sangita looked at me strangely and I bit my lip, trying to contain my excitement.

'Well, we'll get them round, maybe Raymond too. Can't do any harm, can it? She'll probably turn up in one of her mini-skirts and Barry won't be able to keep his eyes in his head, so you'll have to watch me and make sure I don't say anything to make things worse!' She laughed and stood up, 'Once I get going you can't shut me up. Ah well, I've done my bit, at least. You just carry on and come to me if you have any more problems with her. I doubt very much she's going to pursue it further. It'll all blow over by the end of the week.'

Sangita was moving towards the door and I followed her, clutching the biscuit tin in my hands and rattling it anxiously, suddenly beset by nerves.

'Shall I bring something? And what shall I wear? Will you put it on the invitation?'

Sangita chuckled, 'I can see you're used to much better things than what's on offer here! No no, you just come as you are and leave the food to me. Don't worry about a thing, and,' she dropped her voice, 'keep your chin up. You'll get through this now I'm here to help you.'

'I'll try to be extra friendly to Lucy when I see her,' I said thoughtfully, 'it's likely that she and Neil are having a few problems together:

she can't be a very happy person to be making up things about someone.' I shrugged, 'It's sad really, but none of us knows what goes on behind other people's closed doors.'

'Yes, yes,' Sangita was putting her coat on, 'but don't feel too sorry for her. It makes me mad after the tragedy you've been through, it really does. I've a good mind to let her know, just to shame her out of telling these silly stories.' We moved towards the door, 'But you're right, of course. Least said soonest mended. You come to me if you're feeling down or want a cup of tea with someone in the afternoons. I'm always about during the day.'

She waved, and I followed her out to watch her as she went down the street, the bright pink and green of her sari sticking out of her blue anorak and picking up dirt from the pavement.

I was unsettled after Sangita left, my guts churning so much I couldn't set my mind to anything I'd planned for myself that morning. I was hardly in the mood to hop into the bath and start doing my hair after her little revelation about Lucy, and I didn't want to turn up at Neil's with a sour face. It irritated me: another day wasted when I'd decided to strike when the iron was hot, and now I wasn't fit for company. I don't get angry very often any more but this time was an exception and it wasn't as if I hadn't been given justification.

I tried to think about the impending dinner party. I had preparations to make, and with a bit of luck, the occasion could mark the start of something special between Neil and myself. I tried to stay positive but the idea of Lucy trying to turn a new friend against me made me boil inside and I couldn't concentrate. I hadn't really taken her seriously. That was my mistake. Obviously, I'd underestimated her; let my guard down. The thought of her trotting round to Sangita's to tell tales about me made me want to bang on her door and tell her exactly what I thought of her.

Controlling Your Anger, Freeing Yourself was full of insightful and practical suggestions on how to deal with the spectrum of negative feelings from irritation to violent rage. I had read it three times already, and after Sangita left I went upstairs and found the book so I could lie on my bed and read some of the more useful sections again. It was very important to me that this house, which represented a new life and a new start, did not become associated with the problems of my past. As I lay there I realised, with an increasing sense of irritation, that my previous life was still trailing its influence over my current one. The house-warming party, which had seemed like such a good idea at the time, had actually been the occasion when these people had started to embed themselves in my life and I had allowed them to become unnecessarily embroiled in my history.

My anger has often got me into troubling situations, for example, the incident with Lorraine Morris. I pondered it deliberately, trying to gain some insight into my own angry impulses in order that I could decide what to do next.

Boris had been sitting on the closed lid of the toilet fumbling with stolen cigarette papers and tobacco. The screwed-up pellets of his former attempts were scattered on the lino between his feet.

'Don't think you're smoking that in here,' I'd said to him. I remember the weather that day very clearly: the rain was sliding down the window, condensation pooling on the sill, and outside in the garden below, my mother's gaudy tea roses had come into bloom. When I was younger I liked to fold the petals into tiny envelopes and eat them, or rub them on my wrists and neck, bruising the flesh and spreading the perfume over my skin. Even more recently, I'd used the petals of Lucy's primroses to do the same. At this time my mum's roses were leggy and neglected and the blowsy flowers were shedding browning petals on the grass. The wind made the stems sway and buckle towards the lawn, red drops falling like the rain that battered them.

'If my dad smells that in the house he'll kill me.'

'Don't be a dick, your dad smokes himself. He won't smell it, they never do.'

'He'll know,' I insisted. 'They're not his brand.'

Boris raised his hands precariously to his face and licked the edge of the paper. He dropped half the tobacco onto his trousers as he tried once more to roll a cigarette. Natasha, who could do it with one hand, had said there was a trick to it but refused to tell him what it was.

'Shit! I nearly had it then.' He looked up at me and frowned

irritably. 'Open the window then. You can have some too, if you like.'
He managed it then, and held up a crooked, twisted little tube of
tobacco for me to admire. 'Look at that! Look at that! Not bad, you
reckon?' We must have been about fourteen.

'You're not opening the window in this weather. He'll be back any
minute.'

Boris flicked his lighter a couple of times and held the cigarette
between his lips. It was a favourite trick of his, to let it stick to his
bottom lip, the paper adhering to saliva, and then carry on talking
with it bobbing about to his words. I'd seen some of the others doing
it: the sixth formers waiting at the bus stop, identifiable by their lack
of uniform and Zippo lighters.

'Go on,' he said, smiling. 'Tell me what Lorraine said.'

'When?' My hands were in the sink, which was full of water, and
I sloshed and swirled something about until my forearms were wet.
I pulled out the plug, and Boris handed me a towel.

'You know when,' he put the cigarette into the chest pocket of his
school shirt. The front of it was speckled with ink and grubby with
mud from his hands. The material was thick cotton and frayed at the
cuffs and collar. Caroline probably bought it for him like that, the
way she bought shabby floral sofas at auctions and rubbed the paint
from her dresser with sandpaper to make it look older than it was.

I've never understood the lengths rich people will go to in order
to look poor. And my mother, even when she was ill, attacking my
shoes with a black marker on Sunday evenings so she could cover
up the white marks where the patent covering had been scuffed off.
I thought that once I crossed the magical line and became an adult
I'd be able to understand things like that and stop making mistakes.

Lorraine was a girl at our school who'd noticed that my uniform
had been getting shabbier, that there was a hole under the arm of my
sweater and the scuffs on my shoes weren't being filled in anymore.
She never let it pass. She had blonde hair, skin stretched so tightly
over her skull that purple veins showed at her temples like bunches
of broken twigs. She got her school socks from John Lewis and not
the market and they had the right diamond pattern on them and
enough length to build up into a good concertina at the ankle before
pulling them up to the knee.

'I'm going to get knackered for this,' I said, going back to the wet shirt lying against the plug hole and turning the cold tap on full blast to try and flush the stains away. 'What am I going to say?'

'Hide it or something,' Boris suggested, 'you've got more than one shirt, haven't you?' I didn't answer. I could see him in the mirror behind me, his eyes grazing the area between my shoulder blades and looking at the way the straps of my bra tracked through my flesh. The elastic part around my chest made me feel like I was caught in a harness, the kind they put guide dogs and pit bull terriers in. My skin swelled softly around the garment, leaving it half embedded in my torso as if I was made of quicksand or custard and anything left on my surface too long would be slowly absorbed and suffocated.

'You're going to get a letter back anyway; you might as well come clean before he gets it. It'll go easier on you that way.'

He was still examining me as I leaned over the sink and scrubbed at the shirt, now with a bar of soap, and blowing my hair, still damp from the rain, out of my eyes.

'He never reads them. It doesn't matter,' I said, reluctant to turn around because I knew he was still staring at me. I could almost feel it, his eyes nudging against my hips. It didn't make sense to feel embarrassed. But no one had ever looked at me so interestedly before. He was trying for another roll-up and he dropped it again, the tobacco scattering on the black and white squares of the bathroom lino.

'You've got it on your skin as well,' he observed.

I leaned into the mirror. He was right: there was a rust-coloured smear between my collarbones.

'Where? I can't see.' I moved towards him and leaned over. I felt aware of my presence looming over him in the cramped bathroom. I smelled the white soap on my hands and I was filling the air with sugary Impulse spray as it evaporated off my warm body and mingled with the smell of the chips I'd eaten in the canteen for lunch.

'Show me.'

Boris stood up and made himself taller than me again. He licked his finger and dabbed it into the hollow of my throat without looking at me.

'There.' He looked hot. 'I bet you get AIDS now. Ugh. You're going to die of Lorraine's AIDS.'

I laughed and went back to the sink. 'You're such a prick. She's too skinny to get AIDS – they'd have nothing to feed on. And anyway,' I dabbed at my throat and the upper part of my chest with the flannel, 'you're going to get it now as well.'

Boris screwed up his face, looked at his finger and then gravely wiped it on my toothbrush.

'You're disgusting. I'm not using that now!' I laughed.

'Go on, tell me what she said to you again.'

'I don't remember. Are you supposed to use hot water or cold?'

He shrugged, tucked the tobacco packet into his pocket and looked at me admiringly.

'Well, whatever it was, she won't be saying it again, will she? I couldn't believe that!' He made a fist and punched the air, 'I mean, that was like, so harsh! Her nose just *exploded!*' He mimed the punch again, hitting the cord for the light with his flailing fist and making the wooden bulb at the end of it bang against the window.

'You're exaggerating,' I said, 'I only gave her a little poke. It's her own fault for being so… flimsy.'

Boris shrugged, and then the look of admiration returned to his face. He pushed his glasses back. 'If you'd done that in school you'd have been expelled for it.'

'I don't care,' I said. I was more curious to hear what Boris was telling me than I wanted to admit. It all happened in a blur: that's what people mean when they say something happened on the spur of the moment. I remember my head getting hotter and hotter, gritting my teeth, and when she turned around in her seat to sneer at me again something popped, like a bubble under my skull, and I had her blood on my shirt. The girl who was sitting next to her was screaming.

'Maybe nothing'll happen,' Boris said. 'I wouldn't dare tell the teachers, not if it was me.'

'I'm sure you're right,' I said, scrubbing.

'You might get a letter, but so what? She's a silly bitch. Muff-diver,' he paused, because he'd never said 'muff-diver' before and it was one of his favourite things, to try out a new word on me and giggle through an explanation of what it meant. I was concentrating on the shirt and didn't ask.

'She's a lezzer with Janine, you know,' he said seriously. He punched the air again and looked at me proudly, 'You did right, Annie.'

I turned off the tap and started wringing pink water into the sink, the white fabric of my shirt squeaking between my fists. Boris came and stood behind me and looked over my shoulder. I could feel his breath on my neck, knew his eyes were half on the shirt I was shaking out in the sink and half on my chest. I very gradually straightened up so that Boris's chin was against my shoulder. He left it there for a second, then stepped back.

'You're going to have to bin it, or soak it in bleach. Tell your dad you had a nosebleed or something,' he said loudly.

'I'm going to have to, aren't I?' I leaned over and inspected the front of my skirt. 'This is all right, isn't it?'

He'd stopped looking at me now, and whatever the moment was or had signified quickly passed. When he came over to me to look for any telltale drops of blood there was nothing loaded about his hands spreading the pleats of my skirt against my thighs and making me turn about on the spot so he could examine the back of it.

'Nah, you're all right. I have to go though. My mum's having people round tonight and we've all got to be there.'

We went out onto the landing and as we went down the stairs I shrugged my way into a T-shirt. Boris put on his blazer in the kitchen and picked up a carrier bag with a muddy football inside it from the back step. He stood on the path outside the door for a minute, kicking the carrier bag against the wall and letting the rain fall onto his glasses.

'You reckon it'll be worse tomorrow?' he said, squinting through the drops obscuring his vision. He squinted quite a lot which gave him a reputation for being clever, and that caused him his own problems. Because of that, we had an unspoken understanding that we wouldn't hang around together in the breaks at school. I sat in the library if it was cold, or wandered around the car park if it was warm, and he took his ball and practised taking penalties between two paper cups on the empty end of the sports field.

'Worse than what?'

'Good point,' he smiled, 'just keep your fists to yourself when I'm about, right?'

We both laughed weakly at his little joke and then he went, stopping at the end of the garden to turn his ball out of the bag so he could kick it home. I ended up soaking that shirt in bleach solution as he had suggested, and it came out better than before: no tomato sauce stains either.

Looking back I can see that Boris had viewed the whole incident as a kind of triumph on my part, and really there was no reason not to think of it in that way. Even though my actions didn't help matters for me at school it did constitute a very clear communication to Lorraine Morris. Furthermore, Boris had been very proud of me, and I think our conversation in the bathroom was a turning point in our relationship. He began to make the transition from seeing me as his childhood friend, to noticing that I was becoming a woman and could have other uses.

I came to with the book spread flat over my chest. I listened carefully for a few moments before moving but I heard nothing. The short nap had done me good and I was certainly in better spirits than when Sangita had left me. In a strange way I began to see that Sangita's visit was a positive sign: Lucy's gossiping and jealousy actually comforted me. She was clearly worried about her own position in the community, and more importantly, in the scale of Neil's affections. All in all, it was nothing to get irritated about; I got up and went downstairs humming, having totally forgotten my momentary anger with her.

11

Not long after, I found myself absent-mindedly cleaning ornaments on the windowsill in my bedroom. I'd chosen the largest of the three bedrooms in the house for myself, and it just so happened it was at the back and had a clear view over my own and Neil's garden.

My own garden was a mere strip of chipped patio with a square of grass beyond. The lawn was shaggily in need of a cut and migraine-vivid in its greenness. I'd not got around to doing anything with it since I'd taken possession of the place, and apart from some round stepping-stones under the washing line, it was bare. Neil's too was masculine in its utility. I could see the white plastic patio set, the chairs tipped against the table in case of rain, and a little wooden enclosure for the wheelie bin. Other than these superficial additions, our gardens, like our houses, were strikingly similar. I became distracted as I made my comparisons, totally lost in my thoughts, until minutes later I realised that I had stopped dusting the porcelain sheep altogether and found that I was staring at the clothes hanging on the line in his back garden.

Whoever usually hung out the laundry was very particular about having the shirt fronts buttoned up and matching socks next to each other, one to a peg and very orderly: like an advertisement for soap powder. I can't imagine Lucy would have done all that, and she did seem to be out most of the day while it was Neil himself who stayed at home. This time, and the inconsistency is probably what drew my attention, the clothes were hung up, all darks and lights together, two socks to a peg, and the bottom of a bed sheet brushing against the unmown grass. I began to wonder if Neil was having problems at home.

There was a dress hanging on the line, black with ruffled sleeves and green ribbon sewn around the hem and neckline. Looking at it, I had a moment of inspiration. Since Sangita's invitation I had been biding my time, waiting for a few days before I sent an acceptance card so as not to appear over-eager, but formulating in my head the way things would work out when I did go around for the meal that had been offered to me. During this interval I had toyed with the idea of buying something new to wear for the occasion.

Loving Yourself: Tips for the Single Woman had contained a whole chapter about the effects personal grooming and fashion could have on a person's self-esteem, and had suggested that a woman who makes the effort to present herself in the best possible light would exude confidence and therefore become more attractive to others.

I decided that I would borrow Lucy's dress from the line for the afternoon and take it with me to town so I had something to aim for while I shopped. It was a great idea: I already knew Neil liked the colour and style because it belonged to someone he had (at some point) found attractive enough to set up home with. I thought choosing a garment with his tastes in mind would be a nice touch and create the best possible outcome for me.

Obtaining the dress was no small undertaking. Both our houses had doors in the back fence into the alley that ran behind them and these doors were rarely used except for taking out the dustbins. Neil's had both a bolt and a padlock but with the help of the added height provided by my own wheelie bin I was able to make my way over the top of the door, and use one of the chairs from his patio set to get back into the alley once I'd accomplished my mission. I'm not well known for my athletic ability, but the scrapes to my calves I gained sliding over the door and onto the top of the bin on my way out were a small price to pay for the damp dress I clutched carefully between my arm and my body as I descended.

I went into town that afternoon. After looking at the label inside the dress I knew it had been purchased from a discount store in Freeport that I knew well and, if I was lucky, would still have the items in stock. Imagine Lucy buying her clothes from a cheapie shop! It tickled me, and I giggled as I walked along the main road and turned into the entrance of the shopping centre. It was raining, so I didn't dawdle at the chocolate shop or hang about looking at books as I normally did, but headed straight to the store in question and made my way to the sales desk.

The girl serving behind the counter frowned as I pulled the still damp and slightly crumpled dress out of my carrier bag and slid it across to her.

'Returns are on the next floor,' she said in a bored monotone. I could see she had her tongue pierced because she didn't stop chewing on her gum once during our exchange.

'Oh no, there's nothing wrong with it. I like it very much. I was wondering if you still had them in stock?' Her hair was scraped back into a ponytail so tight and so high it pulled her charcoaled eyes upwards and gave her what Boris's sister Natasha had once referred to as a 'Croydon facelift,' so called, I believe, because that kind of style is very popular in parts of the South East of England.

'Should do. Try over there,' she gestured vaguely. I turned around to the rack I thought she was pointing to but not before seeing her smirk and hearing her mutter, 'Not in your size, love,' under her breath.

There may be lots of things that I don't quite understand, but I know what happens to people like me when they go into clothes shops and ask for the help of the assistants. So big I take up more of a person's vision than is strictly fair, and yet suddenly invisible, almost transparent, when it comes to help in the fitting rooms and advice from the staff. Luckily, Caroline had taken me under her wing at an early age. It was she who bought me my first handbag, took me to be measured for my first bra, and gave me the wise advice that I should avoid wearing the bra and the handbag together with the strap diagonally across my body. She let me know, in that polite, motherly way she had, that it had the effect of forcing my breasts apart, prominent as torpedoes. It could, she warned, result in the 'wrong sort of attention'.

'You've got a lovely smile, sweetheart. That's what you want to accentuate. Try these earrings, and a smudge of lipstick. It'll help to divert attention from your chest.'

As I fingered the dresses on their hangers looking for the largest size I remembered my amazement when on a shopping trip I'd stumbled into a shop that specialised in clothing for the woman of more ample dimensions. I'd never known choice like it. I was married by this point, and searching for something to wear to a dinner dance Will had wanted us to go to. The curtains in the changing cubicles, as always, didn't quite fit and it didn't take me long to notice there was a man hanging around in the waiting area outside. It was the sort of shop that had a few chairs and a coffee table with various magazines set up near the cubicles so that husbands and boyfriends could wait for their women in comfort.

At first I'd thought that this man, the one with the fuzzy chin who wore his hood up even though he was indoors, was with one of the women who were changing, but as the cubicles emptied and filled up he remained where he was, craning his neck every now and again and clutching at the pockets of his jacket as if his intestines were troubling him. It struck me, as I looked at his reflection in the mirror, that he wasn't with anyone at all but only waiting around to catch a glimpse of flesh between the curtains as large women like me struggled out of one garment and into another.

I came out of the cubicle curiously, wanting to catch his eye, and when I did I staggered and nearly fell over. He squinted at me, then pulled a pair of glasses from his pocket, unfolded them and put them on. With the motion, his hood fell back and revealed a mess of over-long curly brown hair that fell over his ears and caught in the collar of his jumper.

'Hello Annie,' he said, and it was Boris.

It had been such a long time, and I was so happy, and I didn't mind being late for Will because I wanted to take a walk along the beach and listen to everything that had happened to Boris in the time since I'd seen him last.

'You can spare a couple of hours, can't you?' he said. 'For old time's sake?' and he smiled, and looked as if he'd be disappointed if I said no. I thought about Will waiting at home, frantic about the dinner dance, wanting to check me over and supervise the putting on of make-up.

'I can,' I said, and was dithering with my bag and my coat so much, blocking the entrance to the changing room, that I let the dress slide off the hanger. Boris leaned down to pick it up, and we didn't bump heads, and when he came with me to the till he actually took a green credit card out of his back pocket and paid for it himself!

I was nervous at first as we walked. I had my shoes off, feeling the sharp edges of shells prick the undersides of my feet. Boris carried my bag and seemed quite happy kicking drifts of sand and clumps of seaweed about, occasionally stopping to unearth some buried object with the toe of his trainer. We caught up on all the things he'd been doing. He lived on his own, and was surprised to hear that I'd been married.

'We're still young, Annie,' he said, shaking his head, 'what were you, nineteen?'

'Eighteen,' I said, 'I met him the year after you went. It was all very quick.'

'A whirlwind romance,' he laughed, 'just like you always wanted,' and I would have stopped and corrected him but I didn't want to interrupt.

'You're lucky,' he said, 'I've not got anyone. Natasha, Karina, Alex – they've all got married. Cost my dad a fortune! Natasha's even got a couple of kids,' he looked at me, and I shook my head.

'Not for me,' I said, 'I couldn't stand it.'

'Still,' he said, as if what I had was better than nothing, 'I bet it beats going back to your dad's house for Christmas dinner.'

'Oh yes,' I said, 'now I get to go to Will's geriatric parents and watch them try and make a midget chicken and six roast potatoes stretch between all of us.'

Boris laughed, and leaned over at the waist to pick up a stick from where it was half buried in the sand. I think he planned to throw it out onto the water, but as it came up it was bigger than he expected and he drove it back into the sand between his feet and leaned on it. We stopped, and I pulled my hair out of my mouth and looked at him.

'I can't believe we'd just bump into each other like this,' he said.

'Do you live round here?' I asked hopefully. 'I did try to look you up in the phone directory for Keswick, I even rang around some of the schools there to find out which one your dad was at…'

Boris shrugged. 'No. I was meeting someone, they didn't turn up.'

'A girlfriend?'

'No.' He kicked the stick over and took my hand. We started walking again and he looked away from me, out at the bobbing red buoys far out on the water. The sea rocked them backwards and for-wards, up and down so much that I couldn't follow his gaze and look out at them without feeling sick.

'What do you think we go over there for a bit? Just for a couple of hours. Do you have time?'

He was pointing to the hotel that looked over the beach, a big grey box of a building with wide windows and blue paintwork. It was the only hotel in Fleetwood, as a matter of fact. Most of the people that come stay in the row of bed and breakfasts behind the crazy golf, but this hotel was expensive, and had its own bar. I'd often walked past it. It has its own little gardens with bristly, sand-choked grass, and it curved around the edge of the land like a letter C. The North Euston.

'There are cheaper places to go if you want to get a drink,' I began, feeling guilty because he'd already paid for the dress.

'No,' he said irritably. It reminded me of when we were younger and he'd say something I wouldn't quite understand. That tone of voice let me know I had missed his point, as it did then, but he'd never lower himself to explain. He'd hurry along with whatever he was saying and I would do my best to catch up. Most of the time I did, but as I said, he was very clever. I didn't wear a watch, but I'd almost forgotten about Will anyway.

'I suppose we could. It'd be a treat for me, anyway!'

I was very naïve then. I hadn't realised how frank and blunt some people can be about their requests, even when they are in a kind of code. Often, when I don't quite catch the full implication of what someone is saying I just go with the flow so as not to embarrass myself and hope that things will end up making sense to me later on when I've had time to ponder it.

'Just for a couple of hours,' he said, and then touched my chin lightly with his finger, 'so we can be on our own. I'd like that, wouldn't you?'

I smiled then, I couldn't help it, and my stomach was turning up and down inside me. I hadn't noticed it before, but as he leaned towards me I realised how nice his aftershave smelled.

'Come on then,' he said, grabbing my arm and setting off into a trot so quickly I didn't have time to put my shoes on and almost fell.

The bar was full of dark wood and patterned carpet. It smelled very strongly of cigarettes and furniture polish. The walls were painted cream and decorated with black-and-white pictures of trains. Long ago those trains had run along the now abandoned line that had given the hotel its name.

I kept silent while Boris purchased us drinks, still marvelling at him recognising me when I no longer felt like the person he had known. Perhaps life had decided we really shouldn't have lost touch, and had leapt in with a helping hand to push us together again. He pulled the table out from the wall so I could sit in the corner away from the window.

'This is lovely,' I said, and because he'd paid for the drinks, I thanked him. 'I'm going out tonight too, to a place like this. For dinner and dancing.'

'Sounds like fun,' he replied neutrally.

'Oh, it isn't really. Not as nice as this. It's full of dentists and their wives and everyone's a lot older than me. I have to listen to them going on about contracts and premises and the stuff they make the fillings out of. Will always sits at the same table as the man he wants to work for so I'm not allowed to say anything. It's very boring. The dancing goes on late but because Will never lets us stay overnight we always have to leave early. This is much better.'

I rattled the ice about in my glass and Boris took a few good gulps of beer and patted at his pockets. I knew he was searching for cigarettes, a packet of tobacco, something like that. The gesture was an old one. He found the tin and started to roll his cigarette.

'They have bars in the bedrooms, don't they? And you can ring up the kitchen and get them to make you things and they'll bring it right up to you,' I said, just to fill up the silence. 'I wish Will would let us stay over.'

'Why doesn't he?'

I shrugged. 'The money, I think.'

'We should get a room and test out the room service,' he said, and before I could answer, waved his credit card at me, 'it'd be fun!'

'I don't want to be late,' I said doubtfully.

'Why? What's he going to do? Smack you and make you go without pudding?'

I laughed and shook my head, 'You don't need to humour me. I wasn't hinting.'

'I've never stayed in somewhere like this before either,' he said. He gestured around him at the room. The bar was empty and everywhere I looked the light was bouncing off some spotless surface or other. I leaned back in the chair and the curved wood cupped me comfortably. I was happy even though the easy conversation we'd shared along the beach reminiscing about our school days seemed to have dried up into a companionable silence.

'How are your parents?' I asked, when we'd been sitting quietly for so long that we'd both nearly finished our drinks.

'Mum's just the same – Dad had a heart attack last year – he's all right though, just can't drive. You? How's your dad?'

I shrugged, and he smiled. He knew me, and that was enough. He spoke for a little longer about a half-finished computer science degree, his hopes to start his own Internet site for people who liked to play role-playing games with each other online, and the fact that he could make quite a bit of money doing it. After a few minutes of this, he finished his drink and stood up. Disappointed, I reached for my bag.

'Shall we give it a whirl then?' he said, smiling out of the corner of his mouth.

'What?' I asked, confused.

'The room service?'

The hotel room was like nothing I had ever seen before. All-white bed linen; a little kettle with cups and saucers on a table under the window; spotless mirrors and bath in the en-suite. Boris left his jacket on the bed while I explored. I couldn't help myself. It was so different from the dank little place Will had taken me to on our honeymoon. We'd spent five days in Brighton, sleeping in a hotel that smelled like frying pans, with bristly carpet, and tea stains on the bedspreads. Here at the North Euston there was even a little glass ashtray with the name of the hotel engraved in the bottom. The air smelled vaguely of fabric softener and potpourri. I went over and twitched the spotless nets for a view.

'Some weather, eh?' Boris drew the curtains – they were so thick it could have been midnight. 'I don't have a lot of time.' He went over to the bedside table and put his hand on the lamp.

'Shall I leave this off?' he said. By then I'd guessed what was expected of me, and it wasn't as if we hadn't done it before. I nodded and he took off his jumper, and it was as easy as that.

'What have you got for me?' he'd murmured, his eyes half closed as if he was imagining I was someone else.

'Show me, sit up like that and move your hands, down there. Show me that. What have you got for me? Can I touch? Here?' And then he'd stopped talking and let his hands and eyes move across the latitudes of my skin.

I let him heave me on top of him and lie still with his cheek pressed between my padded sternum and the bed. He liked that best of all I think: to feel smothered, cuddled in, I suppose, and held tight between a soft mattress and me. He moved, panting, and lay on top of me, rocking like he was floating on saltwater. I was a soap-smelling mountain; he climbed me, fell down, and slid between my legs. He shuddered out his orgasm buried inside me, his fists full of my flanks. Later, his head on my thigh, he traced the red pin-pricks around my navel.

'What's this?' They were beginning to bruise.

'Acupuncture. That's what I was doing this morning.' He traced the bluish haloes lazily with his tongue, probably tasting the copper tang of dried blood.

'What for? Not weight loss, I hope.'

'Will thinks it'll help us have a baby.'

'Oh. I see. You can't?' Without his glasses he looked younger. He didn't appear sympathetic or concerned, just plainly interested, the skin on his face empty and slightly pink. I liked it that he didn't start by assuming I was withering away inside due to anovulatory cycles, but it was obviously important he knew what I wanted from a relationship right from the beginning. I wanted it to be honest.

'I don't want to. I use a diaphragm. Put it in every night – he doesn't know, never notices it.' He huffed through his nostrils and smiled briefly as if my answer was more or less what he expected.

'I wondered about that,' he said, and blushed slightly. 'Got a bit carried away there and forgot to ask.'

I laughed. 'It's very hard to have a baby if it's the wrong time of the month,' I said, 'isn't that your theory?'

'What?' he said, confused. I could see his face change as he remembered and he smiled.

'You should leave him,' he offered. 'Find someone else, who you will want to have a baby with.'

When he said that, my heart started to pound very loudly and I started to see, in my head, a whole stretch of time in the future that was quite different from what I had been living through so far. I hardly knew what to say, so I just smiled to myself and allowed myself to touch the top of his head very gently with my fingertips.

Boris sighed and rested his forehead on my hip. His next words were muffled and I felt them vibrate along my belly with the heat of his wet breath.

'I've got to go now.'

I expected, of course, that he'd have to go back to his own house for a few days, that it would be as long as a week before I saw him again. I told him that was quite all right, and then, as soon as I'd said it, a thought started to nag at me and even though I knew it would spoil the moment I couldn't keep it to myself.

'You didn't keep in touch after you moved away. Did you mislay my address?'

He sat up and I looked at the small pockets of fat beginning to form around his nipples, marvelled again at the dark scattering of hair on his chest that had not been there before.

'Shit, Annie. We were kids.' He shrugged. 'I didn't realise it was that big of a deal.'

The air had cooled quickly, as if the heat of our exertions had left the room, sweat drying to a chilly film on the body, and Boris shrinking back to a virtual stranger.

'I just wondered. It doesn't matter. Like you say, we were young. Our parents were in charge of our lives back then. It's different these days.' There was a clock on the wall over the door and I saw him glance at it without trying to hide it.

'But you have my phone number now,' I said. There was a moment or two of silence.

'I do.' He stood up and started picking his clothes up from the floor.

My hands smelled like his hair and I remembered the coats of Meg and Fly, alive and shinily shaggy with sebum.

JENN ASHWORTH

'Do you ever think about it?' I asked, and he was dressing now, buttoning his flies and poking his feet back into his shoes. 'When we were younger, I mean.'

'It was a long time ago,' he said, and I laughed, but I didn't feel like it, because I was remembering all those times he wouldn't sit next to me on the school bus, the air stinking of Lynx and Impulse and Embassy cigarettes. Picking mud out of my hair and shaking cling-ing gobs of phlegm from my coat sleeves. Washing blood out of a school shirt. But I knew he thought I was beautiful.

'My dad says you're like a Rubix,' he'd said once. 'Not the puzzle thing – he's a painter. Pretty girls. Big, um, bazookas.'

He'd squeezed the air in front of him, caught me looking at his enthusiastic hands and stopped, blushed, and pulled a cigarette stub out of his pocket which he started turning around between his fingers and made no effort to light.

'When you walk about, Annie, it's like when some girls run. Like a porn film, but with clothes on!' He laughed because I was laughing then too, and pushing him into the road with my shoulder.

The memory comforted me. There was a short time in my youth when we had been friends that my life had been filled with compli-ments like that, and I was hoping, no, I was almost certain, that I was about to embark upon another period just like it.

He was dressed now. Calling an end to it and putting all the clothes back on was more awkward than beginning things had been.

'I'll sort out the bill,' he said. 'You hang about for a bit, if you like.'

'I won't be long,' I said cheerfully, wrapping the sheet around myself and feeling shy now that the light was on. He put his head on one side thoughtfully.

'I'll leave something for you,' he said, 'you might find it interesting.'

I watched as he rooted around in the inside pockets of his duffel coat and finally produced a tattered, rolled-up magazine. He saluted me with it, then dropped it into the bag my dress had come in.

'Have a look when you get home,' his hand was on the door handle, 'thanks. See you. All right?' I nodded and then he went.

I lay alone in the still-warm bed for a few minutes, swishing my legs about between the sheets and smelling the smells that we'd left on the pillows. I tried the chocolates that were left on the bedside

126

table, and then caught sight of the time on the clock. I was so anxious about the fact that I was going to be much, much later home than I said I would be, that as I hurried to dress, I didn't have time to look at the magazine Boris had left for me. I was preoccupied, wondering what I was going to say to Will when I got home.

In the end, I decided to say nothing. While I had high hopes, nothing had been decided between Boris and myself just yet, and troubling Will with unfounded concerns when the facts of our arrangement were cloudy even in my own mind would, I reasoned, be nothing other than an act of selfishness. And of course, we had the dance to go to.

As I approached the house, place of the brown three-piece suite and scalloped net curtains, I saw Will was waiting for me, anxiously stroking the heads of a pair of porcelain horses on the windowsill. He'd opened the door while I was still rooting for the key in my bag.

'Annie!' he said. He'd changed from his work clothes into some grey trousers and a blue short-sleeved shirt.

'You're late. I was worried. What were you doing? Did you forget about the dance?'

'I went shopping for something to wear,' I said. 'I found a really good shop. Got a bit carried away actually.' I rattled the bag that contained the new dress and the magazine. Will smiled.

'Good girl. There's still time for you to eat something before you get dressed, some biccies, maybe, and there's something else in the oven. Fill up before we go, okay, love?'

He herded me into the sitting room, deposited a tin of biscuits on my lap and knelt to take my feet out of my shoes. I was feeling groggy and wished I could go to sleep.

'Did you get something nice? In black, like I said? You made sure it was discreet, didn't you?'

He always got worked up about these parties, cuffing my elbow with his hand to guide me into dining rooms as if he was steering me, and I was the only one that knew his hands were shaking.

'It's just like you wanted. Black, high at the neck, no split at the side and a material that doesn't cling,' I recited, hoping he wouldn't take it into his head to inspect the carrier bag and discover the magazine that was in there.

'Righto.' He seemed distracted and I thought for a moment that he didn't believe me. I clutched at the bag. The magazine was still in it, had been banging against my calf all the way home.

'Pass me that glass, will you?' He darted about the front room, fussing with the curtains and looking at something flying about in the air. There was a blue-bottle hovering around the light shade and he proceeded to usher it away from the centre of the room with a rolled-up newspaper. He started to scale the furniture in pursuit of the fly which was teasing him, alighting tantalisingly within arm's reach and then flicking away as soon as he got his glass within catching distance.

'There's spray, under the sink,' I said, beginning to get out of my chair. 'I'll go and get it.'

'No, the fumes.'

'What?'

'They're bad for you.'

'I'm not expecting yet, Will.' I said it as mildly as I could but the subject had become a difficult one between us, which didn't stop him broaching it on an almost daily basis. This time it was me. I was feeling so overwhelmed, so changed by the afternoon I'd had, that I barely knew what I was saying.

'All the same. Might as well start as we mean to go on. Get into good habits. I've nearly got it now. You sit where you are, drink your tea. There's something in the oven to eat if you're still hungry. Leave this to me.'

The fly was walking along the wall above a framed photograph of Will's mother and father. Will jumped at it a few times with the glass but only succeeded in knocking the picture crooked. He put a finger to his lips and then slammed the glass against the wall so quickly it banged and I thought he'd broken it. By standing with one foot on the arm of a chair and the other on top of the sideboard he'd managed, finally, to trap it under the glass. It buzzed and bounced itself off the curved interior. Precariously balanced, Will slid a sheet of the newspaper between the wall and the bottom of the glass and then stepped down.

'Look at him, he's a big one, isn't he?'

The fly continued to head-butt the sides of the glass. Its wings buzzed and I could see the green, oily-looking scales on its body.

'Ugh. It's filthy. Couldn't you just whack it?'

'No need for that, I'll take him outside.' He opened the front door and moved the paper away from the top of the glass. The fly, probably quickly acclimatised to its prison, was busy sticking its proboscis to the bottom of the glass and rubbing its hands together as if eagerly anticipating the flavour of whatever it had found to suck up from the bottom. Will had to shake the glass in the air over his head and then tap the bottom against the cladding to get it to fly away.

'Not expecting yet, but maybe very soon,' he said. 'I haven't forgotten what day it is, you know.' He tapped the side of his nose and I knew he was referring to the temperature chart in the bathroom that I filled in more or less at random each morning.

I almost shuddered, but he didn't notice. There wasn't going to be a baby. I disliked myself for deceiving him, especially over something as important as this, but I didn't feel I had much choice. Because it was important, and because he was so fixated on this 'baby' I'd been forced to take measures to protect myself. Reasoning with him would have been pointless, when he had convinced himself that, on this issue, *what he wanted and what I wanted were the same thing.* And so the diaphragm was there, safe and sound like a little plastic hat in its pink case in my knicker-drawer.

The evening passed quickly enough: probably because I'd managed to get slightly drunk by going to the bar and ordering drinks that looked like lemonade. The important conversations Will was supposed to be having receded into a blur, and because he was in a state of anxiety about missing my most fertile time slot, he dragged us away home before the dancing began. At home in the bedroom I saw that I wasn't the only one who had been out shopping that day. Draped over my side of the bed in a puddle of shiny blue material there was another one of those silly flimsy things he sometimes bought for me. God knows where he got them.

I dutifully went to the bathroom and had a quick wash, greased the plastic disc, put one foot on the pan and inserted it. Naked, I brushed my hair in the mirror. The yellow strip-light above the medicine cabinet had always made me look awful: a cancer patient. My skin glowed pink and green as if I was dying.

Next door I heard Will rustle under the sheets and fold himself into the bed like he was sliding a letter into an envelope. It would be pitch black in there. His pyjama bottoms would be folded neatly on the floor next to his side of the bed for later and he would be lying there with his arms crossed over the front of the pyjama top, his fingers nervously playing with the nubs and whorls on the candle-wick bedspread. There was a smudge of toothpaste on the bathroom mirror and I took out the cleaning things from the cupboard over the toilet and started to work at it.

Five or ten minutes passed and I heard him cough gently. There was no chance of him nodding off to sleep so I turned off the taps and used the squirter to shove some more spermicide from the tube inside myself. Finally, I pulled off the tags and slipped the cool electric-blue nightdress over my head. It had a low v-neck that left nothing at all to the imagination and fell garishly to just above my dimpled knees.

I wondered about the kind of things I would be free to say if it was Boris in the bed with me that night. Sometimes I did ask Will to change things a little. I'd read an article in a women's magazine on the matter once and had suggested we implement some of the variations they'd illustrated in our own relationship. My comments were always met with silence and a stubborn refusal to vary the met-ronomic rhythm of his prodding.

Will climbed on top of me and worked his way inside. Soon his mouth was open and sealed against my shoulder and he began to rock industriously on his knees. Usually, that was it, but this time, because he was a bit tipsy, I suppose, he played a counterpoint with his hand, regularly tweaking my left nipple.

'Do you want me to get on top?' I said, my quiet voice in the dark-ness the biggest breach of our silent bedroom etiquette yet.

Limpet-like, the noise his mouth made coming away from my skin was louder than the regular squelching of him working away between my thighs.

'Shush, love,' he whispered, 'I don't like it when you're crude. It isn't ladylike.' He coughed out a little dry laugh, 'Anyway, you'd suf-focate me, you would!'

He kissed my cheek chastely, re-arranged the sheets around us and continued. It was workman-like: nose to the grindstone, back to the coal-face. He took a deep breath, nipped my shoulder with his teeth, and ejaculated. There were always, after this moment, a couple of minutes where he would lie limp on me and rest his throat against my shoulder as if I were a couch. A big, jiggly waterbed. He never said anything. No endearments, no words of thanks or reassurance. His ribs and hips stuck into me and I inhaled, feeling my chest roll and throw him off-balance. Then he moved away, returned himself to his pyjama bottoms and shuffled around under the bedspread.

'Stay lying down for half an hour, Annie,' he said, like he always did, 'let it do its work.'

We fell asleep, him probably dreaming of his baby and me thinking of Boris, anticipating the phone call that I knew would be coming soon.

The next morning I was tidying in the front room when I came across the carrier bag tucked between the cushions of the couch. I pulled it out and noticed that the magazine was still rolled up inside it. I took it with me into the kitchen and sat at the table to finish the leftover toast from breakfast. Guilt had worked on me in the night, and I'd planned to throw it away and consign the whole confusing incident to history but curiosity got the better of me and I unrolled it expectantly.

The cover was bright yellow and there was a large naked woman sprawled on all fours on the front, with text modestly covering the area where her private parts should be. The writing said: 'Fat whores sucking dick, lardy bitches on heat, stories, pics, personals and more!' and the magazine was called *Abundance*. I flicked through its pages as I ate. The personal advertisements were on five pages at the back and a few were circled in what looked like a blue felt-tip that had seen better days.

I was amazed.

I forgot about the toast and sat there for several hours examining the magazine from cover to cover. It was very unlike my usual reading material, which at that time consisted mainly of romance novels I picked up at the library and out of date women's magazines Will brought back from the surgery for me. It would not be too much of an overestimation to say that my experience of reading

Abundance constituted one of several great turning points in my life, an epiphany almost catastrophic in its eventual consequences.

It was the thought of Boris and all the others like him that cocooned me from the glances of the staff and the other shoppers as I walked around the shop and felt the silky material of Lucy's dress sliding between my fingers. I could feel, in the midst of the other people pricking at me with their disapproval, an unexpected gaze like a caress over the flanks. Thanks to Neil and the promise of something more substantial than brief connections in otherwise empty afternoons, that part of my life was in the past. Even so, it was still a comfort and a confidence boost to know that somewhere around me in the shop a man was looking, not staring or wondering, but just looking, and running his eyes over me like a firm and appreciative hand.

I hunted through the racks until I finally found the dress in a size that I thought would do. Taking it to the counter, I looked all around me as I went, searching for the owner of the pair of eyes that had gazed at me while I was browsing. There were no men in the shop at all, just harried women with their heads bowed over the hangers contemplating halter necks and boot-cut jeans.

'I'll just take this one, please,' I said, and opened my purse. The girl was there, still chewing her gum. She took out the hanger, threw it into a basket behind her and scanned the ticket at the till. I handed over the money and she held the dress up to fold it, looking at me and back at it doubtfully.

'We can swap it if you keep the receipt,' she said, 'if it's too small.'

'I'm sure it'll be fine,' I said firmly, and took the bag from her. I could feel her staring at me as I walked out of the plastic-smelling shop and into the street and I wanted to laugh, because I had my secret, and that sixteen-year-old was still to discover it. The more there is, the more they want you. They even paid sometimes, I'm so rare.

It was still raining, and I hurried back home, dodging the trams in my haste to get back to the house and return Lucy's dress. Unfortunately, when I turned the corner onto my street I saw she was kneeling in the front garden and as I got closer to her I noticed she was digging holes into the soil with a trowel and planting primroses into the bare flower beds. She turned around when she heard my steps on the path and I leaned over the fence to talk to her. It was still drizzling lightly, she had the hood of her coat up and the knees of her jeans were black with wet soil. Because I'd managed to buy exactly the right dress, I was in very high spirits and decided to engage her in conversation.

'Doing a bit of gardening, Lucy?' I said. 'It's hardly the weather for it.'

'Just replanting those primroses. Neil went to the garden centre yesterday and bought some more for me,' she said curtly.

'How nice. They'll look lovely once they settle in.'

'Annie, you didn't see anyone messing about round the back this morning, did you?' She leaned back on her heels and looked up at me.

Even though it was raining I imagined for a minute what I must look like, towering above her and totally blocking out the light. She was sitting in my shadow. I did remember thinking exactly those words, that's how giddy I had become with the success of my afternoon's shopping.

'In the garden?'

'When it started raining I went out to take the washing in and I noticed one of my dresses was missing. I didn't like it much anyway. It's just a bit weird.'

'I've been out myself, actually,' I said. 'Doing a bit of clothes shopping, you know, treating myself.' I rattled the bag and smiled.

'So you don't know anything about the dress then?' I shook my head but she carried on looking right at my face. The rain was hitting my ears and dripping down the back of my neck. I wanted to go but Lucy stayed sitting where she was as if she hadn't noticed how wet it was getting.

'I'll probably have to mention it to Sangita the next time I see her. See if she can get the Neighbourhood Watch onto it. Hasn't she been to see you?'

I smiled. 'She has, as a matter of fact. A very nice time we had too. She's invited me round to her house for tea.'

Lucy shook her head, exasperated.

'She didn't mention it then? She's having a dinner party: this weekend, I believe, once she's cleared it with Barry. I'm surprised she hasn't been in touch!'

Lucy sighed. 'I'll mention the dress to her when I see her,' she said pointedly. 'She'll be able to get to the bottom of it. This is the third time I've had to put these primroses in.'

'At least planting out when it's wet means they won't need a watering.' I laughed in as friendly a way as I could manage and she turned her head away from me and back to the soil.

I went inside, went straight through and into the back without even taking my coat off and threw her dress over the fence and into the garden. She'd probably assume it had blown away somewhere and the wind had brought it back. I was unsettled, of course I was, but I was also sure that with the way things were progressing the dinner party would mark a turning point and she'd be gone from Neil's life very soon.

It seemed to me I had made an ally in Sangita against Lucy, and she could be relied upon to view both my actions and myself with sympathy and understanding. She, like me, could see Lucy for what she was and was not about to be taken in by rumours and gossip.

Lucy's need to blacken my name in the local community could only mean one thing: she was feeling threatened by my growing intimacy with Neil. Her jealousy comforted me: it obviously meant she could see the special connection Neil felt he had with me, and it worried her. All in all, it was nothing to get irritated about, I thought, as I took off my coat and shook the dress out of its bag excitedly.

I went into the kitchen for something to eat and my eye was drawn to the little mat near the washing machine where I placed the bowls for Mr Tips's food and water. The water bowl was dry and the food that was left had a cracked, glazed appearance that suggested it had been lying there untouched for some time. I tried to remember when I had last seen him about the house, and the sudden apprehension he had not returned in more than four days made me jump as if someone had thrown a pail of icy water down my back.

Four days and I had completely forgotten about him!

It just goes to show how much I had been distracted by the events unfurling in my life at that point. Mr Tips was, well, he was like a baby to me. We'd been through a lot together and he'd never once abandoned me. The thought that he could be out wandering somewhere and thinking, justifiably, that I'd forgotten all about him brought tears to my eyes.

I immediately went out into the back alley, banging a knife against his bowl and clicking my tongue. I knew if he was in the vicinity he would hear me and that would be enough to restore him to me, but even though I paced for several minutes he didn't make an appearance and I became more and more anxious about what had happened to him. My mind was filled with visions of him alone, lost, unable to find his way home. Or worse, trapped somewhere and slowly starving to death.

I was just kneeling to look under the hedges that backed onto the alley, wondering perhaps if his collar had caught on a twig and he was in fact trying to get to me but couldn't, when there was a noise of a window opening above my head. I stood up sharply, looked at the back of the houses and realised it was Lucy, opening her bedroom window. She leaned out and peered down at me.

'Are you all right, Annie?' she called, frowning. Her face was framed by purple curtains, white windowsill and orange brickwork. The colours jangled against my eyes and I squinted back at her.

'Yes, quite all right,' I called back, my voice cracking a little because I was quite close to tears, having been inwardly berating myself and my selfish carelessness for the previous ten minutes. I brushed the mud and leaves from the front of my jeans with my hands and waved to her.

'What's that?' she asked, suspiciously. I was confused, and then realised I'd waved to her with the hand that was holding the knife I had been using to bang on the food bowl. I looked at it, almost surprised to see it there, and put my hands behind my back.

'It's just a butter knife,' I said, trying to sound reassuring but failing because I had to raise my voice in order for her to hear me, 'I'm looking for my cat.'

'Right,' Lucy said, 'just checking,' and started to close the window. She glanced away from me, down into her garden where I couldn't see because of the fence.

'Is that my dress?' she asked.

'I don't know,' I said, 'is it?' She disappeared from the window and a few seconds later I heard the back door open.

'It is!' I heard her say. The alley door opened and she looked out angrily, holding it in her hand.

'It's covered in mud,' she said. 'What do you think you're playing at?'

'I'm just looking for Tips,' I said again, 'he's gone missing, I don't suppose you've seen him, have you?'

Imagine her, fussing over a supposedly missing dress that was safe in her hands while I was standing there, dreading to think what impression I was making but in my distress even willing to overlook that and turn to someone who had declared herself my enemy.

'No, sorry,' she said, and banged the door shut so quickly I had to jump back or it would have hit me.

12

Sangita did as she had promised. After a consultation with Barry, she invited myself and Neil (as well as Lucy and Raymond) for a meal that very weekend. The interval passed slowly, and there was still no sign of my cat. Only a cat, you might say, but when the day of the dinner party finally arrived and I'd exhausted all the usual ways of occupying myself, I found myself bereft of distraction, wearing the pattern off the carpet with my pacing, and missing him. I'm ashamed to say I was too excited to go out and look, preferring to remain indoors and fester, waiting in agony as the hands of the clock crept more and more slowly onwards.

'We'll eat about seven,' Sangita had said, and I'd promised myself I wouldn't start dressing until at least five. I spent the time between lunch and the appointed hour carefully hand-washing and pressing my new dress. When the hall clock chimed and I finally allowed myself to slip the fabric over my shoulders I was trembling. Even though I was alone, I was too shy to look at myself in the mirror, and when I did, I was awed by the transformation.

The hours spent over the sewing machine had frustrated me terribly at the time: the seams were so sparely cut there was barely any material to let out and I'd been in a fever of impatience, desperate to trot next door and show it off. Now, looking at the sophisticated fall of the black fabric as it ruffled around my knees, I was grateful for the effort I'd made. I had the chance to appear as I really was: worldly and calm, well turned out and confident that Neil would be impressed. If he could find the frock attractive on Lucy, who had the curves of a coat hanger and nothing to speak of in the way of breasts, how much more would he enjoy the sight of it presented on a woman who had the figure to fill it properly?

Finally, I applied my lipstick, thinking that the only thing I needed to make the whole day perfect was someone to tell about it. How tempted I was to take a bus back to the old house and call on some of the neighbours!

'I can't stay for long,' I said to the mirror, imagining being pressed to remain for just one more cup, 'I have a dinner date to be getting to. Oh yes, a new friend of mine. We're on good terms with the local doctor and his wife, and they've been begging our company for days!' I practised laughing until I got it right, thinking of Lucy and deciding there was nothing worse than a screecher.

As well as my date with Neil, there was one other reason that I was looking forward to the evening. I'm no great cook myself, and while the attraction of being able to eat a tin of cold rice pudding for breakfast and four vanilla slices for lunch had taken a good few weeks to wane, wane it had, and I was eagerly anticipating a home-cooked meal. You don't bother so much when you're on your own. I'd tried, of course I had, despite the fact that my skills were limited in that particular department. You know what it's like.

You get to the shops and put the things you think you'd want to eat later into the basket, but it all looks so meagre and pathetic that you put a few extra things in there just so the shop assistants won't go into the back and laugh at you for being on your own and having no one else to cook for. You lug it home on your own, unpack it onto the kitchen worktop and stand staring at the single plate and mug lying dirty in the sink from the morning. Life goes on, and whatever happens, you have to eat.

So you cook. You put the pie in the oven and you cut up your single potato to make mash, and no matter how carefully you work it out you're eating chicken and leek pie for three days and it still isn't finished when on the fourth it goes rancid in the tin.

So you rely on the freezer, more and more, and those special meals for one that you can do in the microwave and aren't so heavy to take back. Eventually, when you're standing in the kitchen waiting for the ping to let you know you can start eating, the thought occurs to you that you might as well just eat it out of the plastic tray it comes in. It'll save the washing-up and of course no one is watching. You've already graduated from the table to the armchair in front of the television, and now you can stand in front of the microwave and take a spoon and gobble it out of the tray. It's over with quicker that way and everyone knows eating is more of a social event anyway. No point bothering when you're on your own.

For a while it's like that, hearing nothing but the sound of yourself chewing as you stand over the bin with your foot on the pedal, just so you can drop the container in afterwards and never have to think about it again. No one's watching, so eventually you stop buying washing-up liquid and don't even bother with the microwave meals, which were too small anyway. It happens by degrees. Just once, you think, you might as well buy cake and biscuits and all of your favourite things. Things that are sweet and soft, that you don't have to share, don't even have to unwrap, and that you can take upstairs and eat in bed. You might pretend it's your birthday and the person who's brought you all these treats and tucked you up in bed to eat them has just popped out to buy you some flowers.

I was worried about eating too much and embarrassing myself at Sangita's house. My stomach grumbled at the thought of the pasta and I eyed the bag of toffee popcorn I'd bought to offer as a pre-dinner nibble. As a compromise I made myself two rounds of buttered toast and ate it leaning over the sink. I didn't want to get any crumbs on the dress.

I arrived at the Choudhry's twenty minutes early. It was just Sangita and I on our own for forty minutes, which was pleasant enough. She let me help her with small jobs around the kitchen and although I'm clumsy with a paring knife, I did my best and I think she was pleased. She'd set the table with a white cloth and two dignified glass vases of understated white carnations.

'It looks lovely,' I said to her, spreading my hands out in front of me and making a little circle to encompass the table, the white flowers and plates, and Sangita herself, hovering near the cooker with a spoon. She was wearing a black sari that showed off her tiny rounded stomach. It had gold leaves and flowers embroidered all over it and it sparkled in the hood-light from the cooker.

'You look like a little Christmas tree,' I said, 'and this, it's just like Pappadum Palace, those little white flowers. It's beautiful!'

Sangita swiped me playfully on the arm with a tea towel and started giggling.

'You're wicked, Annie, wicked! If Barry hears you comparing this house to the Biryani Barn there'll be hell to pay! Shh! This is him now!' and she turned back to the cooker with her hand over her mouth, her shoulders still quivering.

Barry appeared from upstairs smelling of soap and wiping shaving foam from his ears with a hand towel.

'Should my ears be burning, ladies?' he said, but there was no time to answer because someone banged on the door and Barry went to open it. Neil, Raymond and Lucy piled in, smelling of cigarette smoke and alcohol.

'Not late, are we? We're starving!' Lucy trilled loudly, and Sangita turned from the cooker and gave me a little 'thumbs up' just before they traipsed into the kitchen, putting handbags and mobile phones down on her table and knocking the cutlery askew.

Lucy was wearing a very short white dress with little blue flowers all over it. It wasn't a bad dress, in fact, the colour quite suited her, I'll give her that. Still, it was more a summer dress meant for a walk along the beach than a casual meal with friends. Neil had brought Sangita a bunch of flowers, kissing her on both cheeks and dropping them into the sink. I stood up to open the toffee popcorn I had brought but Sangita must have put it away, and everyone was talking and I didn't want to interrupt and ask her for it.

The quiet kitchen where we'd been drinking tea and laying the table was filled with people opening cupboards and clinking bottles and I was quite overwhelmed. I sat quietly wondering what to do with my empty teacup and smelling the food bubbling on the cooker when Lucy came over and sat down beside me. She'd brought a bottle of wine with her and opened it to pour herself a glass.

'None for me thanks, Lucy,' I said, and covered the top of my glass with my hand. She left the bottle where it was on the table and looked at me as if she'd never met me before in her life.

'What is that you're wearing?' she said loudly. Raymond, Neil and Barry were talking about films or something, and Sangita had her back to us, discreetly chopping garlic and scraping it from the chopping board into one of the shiny silver saucepans on the cooker. They all stopped what they were doing and turned to face me.

'A dress,' I said slowly. I've noticed sometimes people ask you questions that you just can't answer without making you or them sound stupid. 'It's new,' I added, so as not to embarrass her.

'New?' she said, agitated. 'It's that ratty old thing that went missing from the line, isn't it? Neil! Come and have a look at this.'

Neil turned, raised his glass to me and nodded a greeting.

'Neil!' she barked. 'Look at what Annie's wearing!'

'It's, ah, it's very nice?' he said, raising his eyebrows and looking at Lucy doubtfully. Sangita turned from the cooker and looked at Lucy, exasperated.

'You don't mean to say I've been cooking all afternoon only to be serving refreshments for a bun fight, have I?' she said, as if she was telling a joke. 'Surely not?'

'It's that dress I was telling you about, San. The one that went missing,' she pointed at me, 'and she's wearing it!'

Raymond looked at Neil enquiringly, and he shrugged again. 'I thought you said you found it, Luce?' he said gently, and touched her hair.

'Well I did, but that's not the point,' she said, as if whatever her point was should have been obvious.

'So the dress that went missing isn't actually missing at all,' Sangita said, and laughed, 'you've got me into a right tangle, and just as I'm about to serve up too. There's more than one little black dress in the world, and more importantly, the garlic bread's getting burnt. Raymond, could you give me a hand getting it out of the oven? Perhaps Lucy would like a cup of coffee to go with her wine?'

Lucy 'humphed' and turned back to her wine glass. I smiled into my chest and clasped my hands together on my lap. My outfit, as I had hoped, had obviously gone down a storm. She drank steadily, topped herself up, and drank again. We sat together in silence as Sangita bustled around Raymond at the cooker, finally sending all the men to the table to 'get out of the way'.

When Lucy had emptied another glass she turned to me. 'Have you found your cat yet?' she asked stiffly.

I shook my head.

'Not yet. I'm not too worried, he'll come back on his own, I think.'

'No more prowling around in the bushes with bread knives then? Did I tell you,' she said loudly, and to no one in particular, 'that's what she was up to the other day? A knife!'

I was feeling confident, and decided that from now on I would take all of her attempts to upset me as mere jokes, the way Sangita did. Little rocks in an otherwise easy path I could skip over without a second thought.

'Oh no, that's not the sort of thing a girl does more than once or twice a month,' I said, and laughed. Raymond snorted, but Lucy only frowned and made herself busy chasing a drip of wine down the stem of her glass with a finger.

'I'm sure he'll be okay,' I said, 'it's not like having a baby: I'm entitled to go out for an evening once in a while.'

The truth is I was feeling guilty about wasting my afternoon, Lucy-style, on thinking about my clothes when I could have been looking for him. Her questioning made me wonder if she had something to do with his disappearance. I wouldn't put a cruel act of revenge like that past her, I really wouldn't. She was just the kind of vindictive little madam who'd think nothing of parcelling him up in a cardboard box and leaving him at an animal shelter. Or worse, but I didn't let myself think about that.

'Why do you ask?' I said. 'Have you seen him?'

'Cats,' she said vaguely, looking away, 'they all look the same to me. Are we eating soon, Sangita? I'm absolutely famished!'

Sangita ate her meal quickly in precise little bites, her teeth clacking together cleanly as she chewed. Her fingers scurried neatly over her cutlery and napkin, and while Lucy was still waving her fork about and helping herself to more wine, Sangita was finished and lifting the napkin from her lap. Her hands were tiny and brown with small round fingernails almost overgrown with a rind of cuticle, and I looked at them while lifting the fork slowly towards my mouth and wondering what I looked like as I ate.

Barry didn't seem to eat at all, but supervised, pressing Sangita back into her chair every time she rose to get someone a clean glass or a second helping of something. He'd rolled up his shirtsleeves as the steaming bowls were paraded onto the table. I expected him to dive hands first into the platter, such was the gushing praise and admiration he heaped on it, and, by association, his wife. But he allowed himself to be served only a taste of each dish, and pushed these around on his plate, abandoning it entirely after a few minutes to lean back in his chair and sip a glass of sparkling water silently and meditatively.

Lucy seemed to keep one hand under the table throughout the whole meal, and rested her other elbow on the edge, letting her wrist flap about as she spoke and giggling unashamedly when she let food fall from her fork and mark the tablecloth. Whenever I tried to initiate conversation with her, she ignored me, drawing attention not to me, but to herself. My feelings weren't hurt in the slightest. It was quite clear she was only making herself look foolish, and I enjoyed taking the opportunity to show her up in her true light by being especially solicitous to her, offering her the last tomato slice from the salad bowl, for example, and relishing Neil's attention when he stepped in to take it to cover up for her rudeness in ignoring me.

Neil, when left to himself, put his head towards his plate and ate methodically, cutting and lifting and chewing as if to meet a deadline. He gave the meal his full concentration, nodding absently when he was addressed, and only looking up and joining in with the conversation when he was finished. There was something mesmerising about the way he ate, the unhurried diligent way he had of bringing food to his mouth as if the rhythm of his chewing had lulled him somewhere far away from all of us.

He, unless, as I said, pressed by the demands of politeness, paid me no special attention and that made me think he had indeed remembered our first meeting at that bus stop over a year previously. Yes, I had been bleeding and bruised, but perhaps the swelling that had so disfigured my features hadn't developed until later. Perhaps he'd remembered my shoes, or noticed the comma-shaped freckle on the back of my hand. He was, I imagined, the sort of person who'd worry about a woman who found herself in a situation like the one I was in that day. It would be the kind of thing he'd forget only slowly, if at all.

There could only be one reason why he hadn't brought it up already, apart from respecting my own privacy and wish to take things slowly. He'd obviously assumed that it was *me* who hadn't recognised him and he was saving the revelation for when we were alone. A special surprise, perhaps. I thought it would be like going down on Christmas morning and opening the presents I'd discovered under my mother's bed in November. I'd have to pretend to be shocked, embarrassed and touched, but the time to prepare it would only make my eventual response so much more gratifying to him. Every time I thought about it I had to press my napkin against my mouth to hide a secret smile of pleasure.

Raymond, who I'd been seated next to, ate just like my father. This meant he bolted the food so quickly his elbows jabbed me. He washed down his huge mouthfuls with great draughts of beer. It seemed he didn't leave the house without dangling four cans of something from his fingers.

'You cut your hair, Annie?' he asked, and tore off a wide chunk of bread, screwing it into a pellet before feeding it into the hole in the bottom of his face. He chewed with his mouth open and laughed loudly whenever anyone made a joke. My forearm was sprayed with little flecks of saliva.

'Not myself,' I said, 'but I did go to the hairdresser last week, yes.'

Lucy looked at me carefully, probably remembering it was she who recommended that I have it done.

'You decided to keep the side parting, then?' she said. 'I thought you were going to go for something a bit different?'

'Annie's hair looks lovely the way it is,' Sangita interrupted, but in so gentle a way as to make it seem it was she who had started the conversation in the first place. She picked up her plait and looked at the end of it, flat and pointed like a paintbrush.

'I often think about getting this lopped off,' she said, 'you would not believe the split ends on it, but Barry won't have it, will you?'

He laughed, 'You make it sound like I'd beat you for it,' he said to her, and then looked around at the rest of us, 'I just believe, person-ally, that a woman's hair is her best feature. Eve tempted Adam with her hair back in the Garden of Eden, if I remember the story right...'

'I'm a leg man myself,' Raymond said. 'Can't beat a nice pair of legs, can you, Neil?'

I put down my fork (I was having trouble with the spaghetti: I've always found the kind in packets is so much longer and more unwieldy than the ready-cooked kind that comes in tins) and tucked my hair behind my ears. I was interested in what Neil would add to this conversation but it was Lucy who spoke next.

'For God's sake,' she said, amused, 'did I fall asleep and wake up in the 1950s? Do all you men prefer your women barefoot and in aprons too?'

I thought Raymond would be offended, but he just laughed.

'Don't get all hairy armpit on me, Luce,' he said, 'you're reminding me of the wife,' and he and Neil laughed. Lucy gave him a sharp look and topped up his glass of wine.

'I like my men rich and stupid,' she said cattily, and Neil flinched. 'What about you, Sangita?'

'Well,' she looked at Barry out of the corner of her eye, 'I'm more than happy with what I've got, so I suppose I'd have to say a nice smile and a sense of humour.'

'Boring!' Lucy said, and snorted.

'Luckily for me,' Neil said, laying a hand on Lucy's forearm, 'I like a girl who knows her own mind.'

This seemed to strike Lucy and Raymond as hilarious and they guffawed loudly, Raymond going as far as to push back his chair so he could thump his knees. I glanced at Sangita and when she caught my puzzled look she make a little 'eek' expression with her mouth and looked pointedly at the now empty bottle of wine standing near Lucy. I cleared my throat.

'I think the most important thing is to find someone you can be friends with,' I said. 'Legs and hair, they're not going to be there when you get older, but if you're friends…'

'I hope my legs don't drop off when I'm forty,' Lucy said, 'whatever you're planning to do with yours!'

Raymond spluttered so much he covered my arm not only with another spray of saliva, but with tiny white lumps of the bread he'd been chewing. I laughed along with the others and wiped it surreptitiously on the tablecloth. I thought Sangita would have understood.

'That was lovely,' Lucy said, getting her breath back and wiping a crust of bread around her empty plate, 'I was so hungry! You wouldn't think it, to look at me, but I eat like a pig, I really do.'

'I only opened a jar of Ragu,' Sangita said, and winked at me, because we both knew that was a lie, 'but I'm glad you enjoyed it. We should do it more often.'

'It's not often we get the chance,' Lucy said, 'we're so busy these days, aren't we, Neil?' Almost the only positive thing to come from her inebriation that evening was that as it wore on, she finally forgot to sulk.

'You just wait until a baby comes along,' Barry said, and Raymond nodded, 'you don't know what busy means until that happens!'

'Where are your lads tonight? It is half term, isn't it?' Raymond asked. 'You chucked them out for a few hours?'

I smiled. I did enjoy being around Barry and Sangita. Of all the couples I've known they seem to be one of the few that have achieved something special between themselves: something genuinely unique. Just what that something is remains impossible to describe, especially for someone on the outside of it like myself. And I don't say that with jealousy: part of the desirability of these connections is that by their nature they exclude everyone other than the man and the woman involved in them, even, and perhaps particularly, the children that are their by-product. It was enough for me that night to sit in the reflected glow that seemed to rise around them like a halo, learning what I could and preparing myself for when it was my turn. And that, after Lucy's indecorous behaviour, would happen sooner rather than later.

Sangita shook her head, 'They're upstairs, possibly doing their homework.'

'But more likely glued to that game gadget of theirs,' Barry broke his silence to finish her sentence knowingly, 'it's too quiet up there for anything else.'

Sangita laughed, 'Listen to him! You couldn't tell he's up there playing it himself whenever he gets a chance,' she said, pursing her lips at him affectionately.

'We still haven't had the pleasure of meeting your little one,' Lucy said to me, looking at me through half-lowered lids. 'She will be visiting during half term, won't she? That'll brighten your week.'

Sangita glanced quickly at me, 'We're all having a night off from children,' she said. 'There's nothing more boring than parents who harp on constantly about their wonderful offspring,' she added, and looked kindly at me over the candles. I smiled back, full of gratitude, and Lucy caught it, frowning curiously then tossing her hair over her shoulders as if to throw the thought away.

'Tell us something about yourself then, Annie,' she said, leaning forward and dropping her screwed-up napkin onto her plate. It was shiny with oil from the pasta and I saw the thick cotton soak it up hungrily, knowing Sangita would have a devil of a job getting it out. That's the benefit of disposable serviettes, such as the ones I provided at my house-warming party. They allow the hostess to concentrate on the food and the company and free her from worrying needlessly over domestic matters. Sangita gave no signs of noticing.

'I gather that's why we're all here? To get to know each other better? You've hardly said a word.'

We were all finished now, leaning back in our chairs with full stomachs. Neil's mouth was shiny with residue from his food. I pictured my face glowing softly in the candlelight, the soft shimmer of my make-up and the green ribbon at the neckline of the dress perfectly complementing the colour of my eyes.

'Did I see you coming down the street with an armful of books the other day?' Neil asked. 'I'm sure I did. I nearly came out to help you.'

'Did you?' I said, realising uncomfortably, stupidly, that my house wasn't the only one with windows. 'I must have been on my way back from the library.'

'Are you working on something? A project? Are you at university?' he asked.

'I suppose you could call it a project,' I said hesitantly, 'I do read a lot. It's so much better for you than television, isn't it?'

He nodded, 'I'm always trying to get Lucy to crack open a book. If it's not house makeover programmes it's celebrity game shows. Gives her ideas, it does.'

Lucy frowned slightly and touched Neil's arm.

'I'm only joking,' he whispered, and turned back to me expectantly.

'I'm not working at the moment,' I said, 'I have a background in, well, medical administration, I suppose you could call it. Briefly, though. My husband, well, I didn't need to work.'

'I see,' said Neil, 'and you're brushing up on your skills now? Thinking of getting back into the market?'

I nodded, 'That's exactly it. Couldn't have put it better myself.' I felt excited.

It isn't often I feel comfortable talking about myself, but the others had fallen silent and in the dimness of the kitchen it was as if they'd ceased to exist, or crept silently into the shadows like mice in order to leave Neil and I to ourselves. I was reminded of the Disney film *Cinderella*, when she and the prince dance together and the valet hastily draws a curtain between them and the rest of the ball to give them silence and privacy, away from the jealous peering of the ugly sisters.

The thing that had entranced me most about that film was the way she'd done her blonde hair up in an impossibly simple fold at the back of her head. I'd tried to recreate the style myself on numerous occasions and failed. Distracted by the train of my own thoughts, I touched my hairband and wished I'd asked Jessica to show me how to do it.

'It's not for work, it's more a hobby of mine,' I began. Lucy held her fingernails in front of her and started to admire them, the light glinted off them and I was annoyed by her presence. It would be so much better to have these 'getting to know you' conversations without her being there to put me off, but I had to make the best of it.

'It's self-improvement,' I said, 'learning about people, about myself. There's nothing you can't find out from a book, nothing at all.'

Lucy glanced away from her fingernails and poked Neil in the ribs.

'Not everything!' she said coyly, and licked her lips at him. Neil slid one of his hands under the table and she giggled.

'Barry and I actually met in a library,' Sangita said. 'Did you know that, Annie?'

'I didn't,' I said carefully, and she stood up and started transferring plates from the table into the dishwasher, throwing the napkins into the washing machine without checking if they were really dirty or not.

'I worked in one, for a little while. He was a student and was coming in to pick up a book he'd ordered. He'd filled out the reservation card all wrong and I was the one who helped him sort it all out.'

'I took her out for dinner that first night,' Barry said, and Sangita let her hand fall onto his head as she passed behind his chair, 'and here we are. Shall we go and sit down?'

Lucy settled herself on the settee. I'd headed over to sit between her and Neil but she lifted up her legs and put her feet into his lap.

'Sorry, Annie,' she said smiling, 'I've been on my feet all day and Neil's promised me a rub, haven't you?'

Neil stroked her shins and started to knead at her feet. The Choudhrys had taken the two armchairs either side of the door and sat there showing their teeth like ornamental lions. Raymond had already claimed the piano stool without a thought in his head for me and I looked about desperately for somewhere to sit. There was a kind of footstool upholstered in the same material as the three-piece suite, and I, with great difficulty, lowered myself onto it.

'Would anyone like coffee? Or tea?' Sangita asked.

I was about to nod when Lucy shook her head, 'We brought something to share for afterwards, didn't we, Neil?' She leaned over the side of the couch and handed him his rucksack.

'Someone gave it us last Christmas and it's been knocking about for ages. Might as well get it drunk, if that's all right with you?'

'Just because we choose not to, doesn't mean we forbid it our guests,' Barry said, gesturing towards a row of short glasses lined up along the top of the piano. 'Please, help yourselves. There are some chocolates up there too, if anyone would like some?'

I eyed the box as Lucy clutched at it, poked her narrow fingers between the sheets of tissue paper, and then handed it to Raymond, still chewing. By the time it came around to me all the soft-centres were gone. I think Sangita, probably with all the stress of cooking the meal, had forgotten about the toffee popcorn. Or maybe she hadn't understood that I meant for it to be shared out and she'd assumed it was a present. Oh well, it wasn't expensive.

'You know, me and Lucy met at her work too,' Neil said. Lucy smirked and hit him lightly on the arm.

'Don't,' she said, smiling and turning her face into the cushions on the couch, 'they don't want to hear about that!'

'I needed a new shirt. My dad and me were meeting with a man we wanted a big contract from. I needed to look the dog's...'

Barry coughed.

'And so I got the bus into Freeport and went into the shop where Lucy works. I'm wandering up and down the aisles not knowing what the hell I'm doing,' he said, 'when she comes up to me.' Lucy hit Neil on the arm and shook her head.

'Go on, tell them what you said,' he spoke loudly, the way people do when they're wearing a personal stereo, and as he leaned towards Lucy the light from the standard lamp next to the sofa illuminated his face and I saw his cheeks were flushed.

Lucy, with that solicitous topping up of his glass she'd indulged herself in all evening, had succeeded in getting him quite tipsy and I cringed inwardly, wanting to take him away and shield him from the embarrassment that would follow if he kept talking when he wasn't in full control of himself. He poked Lucy again, and raised his eyebrows eagerly,

'Go on,' he repeated, 'tell them. It was great!'

'No one wants to know, Neil,' Lucy said, pretending to be irritated, but cracking that coy little smile she had that made everyone else in the room feel invisible.

'Well I do,' Barry said warmly. He was obviously trying to diffuse what could have turned into a nasty row, and while I admired his sentiment, I wasn't too sure about his method. What Neil did not need at that moment, after all the wine Lucy had poured down his neck, was any encouragement.

'Well, it's nothing really. He gets me to tell him this story all the time, as if he wasn't there,' she shrugged, 'he just likes hearing it. You're like a little boy, aren't you?' she put her hand out and rubbed his chest and Neil grinned.

'I just saw he was having a bit of trouble choosing, so I went over and pointed out a couple of shirts that looked about his size, you get an eye for it once you've been doing the job for a while. He was holding them up against himself and kind of twirling in the mirror,' she let her mouth drop open slightly and her eyes go blank, 'like this, and I said, well,' she ducked her chin to her chest and dropped her voice, 'I said if he was having that much trouble dressing himself, he'd probably need a bit of help with the undressing!'

'And she came right in there with me!' Neil said, and Raymond started guffawing loudly, although by the sounds of it he had heard the story many times before. Sangita laughed politely and Barry stared at the curtains. I myself was so crippled by embarrassment for

Neil and irritation at the way Lucy persisted in making a mockery of him that I sat quite still, neither talking nor laughing.

'It's funny that it should come up,' I said, 'because the very last thing I read was a book on the psychology of mating behaviour in human beings.'

'Not another story about transsexuals then?' Lucy said. I ignored her.

'Some people did an experiment. It was very interesting. They found a pretty woman and got her to approach a few men in a comfortable room where they'd been waiting for her and passing the time by watching a little television. They asked the men how they'd liked her, got them to give her marks out of ten,' I said.

'God,' Lucy said, 'what poor bitch would volunteer for that? How desperate would you have to be?'

Barry was nodding, 'She was a research student, actually,' he said, 'probably being paid a lot more than any of the men taking part in the study.' I looked at him, surprised.

'I've heard of this experiment,' he explained, 'read the literature as an undergraduate. Fascinating, although tendentious. Go on, Annie, go on.'

'I will,' I said, pleased. 'A few days later they got the same men back, and asked them to cross a dangerous rope bridge. They got the woman to wait in the middle and chat to them a bit, and after that, they all had to give her marks out of ten again.'

'The same woman,' Barry added.

'Yes,' I said, shifting backwards to stop myself from falling from the footstool onto the floor. 'And do you know, they thought she was prettier on the rope bridge than they did in the waiting room. It's strange, isn't it?'

'And what was the point in that?' Lucy said. 'Doesn't sound like anyone was doing any mating to me.'

'Well, the point, as you so succinctly put it,' Barry said, 'is that it helped the psychologists to gather evidence that backed up an idea scientists in the field have long suspected.' Sangita put her hand over his and looked at him, frowning slightly.

'I am sorry, Annie. Continue,' he waved his hand like the queen.

'They say that falling in love is the same as being scared,' I said simply, 'the men on the rope bridge were scared, and they mistook it for falling in love. Most people have it all tangled up in their heads.' I paused as Sangita handed the box of chocolates back to me. There was a second layer that I hadn't discovered on the first round, and I scrutinised the inlay card before settling for a strawberry crème. It was unlucky that my next sentence, which was the conclusion of all I'd said before, was muffled by the melting chocolate and pink filling that was clinging to my teeth: 'Some people get it all mixed up.'

'And that's it?' Lucy said. Neil squeezed her knees with both his hands in order to pacify her.

'I wish I'd read that a few years ago,' Raymond said. Neil lifted his chin, waiting for the punchline.

'I was terrified when I met the wife, and stayed that way!'

It was a weak joke, but we all laughed.

'I wasn't scared when I met Luce,' Neil slurred. Lucy smiled, and started playing with her hair. 'It was the best shopping trip I ever had: I've never spent so long in a changing room!' he added, rubbing her calf. 'Good job we hit it off so well, seeing as you got the sack!'

Lucy wriggled against him and pushed her feet into his lap.

'What are you like,' she said, without making it into a question. She let her head lean against the cushion and rolled her eyes, 'I feel pissed all of a sudden, since I've sat down. Maybe we should have some coffee after all?'

The foot massage had turned into a thigh rub and was becoming quite indecent. From where I was sitting, I could see, if I had the misfortune to incline my head a half-centimetre to the left, the smooth line of Lucy's upper thigh running uninterrupted to the taut bulge of the red material stretched over her crotch. I shuffled along the foot stool and felt lucky I was so big: if I slouched a little I could at least protect the Choudhrys from the view. Neil leaned forward and rubbed his nose against Lucy's hair, and she giggled into his throat and squirmed under his hands.

I thought someone should take control of the situation and pour some coffee down Neil's throat before Lucy could humiliate him any further.

'Sangita,' I said, 'I can't let you wash up after cooking such a lovely meal. Would you mind if Neil and I went into the kitchen and got started on those dishes? I'd hate for you to come down and see it all lying there in the morning! We can boil the kettle while we're in there, can't we?'

Neil nodded limply, his face still turned to Lucy.

'I've already loaded up the dishwasher,' she said lightly, flushing pink with pleasure, 'but the glasses and cutlery are soaking in the sink. I wouldn't stop you running those under the tap if you insisted.'

I stood up.

'No, Annie, you sit down,' Lucy said. 'I've done nothing tonight, let me go in and help Neil,' she raised an eyebrow at Neil, who had already risen to his feet and offered an unsteady hand to her.

'Up you get, gorgeous,' he said, lisping. Lucy reached for his hand once or twice but missed each time, squinting and shaking her head as if what was obvious to everyone else was totally beyond her comprehension. Eventually, she swung her legs onto the carpet, pushed her hands against the sofa and tried to stand on her own.

'Oops!' she giggled, dropping back heavily onto the couch.

'I think you should stay where you are, we don't want any accidents, do we?' I said firmly. And that was a lie. Should there have been an accident involving Lucy, few tears would have been shed for her at my house.

'Annie, you're like a mother hen,' she babbled, putting her feet back onto the settee and snuggling herself into the throw. 'Look at the fush you're making, it's only a few dishes.' She patted the couch between her knees, 'Come back and sit with me, Neil, I'm getting lonely.' She probably would have continued her fluttering and twittering, but hiccups seized her and she held her breath ostentatiously, clamping her nostrils shut between her fingers and waving her other hand in the air if she was drowning.

I chose to ignore her.

'We'll have it spic and span in a jiffy,' I said to Sangita, and led Neil between her chair and Barry's and into the kitchen.

Sangita was right: there was hardly anything to do. Neil leaned crookedly against the cooker and sipped at the coffee I made him while I rinsed glasses under the tap and upended them on the draining board. It felt strange, to be let loose in someone else's kitchen together. It almost felt like we were in our own house and we were just getting the kitchen straight before we went to bed.

When I first moved into Will's house I didn't dare touch anything in case I broke it, and it had taken me a very long time to learn where everything went in the kitchen. Trying to find the right cupboard for the Choudhry's delicate glassware took me back to that place, and rather than fumble and break something, I concentrated on the drying and left the glasses in a neat row along the centre of the now bare table. It also gave me an excuse to look away from Neil and concentrate on something else, to keep my hands busy and pretend to be engrossed in getting the glasses smear-free rather than battle with my nerves and attempt to engage him in conversation.

'I probably need this,' Neil said, once the glasses were finished and I was folding the tea towel and laying it neatly across the taps. He rubbed his head and held out his mug for more coffee.

'Lucy's a wicked one when it comes to alcohol – she won't let you go without a refill.'

'It's naughty of her,' I said pleasantly, 'you shouldn't have to put up with peer pressure from your nearest and dearest.'

'Peer pressure,' Neil said, 'I like that! I'll have to tell her,' he laughed through his nose and his mug tilted dangerously towards the floor. I reached over and pushed the rim back with my first and middle finger. Was I stupid to think that when our eyes met this could very well be a significant moment between us? My foot bumped his and I stepped back, leaning against the fridge the way he was leaning against the cooker, leaning the way people did in kitchens during gatherings when they wanted to go somewhere away from the general noise so that they could talk.

'It's not Lucy's fault,' he said, 'Raymond came round in the afternoon and we watched a video together. She was working. When she came back we ducked out to the pub and...' he shrugged, 'you know how it is.'

'What video did you watch?' I said. 'I like films.'

'A classic! A real classic! Well, two actually. Raymond didn't have Liam today, so we put on *Rocky IV*, you know, the one where he fights He-Man? And after that, we watched *Con Air*. We've watched them both so many times the tape's worn thin. I'll have to get them on DVD, I reckon. You seen them?'

'I can't say I have, actually,' I said. 'I watched *The Sound of Music* yesterday though. I taped it from the television a few Christmases ago and I never stop kicking myself that I didn't pause the recording when the adverts were on. There's nothing like advertisements for Christmas presents watched in July to make you feel miserable, is there?'

Neil looked at me blankly and lifted the mug to his face.

'And what was it that you said you did again?' I asked desperately, knowing he was about to finish the second coffee and that we'd have to go back in and our moment 'behind the curtain' as it were, would be curtailed.

'Oh, nothing much,' he said, dropping his mug into the sink. I watched him as he turned on the taps and began to wash his hands. There aren't many people who wash their hands after a meal. I found it almost old-fashioned and oddly endearing. Watching the bubbles slide from his fingers and chase each other around the plug hole before disappearing, I wondered what Neil was like in his private moments. I felt like I knew him already, although I realise there's a difference between being able to hear someone through a party wall and being there with them on the other side of that wall.

I always imagined Neil as the type of man who'd shave with a bar of soap and a real shaving brush. He'd dislike finding hairs from his head in his comb in the morning and need constant reassurance that his hairline wasn't receding. He'd probably enjoy time alone with a newspaper and like to take the woman in his life out on long walks at the weekend, perhaps followed by a meal in an up-market pub. I was sure he, like me, wasn't overly keen on children, and had such aspirations in life that he had very little time for domestic matters. I was going to have to learn how to cook, and iron too, probably.

'My parents own a business,' he said. 'A mail-order company.'

'How interesting,' I said. 'I didn't imagine you in retail. I thought you worked with computers?'

Neil shook his head, 'It's not interesting at all. They sell hardware to heating and plumbing contractors. Job lots of radiators. Lengths of piping. Replacement parts for old boilers.' He shrugged, 'It's all product numbers to me. I might as well be selling tins of beans. I do the invoices, the web orders, stuff like that. It's an excuse for them to give me money, really, which I'm not complaining about. Every now and again it gets really busy and sometimes it isn't much fun working for your dad.'

'I can imagine,' I said.

'But you can live off it, and, like I'm always telling Raymond, at least it's not robbing fruit machines!' he laughed loudly at this, and I realised he was probably alluding to a joke that he and his friends had worn thin between themselves and I myself, as a newcomer to the group, hadn't yet had time to memorise it. I wasn't sure whether I should be honest about my incomprehension and ask for an explanation, or fake a laugh and risk being caught out later. I decided on a hybrid of the two approaches and smiled gently while turning away to rinse his mug under the sink.

'Perhaps the next time you and Raymond have an afternoon set aside for video-watching, you could bang on the wall or something and I could come over too?' I said, while my back was still turned to him. I wouldn't have had the courage otherwise. 'I could always bring something to eat, and help tidy up afterwards before Lucy comes home. You never tried my cakes, did you? I do a lovely jam sponge.'

I turned back to him and wiped my wet hands on my jeans. Neil looked as if he'd dropped something on the floor.

'It's more of a guy's thing really,' he said after a while, 'I don't think you'd like it.'

'We could all take turns?' I said. 'I could choose a film one week, and you or Raymond could choose it the next. That way,' I said, and I remember gesturing a lot, 'we all get to learn something about each other. It's natural for boys and girls, well, men and women, really, because that's what we are, aren't we, it's natural for us to like different things. It'll do us all good to have a change, won't it?'

It makes me curl up when I think about it. I always gesture too much when I'm excited about something, and I always vow to myself that I won't do it next time, but next time, of course, I'm always excited and I never remember to stop myself until I'm alone in the dark with a red face, huddling under the duvet and grimacing at what I must have looked like.

The kitchen door opened and it was Lucy with her high heels and little fluffy coat back on.

'Come on, Neil,' she said, holding herself up by the door frame. 'Are you talking about washers and pressure gauges again? You've been in here ages!'

Neil sauntered over, running his hand along the edge of the table as if to keep his balance. I'm not sure that coffee did him much good.

'Just telling Annie about the films,' he said.

'Oh, it'll be a good while before we do that again,' she said briskly, more to him than to me, 'you're going to be busy getting those bookshelves up: something to *soundproof* the adjoining wall. No more lazy Saturdays in for you while I'm out earning.' She nodded the briefest of acknowledgements my way and then turned back to Neil. 'I'm tired now, I want to go home.'

Neil turned towards me and shrugged, 'You heard what the lady said, we're off now.'

Through the open door I could see Raymond zipping up his funny padded jacket and I realised with a sinking heart it was time to go.

'So, what do you think,' I said to Neil, 'about that film night? It sounds like fun, doesn't it?'

'I don't think Ray would be too impressed with *The Sound of Music*,' he said. 'But you could always ask him? He's got a bit more spare time than me.'

'It doesn't have to be *The Sound of Music*. I have a library card. I bet I could get *Con Air*.'

'What?' Lucy interrupted without looking at me. It hadn't been going as well as I'd hoped, but it was foolish of me to press matters with her standing there.

'Oh, for God's sake, Neil, come on!' Lucy wasn't angry when she said that, just impatient. She turned to the side and wiggled her bottom at Neil and he reddened, and started checking his pockets for his phone and keys.

'I'll have to talk to Raymond about it,' he said, turning towards me just once before he followed Lucy out. 'See you!'

By the time I'd got my own coat on and said goodbye to the Choudhrys Lucy and Neil had already left and only Raymond was waiting for me outside on the path.

'I think it went all right, didn't it?' Sangita whispered into my ear as I passed her at the doorway. I couldn't say much, because Raymond was there, kicking at something he'd found on the path and clearly both determined to walk me home and anxious to be gone. I smiled broadly and gave her a little 'thumbs up', but of course I was disappointed it was Raymond and not Neil there waiting for me.

'I'll call you in the week,' she said, and waved before she closed the door on us.

Outside it was dark, and I could see Lucy's white legs gleaming in the distance like scissor blades snapping open and shut from under the high frill of her skirt. Even though it was a summer evening, I felt the cold and pulled the edges of my good jacket together. Raymond walked beside me in silence for a few seconds, his hands jammed into his pockets and his elbow brushing my arm. I was trying to think of something neutral and friendly to say to break the silence when Lucy started hooting and calling and turned to wave. Neil, already at the door, gathered her up in a hug from behind, lifted her up off her feet and bustled her indoors to the sounds of shrieking and stiletto heels sparking off the doorstep. The front door banged shut before Raymond and I had a chance to catch them up.

'Three guesses what they'll be getting up to now,' Raymond said coarsely, and laughed.

I was feeling distinctly uncomfortable alone with him in the dark and chose not to answer.

'You not talking tonight?' he said, in that slightly sneering, over-familiar way of his that he probably imagined was dashingly flirtatious.

'You must excuse me,' I said, 'I'm just very tired all of a sudden.'

'It gets you like that, when you get out in the fresh air, doesn't it?' he commiserated. 'We started in the pub this afternoon, so I'm feeling quite *tired* myself!' The tone of his voice let me know what he was implying and I hurried to correct him.

'I drank hardly anything at all, actually,' I said. 'It's not really for me. Not that I'd turn down an invitation to join you all the next time you take an afternoon out. It's just that I prefer to have my wits about me when I'm out in public, you know.'

'Each to their own,' he said, and let the silence stretch for a few moments.

'It was all right, tonight, wasn't it?' he said, obviously uncomfortable at hearing nothing other than our footsteps. 'I had a laugh; shame it finished so early. Things were just getting entertaining!'

'I don't think watching a friend becoming inebriated and making a fool out of himself would count as "entertainment" in most people's estimation,' I said sternly, and not because I was irritated at him mocking Neil, but because his hint about the evening finishing early had shocked me. I realised if we were to prolong the conversation any further he'd probably suggest we continue it at one of our houses over more drinks. That was something, understandably enough, I wished to avoid, both for my own sake and for the impression that it might give Neil. It wouldn't do to have him think that impatience had made me transfer my affections to his friend. I quickened my step. Raymond belched loudly, banged his chest and laughed.

'He's a lucky bastard, is Neil. I bet she tires him out, eh?'

'I wouldn't know,' I said uncomfortably, 'other people's private lives don't really interest me that much, I'm afraid.'

He laughed again, 'You might fool the others, but not me. Anyone would think you were royalty, the way you go on. I saw the way you were looking, missing your husband, is it? Bed feeling cold at night?' he cackled, and I stepped away from him as he lurched into me.

'My husband isn't any of your business,' I said. 'I think you need a coffee.'

I turned my head away, keeping my eyes focused on my garden gate. Everything looked so different in the dark. The grass was black and purple, the pavement sickly orange in the glow of the street lamps. I looked up at Raymond and his eyes glittered at me.

'Touched a raw spot, did I?' Raymond giggled and I had no idea how seriously I was supposed to be taking him. He was clearly drunk and finding the whole situation very amusing. Perhaps he was enjoying a bit of banter and some light mockery at my expense was his way of trying to make friends? They do say it's good to start a conversation with a joke. And yet, all the same, I felt threatened. The warm glow of the food and company at the Choudhry's had already shrunk into the past, and while spending the rest of the evening with whoever happened to be presenting BBC Radio Lancashire wasn't much of a consolation, it certainly bettered whatever Raymond thought he had to offer.

'There isn't a "raw spot", Raymond,' I said, using his name very deliberately because it shows control and confidence. 'I just like to be private, that's all.'

'Well if you've had a chinwag with Sangita, it won't be long before the rest of us know about it,' he said, grinning. 'She can't keep her gob shut for more than a few seconds, that woman.'

'Really,' I said.

'And you've got to start leaving Lucy alone,' he said, as if it followed naturally from what he'd been saying before.

'I beg your pardon?'

'That dress,' he gestured, 'what were you playing at?'

'I think you'll find,' I said, 'that Lucy's own dress is hanging up safe and sound in her wardrobe. Do you really think she and I could share our clothes? Look at her.' Raymond stared at my stomach and I crossed my arms over my chest.

'Fair point,' he said. 'But Neil's a mate, and she's getting worked up about it. When she gets worked up, he's got to deal with it. And he doesn't need it. He's really come out of his shell since he's met her. If there is something going on between the pair of you, sort it out.'

For a minute I thought he meant something going on between me and Neil. The thought that Neil had confided a special interest in me to his friend had me trembling.

'I've no idea what you...' I began.

'You scare her,' he said simply, 'I don't know why, but you do.'

'There isn't much I can do about that,' I said. 'She seems to be a very highly strung young woman.'

'Well, however she's string ... strung, just pack it in. That's all I'm saying.'

I think I was supposed to nod and feel chastened. My stomach, bloated with pasta and cola, felt weighted with cold stones. I stumbled forward and finally felt the flaky wood of my own gate under my palm.

'Well, this is me,' I said, 'thanks for walking me home, Raymond.

It's very late, and I have an appointment in the morning. I must be getting to bed now.'

Raymond appeared to be amused as he walked away from me. He said nothing else, but I watched him raise a hand as he passed Neil's front window. There was a snail on the path and I stood on it as I walked towards my house. It crunched under my shoe, as if I'd stood on a crisp packet. I didn't look or turn back as I opened my door and let myself into the dark of the empty hallway, taking care to wipe my feet carefully before I went any further.

The appointment I had the next morning was only with myself. I'd reserved some books at the library and I wanted to go in and see if they'd arrived. I was always too impatient to wait for the letter. If they'd let me, I'd have paid extra for them to send it first class, but I'd already been informed that the letters came from a central computer somewhere quite outside the town, and I could either come in and ask when it was convenient for me, or wait for the postman. When I didn't have anything pressing to do, which was most mornings, I went in and asked.

I am not unselective about what I read. Far from it, I have a plan and a system which would be unintelligible to anyone else, even those perpetually amused library assistants, even to myself, were it not for my File. I can still remember that File very well: I don't have it with me now although I am in the process of recreating it with the stationary I have to hand. Still, it illustrates my point perfectly so I will describe it to you.

At first, I kept notes and small summaries of the books I had read in a spiral bound notebook I kept in my handbag, the pages secured with an elastic band. When this filled, I decided to invest in a proper ring binder with dividers and colour-coded file paper. During the first month I was in my new house, before I started making friends and was forced to spend most of my time amusing myself with books and observations of the people around me, I'd transferred most of what was useful from the old book into it. The dividers came in very useful: pink for romances, blue for psychology, red for sociology, green for current affairs and orange for self-help. They came in packets of eight and it was a stroke of luck that they did, because once I moved, I saw the need for a section detailing my observations of those around me.

Behind the seventh, which was yellow, I noted down the usual movements of Neil and Lucy and their preferences in terms of groceries and newspapers that I gleaned from my keen eye and our proximity. In this section also, went the names of the Choudhry's children and Liam, conversational topics I had tried and my estimation of their success.

The eighth section (purple) I used as a kind of journal to make notes on my own development, my goals, aims and ambitions. The whole thing was cross-referenced very carefully, so, for example, on page twelve of the purple section, I had written:

Make sure you do something about the garden sooner rather than later. You could have a party in mid-August for your birthday and for that you will need a patio set, something like a rockery or a flower bed and pots of culinary herbs for the patio.

See yellow nine and blue twenty-seven.

If you turned to those pages, you would read, first in the yellow section, my observations of Lucy and Neil's barbecue, and in the blue section, a summary of a book of etiquette for the modern hostess and a quotation from *Making A Good Impression: What You Don't Know About How Others See You And Why You Need To Know It*. I am sure if I had still been there for my birthday, the celebrations would have been a success thanks to my careful preparation.

The File was very intricate in this respect, useful to me in all sorts of ways, and although it was a shame it was too big to carry around with me, I always had a notebook in my handbag and it was never a problem for me to transfer my random jottings made while out and about into the proper section when I got home. Whenever I returned from the library, I would make a list of the books I had just returned and write the summaries, cross-referencing my insights into what I had recorded behind the last two dividers. On returning from the party, I had immediately pushed all worries about Raymond's behaviour out of my head and busied myself making notes of the information I'd learned about the others for use in future social situations. This is really no different to the way some people keep business cards in their wallets so they're never in the embarrassing situation of forgetting a name.

I doubt anyone else has a method as detailed as mine, and I'd often thought how valuable a system I had worked out for myself and how I could best share it with others so that they too could profit from it. Having said this, in the aftermath of the Choudhry's dinner party I began to doubt my own system. My conversation with Neil had not gone as well as I'd hoped and I wondered if my preparation had been inappropriate in some way, and I had missed some vital opportunity to connect with him because I had unnecessarily confined my studies. It seemed to be apparent that a specialist such as myself might find it difficult to locate a common ground with the more general reader. It might, I reasoned, do me some good to widen my interests, if only for the purpose of having a more varied assortment of conversational topics at my fingertips the next time I was invited to a social event.

If I could put it into an image, I would say my reading life so far has been shaped like a funnel. During my teenage years, I was just beginning at the widest part: I read anything I could get my hands on and finished every book whether I was enjoying it or not. In my late teens the funnel started to narrow as I began to specialise into what I found most useful, and now, as an adult, my reading life exists solely in the cylindrical tube you can find at the bottom of the funnel. I browse only two or three shelves in the library, ticking off what I have read in my File and ignoring everything else. Within this narrow confine I thought I would find everything that I needed.

At the library the morning after the party, I used the computers to consult the catalogue and after a few false starts, managed to locate and order some of the 'great classics' Neil had referred to in the hope that watching them might help me to understand him better, and, at the very least, give us something to chat about the next time we met.

Part Three

13

After the North Euston, I'd waited two months, but Boris didn't call. I did try to find out his number, but he hadn't told me where he lived or where he worked and it quickly became clear that contacting him was going to be impossible. Things between Will and I had been unsatisfactory before but now there was an additional burden: I was constantly tormented by that glimpse of what I could have had. It was like catching sight of a party through a chink in some hastily drawn curtains as I walked past alone in the street outside. I think I became quite depressed.

The weekends were especially difficult because Will liked to take me out. We often went walking along the promenade, his long legs and broad stride leaving me breathless and trotting a few steps behind like a puppy. Or we went shopping in Freeport where they had a Thornton's discount store that he didn't like me going into. If he was 'feeling flush' (which was rarely), we went out on the ferry for a nasty day trip to Knott End, or on a special occasion, my birthday for example, we went to Blackpool for a game of bingo.

The weekend routine was punctuated every third Sunday by the worst trip of all. He would take me in his car for lengthy visits to his parent's house in Wigan. I would sit silently for hours making pictures out of the patterns in the wallpaper while they drank tea brewed so strong it was orange and nibbled on cardboard-coloured plain biscuits. I once saw a jar of chocolate biscuits in a kitchen cupboard and Ada, catching me glancing at them as she brought out the tea, looked at my girth pointedly and placed a saucer of the plain ones on the tray. In that way she let me know I wasn't quite what she'd imagined as a daughter-in-law. I think they missed Will's first wife, and her baby, and although most of the time they talked about gardening, council tax and asylum seekers, we'd never be there long before they'd start to hint about how much they'd like grandchildren.

After one of these visits Will bought himself a copy of *The Natural*

Fertility Handbook, and I went back to the doctor and got a new diaphragm.

And for months, whenever the telephone rang I jumped for it and answered breathless and happy, already having decided which suitcase I would take and what I would fill it with. I've lost count of the times it was just someone trying to sell me something and I let the receiver fall back into its cradle without saying goodbye. Whenever I stopped to think about my situation I cried and felt like giving up hope, but most of the time I tried to console myself by saying that I was just being patient, that the best things came to those who wait, and that really, in the great scheme of things, it hadn't been that long.

Eventually, out of sheer loneliness, I went and got the magazine that Boris had given to me. It had been in the airing cupboard for months but I'd never forgotten about it, never wanted to throw it away. It was my only link to him, and I wondered if one of the advertisements at the back was from him. He'd said he'd been in Fleetwood to meet someone, someone who wasn't a girlfriend. Perhaps it had been a friend he'd made contact with from *Abundance* and I'd be able to find him that way.

I unrolled the magazine and pressed it flat on the kitchen table while I waited for the kettle to boil. As always, Will was at work, and this seemed as good a way as any to pass the long interval of time between lunch and his return home. I remember Mr Tips, who was still a kitten then, sitting on the sofa next to me and pawing at the pages as I turned them. I went past the pictures quickly, blushing even though I was on my own, and hastily got to the page at the back where the personals were.

Most of the advertisements were from men, wanting to meet women of a particular dress or bra size, 'for good times and more'. The 'more' intrigued me, and in spite of my better judgement, I picked up a pen and began circling the ones that interested me most. I wouldn't say a plan had formed in my mind at that stage, but the pictures and the stories and the idea of all those people waiting for someone like me to read their words and contact them had sparked a little bit of hope inside me.

What was I hoping for? The same thing that everyone wants: a more satisfactory interaction with another human being. I'm not just talking about the bedroom aspect, although that was, I admit, one of my motivations. There were, I realised, plenty of opportunities to make friends, to meet someone during the day. I could make a friend or two and live a life of my own in the hours that Will was at work. A life just for myself that wouldn't disturb the balance of the life I had fallen into with Will because he would never know about it. I wasn't going to leave him (our marriage had its good points) but meeting someone else would, I hoped, complement it by the addition of a certain kind of intimacy.

The first few phone calls I made were awkward. I found it difficult to say what I wanted, and when I did, I was often met with incomprehension. The magazine was months out of date and I suppose some of the mobile telephones had changed hands, or the men in question had forgotten that they'd even placed an advert. On the ninth call I spoke to Michael, and once he'd ascertained my dress size and my age, he agreed to meet me in a bed and breakfast in Blackpool for a few hours the very next afternoon.

He was offhand on the telephone, as if he'd done it a thousand times before.

'You sure you can't accommodate?' he'd asked irritably. I didn't know what he meant; it was a whole new language for me. I stuttered and he interrupted.

'It's fine. You'll have to bring some money though. We'll split the room, yeah?'

I thought of Will's penny jar and my secret post office account. I'd never had reason to tell Will about it, and all the birthday money I'd ever been given as a child as well as a few hundred pounds from my mother was resting in it, quietly growing and waiting to come in useful.

'Yes, I can do that,' I said, swallowing past the lump in my throat.

The room was grimy and smelled like cigarette smoke. Michael had brought a stick of rock and a shower curtain. He asked me, very politely, if I wouldn't mind taking all my clothes off, lying down on the shower curtain which he'd put on the bed over the sheets, and eating the stick of rock. Confused, I did as he'd asked. It was pink, and the letters running all the way through it said 'my girl', like one of those love heart sweets the other girls used to pass about at school. Michael had stood on the other side of the room watching me suck the rock into a point, urging me to continue when I felt sickly and took it out of my mouth. This went on for approximately half an hour. At that point, he removed most of his own clothes (he left on his vest) and advanced towards the bed. I put down the rock and raised my arms to him but he shook his head, kneeled with his knees crunched up between my open thighs and began to manhandle himself.

He didn't even want me to touch him. All I had to do was lie there and eat the rock. It wasn't bad rock, my skin felt clammy where it touched the shower curtain and I grew quite uncomfortable as the bed jogged against the wall, vibrating in time with his forearm which was moving so fast it blurred. That passed the next twenty minutes. After that, he showered and dressed and I did what I could with paper tissues while he was in the bathroom.

When he came back, he thanked me, folded up the shower curtain and left. It was disappointing, but the disappointment only made me want to try again in case it was better next time. It wasn't as if it was costing me anything. The men almost always paid for the rooms, sometimes a drink and a meal too, and I didn't have to do anything that hurt. There were lots of them over the next few months.

I remember John, who brought a green and silver tin of golden syrup and wanted me to scoop it out with my fingers and eat it. When I'd had half of it and felt thoroughly sick and sticky, he'd made me lie on my front while he poured the rest of it over my behind and moved backwards and forwards inside me. He was an odd one, and to add injury to insult all that sugar about my undercarriage resulted in a very nasty yeast infection. I had to pay *six pounds* for some cream to treat it.

Alan, who I met a few times and grew quite attached to, promised me flowers and a real evening out at the pictures if I would just let him put the end of his pecker into my belly button. I used to pretend I was reluctant to do it because it would make the bunches of flowers grow bigger and bigger, the trip to the cinema turn into a weekend away, and he'd beg and he'd plead until eventually I'd say, 'Go on then, but be quick,' and he did, and he was.

After Alan, there were a few others, none of whom were that memorable. It had become a habit by then. Something interesting to do in the afternoons. Lots of them just wanted me to take my top off and lie on top of them so they were squashed into the bed, and that reminded me of Boris, so after a while it became one of my favourite things to do. Some of them would give me a bit of pocket money, and that was nice too, because by then the post office account was empty and I'd become familiar with the kind of clothes they'd like to see me in. It all cost money I didn't want to ask Will for. I subscribed to *Abundance*: the envelopes arrived while Will was at work and went right into the airing cupboard.

I still thought of Boris, knowing that he had my phone number, and even though there'd been so many men since him, I was kidding myself that I was, in a roundabout way, still looking for him, and I would stop as soon as one of the mobile phone numbers I harvested from *Abundance* gave me his voice.

It wasn't that I didn't worry about Will catching me out. Sometimes I didn't get home until he was already back from work. I'd panic at seeing him in the kitchen making the tea and have to rush up the stairs to hide the ladders in my tights and wash off the sticky trails of semen and ice cream drying flakily on my tummy. I'd claim I was bursting to use the toilet, and he'd be pleased, wondering if it was an early sign of pregnancy. It was hardly ideal, and a world away from how I'd imagined my life to be when I'd agreed to marry him. It wasn't hurting him, was it, but still, I felt a bit guilty about it sometimes and on these occasions I was extra attentive to him, making sure that I carried on taking the folic acid and filling in the temperature charts that dictated the timing of our infrequent couplings.

I was so smug, and of course after a year or so of this I did get caught out, after a fashion. I fell pregnant, and there was no way of telling who had given me the baby. Will discovered me wailing over the test in the downstairs bathroom and mistook the noise I was making for joy. Of course he was ecstatic and I couldn't cry again until I was on my own, holding up the traitor diaphragm to the light bulb and checking it for holes.

Will took over the cooking and all of the housework so I was even more bored than I had been before. He started to take more of an interest in the kind of things that I ate, and often sat me in the kitchen so he could explain the health benefits of what he was preparing for the foetus and me that evening.

'This is the week that the optical nerves are being formed!'

I remember the book he had, a week-by-week dissection of what was going on inside. He was standing over the sink peeling carrots with a tea towel over his shoulder. Swish, swish with the peeler, and the dirty orange skin of the carrots curled into the sink. I leaned over and picked the peelings out to eat them. The dirt tasted gritty between my teeth. He let it pass without comment.

'You should rest more. Stay in bed in the mornings, don't get up. You'll appreciate it later. It's going to be hard work.'

'It's not going to be that bad. They sleep all the time, don't they?' Will called me naïve and laughed quietly under his breath. I carried on chewing the carrot tops while he started to slice.

'You'd better get that idea out of your head. It's going to be a shock to your system. I'll only be able to take a week or so off work, then it will be up to you.'

'There's nursery, I suppose,' I said, and watched Will stirring at the cheese sauce and picking out black flecks of burned milk from the pan with the edge of a teaspoon, 'we can afford something like that, can't we?' He replaced the lid and leaned against the draining board thoughtfully sipping a glass of parsnip wine.

'I'm glad this came up. We should talk. Make a few decisions about parenting style. You can't start too early and it's important we're both singing from the same hymn sheet.'

'Mmm,' I said, pretending that my mouth was still full.

'We need to be prepared – there's going to be a lot of changes. Everything's going to be different and it's going to be harder on you than it is on me – '

I never took him too seriously because at this point, although I was late on in the second trimester, I had every confidence that I would soon be hearing from Boris. In fact, I even indulged myself in little fantasies from time to time; that he'd used his computer to find my address and was watching over me to make sure I was growing well and living somewhere nice. While I waited, I pictured him hurrying to make the necessary arrangements so I could come and live with him. Will could keep the baby: I expected to have very little to do with it.

'I'm going to be stuck in the house all the time while your life carries on as normal,' I said. I was only teasing: it was a light-hearted conversation, as far as I remember.

'No,' he said, running the cold tap over the carrots he'd just finished peeling. He was very careful about that: scrubbing the root vegetables to get rid of the toxoplasmosis.

'Well thank God for that,' I said, chewing on the peelings again and enjoying the sight of him wincing, starting to change the subject to warn me about the deadly organisms in the dirt, and then abandoning the topic because he didn't want to put me in a bad mood.

He glanced at the hard lump of womb stretching the front of the T-shirt that I was wearing.

'The bulk of the physical work is going to be on you: breastfeeding and that. It's not easy, you know, but what I meant was you in particular, you don't like change: you don't like not to be in charge, and to know what's going to happen next. I know you, you like to have everything arranged to your satisfaction, and it's not going to be like that anymore. Someone else is going to be in charge, aren't they?'

I saw my own reflection distorted on the pan-bottoms draining in the sink. Will's assessment of me had been startlingly accurate. What more about me did he know? That he was one of the objects I liked to have arranged to my satisfaction? Not the sole object, not the solar centre of my life, but one of a carefully arranged number of stars all sparkling and orbiting around me? I spat grit into the sink and turned on the tap to flush it away. What he'd said about someone else being in charge had dried out all the saliva in my mouth and all I could taste were the sharp grains of soil between my teeth.

'It won't be that bad,' I said, keeping my back to him. My tongue worked at the dirt caught in my molars. I imagined it squirming into the cracks like a fat pink eel and felt like I was going to be sick.

'People wouldn't have second kids if it was so awful – if your life was over just like that. Would they?' I wasn't even convincing myself, not really.

'Oh ho ho, that's what you think!' he said, as if he was some kind of expert. I forgot, sometimes, that he'd been through pregnancy with a woman before. Perhaps he'd chosen me because I didn't remind him of her.

My pregnancy was a time for waiting, the same as most people's. I wasn't waiting for the birth, which I dreaded, but for Boris to resume contact and let me know what his plans were for our future. It would be very easy, once a couple of years had passed and I was well established in my new life, to pass off my time with Will as an error I made in my youth and inexperience. I would not think of it often and what seemed now to be one of the main features of my life would dissolve into a short period that the present would make irrelevant. As a consequence, I paid hardly any attention at all to the irritations of pregnancy and the way time was passing, preferring instead to distract myself by turning over and over in my head the time Boris and I had spent in the hotel.

You'd think the constant rehashing would have engraved the scene on my memory perfectly, but it was as if I wore the picture out by looking at it constantly, and slowly, the details became less distinct. At first, whenever I remembered our time together my hands would start to shake, my face feel hot and I'd be hard pressed to keep the grin from my face. Will would say, 'Thinking about the baby again?' and lean over from his armchair to squeeze my hand or pat my knee, and I would nod.

First it was sickness, not vomiting, just nausea, then strange tastes in the mouth, darkening of the nipples and a blue network of veins over my breasts, the front of my chest, even my throat: it was horrible, like mould in cheese, or marks on a road map. By month three the sickness had abated, as the midwife had predicted, but now I was constipated, salivating constantly, sleeping at least fourteen hours a night, and plagued with dreams involving removal men trying to get large items of furniture through oddly shaped doorways.

The discomforts of the first trimester were equalled in irritation only by the attentions of Will, who was frantically eager about his long-awaited conception and would not let me lift so much as a teaspoon without clicking his tongue at me and saying, 'Not in your condition, my love.' The thing was smaller than a baked bean, nowhere near sentient, and yet I was counselled to avoid violent television, loud music and strobe lights in case they disturbed the being-to-be, sleeping in its little pink palace behind my navel. There was no need to bite my lip and restrain my annoyance at his petty ministrations because suddenly pregnant, anything and everything could be blamed on the great Goddess Hormone and every outburst was another symptom of a healthy, functioning reproductive system and so was cherished.

As time passed and it became clear that despite my desperate and increasingly detailed research I was still unable to contact Boris, I became more and more irritable.

'Are you ready to go to bed yet, Annie? The Sears book says you need plenty of sleep,' he'd say, sitting up in bed with a dental journal cracked over his knee, turning a glass snow globe with a miniature Blackpool tower in it over and over in his hands.

'Get lost, Will. I'm reading. Are you blind or something?'

'Okay, sweetheart. I'll just pop off to the spare room then, the lamp's keeping me awake. That all right by you? Or would you rather I stayed and kept you company?'

The fourth and fifth month came and went: there was no anomaly scan because Will wasn't sure of the ultrasound and its affects on his foetus: no amniocentesis, because of course we wouldn't terminate the pregnancy even if the product wasn't perfect. No call from Boris. I scanned the ads in *Abundance* for some kind of clue that might lead me to him, but once the pregnancy started to show I didn't dare contact anyone.

Will questioned me daily for signs of movement and bought boring classical music to aid the formation of a growing brain. I confessed nothing until the seventh month, although by then I'd been feeling insistent prods for some six weeks. It wasn't thrilling, it was frightening: an alien inside me unfurling its limbs and kicking me awake in the night. Pain in the pelvis. Insomnia. Yellow oil leaking from my breasts and staining the bed sheets. Heartburn. Loss of breath.

The eighth month: tour around the maternity ward, a look at the Entonox and TENS machine, the packing of the bag, which of course Will supervised and checked against his list on a daily basis. Brown rice, spinach, scrambled eggs. Knitting. Will heaving the pieces of a cot up the stairs. The painting of the junk room in pale, hopeful blue. The discussion about names: predictions with wedding rings on pieces of cotton – boy or girl? Brown bread, marmite, iron supplements to turn my faeces black.

And all the shopping! Mothercare: lemon cot bumpers, green babygros, off-white flannel dungarees, white knitted cardigans. Boots: terry nappies, breast pump, Avent slow-flow teats, Johnson's baby lotion, bath, talc, and of course, the big yellow plastic bath with a hole in the bottom to attach a tube to for siphoning out the dirty water. Argos: pram, car seat, bouncing cradle, bath stand, electric steam steriliser, musical night light, monitors, stair gates, rocking horse, stroller, baby gym. The chemists: breast pads, maternity sanitary towels, baby wipes, paper knickers, antiseptic soap, glass bottle of medical grade olive oil and the instructions for massaging my perineum.

I poured the oil over my fingers and licked it off, feeling angry that Will had never given me a credit card of my own for treats until now.

Ninth month: earliest contractions – mild period pains, tightening in the hard wad of muscle that protruded slightly from the softness of the rest of me. Forty-week midwife's appointment, blood pressure, morbid obesity, pre-eclampsia, caesarean section.

And then afterwards: looking at the round-headed thing my body had made. A darkish fuzz already starting to curl at the ends like wispy pubic hair. No eyelashes or eyebrows. And all the time through the contractions, the epidural and the cutting, and the splash of water I heard as the scalpel punctured my womb, I'd been hoping that Boris really had been watching over me and would come to the hospital and take me away as soon as it was over. They plopped the slimy thing on my chest and I moved the cord to see; there was nothing but a dimple between the legs, a hairless vulva in miniature – axe wound, as Boris would have called it, nestled between splayed-open frog-legs and swollen with my oestrogen, leaking its own slimy discharge in a stretchy string of mucus onto a mottled thigh still vernix white.

They stitched up the smile-shaped gape in my abdomen while I lay still and observed as Will bonded with his daughter. Just the face and the top of the head poking out of the blanket they'd wrapped her in: cheek to cheek with him, who was trembling and weeping silently.

'Isn't she perfect? Haven't you done well?' His tears dropped onto my arm and I concentrated on my own view: the bloody slit in me slowly being sutured. They'd put up a screen between me and the business end so the sight of it couldn't traumatise me but forgot about the bright lights and the reflective surface of the surgeon's spectacles which revealed everything. The needle darted in and out of my flesh and curiously, I felt the tugging as they pulled the split strata of muscle and tissue back together, but no pain, nothing at all.

'We'll hire a maternity nurse, so you can have total bed rest while you recover. Lots of little treats and plenty of skin contact with the baby. You haven't let me down, and anyway, we can try for a natural home birth next time, can't we?'

And that's what he was like, planning everything from the very beginning. I pretended to be asleep. He was, perhaps, dismayed at my lack of enthusiasm, because he held the baby close to my face so it could stare at me and open its pinched, beak-like mouth towards my neck. She smelled of blood and salty water and umbilical cord. I looked closely and for the first time her eyes met mine. She had a poached, waterlogged look, her fingernails still swollen and her skin pruned from her life-long immersion. A little amphibian, something escaped from a mermaid's purse.

'Look, Annie, just beautiful. Look what you made for us!' I turned my head and he moved the baby back up to his chest.

'Your wife is very tired now.' The midwife who was cleaning me up under the modesty sheet ducked her head up between my knees so I could see her, but she was looking at Will. 'She's going to need a long sleep. Perhaps you'd like to dress baby while mum has a nap?'

Will kissed my forehead chastely and the midwife stripped off her latex gloves and led him out of the room. For a few moments I was alone and I closed my eyes again and slept.

14

The Friday after Sangita's dinner party I decided to get out of the house, get a bit of fresh air to clear my head and pay her a visit. I'd spent the week fruitfully and had immersed myself in a two-pronged approach to my goals. The first prong consisted of watching a selection of 'classic' films borrowed from the library in order to bring my own interests in line with Neil's ('widening my funnel', as I put it in my File). For the second prong, I prepared a speech which would help me to embed myself even further into the fabric of the community. With Raymond being quite clear about whose side he was on, it became very urgent that I capitalise on my friendship with Sangita, just in case things escalated with Lucy and I needed her in my corner. My visit to her would be the occasion where I would announce my willingness to give the speech, and book a date convenient for us both.

The street I lived on was a cul-de-sac with a large turning circle at the bottom. I imagined that from the air it would look like a giant exclamation mark. The disappearance of Mr Tips was still on my mind, so I took the box of cat biscuits with me and walked up to the main road, shaking them and peering over walls and hedges, following the street right around instead of taking the most direct route. Despite my shaking and calling there was still no sign of him. The corner shop was at the top where the street met with the main road, mine and Neil's houses were somewhere near the middle, and Sangita's was right at the bottom on the curve. This meant she was lucky enough to have a garden larger than most, and as I approached it in the light of day I noticed she or Barry had put their own stamp on the garden and it stood out positively against the rather bland lawns and flower beds the rest of us had.

There was a small rockery at the front, a water feature with a tinkling fountain and an array of shiny silver containers that overflowed with green, healthy-looking foliage. The sight of the garden, especially the rockery, pleased me very much and I stooped to hide the cat biscuits in one of its nooks. I realise it sounds odd, but I had sound reasons: the box wouldn't fit in my handbag and I didn't think knocking at someone's front door with a box of pet food in my hand would create the right impression. My task accomplished, I straightened and admired the rockery for a few moments, counting myself lucky that I had linked myself with the right kind of person.

In my mind I compared the garden with my mother's bedraggled roses and my father's half-hearted attempts to start a vegetable patch around the side of our house. It goes without saying, but I forgot my worry for a second and grew pleased at how far I had come under my own steam. Even as I knocked, I was thinking how much my mother would like the garden and how pleased she would be if she knew I was busy making connections and becoming a figure of influence. I hoped that somehow she *was* able to see me, and appreciate my efforts, perhaps even enjoy the sight of me perched on the brink of success. Giving a talk to the community would be one more in a list of my recent achievements.

Sangita answered the door. She was wearing an apron and her hands were white with flour.

'Come in, Annie, come in. You've come at the right time, you must have smelled the baking!' I stepped inside and we passed through the front room quickly and went right into the kitchen.

'Is everything all right? Nothing's happened, has it?' she asked, bending over the kettle and then gesturing for me to sit at the kitchen table. I did, and she pushed her hair out of her eyes with her forearm and returned her hands to the bowl.

'Oh no, everything's absolutely fine. I've been reading those leaflets you left for me last time,' I said, 'and I think I should get more involved.' So far, so good.

'That's great news!' she said, obviously pleased. 'Sometimes I feel like I'm fighting a losing battle – Barry says it takes too much of my time away from the family, but I think I'm doing it *for* the family, do you know what I mean? The boys need somewhere decent to come back to at weekends.'

She turned the dough out of the bowl and started to knead it on the counter. The whole kitchen smelled like sugar and butter and my stomach started to rumble. I coughed so she wouldn't hear it.

People always assume that larger people eat all the time, and never consider that my size is the result of a normal variation on human metabolism and gland activity.

'You can help me deliver leaflets, if you like? There's a meeting with our local police officer about the graffiti on the bus stop at the top, and I'm trying to drum up as much interest as possible. I really need some help with the legwork because the boys are back this weekend and I don't want to be busy doing that the whole time they're here.'

'Your boys?' I said, feeling pleased that I'd remembered to ask questions. The conversation was going quite well, I thought. It's like a tennis game really, one person says something, you say something back, and you have to keep the ball going backwards and forwards, sailing through the air, being careful never to get distracted by your own thoughts or details about the environment you happen to find yourself in.

'Barry's been teasing me about it, all the cooking I've been doing. "They do eat at school," he says, "we pay enough, they don't starve them you know, it isn't bloody Dickens!" That's what he says to me, he calls me a mad old bag but we can't help it, can we, us mothers? It's in the genes, it's the way we're built.' She started rolling the dough out with a pin, remembered the kettle and left it so she could fill the teapot.

'I was thinking something more like a talk actually, a short speech. I've been reading a lot, and in light of my current experiences since I've moved into the area,' I said, nodding slightly so she would know what I was alluding to, 'I've come up with some good ideas.' Sangita took two cups out of the cupboard, china cups with pictures of leaves and berries all over the side, and came and sat down with me at the table.

'I'm due a break,' she said, and poured the tea.

'It wouldn't be a long speech,' I went on, 'just enough to introduce me to everyone, make my face known properly, bring up some of the important issues. What do you think?' I lifted my cup and prepared myself to receive the compliment I was sure would follow.

'You are keen, aren't you?' she laughed. 'And there's nothing wrong with that either. Most of the time it's just me and a couple of the old dears from the bungalows on the main road.' She paused and I opened my mouth to explain what I had planned in more detail but she carried on speaking.

'The thing is, we're all booked up, Annie. The agenda is sorted out a few months in advance. This month it's going to be teenage alcoholism and its link with anti-social behaviour – very relevant to your own little situation with Lucy, I shouldn't think, and the one after is the importance of the door chain, and after that, what have we got,' she flicked open a notebook that was lying on the table, 'oh yes, you'll like this one, we've got someone from the council coming to take ideas over what to do with that bit of grass at the top. Someone suggested a kiddies' play area but I thought a peace garden would be lovely, somewhere for people to sit and reflect. Very appropriate in the current political climate too, don't you think? We need to be concentrating on what brings us all together, not our differences.'

'Oh yes,' I said, 'we're all people, after all, no matter what kind of religion we follow, or if,' I nodded at her, 'we're foreigners or not. In fact, that links very nicely with the topic of the talk I've been preparing. Perhaps you'd like to hear some of it?' I didn't have it written down, I'd managed to learn the whole fifteen minutes off by heart the previous afternoon, and while I was stuck for a title, I thought if Sangita could hear the whole thing, she might be able to suggest one that we could then put on the front of the leaflets.

'It starts like this,' I began, 'Ladies, Gentlemen and Children, as a newcomer to this fine street of yours, I have been pleasantly surprised by your friendliness and hospitality. Nevertheless, of late there have been two or three occasions which it is my duty to draw your attention to. Many of you may remember me from...'

I was about to go on but Sangita leaned over and tapped me on the arm. I'd been focusing my gaze on a wildlife calendar she had tacked up on the wall near her back door while I spoke, because I thought it would be good practice for the real thing when I'd need to use techniques like that in order to avoid stage fright. I refocused my eyes on her.

'The thing is, Annie,' she said carefully, chewing the skin on the side of her thumb, 'I don't think something so personal in nature would be quite appropriate in that kind of setting. What kind of thing were you talking about? Are you still having problems with Lucy?' I had been so caught up in remembering my speech and making sure my tone of voice was perfect that it took me a minute to catch up and answer her question.

'Things didn't go as well as I'd hoped last week,' she added, 'but all that wine she had won't have helped matters.' She rolled her eyes.

'I did have a pleasant chat with Neil,' I said, smiling as I remembered, 'she didn't spoil the whole night. I just think if I could do a little talk, perhaps let people know...'

Sangita shook her head gently, 'Don't be disappointed, you should still come to the meeting and introduce yourself. You'd enjoy it, I'm sure you would. And you'd get to meet Charlie. He's lovely,' she giggled, 'I probably shouldn't say, but he's single too!'

'Charlie,' I asked faintly, 'who's Charlie?'

'He's the police officer assigned to our area. Didn't you see his picture in the leaflet? He was married, I think, or living with someone, but she ran away with a colleague of his – someone much younger. Took the baby with her as well, poor man. You should meet him.'

'I don't think so,' I said, wishing she would offer me a bit of whatever it was laid out under a tea towel on the draining board. I was feeling horribly disappointed, and wondering if there would be a different venue for my speech. Perhaps borrowing Neil's computer for an afternoon and getting him to print it out for me on coloured paper for local distribution would be a better way forward.

I looked back at the draining board. Cakes or muffins, something like that, I was sure. They were still warm, I could tell, and the smell was wafting over to me. There wasn't a polite way to ask, I knew, so I abandoned the idea.

'Oh, I'm sorry, Annie. I've been tactless, haven't I? Barry warns me about it all the time, says I open my mouth and let my belly rumble, never think before I speak. The boys are always telling me to shut up.' She leaned over and touched my hand. 'Are you feeling all right today? You're not upset, are you?'

'It's not that,' I said, removing my hand. I didn't want to mention Mr Tips to her. It seems strange now, but I didn't want to let her know how important he was to me and just how worried I had become since his disappearance. The efforts of the past week, spent

watching so many 'classic' films that I'd lost sleep and suffered with
headaches, were beginning to catch up with me. My exhaustion and
the worry about my cat left me feeling quite subdued.

'Are you sure? You can talk to me, you know,' she was going to pat
my hand again, I could tell, so I put it under the table and tried not
to glance at the cakes.

'No, it's nothing like that.' Making the best effort I could, I laughed
lightly and looked up at her, 'I just don't think I'd like to date a policeman, that's all.'

She shook her head and laughed. 'What are you like, Annie? He's
very good-looking. You might change your mind when you see him!'

'I don't think I will,' I said, and then smiled, trying to look away
from her and make myself look shy and full of hidden secrets. I
started enjoying myself then, in spite of everything, and I realised
coming to Sangita had been a good idea after all – much better than
going to see Jessica again, and I didn't have to pay fifty pounds for
the privilege! This was how I had always imagined it to be amongst
the other girls at school· women friends sitting at the table talking
about boys and gossiping harmlessly between themselves. Apart
from Caroline I hadn't really had any female friends before, and I
started to see what I'd been missing.

'I'm kind of seeing someone at the moment,' I said, 'it's in the
early stages, but it wouldn't do to complicate matters.'

Sangita leaned back in her chair and raised her eyebrows. I
noticed, for the first time, that she had a little red dot painted on
the middle of her forehead, and I wondered what she put it on with,
what it meant, and whether it itched or not.

'Well, well, well,' she said, smiling and putting her elbow on the
back of her chair. 'You *are* a dark horse, aren't you? I thought you
looked a bit different. You done something with your hair? Lost a bit
of weight? In love?' she laughed. 'Don't keep me in suspense then,
tell me all about it. Do I know him? Where did you meet him?'

'He's got a good job, very well respected in his company, I believe
– and a lovely house, very modern.' Sangita tipped her chin towards
me and winked.

'Go on,' she said, putting her elbows on the table and resting her
face in her tiny hands, 'I love a good story.'

'It was quite unexpected, really. He's very quiet, but romantic in his way.'

'A strong, silent type?'

'Exactly,' I said.

'And is he tall, dark and handsome too? Just like my Barry? You lucky thing. What's his name?'

'Oh, I'm not going to go into detail just now,' I said. I'd made a mistake and gone too far. Clearly, it was more complicated between Neil and myself than Sangita could realise, and I doubted my ability to make her understand and for her to accept without judgement. All in good time, I thought to myself, and looked forward to the time when she, Barry, Neil and myself would go out for meals together, or perhaps sit around this very table drinking wine out of crystal glasses and chatting while coffee brewed in one of those glass plunger things.

'You'll just have to wait and see,' I said mysteriously.

'You're such a tease!' she said, standing and taking our cups away to the sink. She rinsed them out and then opened a cupboard door. I thought for a minute she was just going to put them away like that, wet, and not washed properly in soap and hot water, but then I saw the cupboard was actually hiding the dishwasher, and she put them in that and closed the door on them.

'I'm glad you've found yourself a bit of happiness,' she said, 'I can't think of anyone who deserves it more than you do.' She smiled, but didn't sit back down or return to the dough half-rolled on the counter, and I realised it was time for me to go home. I stood and picked up my handbag from the floor.

'Well, I've a lot to get through this afternoon so I'd better be heading off now,' I said. 'Say hello to your boys for me.'

'I will do,' she replied, 'and I'll pop around in a couple of days so we can do that leafleting. Maybe you won't be so secretive then!' Laughing, she walked with me to the front door but it opened before we got there to reveal Barry, with two little boys standing in front of him. They rushed into Sangita's arms and for the next few minutes my presence there went quite unnoticed.

'Aakash! Vimal!' she cried, and gathered them to her, laughing. Barry stood in the doorway looking at the scene proudly for a few moments, then squeezed his way in. I stood behind them, not quite sure of where to put myself, and then, not wanting to be in the way, quietly sat down on the sofa to wait.

'It's Friday afternoon!' she said. 'Boys, you haven't got yourselves into trouble again, have you?' She looked up at Barry.

'A bit of a surprise, that's all. I thought you were missing them, so I rearranged a few things and went to pick them up early.'

'Is that allowed?' Sangita asked. 'They really shouldn't be missing lessons, Barry.'

'Mum! We don't do anything on Friday afternoons anyway!' one of them said. I looked again at their little green school uniforms and matching satchels, their identical shiny black haircuts, and realised they must be twins. 'Aren't you pleased to see us?'

Sangita laughed, hugged them both again and then shook her head at Barry. 'Of course I am! I've been baking all afternoon. Go and see what's in the kitchen for you,' she said, then turned to Barry, 'and you! You're not getting any!' She waved her finger at him, 'It's very bad of you – what will the other parents think!' but she was smiling and I could tell she wasn't annoyed really. The boys dropped their bags and ran into the kitchen. Barry went over to Sangita and kissed her, rather longer than was necessary, I thought, and then noticed me just as I was starting to feel 'spare' again. He stopped, and wiped his mouth.

'Annie,' he said, 'to what do we owe the pleasure?'

'Just a flying visit,' I said, 'I was on my way out, actually.'

'Ah,' he said, then paused for a second, frowning. I was hoping he was going to ask me to stay a little longer. There was a crash from the kitchen and the sound of something being scattered over the floor. He looked over my shoulder and said something sternly in his own language, and Sangita vanished into the kitchen. She shut the door behind her and I could hear the sound of muffled giggling.

'Those boys,' he said. 'Their mother hasn't heard of the concept of discipline yet,' he smiled and shrugged, 'but what can you do?'

'It's really not my area,' I said, not sure how much of what I had told Sangita had filtered through to Barry. 'They seem very happy though,' I added, then stood and picked up my handbag from the floor at my feet.

'Just one moment, Annie,' he said, seriously. I remained standing, and the pleasant feelings I'd been experiencing at witnessing the boys' homecoming evaporated. I started to pick through what I had just said, hoping that I hadn't offended him. The biscuits. He'd found the cat biscuits and they'd damaged the nice rockery, and I was in trouble. I wound the strap of my handbag around my fingers and tried to suppress a cough.

'Yes?'

'You wouldn't happen to have a black and white cat, would you? I seem to remember there being a little creature ambling about at your party...'

'Yes!' I said. 'Have you seen him? He's been gone days now and I've been really worried. I was looking all over the place for him last night.'

'Oh,' he said. 'Perhaps you should take a seat.' He patted my shoulder then opened the kitchen door. The cake smell, giggling and lots of chattering in a language I couldn't understand rushed out.

'Sangita! A pot of tea in here, please, and when you've done that,' she poked her head around the door and he lowered his voice, 'a cardboard box, and an old blanket too, if you can find something we can spare.'

Barry had seen a black and white bundle lying in the gutter at the side of the main road and had slowed the car down as he passed to check what it was. He hadn't stopped, not wanting to upset the boys, but he'd seen enough to identify the crumpled body of Mr Tips. While I drank tea and took the tissues Sangita kept handing to me, he went out to the top of the street with the box and came back five minutes later.

'You probably don't want to have a look inside,' he said, handing me the little box, 'but if it's any comfort to you, I think he will have died more or less instantly. The car must have knocked him to the side of the road, there wouldn't have been any suffering.' He meant it as a comfort.

If there had been a chance of saving Mr Tips, Barry would have been able to do it. He was a doctor. I knew all these things, but I still wrapped my arms around the box and turned my head away from him. It was an old crisp box, cheese and onion, and after the crisps had been eaten one of the boys had used it to keep something in because 'keep off' was written on one of the lid-flaps in red felt-tip and a childish hand.

Sangita had sent the boys upstairs and although I can't remember what we talked about I must have stayed in their front room another hour or so because eventually the sounds of banging and shouting above our heads became too loud to ignore.

'I'm sorry, Annie, I'm going to have to start making their tea,' she said gently. 'Would you like Barry to walk you home now?'

'It's quite all right,' I said, wiping my eyes. 'It's silly of me to be making such a fuss.' I stood up to leave.

'I *will* come and see you soon,' she said, 'after the weekend if I don't get time during,' she nodded at the ceiling and rolled her eyes. 'You'll be glad of the peace and quiet.'

When I got home I placed the box gently on the kitchen counter and took the biggest metal spoon out into the garden. I didn't have a trowel, but the ground was soft enough for me to make a decent hole with what I had. The job done, I stood for a little while looking at the dark patch on the grass.

I never doubted for one minute it was Lucy who had been responsible for the death of my cat. She knew he was missing, she knew I was looking for him. She'd even made a point of asking about it at the party. Just to rub it in. She'd been out to get me from day one, but this was one step too far. Up until then her evident jealousy had been comic. Now, she'd succeeded in really hurting me. She'd taken away the only thing I had that really mattered to me. I checked the cupboard for a tin of rice pudding and reached into the sink for a spoon.

Every time I wasn't thinking about something else, my mind went back to her. I saw her jerking the steering wheel in order to run him over. Pointed shoes on the pedals and red fingernails scrabbling over the gear stick. The bump under her wheels, and her slotting the car into reverse and making the tyres squeal as she made sure the job had been done properly. She was cackling as she sped away without a cursory glance in her rear-view mirror. I could hear it, and none of my affirmations would blot her out. Poor Tips. I saw him struggling onto the verge, lifting his head to look at the car uncomprehendingly as it screeched away in a cloud of exhaust fumes. Tyres spitting out gravel and her witchy nails clicking against the wheel, Tips softly mewling with his last breath. I had to keep taking deep breaths and counting to ten just to stop myself from exploding.

I went upstairs to shower and calm down and I was just folding the towels and draping them over the side of the bath when I heard sounds echoing from the other side of the wall. As I have said, the walls are thin, and especially if I happened to be standing close by them, I could hear most of what was going on in Neil's house. There was the sound of the shower being switched on, and, I realised with a sinking heart, the high-pitched giggling that was characteristic of Lucy. If I could have punched my way through the wall and got my hands around her scrawny little neck at that moment, I would have.

To my surprise, what I heard next revealed that she was not alone in the bathroom, and that indeed, Neil and she were taking a shower together. I sat on the end of the bath and leaned my face against the tiles because the steam in my own bathroom was making me feel faint and I thought that the coolness of the tiles against my cheek would help to revive me. Coincidentally, my proximity to the dividing wall had the effect of making Lucy and Neil's antics next door all the more audible to me and for a few moments I was at a loss to explain their significance to myself.

It became clear, in the course of the next fifteen minutes or so, that Neil had somehow picked up on my intention to visit him in the coming days in order to tackle seriously the matter of our burgeoning relationship. It would no doubt mark the beginning of something that would change life immeasurably for the three of us, and with foresight and kindness he had taken it upon himself to comfort Lucy in the only way that most men know how. While it was true that Neil's method lacked tact, the thought behind it was well meaning and an example of the way he would always try to comfort and nurture an intimate partner. Such clumsiness, I realised, was nothing more than a symptom of the way his own needs for guidance and care were being left unmet in his present relationship and a further indicator that he was with the wrong woman.

Opposites Attract: Why We Need Each Other So was a book I had referred to often, and which had filled me in on a lot of the differences between men and women. Far from making intimate relationships between them impossible, these differences actually served to foster a sense of closeness and dependency between couples of the opposite sex just as a dog and a blind person can learn to depend on each other despite their obvious and marked differences. With these comforting thoughts in my mind I finished tidying the bathroom and went downstairs. I decided to give them fifteen minutes, and then go over myself and see what the state of play was.

15

'Annie? What are you doing here?'

Disappointingly, Lucy had answered the door. Her hair was wet, but at least she was dressed. I'd imagined Neil flinging it open to enable me to rush into his arms and receive the comfort I so badly needed from him. As it was, I could hear him moving about in the front room, so near to me and yet totally unavailable. I clenched my fists, at once overcome by my anger.

'What have you done?' I shrieked.

'What?' she said, managing to both step back from the doorway and look genuinely puzzled. Well, of course, she'd seen me bringing the cardboard box back and had time to prepare a story. She'd probably had a good laugh to herself at the state I was in as I dug the hole. Neil's face appeared at the door next to hers and they both stared out at me.

'You've killed my cat. Don't try to deny it! You were asking about him the other night. You knew I was looking for him. It was you, wasn't it? To get me back for that dress!'

'I haven't done anything to your stupid cat, you mad cow,' she said. She started to close the door but Neil caught the edge of it in his hand and came out onto the path.

'What is it, Annie? Tell me what happened,' his voice was soothing and he looked concerned, genuinely concerned. I wiped my eyes on the edge of my sleeve and found it difficult to begin.

'Neil! She's just come round here and accused me of killing her cat! Don't stand there patting her on the back. Neil!'

'I've just buried him in my back garden,' I said quietly. 'Barry found him by the side of the road. *Someone* ran him down. A hit and run!'

Neil put out his hand as if he was going to pat me, then let it fall to his side and turned back to Lucy.

'You can see she's upset, Luce, go and put the kettle on. She didn't mean it. You didn't, did you, Annie?' He looked at me carefully and I forgot what I was going to say.

'Annie, Lucy can't even drive the car. It's mine. And she wouldn't have done something like that on purpose, even if she could. You know that really, don't you?'

Lucy had disappeared from the front door and I heard things being banged about in the kitchen. He grasped my elbow gently and led me inside.

'It was the shock,' I sniffed. It occurred to me that Neil wanted his relationship with Lucy to end as amicably as possible. I could play a part in that, if he wanted me to. Perhaps he was worried about her taking the house away or destroying some of his possessions. She would, if she knew he was leaving her for me. And then he would suffer, and I didn't want that to happen. It wasn't going to be easy, but I could do it, if he wanted me to. I could be nice to her if that was the way he wanted to play it. Neil was a very admirable man in his own way. Goodness only knows how long he'd been unhappy just because he wouldn't have been able to live with himself if he'd hurt Lucy's feelings.

'Of course it was,' he said gently, 'that cat's all you've got. Come on now and sit inside for a minute until you calm yourself down.'

The front room was exactly as I'd remembered; the books and knick-knacks lying about neatly as if no one had touched them since I'd last been round. Lucy had left the kettle to boil and stomped off upstairs, but Neil didn't make any tea. He left me on my own for a few seconds while he went upstairs, and then reappeared with a roll of pink toilet paper in his hand.

'I don't have any tissues,' he said sheepishly. I took a piece of the paper and blew my nose.

'Better now?' he said, and I nodded.

'You know, it really wasn't Lucy,' he said. 'All that about a dress,' he shrugged, 'I don't know what's been going on, but she really wouldn't do anything like that. It must have been an accident. On the main road. A horrible, horrible accident.'

'I'm sure you're right,' I said, not believing a word of it. Of course she was going to have him fooled.

'You could always get another cat?' he suggested. 'It's a nice bit of company for you, isn't it? While your family is,' he looked away, 'elsewhere?'

'I suppose so,' I said, knowing that I wouldn't.

'There's always kittens in the newspapers. Free to good homes,' he added, and reached under the coffee table for a newspaper.

'That's yesterday's,' he said, 'take it with you when you go. You can get another one by the end of the week. It'll make you feel better, won't it?'

The thought of Mr Tips uncurling and looking at me in surprise when Will had first brought him home set me off again and Neil handed me the toilet roll.

'No need for all that,' he said gently, and then sat and waited in silence, sliding the coasters about on the coffee table and making them tessellate as I got myself together.

'I was at Sangita's house,' I said, 'we were talking about you, as a matter of fact, and then Barry came home and he said he'd seen a cat and was it mine and…'

'If it makes you sad, don't think about it,' he said helpfully. 'Think about what you're going to do tomorrow instead. You got anything nice planned?'

I shook my head.

'He was too small when I got him. I had to feed him with an eye dropper. Every three hours, even at night.'

Neil nodded, and went back to the coasters.

'His mother died, you see. If I hadn't taken him on, who knows what would have happened to him. He wasn't even that old.'

'Think about something nice,' Neil said, 'what will you do for the weekend? You could always treat yourself. Take a day out on a tram.'

'Could we?' I said, my tears drying instantly. I heard a door slam upstairs. Lucy was locked up in her bedroom now, probably throwing things about and sulking like a teenager.

'Well, I'm going to be working tomorrow,' he said slowly, 'but I bet Sangita wouldn't turn down a day out shopping.'

'Her boys are back this weekend.'

'So they are,' he said awkwardly, then stood up. He looked uncertain, and didn't meet my eye. A sure sign he was shy too. And that was good: it showed that he thought a lot of me and cared about the impression he was making so much it was making him self-conscious. I was worth being shy around, as far as Neil was concerned.

'Annie? Are you all right?'

'Of course,' I said, smiling. 'Much better now. You've been very kind.' I adjusted the cardigan, and patted at my face a little with the toilet paper to make sure my make-up hadn't run.

He stood up uncertainly, 'I'll make us a quick cup of tea, shall I?'

I nodded, 'Thought you'd never ask,' and waited quietly while he was in the kitchen.

'You have such a lovely house, Neil,' I said. I always feel it's best to pay plenty of compliments, it puts people at their ease, and of course there's the old saying, give and ye shall receive.

'Such nice, expensive pictures. And I really like what you've done with the fire piece thing. It'll be lovely once you get carpet down. Your job must be going very well for you.'

Neil poked his head around the kitchen door, 'The hours I have to put in, you wouldn't believe.'

'And Lucy doesn't help you out much? You do look a bit tired,' I said.

He came back into the room with two mugs, the spoons still sticking out over the rims. Not the way I would have served tea, but of course you make less effort when its someone you know well, and in the time to come I expected to take over that aspect of life and would make sure it was all done properly, to give the right impression of us as a couple.

'Lucy's all right,' Neil said.

'Well, I don't think –'

'I don't want you to take this the wrong way, but –' he stood up and started fiddling with the buttons on his CD player, 'lets get a bit of music on, shall we?'

I didn't recognise the music and waited patiently for him to return to his seat and finish his sentence. Some men don't like to be interrupted.

'I can see why you might have thought that she… things have got out of hand, haven't they?' He looked at the backs of his hands. 'She's a great girl, she really is, but she's got a tendency to get things out of proportion, exaggerated in her mind, if you will, and obviously, we all know, we're all adults and there's been a couple of misunderstandings along the way – well. Maybe after today we could, kind of, clear the air.'

'This tea is making me all hot,' I said, and fumbled my arms out of the cardigan, 'it's a good job I wore my new dress today, or I'd be sweltering.' I tossed it over the back of the settee in what I hoped appeared to be a self-confident and relaxed gesture.

'Ah,' Neil said, staring at me, 'that dress, you've got it on again.'

I brushed my fingers over the fabric. 'Yes,' I said, 'so I do.' I looked up at him and opened my eyes wide, clenching my jaw to stop myself from blinking. I'd practised this in the mirror until my eyes watered after I'd read that it allows members of the opposite sex to see your pupils, which apparently helps them to judge whether you like them or not. Perhaps, I was thinking, Neil needs a little reassurance that his feelings for me really are returned.

'I wouldn't let Lucy see you in that,' was all he said. 'That's what I'm trying to say. She feels like you're antagonising her deliberately and she doesn't know why. You could make things a lot easier,' he waved his hands towards me, 'black isn't really your colour anyway, is it? I'm sure you've got lots of dresses?'

'We don't have to talk about Lucy,' I said gently, as I could see the subject was still troubling him. It is important, in matters of the heart, to tread very lightly: I understood this and I wanted him to know it.

'No,' he agreed, 'that's not really the point, is it? I don't know how things have come to this: Lucy storming out, threatening all sorts.'

'Threatening?' I said. She could try, was what I was thinking, she could blinking well try.

'Things got a bit heated just now,' he stated, and shrugged. 'You were upset. Understandable. And Lucy, she gets tense. She worries. I wouldn't worry, wouldn't take it personally. The thing is, she's on the blob and it makes her a bit, well, you know.'

He grimaced, rubbed his palms over his knees and stood up again to do something to the stereo. While his back was turned I deposited the damp, disintegrating tissue from my palm into a crack between the sofa cushions. He turned while I was brushing the remnants from my hands and I froze, but he was talking again and it didn't look like he'd noticed.

'We'd, that is, Lucy would, and me, the both of us,' he swallowed and went on, his knees popping as he sat back down. 'She does want to try, and I know she gets a bit emotional, God love her. She's been wanting us to have a conversation for ages. For me to tell you, that, well, we want to make a fresh start. We can't carry on like this, and seeing as this is where we live, there's no avoiding each other.'

It was what I had been waiting for. I leaned over to him slightly and he shifted backwards in order to look at my face better.

'Yes, that's exactly what we need to do,' I said. 'A fresh start. I couldn't have put it better. It began badly, I know that, but it doesn't need to carry on like this. I'm glad she thinks the same. It's very sensible of her.'

He smiled, and I realised how worried he must have been because I don't think I'd ever seen him smile like that at me before.

'Good,' he said, 'that's just what she wanted to hear.'

'I'm pleased too,' I replied, 'things are going to be very different for me now.' I stopped for a minute, smiling and getting carried away in my imaginings.

'I don't mind saying, but I've had a really hard few years. People can be very cruel, very unfriendly, especially men. Present company excepted, of course,' I giggled a little, feeling shy again all of a sudden, even despite the inroads we were making.

'There are people out there who have no idea how to behave, no idea what's expected of them in relationship situations. I've been hurt, let down and disappointed. I'd almost lost all my faith in other human beings, I really had.'

Neil was nodding in time to the music and had broken our eye contact so he could immerse himself more fully in the true meaning of my words.

'I can honestly say,' I went on, my nervousness disappearing as I spoke, 'that I've never done anything but make the effort to connect with other people, to really get close to them. Where all this with Lucy has come from, I don't know. I realise the situation is... difficult for her?' I blushed, but Neil nodded.

'Well, I hope everything will settle down now,' Neil said. There was a loud thud from upstairs and he flinched. 'Give it time to blow over. Everyone keep their heads down.'

I smiled, not really listening to what he was saying because I was trying to memorise the pattern, no, the constellation of moles on the side of his neck. Every time I closed my eyes they dissolved from my imagination. It didn't matter. I knew that soon after we had, as he suggested, 'settled down' together, we would be able to hold each other at arm's length, smile, sigh and say, 'Yes, there are no mysteries between us now.'

'Do you want that paper?' Neil said, and stood up again. He reached for my mug and even though it was still half-full, took it with him into the kitchen. I put my cardigan on just in time, for Lucy came thundering down the stairs again and thrust herself into the room.

'God, Neil, why don't you cook her a meal as well!' she said, seeing the mug in his hands.

'She was just going, pet,' he said, 'a cup of tea, for the shock. You're better now, aren't you, Annie?'

'Much better,' I lied. Lucy was scowling at my dress but I pretended not to notice.

'Annie knows you didn't do it. She's sorry,' Neil said. I nodded, happy to collude with him in this, even though in usual circumstances dishonesty is beyond me.

Neil went over to Lucy and squeezed her around the shoulders. 'I'll just see Annie out and I'll get the tea on.'

Lucy nodded, mollified, and stalked back into the kitchen.

'You'll be all right,' he said, once we were at the door. 'Soon enough you'll be feeling much better.'

Soon! There it was. All right, I'd leapt at the chance of us taking a day out together. I love going on the trams, and with someone else there to work out the timetables and choose where to go for lunch it would have been perfect. Not just someone, but Neil. I suppose I jumped the gun a bit. He could hardly start arranging our future before he'd fixed things with Lucy.

And the next day was a Saturday. No one worked on a Saturday. Clearly, after the comforting that he'd been doing that afternoon, he'd decided to strike while the iron was hot and talk to her the next day. It would have been highly inappropriate to take me out before he'd properly finished things with her. I was worth more than that, and he, by the way he was behaving, was letting me know this. Not a short tram ride leading to a nasty bed and breakfast in Blackpool. Oh no! That was for the old days. My future held something altogether more substantial than brief connections in otherwise empty afternoons. Soon! That's what he'd said. Soon!

When I got home, I began to feel quite sorry for Lucy. She was only nineteen, not much older than I'd been when I married Will. I knew more than anyone that she had a hard time ahead of her. I'm not heartless, you know. I chose one of the books that had been most helpful to me, something aimed directly at single women. It was a good one – full of tips for getting used to your new situation, where to find out about DIY and car maintenance, and how to go about meeting someone new once you'd done the quiz at the back and found out you were ready for it again. I took an eraser, rubbed out the notes I'd made in the margins and then wrapped it up nicely with her name on the front. I snuck out quietly and posted it through her door.

When I first heard voices coming from behind the wall the thought crossed my mind that it might be Neil, trying to communicate with me in some way, but then I heard Lucy's voice too, raised in anger, and I realised I was inadvertently eavesdropping on what sounded like quite a heated argument.

'I am not being paranoid!' she shouted. 'Look at this, look at this book. What the hell do you think she's trying to say by that?'

'She's just trying to make it up to you. She's trying to say she's sorry. She didn't really think you'd killed her cat.'

'Make it up to me?' There was the sound of something hard being thrown against the wall. It may have been *So Now You're On Your Own Again: What To Do Next:* I'd bought it in hardback.

'Come on, Lucy, she was upset. Look at her. Don't tell me you don't feel the slightest bit sorry for her.'

'Sorry? Sorry?' Every time she spoke her voice rose an octave. I don't know how she did it. In another life, she could have been a singer.

'This is the woman who's been turfing up our garden and

opening our post for the past three months! And you feel sorry for her?'

I didn't catch what Neil said in reply. In fact, I caught very little of his part in the argument, because Lucy seemed to be doing all the shouting and it was her voice that carried most clearly through the walls.

'A chance! Don't you think we've given her enough chances already?' There was the sound of a slammed door and Lucy's voice became too muffled to hear. I smiled at Neil defending me and trying to get her to see the truth of the situation by persuading her out of her own skewed perspective even at this late stage. For some reason it comforted me to sit a while and listen, to imagine them standing on the landing, very close to me, Neil sighing wearily as he watched Lucy swing her ponytail about and go into their bedroom. I heard the door open and bang closed a second time. Her voice came through clearly again and she was obviously quite close to tears. How Neil coped with her emotional outbursts for so long is beyond me, and yet loyalty is a quality I find very attractive in a person and I looked forward to the time when this slow process would be complete and his loyalty, his kindness and his concern would be transferred solely to me.

'You need to go and talk to her. Properly! Tell her to pack it in! Sort it out once and for all,' Lucy shouted. Neil said something back to her but no matter how close I got to the wall, only the low rumble of his voice carried through the bricks and wallpaper.

'No! No, you can do it this time. I mean it! Do you realise how close I am to going back to my mother's? Do you even give a fuck about me? Don't you even think about fucking off to Raymond's!'

She started crying noisily, and then the voices faded as she went into the bedroom again and Neil followed her, no doubt to comfort her a little before, I hoped, doing as she requested, taking the golden opportunity she'd presented him with and coming round to me. I brushed my hair and waited, but after an hour passed I realised Neil was the kind of person who would act in his own time and in his own way.

Considering it calmly, I realised that his refusal to obey Lucy in this sent a much clearer message to her than immediately coming to see me would, and of course, he would have been well aware I had heard every word of his defence of me and that would, for the time being, be enough.

16

It was a shame, but even though Neil had said he didn't have time to take me out that Saturday, I'd hoped he'd find time to pop round and reassure me at some point during the day. It was a long day. I'd folded and unfolded the newspaper he'd given me, knowing that I wasn't going to look for another cat, but wanting to keep it anyway because it felt in some ways like a lover's token, a little indication of his concern for me. Of course, he may have been telling the truth and he really did need to work. Or perhaps he'd been caught up in an extended conversation with Lucy. They must have had lots of joint possessions, and sorting out who would have what was bound to take a long time. These things happen, but I wish I could have let him know he could let Lucy have everything and he could share all my new things at my house. He would probably see it as a threat to his masculinity. A lot of men are like that.

My heart lifted as I saw him leave his house around lunchtime but when after a few hours he still hadn't returned, I began to worry that he wasn't going to come back. Who knew what that woman was capable of? Perhaps the stress had driven him to abscond?

I'd been wandering about the house with my thoughts going on in this way, drifting about and half-heartedly doing a little cleaning, starting to bake a chocolate cake and leaving the mixture unfinished in the bowl. After a while, I found myself at the front window looking out over my little garden and past the low wall onto the street and the houses opposite. I was waiting for him to come back. I wanted to be available, nice and visible to make things easier should he decide to pass on a little message to me, or just a friendly nod through the glass. I peered out, and noticed Raymond sauntering along the street again just opposite my house.

I didn't think Neil would mind me passing the time with Raymond, in fact, given the circumstances, I was sure he'd understand. As I considered it, I wondered if Neil had been on his way to see Raymond and perhaps he had given him a message for me, some little codeword to let me know he was on his way home and would be sending for me soon. It suddenly became very important that I speak to him. I pulled up the curtain and banged on the inside of the window.

'Raymond! Ray!' He looked in my direction for a moment but carried on walking, it was clear he hadn't seen where the noise had come from. I banged on the glass again with a little brass wheelbarrow I kept for decoration on the windowsill, and shouted his name as I had done before, only louder this time. He looked right at the window where I was standing, our eyes met, and then he looked away and walked on quickly. In my shock I quickly left the house, went out onto the street and called after him. He finally turned.

'Hello,' he said, 'I didn't see you there.' He didn't come over to me, and I wasn't about to cross the road because I'd left the front door ajar, so the whole of our conversation was conducted in voices loud enough for the whole street to hear. I was very aware that Lucy was probably sitting in her own front room, perhaps looking out of the window awaiting Neil's return just as I was. It meant I had to be very careful of what I said.

'Have you seen Neil today?' I thought I'd ask, in case the message had slipped his mind.

'Yes,' he said slowly. 'Why? What do you want him for?'

'Just wondering,' I said. 'He's been out a long time, hasn't he?' He scratched under his arm like a monkey, drawing my attention to his faded Doctor Who T-shirt. It needed a good iron.

'I'm sure he'll be back soon enough. He does live here,' Ray said.

That was it, the message. Neil would be coming back to see me before long. He'd probably come round the 'back' way so Lucy wouldn't see him, and I needed to leave the alley door open so he'd be able to come in. Maybe. I was becoming less and less certain of my own estimation of events, especially now that Raymond had taken a step towards me into the road and was frowning curiously. What had Neil said to him? Why was everyone busy popping into each other's houses, going to the pub and watching films together? Everyone except for me.

'You had another falling out with Lucy?' he said, taking another step forward. If a car came past at high speed, Raymond could find himself in serious trouble. That made me think of Mr Tips again, and I cringed away from the images in my head.

'No,' I said.

'Neil told me,' he replied. 'I thought you were going to give it a rest?' he spoke slowly, calmly. It wasn't as if he was threatening me or anything like that, but he was alluding to our earlier conversation on the way home from Sangita's dinner party. The one where I thought he'd been drunk and wouldn't remember.

'Excuse me?' I said, pretending to misunderstand.

'You said Lucy killed your cat. She's been crying. She says she's going to go back to her mother's.'

'Oh, that!' I said, and laughed awkwardly. My voice carried across the street, and into who knows how many open windows as it went.

'I thought you were going to lay off her? Neil's worried sick.'

'Neil was very concerned about me, yes,' I said, bristling with indignation, 'but I'm feeling much better now.'

'Neil,' he said, rolling his eyes, 'is a sucker for a sob story.'

'There wasn't a story, Raymond. I've a fresh grave in my back yard if you're in the mood for inspecting it.'

'I don't doubt it,' he said, and laughed. 'Just see if you can settle things down, all right, Annie? Lucy's talking about moving out, and Neil'll be gutted if she did. He's a mate, you see what I'm saying?'

'I'm sure I can't be blamed for someone else's paranoid fantasies,' I said. 'What did Neil say about it?'

'Seems like you've got enough to be dealing with in your own life without poking your nose into other people's,' he said. 'I'm telling you, leave their bloody bins alone. It's weird and it's freaking Lucy out.'

'Raymond! I'm going to have to talk to Sangita about this,' I said. 'I've had a terrible week and I'm shocked at you, I really am.'

'Sangita? Just because she thinks she's judge and jury round here, doesn't mean anyone else does. You and her are so matey – sitting talking about us all like the mother's bloody union,' he sneered, as if he found the idea of my friendship with the Choudhrys incredibly amusing.

'We *are* mates – I mean, friends,' I replied. 'We have a lot in common,' I said proudly.

'Like your kids? How come we've never seen your daughter? Have you even got one or is that just something you concocted to get on her good side?'

'Raymond!' I said.

He shook his head and turned away from me. 'Leave it, Annie,' he said wearily. I didn't want him to have the last word, didn't want him to wander off and bump into Neil before I could have a chance to put things straight.

'Raymond,' he was hurrying away now, clearly not wishing to carry on the conversation. 'You've got completely the wrong impression of me!' I called, and heard my own voice, rather plaintive and desperate-sounding. He pushed the air with his hand without looking back as if he wanted me to go away, and I turned away, tears stinging the backs of my eyelids. I took myself inside before I could say anymore.

After a few moments of irritation, and yes, I'll admit it, hurt, I realised what had happened and felt stupid for not being able to anticipate it. Neil had been to Raymond, and perhaps let something slip about our as yet still illicit understanding. No doubt, like me, he'd been finding the situation stressful and had wanted to confide in a friend. If I had someone close to me I would have done the same thing: you'll remember I even dropped some very heavy hints to Sangita. Good news is a heavy burden and I was bursting to share it with someone. Perhaps he'd even been drinking again, and I couldn't blame him for that either. Secrets make you lonely, and living with Lucy would drive anyone to imbibe occasionally.

Raymond had quite clearly taken Lucy's side in the matter. Realising his attempts to woo me weren't going to get him anywhere, he'd switched his attentions to someone in his own league. I sighed with relief: it was stupid of me not to have thought of it before, not to have worked it all out from the evidence. It would all have to go into the File too. And it wasn't such a bad thing. Lucy would need all the friends she could get soon enough, and Neil and I would need no one more than each other. Soon. I let the curtain drop and drifted back into the front room.

I did not concoct the existence of a daughter to 'get in' with Sangita.

As I've stated quite clearly elsewhere in this account, there are various occasions when I may have omitted some detail, or elaborated so that something minor would seem to be a bigger part of my life than it really was. I am a human being, after all. And getting all this down in retrospect has its disadvantages too: it's hard to describe events as they really happened without adding in nuances of hindsight and including details that I may not have noticed at the time. But daughters are not details. The baby – Grace – she was there all right. I just didn't want to talk about her.

We brought her home from the hospital, and I gave up hope on Boris and on everything. It was terrible: she never slept for more than an hour or so, night and day. The noise had its normal physiological effect on me: milk spraying from my nipples, a constriction in my throat, a flush to my neck and cheeks. I couldn't tell if it was love or anger because I felt nothing except the desire for sleep and silence that was consumed by the bottomless pit of her desire for something I could never find.

I learned very quickly that it didn't matter what I did. She cried when I held her, she cried when I put her down, she cried when I fed her hourly and she cried when I spent an afternoon refusing to feed her at all. When she did sleep it was between me and Will, her hands batting at my nightdress in the night, nappy leaking onto the sheets, vomited milk leaking from the corners of her mouth onto my pillow. She'd twist herself horizontal and pummel her feet against my back, as if not satisfied with beating me from the inside night and day, she had to do it to me now she was on the outside too.

I didn't like her sleeping in our bed and I complained about it, but Will wasn't having it. I wish he'd listened to me. I wish it more now than I did then. It's regret, isn't it? Where you go on about the past, and feel badly about things you can't do anything about? Useless emotion: consuming and persistent. I wish he'd let her sleep in the cot: he paid enough for it.

I can't really describe her to you. She wasn't a person to me, just a puzzle box with a secret combination I would only find by trial and error but once I'd slotted the pieces into place, would magically close in on itself and fall silent. Even Will wasn't immune to it. He paid ninety pounds to a cranial osteopath who came to the house, drank three cups of tea, asked a lot of questions about the delivery and then placed his thumbs on the baby's head for approximately thirty seconds.

Because I'd given up on Boris, and because it didn't seem to matter what I did, in the end I decided to do nothing. If Will had wondered for a moment about what might have been going on in the house while he probed cavities and drilled holes during the day, he never asked me about it. The baby was going to be in charge. Was that the way life was supposed to be: spending your whole childhood with adults telling you what to do and then after a few short years of independence, living out the rest of your life with a screaming knot of accidental flesh calling the shots? I didn't think so. I stuffed my ears up with cotton wool and ruled supreme.

The cot Will refused to put her in at night became her home during the day; once he had gone to work I put the baby in it and left her there. I gave her the bottle every four hours without touching her or picking her up, and I changed her morning nappy, sodden clothes and bed sheets half an hour before I expected Will back. She had terrible nappy rash because of it, but no one ever died of that.

For the first few days of my new regime she mainly screamed, but after that she just looked through the bars at me, curling and uncurling her miniature fingers in the air as if she were conducting an orchestra. Her expression was either livid or blank but I generally avoided her eyes. The midwives had said she looked like me but I couldn't see it.

When she was six weeks old, Will took the afternoon off. Thank God, I thought, and used my old contacts to arrange something for myself. I'd gone off the idea of bedroom shenanigans since she'd been born, but even a bit of company and a few drinks in a bar somewhere would have been enough. I didn't want much, and Will had said something vague about pushing the pram along the seafront. I fitted the rain covers and folded clean blankets into it. I spent most of the morning putting milk into bottles. Will didn't know about the formula so I added less powder than the instructions demanded to make it look more like expressed breast milk and left the pump wet on the draining board.

The outdoors and everything in it had dwindled to a draft click-ing the letter box but that morning I hovered in the hallway with my shoes on. I'd worn only slippers for weeks and the hardness of the leather chafed my softened heels.

'What's all this?' He nodded at the pram in the hallway, the matching changing bag carefully packed and hung on the handles, the snowsuit laid over the back of the couch. Last of all, I myself caught his eye. He blew the air out between his teeth, a quiet whistle.

'You look nice, very, erm, glamorous. Is that top new?'

'No. You just haven't seen me wearing it before, that's all.' I tugged it straight: I hadn't worn it since before I was pregnant, but it being a little too small for me only seemed to exacerbate its effect.

'Have you done something to your, to your... face?' he stuttered.

'It's called make-up, Will. Mascara. Women wear it when they want to look nice. You've probably read about it somewhere,' I replied irritably.

'And what's all that?' he gestured back to the pram in the hallway. 'Looks like you're not planning on coming back!' he laughed, a little worried.

'Things for the baby. Everything's ready. I've put her milk in the fridge but you can take it out and run it under the hot tap when you need it.' I plucked my coat from the pegs in the hallway. 'I need some fresh air. I haven't been out in weeks.'

Will chuckled and went into the kitchen to wash his hands. The baby was lying on a blanket on the living-room floor and true to form, she started to cry. I did nothing, and Will turned the taps off, went in, and picked her up.

'Hard morning, sweetheart? Has daddy's little princess been a handful? You been naughty for your mummy, have you, little thing?' He tucked the baby's head under his chin and spoke to me.

'It's far too early for her to be separated from you. Look at her, she's looking about for you already.'

I looked. The baby was turning her head and grimacing, sweep-ing her eyes around the room until she found me and locked me into her gaze. There's nothing quite like it. I flinched and wanted to hide, wondering what it was she would want next.

'If you want to walk out to the paper shop and back I'm sure she'll

be fine, but; he looked at my clothes again, 'you weren't planning on
going out properly, were you?'

I nodded and carried on buttoning up my coat.

'Just for a few hours. It's not fair that I'm in all the time. I need to
be outside sometimes.'

'We can go out together. Get some fresh air, go for a cup of tea
somewhere. That's what I had planned.'

I shook my head and picked up my bag.

'On my own.'

He shook his head, 'You can't Annie.' He looked at me sternly,
'You're a mother now, you can't carry on the way you used to,' he said
it carefully, but before I had to chance to wonder what he meant he
laughed again and blew into the baby's ear. She squirmed her head
away and contorted her face. It could have been a smile.

'Come on, Will. Some babies are in nursery at her age. I'm only
asking for an afternoon.'

'Yes, they might well be in nursery, but what about the effect it has
on them? I bought you the Winnicot book, didn't I? Didn't you look
at it? Have you any idea what early separation from the mother does
to the minds of young infants? We don't want that, do we, cheeky
chops? Oh no, we don't, we definitely don't want that.'

I interrupted his babbling angrily. 'And have you any idea what
being stuck between these four walls day and night for weeks has
done to *my* mind?' I'd raised my voice and the baby opened her
mouth and started screaming.

'See, she needs a feed. She needs her mummy. Sit down in your
chair and I'll get you a glass of water.'

I was tired. I probably would have slept as soon as I got a chance
to lie down anyway. Maybe, I thought, maybe he was right, and I
couldn't have things arranged the way they used to be anymore. And
where did that leave me? I took my coat off, threw it onto the sofa
angrily and sat in the new rocking chair. Will deposited the baby in
my lap and went back to the kitchen.

'I give up, just take what you want,' I said to her, quietly, so Will
wouldn't hear, and squeezed her hard under the blanket. She just
squirmed and rooted for the nipple she knew was there under the
layers of clothing and underwear too impractical to feed her in. I

JENN ASHWORTH

let her wait for a few more seconds, but she didn't look at me, and
it was easier to capitulate and hoist up the top than it was to listen
to more of the noise that would surely come from her apparently
inexhaustible lungs.

I gave up. I was tired. You don't believe how tired it's possible to
be until it happens, and what that tiredness does to your mind and
your sense of right and wrong.

Will smiled when he returned, proffering the glass of water (he'd
read that breastfeeding women get thirsty and had been foisting
them on me every three minutes since). It must have been a pleasant
sight for him: lactating mother and suckling babe nestled together
in the rocking chair he'd chosen himself. I was seething: irritation
running over my skin like pins and needles. Inside the now unnecessary shoes I curled and uncurled my toes and under the blanket
my fingers shrank away from her pedalling limbs and knotted themselves into my palm. When Will spoke I didn't hear him at first.

'I think you might be depressed, Annie.'

'What?'

'I said, I think you might have developed a touch of post-natal
depression. It's very common, you know. I'll make you an appointment with the doctor.'

'You think I'm depressed?'

My milk let down: I felt it scalding down the ducts and seeping
through my clothes on the side that she wasn't sucking at. More
laundry. And even after a shower and nice perfume, I'd still walk
about for the rest of the day smelling like a cheese factory.

'Well look at you, you aren't really bonding with the baby, are
you? You're not yourself, always irritable, looking for an argument.
You never used to be like that. Sometimes I hardly recognise you.'
I opened my mouth to speak but he went on, 'Shh! I'm not trying
to criticise you, I've been reading up on it. It's hormonal – not your
fault, nothing to worry about. You might not be the baby anymore,
but we've still got to keep you in tip-top condition, haven't we, love?
You're needed now – you've got to be on top form for the sake of the
baby.'

The Great Goddess Hormone makes her appearance again. I
gritted my teeth and let the words force their way out between them

because the baby had gone to sleep, lolling back on my forearm with her mouth open. The nipple she'd abandoned sprayed milk like a lawn sprinkler and Will looked away and handed me a tissue. I knew from experience that when I moved there would be a tiny red ear-print on my flesh and she would scream as if I was killing her. So I stayed put and let the milk fall onto her hands.

'Your body will just think she needs that milk,' he said, managing to gesture at my breast without looking at it. 'It's supply and demand,' he explained. 'You'd be better off not expressing if you're feeling engorged.'

'She demands and I supply it,' I said darkly, tucking the nipple back into my bra. I was soaked anyway. Might as well keep warm and put Will out of his misery.

'You know in the Third World, mothers stop the flow by giving the areole a sharp tug,' he said. 'It seems to constrict the ducts.'

I laughed slowly.

'It might help,' he said, and rubbed my shoulder again.

'Silly me not to have thought about it,' I said. 'Next time I'm feeling miserable I'll just give my areoles a tweak, shall I?'

He sighed.

'This is what I mean, sweetie. You really are depressed, aren't you?'

'I'm not depressed, Will, I'm tired. Tired, and bored out of my mind. You try living for six weeks on three hours sleep a night. You try spending every waking hour with a baby that's either scream-ing or chewing on your nipples. You try the nappies, the vomit, the stuff over every bloody surface in the whole house. I don't like it, Will. I don't like being a mother! It's not being depressed, it's not a mental illness! Who would like it? Does anyone actually like living like this?'

Will stood behind me and started patting at my hair and knead-ing my shoulders. I was hemmed in: the baby on my lap pinning my arms to the chair and now him behind me rubbing me and pawing me as if I was a Kobe cow. They had me exactly where they wanted me. And where was Boris? Where was he? My only hope had faded through the months of the pregnancy to nothing more than an indulgent daydream I used to pass the afternoons. I shrugged Will off me but he still kept on talking. Him talking and talking, and her sucking: you can see, can't you, that they were ganging up on me right from the very beginning and there was nothing I could do about it.

'But that's the point, Annie. Listen to what I'm telling you, please. There are hormones that go around a mother's system that make her feel happy when she's with her baby: breastfeeding and so on. It's scientific – there's no mystery to it. God help us, sweetheart, I know it's hard work and I know you're not used to it yet, but if you allowed a doctor to treat your hormonal imbalance you'd find your heart was in it a lot more than it is now, I guarantee it.'

'I'm not depressed!' I gesticulated jerkily and woke her up. She started to cry and scratch her face with her fingernails. Will took her off me and tucked her against his chest again.

'There's no need to shout, Annie. You're the adult here, and you're making more noise than she is. I know it's hard, I know it is. Neither of us has had much practice at this, have we? Why don't you pop your coat back on and we can go out for a walk? Eh, love? She'll sleep in the pram and we can enjoy the fresh air and have a little chat about things. Come on, up you get. It'll make you feel better, promise.'

Somehow, he managed to zip the baby into her snowsuit and manhandle me back into my coat at the same time. I spent the rest of the afternoon staggering along the seafront begging for sleep with the wind blowing the beach into my eyes.

17

After the unpleasantness with Raymond the rest of the day passed off uneventfully. I slept late on Sunday and when I did get up, I realised I had again run out of milk. As you can see, housekeeping has never been a speciality of mine. Since my break with Will I'd had to learn a lot about household management and there were still occasions when I made the simplest of errors. The milk I thought I had was lumpy and curdled in the bottom of the bottle and I threw it down the sink irritably, wincing at the smell. My plans for breakfast were ruined and it was with no small degree of annoyance that I put my coat on over my nightdress and left the house for the shop. I was hasty and irritated, catching the hem of my nightdress in the door.

I wish I'd taken notice of how uncomfortable I'd felt in my night-dress, wish the nagging feeling caused by the tear in the hem from where I'd caught it in the door had overwhelmed my desire for milk. I wish I'd gone home to change. Fifteen minutes, half an hour. It would have been enough. I'd been thinking that up until then I'd been doing quite well and things with Neil and the others were progressing nicely. Even Lucy's harassment had proved to be only a setback of the most minor kind when her plan to use Sangita against me had backfired and resulted in the beginnings of a warm friendship, the like of which I'd never had before. Now when I look back, I can pinpoint that morning as the time when things started to go very badly wrong, and it became increasingly difficult to keep everything about my past in its own little compartment.

Milk! The combination of a bottle of milk and a haircut was enough to undo almost everything I'd worked so hard to achieve. But I didn't know any of this then, of course not. It was yet to happen. With hindsight, as my mother used to say, we all have perfect vision.

When I turned from my gate I almost bumped into someone standing on the pavement behind me. Elbows brushed, and embarrassed, I jumped away. I didn't look at the person I'd almost collided with as I hurriedly apologised and moved aside to let him pass. After a few seconds, when he didn't move or walk on, I looked up from the pavement and my slippered feet and realised it wasn't one person, it was two, and that I knew them.

Will's parents: Billy and Ada. Or as I always knew them, Mr and Mrs Fairhurst. It had been a long time and the sight of them standing there strangely out of context made my hands shake. I would have been less surprised if I'd bumped into a character from one of the novels I'd been reading. The watery early-morning sunshine caught on her earrings, their wedding rings, the rims of his glasses, glinting off the hard surfaces and making them look more like ornaments than living things. I opened my mouth to speak, and croaked.

'So this is where you've been hiding yourself,' Billy said. He leaned back on his heels and shook his head slowly, 'Not so far away, after all.'

For a second or two I couldn't speak at all and we stood there in silence, looking at each other the way strange dogs do before their hackles start to rise.

'What are you doing here?' I hissed quietly.

Mrs Fairhurst looked me up and down in exactly the way she had done when we first met. It was the only way she ever looked at me: sweeping her gaze from my shoulders to my ankles and back again. Until I'd announced my pregnancy, that is. After that, she'd just stared at my burgeoning stomach.

'Listen to her!' she said, talking to her husband.

'How did you find me?'

I started to feel very sick. They were hardly a physical threat to me, of course not. He was an old man; I knew he used an angina spray. Ada leaned heavily on his arm, bent over so that her chin nearly touched her chest. She wore a floppy purple hat and bright red lipstick, Billy a blue North Face jacket. She clutched a string shopping bag in which I could see she'd brought a thermos and a copy of *The People's Friend*. Billy was carrying an open *A-Z* in his free hand.

'I've got to go now,' I said uselessly. 'I was on my way out somewhere.'

I tried to pass them, but Billy caught hold of my wrist and the strength in his wasted fingers was astonishing.

'No point running off, girl, we know where you live now,' he said, his voice trembling. They always called me 'girl'. I suppose they'd had Will fairly late, and with the age difference between him and me they were more like grandparents than parents-in-law. I'd experimentally called him 'dad' once, but he'd pretended not to hear and I didn't try it again.

I wrenched my wrist out of his grasp and he toppled, leaning into his wife and she into him, as if they were sheltering against a high wind. I pulled my coat around me even tighter and cursed myself again for being so stupid as to leave the house dressed as I was. The wrong sort of attention indeed!

'Go away!' I said loudly, more scared than angry. 'You've no right to be here, none at all!' I stood my ground, and expected them to melt away, ashamed at their imposition, but they remained there on the pavement, solid as stones and blocking my way to the shop.

I'd go and get the milk later, I decided, I'd just turn around, go home, and lock the door behind me. They could bang as much as they wanted to, I just wouldn't answer and there would be nothing they could do about it. That was the way my mind was working: I wasn't thinking about the ramifications of their visit, the embarrassment and the worry it would cause me. I was threatened, and my mind could only grasp the simplest, most immediate things. Leave the milk, it said, go home and lock the door. Inside my house, I'd be safe. No one could see me and I wouldn't have to talk to them. I didn't think any further ahead than that, not then. Before I could move, Ada spoke.

'Tell her, tell her, Billy,' she prompted urgently. I couldn't think, not after everything that had happened, what kind of message she might want her husband to relay to me, but by the grim expressions on both of their faces, jaws clenched as if they were in pain, I could tell I wasn't going to like it.

They thought it wasn't fair that when the house was sold I got so much of Will's money. It didn't matter to them that I was entitled to it, as his wife, that I'd earned that and a whole lot more during the years I'd stayed at home and hoovered and made sure the books were lined up neatly on the shelves. Took the empty cans out to the recycling, and cleaned the toilets upstairs and down. I even helped out in his surgery when his receptionists went on holiday. When push came to shove, I put the vacuum cleaner in the back of the car and went to do a bit of cleaning after hours. And I never got paid for any of that, never. He'd leave out a magazine and a bunch of flowers sometimes, but that was nothing like a wage, was it? I was *entitled* to all that money, and to the house that I'd bought with it. But of course, they didn't see it like that. I don't blame them in some ways, but they could have stayed in Wigan and kept their opinions to themselves.

'I don't want to hear what you've got to say, that part of my life is over now. There's nothing to talk about. Nothing at all.' I tried to speak assertively but my voice, high-pitched and wavering, cracked, and I became aware of net curtains twitching, curious faces pressed against windowpanes. It made me panic. I wanted to rush about and draw all the curtains, cover all the watching eyes with my hands, stop up listening ears. Everything was getting out of hand.

'We want you to know,' Billy said, waving the street map about breathlessly, 'we know what happened, even if you've got everyone else fooled. Don't think we don't know! Will wouldn't hurt a fly!'

'Shut up!' I said quietly. 'Just shut up and go away!'

'Shut up? After all you've done, after what you've put our family through you've got the cheek to tell us to...'

'I haven't done anything! You could call the police right now and who do you think would be getting taken away? Not me!' I shrieked, rubbing my wrist. To be honest, it didn't hurt that much, but I was trying to make a point.

'I haven't done anything!' I said again. It was foolish, I admit it. Fleetwood doesn't have a train station and neither of them drives, so they must have been up at the crack of dawn in order to get here to see me. Me shrieking words they'd heard before, hundreds of times probably, it wasn't going to change anything.

'You should go back home,' I said quietly, trying to sound reasonable. 'It's going to rain later on, and you wouldn't want to be out in it. There isn't anything else for us to talk about.'

'You bitch!' Ada whispered, and for a second the three of us were standing there on the pavement, our mouths flapping open like baby birds, everyone trying to talk over each other and no one making much sense.

'How did you find me?' I gasped, wondering, now my mind was working at normal speed again, how long it would take to sell this house and find a new one. The thought was brief, and then fast on its heels, in crowded all the reasons why I wasn't going to move. I was going to stay. If they'd found me here, they could find me again somewhere else. I couldn't stand it again, I couldn't do it: all the money, the estate agents, the solicitors. Traipsing round the houses of strangers, having to think of something to make polite conversation about every time. A whole set of new neighbours. The neighbours, friends I'd made here for the first time in years.

And Neil, of course. Neil and that amazing coincidence that had brought us to each other again. He'd helped me when I was hurt and bleeding, halfway through one of the worst days of my life, and when I was scared and lonely he'd turned up again with a key to my house. It meant something, I know it did. I couldn't just walk out on something that had the potential to make everything in my life complete.

'We contacted everyone in Will's address book to see if they'd heard of where you'd gone to. We tried to find your father,' Ada said.

'You talked to him?' I said. I hadn't seen him in years, not since I'd been married. The arrangement was mutually satisfactory, I think, although I wondered why when he'd heard of my predicament with Will he hadn't stepped in to help.

'No,' she said, 'he died. Quite some time ago, actually. There was nothing to inherit, so don't get your hopes up. He'd drank it all away and didn't even have the house any more.' I think she thought she was being cruel, and by talking like that she was going to make me cry. It was nothing. I don't believe that just because people are blood-related it means there's any special link between them. It takes a bit more, and is harder to find than that. Still, I was an orphan now. I'd been an orphan for a good while, perhaps, and hadn't known it. I didn't feel any different.

'It was Jessica who put us onto you,' Billy said, 'Will's surgery girl.' As if there was something morally repugnant about being on friendly terms with an employee. He'd been a dentist too and had made it a point of principle never to remember the names of any of the staff.

'The hairdresser?' I asked faintly, remembering writing my name and address in her big black diary, making an appointment I didn't have the money or intentions to keep. My own fault. Of course it was.

'She was very sympathetic,' Ada spat, 'said you needed as much family around you as you could get. You got to her all right, didn't you? She asked if I could find it in myself to understand that you'd acted when you were in fear of your life, and treat you like a daughter.' She laughed, wheezing with it for a minute, and rocked on Billy's arm. 'Fear of your life? You've been twice the size of him since you were seventeen! It isn't natural, never was.'

I looked at her pale creased face, the grey curls on her forehead and temples, her eyes screwed up with an emotion that can only be called hatred. The red lipstick on her mouth had bled greasily into the crinkled skin around it. It's why they recommend that you don't smoke.

'Daughter?' she went on, asking me more questions that I knew I wasn't expected to answer. 'Daughter? Your father should have drowned you when he first saw you!'

She was so stooped and small I could have pushed her over quite easily. I glanced over my shoulder at the windows opposite, trying to identify who was watching. Shapes moved behind net curtains. It could have been Raymond: I wasn't sure which house was his. The Choudhrys were tucked away at the other end of the street, so that was all right. It was probably someone I didn't know, which in some respects was worse, because people never forget a first impression. Given the opportunity, I could shrug and lift my hands heavenwards. 'Old folks,' I'd say, 'what can you do?' and make a show of being patiently kind to a pair of geriatrics escaped from a home.

'I was very badly hurt that day,' I said to Ada, loud enough for any eavesdroppers to hear because for all I knew it would be my only chance to defend myself. 'I had to go to hospital.' I touched my eyebrow, which was a habit I had of stroking my scar whenever I felt nervous or unsafe. I thought I'd got myself out of doing that, but there I was again, rubbing the ridge over my eye with my thumb as if I could massage it away.

'Really,' she said flatly.

'I had stitches. They took photographs to prove it. You saw the pictures the same as everyone else. It wasn't my fault that happened, was it?'

'I don't care what everyone else saw!' she shouted. 'He was my son, and I knew him better than –'

'Ada,' Billy warned gently, not in defence of me, but in concern about the toll the impassioned attack was having on her. She stopped, and gulped in air, so I got another chance to speak.

'I didn't do anything wrong,' I started off gently but grew more annoyed as I spoke. 'I've not a new life here now. Please leave me alone. If you come around here again I'll call the police.' I said it, but I knew I wouldn't. Hopefully, I thought, they wouldn't realise that.

'The police? The police?' Billy looked dumfounded, and for a minute I thought he was going to have a heart attack. He spat onto the pavement and looked up at me venomously. 'A new life! Tell that to Will!'

Ada had started to sob, dry, coughing little noises, and Billy put his arm around her. I say sobbing, but the motions of her shoulders, the dry exhalations, it didn't sound much different from laughing. Out of context, I would have been hard pressed to tell which was which, and *that* would have got me into trouble somewhere along the line if I'd remained a member of their family. No one, I knew, got on with their in-laws, but this was ridiculous.

The thought of this incident getting back to Neil or the Choudhrys got me worked up again. If Lucy got wind of it and took it into her head to utilise this confrontation and turn it into a major part of her campaign to ruin me, well, I was sunk. After the years I'd spent with Will, those lonely, empty times, I'd finally found a place for myself where I fitted in and where I could look forward to being happy. And they begrudged me that! I couldn't quite believe it.

I moved away while Billy was leaning over Ada, stroking her back and squeezing her knotty hand between his. I headed in the direction of my house quickly, making long strides and quickly outpacing the elderly couple who after a couple of steps, didn't try to follow.

'A new life!' Billy shouted. I turned to look at him and he was standing in the road, waving his arms about as if he was directing invisible traffic. The street map flapped about, reminding me uncomfortably of Will and that donor card. I walked faster, but in the street I had grown to love for its dignified quietness, his words flew along to me like birds. The doors and windows that used to be full of invitations became as inquisitive and vigilant as the ones I'd left behind me.

'Very nice! Very nice, Annie! Settled in then? New friends? Bet they don't know they've got a jail bird living among them! A violent criminal!'

I knew what he was going to say next, I knew it. I walked away shakily and went indoors while he was still shouting. They didn't follow me, but I couldn't get comfortable for hours because I was wondering all the time if they'd be back.

I think after that, the rest of my time in that house was just damage limitation. Their unexpected arrival opened the floodgates until soon more or less everyone who counted knew how unlucky I'd been with Will. Their visit, if it isn't overdramatic to say so, was the beginning of the end. I can't get angry with them for it, not any more. I was so focused on what I wanted for myself I wasn't really thinking about how they might have been feeling, and how it wasn't entirely unreasonable that after losing a son, they'd begrudge a traumatised daughter-in-law finding someone else to make her happy.

'When stressed or upset, take time out to pamper yourself as you'd imagine a lover would. Self-care is the key to self-esteem, and an afternoon spent within the warm embrace of a bubble bath is never an afternoon wasted. Let the hot water run and watch those negative feelings dissolve away in the steam!'

That is a quotation from the opening chapter of *Loving Yourself, Loving Another: Self Esteem for the Independent Woman* and I still know it off by heart. Most of my favourite books have been written by professionals: the top experts in their fields. Even when I was living through my blackest hours and doubted the efficacy of a new lipstick or a bottle of nail polish, I deferred to the judgement of university experts and made the purchase, trusting in the advice of someone who knew enough about the topic to make a living writing books about it. Sometimes it worked and the contents of a little shiny bag from Boots would be enough to transform another after-noon alone into an indulgent period of replenishment.

Back in the house and still without milk, I sat at the kitchen table with a mug of hot Vimto and painted my fingernails. I propped a mirror against the Vimto bottle and soothed myself by stroking periwinkle eye shadow over my brow bone. I tried a smudge of navy blue in the sockets for added depth and glamour and felt quite calm again.

All dressed up and nowhere to go – the cliché flitted through my head and I decided to pop next door. I anticipated that Neil would be touched and pleased by the efforts I had made to present myself attractively. Some part of me must have known that my time now was limited, and I had to hurry if I wanted something to happen between me and Neil. In actual fact, this was to be my last weekend in the house, and although I wasn't to know that then, the sense of urgency was growing.

18

Of course what preoccupied me then is not what preoccupies me now. Sangita, Lucy, Raymond. I can hardly remember what they look like. Was Lucy really so skinny, and Sangita really so decked out in her gold jewellery, constantly wearing the jangling evidence of Barry's love for her? Was Raymond really always strutting about in that ridiculous jacket of his, so proud of his white trainers, so fond of his lager?

When I look back over the notes I have on them in my File, the small details I jotted down after our brief and infrequent conversations seem to have taken a life of their own, and blotted out everything else about them. It is possible they wouldn't even recognise themselves in my account. I can hardly recognise myself in it sometimes. We all seem unreal, like characters from a film. The things that I never wrote down, and never even allowed myself to think about come back to me with the most impact. I can believe these things.

In the last clear memory I have of Will he is standing in the bath with soapsuds clinging to the hair on his chest and genitals. His hips and shoulders jut like coat hangers, and, as always, he is crumpled, his chin bowed to avoid the sloping ceiling. He'd pulled the mirror down and propped it behind the taps so he could shave while he was in the water. He liked to have a good soak every now and again, and it wasn't out of character for him to spend two hours in the water with a copy of *National Geographic* and Classic FM booming out through the landing.

Getting in and finding him still in the bath wasn't unusual: I'm remembering an incident from the time when he'd taken three months off work to get control of his emotions. During that era, the close of our marriage, I would often come home to find him dozing in the living room; his arm dangling down the side of the couch and fingers still limply cradling the remote control. I'd be able to sneak back in under the noise of the shopping channel. I was hoping for that. Hoping for fifteen minutes to take a few aspirin, change my clothes and wash away the blood.

He was leaning towards the toilet so he could grab the red towel and I could see his profile: the child-like curve of his forehead and the blue-shadowed jut of his jaw. His eye too, almost hidden by the lilac complication of flesh beneath it. He'd been crying again. I could see it clearly, because I'd seen it so many times before: him sitting in the bath with his arms around his shins, resting his eye sockets on the cradle of his bent knees. He cried silently, with his mouth closed. Varying extremes of emotion were revealed only by the tempo of his throbbing shoulders, heaving up and down as he sobbed. I could hold my breath and count, and if his shoulders juddered more than a few times before I had to breathe again, I'd sneak away and leave him to it.

He moved his head around sharply when he saw me then straightened up, bumping his head on the eaves. He swore, apologised and stared. As I exhaled, I heard a delicate spatter as the blood from my nose sprayed onto the linoleum. He didn't say anything at all and still didn't reach for the towel, so I sat on the closed lid of the toilet, pulled a length of tissue from the roll and held it against my nostrils. The twenty-pound note that Neil had given me was still crumpled in my hand, and I stuffed it into my pocket to save it from the blood. Will's face looked like someone had just told him a distant and very elderly relative of his had died in the night: a bystander's face.

'I had a bit of an accident,' I said eventually. God knows what I was thinking, turning up without a story prepared. I thought he would be asleep. That was all he did: sit in the bath crying, wander around the house in his dressing down, or sleep at odd times of the day. It was as if I didn't live there at all, and far from the funeral being the point when things started to get back to normal, they'd been getting worse and worse.

He frowned, 'What happened to you? What kind of an accident?' He sounded weary. So tired with everything else there wasn't any room left for him to be bothered about me. In other circumstances, I might have been annoyed at that. But this time, I hoped I could work it to my advantage.

'Don't start, Will,' I said briskly, 'I'm all right, you know.'

'Does it hurt a lot?' he said, studying me. I was glad the mirror was somewhere else. He stepped out of the bath and I handed him the towel. Will never wrapped a towel around his waist like a man; he wrapped it under his armpits like a woman. His dressing gown was hanging on a hook on the back of the door and he reached for it and put it on.

'Is it just your face, or…?' his voice tailed off. I shook my head and he sat on the side of the bath.

'Come on, Annie. You can hardly sit down. You're going to need to go to hospital. What happened?'

'Just my face. A rib, maybe. It's okay.' I didn't dare look at him in case he started flapping, and got going with his amateur dramatics. He leaned over to me and touched my chin, pulling my face up so our eyes met.

'Your eye, you can hardly open it,' he said. He took the flannel out of my hand and rinsed it under the tap. When he pressed it against my face it was cold and soothing and I closed my eyes, leaning into his hand so the pressure made the cut sting.

'I want you to tell me. Who did this?'

I shook my head and he pushed the flannel against my face harder, so that it hurt.

'Some people would say I had a right to know. I haven't asked so far. I've let you get on with doing God knows what in the afternoons. But if this man you've been seeing, if he's… does he know where you live, Annie? Where we live?'

I shook my head again.

'Right. So he's not going to be round here pounding at the door then? Good. If that's the sort of person he is,' he gestured at my ripped blouse, 'you're better off without him.'

He pulled the flannel away from my face, inspected it, rinsed it and handed it to me. I think he felt better, seeing me like that. In a way, I was doing him a favour. It gave him something to do, someone to look after. It distracted him a bit from his own misery.

'I don't suppose you're going to tell the police. No? Well you can tell me then. You come back here, like that, and I'm the one who has to mop everything up and hand out the ice packs. I've got a right to know, Annie. I haven't said it before, but I'm saying it now. Tell me.'

I *did* tell him, I really did. He didn't give me a choice, and when I started, he kept making me go backwards.

'Start at the beginning,' he said, 'I can't understand what you're telling me unless you start from the beginning.' I tried to find a beginning – telling him about Michael, about the magazine, not about Boris but about some of the others.

'What made you do it,' he said, 'was I that bad to you?' I shook my head and spat blood into the bath and told him about the shower curtain, about wondering if it had really happened at all.

'I was just hoping for...' I stopped, trying to explain my reasoning. 'Something,' I said vaguely, knowing that if I could have made him understand I wouldn't have needed to do all that looking in the first place.

'This has been going on for...' he squeezed the bridge of his nose between his finger and thumb as if it was his nose that was bleeding and not mine, 'years?'

'I just met this man once. Today. I saw the advert yesterday. The magazine's called *Abundance*. I'm subscribed. The post always arrives when you're at work.'

I told him about the advert I'd found from someone who lived in Fleetwood itself, which was a first. It's true what they say: sometimes it's a relief to get it off your chest, and I wondered as I told him how I'd been able to keep it all inside for so long. He'd thought, all this time, that I had a boyfriend.

'That, Annie, I could understand. Someone who'd take you out, someone who was richer, more romantic. I could get my head around that. But this, it's so *animal*.' He shook his head. 'I just don't get it. I should be angry, shouldn't I?'

I told him about making the phone call, sorting out the arrangements and setting out in the morning carrying my bag with a change of clothes.

'You were going to stay the night?' Hurt, and before I could answer, 'You've never done that before.'

I pulled the wad of toilet paper away from my nose and examined the jellied lump of blood clinging to it.

'I think it's stopped now.' I held the flannel against the worst eye and looked away from him.

'No, not the night. Sometimes the clothes I'm wearing,' Will flinched, I suppose I didn't need to go on, but I did, 'sometimes they get dirty, or torn. It depends…'

'I see,' he said, the sympathy draining away a little but not gone altogether. 'Go on.'

The advert had asked BBWs to get in touch for 'fun without consequences': it stands for Big Beautiful Women and is an Americanism I didn't like at first and never use myself. Better than 'horny fatties', which I swear to you, was written in one of the adverts I had quickly passed over.

He'd answered the phone after three rings with a nice accent and a calmly confident telephone manner that had put me at ease immediately. I was quite charmed. I'd agreed to meet him (he'd told me his name was Clint, but to be fair, I'd told him mine was Lottie) at the old pavilion. The pavilion, which at one point had sold tea and ice creams but was shuttered up and rusting now, was on top of the grassy hill overlooking the bowling green and the children's paddling pool. It seemed stupid to me, to trudge all the way up that hill just to walk down it, but this 'Clint' didn't give me his address over the telephone and it made sense to meet him in a public place first to get a feel for him. It's what I'd always done in the past and my insight into people's characters had never failed me before.

'And how many times have you done this, Annie? What? Hundreds?' Will couldn't hide his disgust. I could see it in him, in the way he looked at the taps and the water draining out of the bath. He wanted to wash again, just in case I'd given him something. I'd never thought of it before.

I'd got off the bus at the little greengrocer's on the corner of Mount Street and looked at my watch. I was early, quite a bit early, so I'd helped myself to an apple and taken a leisurely detour past some little terraced houses with stone steps leading down right into the street. I walked further on past an old church, which was now a nursery. I could see the children through the windows, crying and snatching toys from each other with sticky, grasping little hands. At the bottom of that street there was a big pub. There still is, for all I know. I thought about going in and getting a glass of lemonade but

I really don't like going into new places on my own so I pressed on.

Despite my wanderings, I still had plenty of time to walk as slowly as I liked and stopped to look at the little wishing well at the start of the path before I began to trudge up to the pavilion at the top of the hill. My breasts swung under the flowery fabric of the blouse I was wearing, and under the waistband of my new skirt the smile-shaped scar from the caesarean started to burn and itch even though it was four months old.

It had been raining on and off all the previous night, and although when I got to the top it was dry, low clouds and mist hid most of the sea from me. I read the graffiti on the rusty metal shutters covering the windows of the old pavilion until I smelled smoke and turned to see Clint appearing around the corner.

I knew right away it was him because he'd said he would be coming from work and so would be in a tie and jacket, and he was, and he knew it was me, of course, because there were no other plus-size women hanging about on the top of the hill waiting for it to start drizzling again.

'Lottie?'

I nodded and he lifted his cigarette to his lips. Perhaps he was squinting to keep the smoke out of his eyes but it had the feel of a frank appraisal. I gritted my teeth and appraised right back. Taller than I'd like, if beggars could be choosers, but it wasn't just a tie and a jacket, it was a suit. And a nice shirt: thick cotton, not a super-market one with fabric so thin I could see nipples through it. When he raised his hand to his mouth I saw the glint of something that looked like a cufflink and I started to get excited.

Clint stared back, inhaled, exhaled smoke through his teeth and then smiled.

'Whoa Nelly, there's a lotta Lottie.'

I paused, shrugged and said thank you, because it was a compli-ment of sorts. Some men are clumsy around women, and you can't blame them for it. It's the way they've been brought up. Still, even thinking that, my excitement faded a little, my own smile dried out and I licked my teeth.

'You're nice,' he said, looking at my hips, 'like the third bowl of porridge Blondie-locks had a go at.'

'Excuse me?'

He chuckled, and sketched a shape in the air.

'Just right!'

When he said that, he elongated the vowels, and I knew he'd said it before, to someone else. I wondered how she had responded and how many meetings like this I'd have to endure before I found what I was looking for, sneaking out, thinking of excuses, putting myself through the wringer every single time. I don't like to judge too quickly: so many people do it to me; but unless this man had hidden depths that included a capacity for affection and mutually rewarding conversation, I knew I was likely to be disappointed.

'Sorry,' he said, 'where's my manners?'

He pulled the packet out of his back pocket and flicked it open, 'Ciggy?'

I shook my head.

'Not your brand?'

'I don't smoke, thanks.'

'Fairy muff.'

He laughed at that, and then held out his arm to me in a very old-fashioned gesture.

'Shall we?'

I took it and we walked down the hill towards the crazy golf and the Ferry Café. I thought he was going to take me there and I was getting ready to claim a prior appointment and hurry home. It's a horrible place. They have vinyl tablecloths that are never properly wiped, and there are grey lumps in the sugar bowls. I smiled as we walked past the open door, inhaling a gust of vinegar and chip fat. He took my relief for encouragement and patted my bottom.

'You're younger than I thought. Prettier, too,' he said. 'No, I mean it. I'm pleased. I've had some right dogs through that mag. Tell you they're big, blonde and busty, and they turn out to be flabby and fucking forty.'

They often do that: treat you to a sample of banter just to pass the time between the meet and the bedroom door. I was supposed to say something like, 'I bet you say that to all the gals,' and titter into my cupped hands so it would seem more like a real date. I didn't.

To tell you the truth, I was out of practice. I'd been looking forward to this afternoon, but now I was here and I'd met him the whole occasion had the feeling of returning to school after a long, if uneventful, summer holiday.

'We'll go back to mine if that's all right? I have to be back in the office this afternoon.'

Clint had guided me back to his flat. It was down some stairs and when I looked up through the window and saw only a row of bin bags beyond the railings above I realised we were underground. When cars went past, the glass in the windows rattled and I wondered what it would be like to live like that.

'Check out my chair!' he said. There was a tattered armchair with a tartan blanket tossed over it. 'A proper little lookout post, that is. I should get a periscope!' He laughed, and sounded a bit like Santa Claus.

'It's very nice,' I said. He crossed the room and took off his jacket, hanging it carefully on a hanger then tossing it onto his bed. The whole flat was in one room, an armchair, a bed, a television, a sink and a couple of rings to cook on. You could see everything, could probably touch everything if you stood in the centre of the room. I thought, seeing as there was only one chair, I should leave it for him, so I went and perched at the foot of the bed.

'It's only temporary. I'm waiting for something big at work to come through, then I'm out of here. Do for the time being. I only sleep here.' He sounded apologetic, and I looked up at him. I'd been bending to take off my shoes and he was scooping empty bottles and cups from the coffee table and dropping them into the sink.

'It's cosy,' I said, 'just right for one. And very convenient for the shops.'

'Leave your shoes on. No need for that. Sit in the chair.'

I moved hastily, worrying that I'd been premature. You get into habits, thinking that all of them have done it as many times as you have. Most of the time they have, but every now and again I came across a nervous one who liked to have a bit of a chat first. I didn't mind it. In fact, I preferred it. I retied my shoelaces and perched on the edge of the armchair.

'There you go,' he said, and rubbed his hands together. 'It's good, isn't it?'

I nodded, confused by his enthusiasm.

'Now look up, look up. That's it. What can you see?'

'Outside?' I said, doubtfully. The chair rustled as I shifted, and I moved to pull a crisp packet out from under me. 'The bins?'

'Jesus Christ!' he said cheerfully. 'It's like watching a spastic doing a jigsaw!' He kicked over the debris on the carpet and rushed towards me.

'Look,' he said, putting one hand into my hair and the other around my jaw. He tilted my head back painfully and I yelped. He probably didn't have women back to his house very often, and didn't know about being gentle. Some men don't know their own strength. That's what I thought and did my best to look where he wanted me to.

'Now what can you see? Look, skirt at two o'clock!'

He laughed, pulled my hair again and tipped my head to such an angle I could see the shiny shoes and short skirt of a girl walking past.

'That's a good one,' he said, rubbing the front of his trousers distractedly, 'on or off?'

'What? I don't understand.'

'On or off, I said, genius. It's not hard,' he giggled, and took his hand out of my hair. 'Except it is.'

'I can't tell what you mean,' I said, and stood up because I wanted to leave.

'Knickers, on or off?'

He shouted and pushed me so I fell back into the chair. Once I was leaning back he carried on pushing me but there was nowhere for me to go: the wood that the chair back was made of dug into my spine through the cushions. He didn't stop. The pushes turned into punches and I was so winded I couldn't breathe enough to answer.

'On or off? On or off?' he said, over and over.

He'd marked out the rhythm of what he was asking me with his fists, as if I was too stupid to understand and needed the meaning underlining. There was a bottle or something poking into my thigh and I tried to squirm away. I didn't think he was ever going to stop. It hurt a lot. I'd never been punched like that before. I tried to look at the tasselled edge of the blanket covering the chair but every time he hit me my head moved so eventually I just closed my eyes and put my arms up around my face. After a while he calmed down. His arms must have got tired.

'She's gone now,' he said quietly, 'we'll never know.'

He sat on the arm of the chair to get his breath back, absentmindedly massaging my shoulder so that even if I'd tried to get up, I couldn't have done.

'Prime location, this is. Like my own porn film. They hardly ever have their knickers off though. Hardly ever.'

His knees bumped me and I flinched.

'Perhaps it's a little cold on the seafront,' I said tentatively, 'what with the wind coming off the water, there could be a draught?'

'No!' he roared. 'For Christ's sake!' He stood up.

'You might have more luck in August?' I started to babble, feeling blood run into my eyelashes. I didn't dare wipe it away in case it made him angry, so I ignored it dropping onto my cheek every time I blinked, as hot as tears.

'Or perhaps, seeing as I'm here, I could trot up and down outside for you?'

Of course I wasn't really going to do that. I just wanted to get out. I tried to get hold of my knicker elastic but he pushed my hand away.

'Why is it, each and every single fucking time I meet someone, they just don't get it? They just cannot get what I'm trying to tell them?'

I knew enough by then to keep quiet.

'We had a right piece up there, and you, so bloody stupid you didn't know what I was on about until she was gone. Halfway to Cleveleys now, and what have I got to show for it? A boner and a pig in my lookout post!'

I thought he was finished but he raised his hand and slapped me across one eye, then the other. My teeth clicked against my tongue, my mouth filled with salt and my nose started bleeding. He laughed, then started pulling at my blouse. The buttons popped and I got up and ran.

Will had listened to me intently as I talked, and he hadn't asked any more questions. It had taken me so long to finish the story that when I got to the part where someone kind had noticed me and given me money for a taxi home the bath had emptied and he was shivering.

'I should have asked for his address,' I said, 'it was a twenty-pound note. I should have asked where he lived so I could...'

'What, go round to his house with a smile and a change of clothes?' Will said sharply. He looked at me angrily, saw my face, relented.

'Sorry. Sorry. I didn't mean that. You're lucky, it was kind of him. I know what you meant.'

Water was still dropping from his hair onto his shoulders, making dark spots on the dressing gown.

'Fun without consequences?' he said, and laughed humourlessly. 'That's got to be some kind of joke, hasn't it?'

'I'm never going to do it again,' I said. I wasn't asking for forgiveness, I didn't even consider what was going to happen between us in the future. Everything I thought I knew about how things were between us had been turned upside down. I didn't feel like he loved me anymore, and it was a relief. We could have a proper conversation now, maybe for the first time.

'No, I bet you won't,' he said.

'I'm not,' I insisted. 'I'm tired of it. It's disgusting. I never got what I wanted anyway. Not once.' I thought about Boris. 'It's too disappointing.'

Will stood up and tucked the gown more firmly around his waist.

'I'm surprised you went back to it. I thought you'd ended the affair, when that's what I imagined you were doing. I thought you'd pack it in once we'd started a family.'

His eyes were fixed on the linoleum and he shook his head slowly from side to side. Something seemed to get hold of him then, some invisible hands squeezing him, wringing out his muscles. He bowed his head, shuddered and took a deep, ragged breath.

'It's as if she was never here at all,' he said. 'You, you just pack up her things and carry on the same as you did before.'

I didn't know what to say, so I waited. Somehow, no matter what I told him, no matter what I did or said, it always came down to the baby. There was a second there when I felt he was indifferent enough to me for us to really talk, and then it was gone.

'Is it grief, Annie? Are you depressed? Not coping?' He looked at me hopefully.

I stood up and dropped the flannel into the sink. My ribs felt like they were crunching together as I moved, the broken ends of them rubbing against each other. It was easier to breathe when I stood up, so I leaned against the wall.

'No,' he went on, 'it's not grief, is it? You never wanted her anyway. You love that bloody cat more than you ever loved her. Don't say anything, I know you didn't want her. I thought you'd acclimatise...'

There were a few moments of silence, I still didn't know what to say, although the landscape inside me was shifting, like an underground avalanche or the slow and building friction at the edges of tectonic plates. I'll always remember looking down at the bathroom floor and finding it impossible to tear my eyes away from it and meet his gaze: grey and white and black squares interlocking in a strange sort of pattern that because of the colours and the geometry gave me the impression there wasn't a floor at all, but just a cascade of black cubes and their shadows falling through white space towards the door. Horrible floor, it was: give me a nice carpet any day: you can always put a mat down for when you get out of the bath.

Will pushed past me gently and I heard him go into our bedroom and rustle the sheets as he got into bed. Boris wasn't going to get in touch ever again, and it had become clear in one frightening and violent afternoon that the method I had chosen to search for his replacement held little in the way of success now, or in the future. I thought about my options. I was stuck with Will, I realised, stuck in this beige, empty house, stuck at home with him knowing almost everything that I had done. How else was I going to meet someone?

19

I know Neil had told me to wait, and that he would come to me in his own time but if *I* was finding the wait intolerable, Neil himself must have been experiencing something like a living nightmare. It made me think that perhaps it was my responsibility, no, my *duty*, as his intimate friend, to hasten along the process and free him from Lucy's clutches once and for all. As well as that, I'd been thinking about Boris a lot, about my decision to wait for him to contact me, and where my patience had got me that time. Perhaps Boris wasn't the kind of man who preferred to make the first move, and I thought he was, and had acted accordingly. And look where that landed me. This time, I decided, things were going to be different and I was going to be a little more assertive.

I rechecked the periwinkle on my eyelids, fixed a smudge and was ready to go when I heard a knock at the door. I wasn't surprised at the interruption, fate has a way of making us work hard for the things that we want, and I've come to realise it is so we value our dreams all the more dearly when they finally come to fruition. I opened the door, welcomed Sangita in cheerily, and guided her into the front room.

'Everything all right?' I said. 'I wasn't expecting to see you today, Sangita. How are the boys?' Her hair was in the same plait, but she'd changed her earrings and the sari was blue and green this time, with a swirling pattern along the bottom that made me feel slightly seasick when I looked at it.

'No, I wasn't planning to come around. Just a flying visit.' She swallowed, and shook her head when I brandished the teapot. 'You look nice,' she said, 'were you on your way out somewhere?'

'Not really,' I said, 'just a little date.' I smiled, but she didn't return the smile and I started to worry. I replayed the events of the Friday afternoon in my head and realised that my presence in her home had probably seemed intrusive. In fact, you could say I had overstayed my welcome. A little apology, and all would be well, I was sure of it.

'I know I was a little upset on Friday,' I said. 'It came as such a shock, you see. He wasn't so old, not really, and he's been a great comfort to me in the past few months. I hope I didn't get in the way of anything?'

'What? Oh no,' she said, 'Barry and I were happy to help. We're not animal people ourselves, but, of course, we understand.' She paused, and I offered her tea again.

'No, really,' she said, looking distinctly uncomfortable. 'The thing is, Annie,' she went on, 'I'm here in a more official capacity. It's not about Friday.'

Ah, I thought, 'The Neighbourhood Watch?' She'd probably realised her mistake, and decided the idea of me giving a speech at the next meeting was too good to pass up. I smiled and waited for her to continue.

'In a way, yes, Annie. I try to get to know everyone, make sure they know there's someone they can talk to if there are any problems. You know that.'

'You've been very kind,' I said, getting impatient.

'I notice there was a bit of an incident this morning,' she said, letting her tone rise so I knew it was a question.

'An incident?' I said, knowing full well what she was talking about. Billy and Ada were probably still waiting for a bus somewhere, and they'd be waiting a good while, what with it being a Sunday. I smiled at the thought of their wasted journey, thinking that they'd only done me a favour by hastening the inevitable.

'Some visitors, members of your family perhaps?'

'Perhaps,' I echoed, knowing I was irritating her, forcing her to come right out and ask me, which of course her natural delicacy should have prevented.

'Annie, I think you know what I'm talking about. Half the street was woken up by your bellowing this morning. If there's some trouble, well, I am the person to confide in, you know.'

She leaned back, looking satisfied and smug.

'It is part of my job, a job that I take very seriously.'

'I know you do,' I said, 'and it's a very important job. You hold this community together, everyone can see that.'

'Annie,' she said, exasperated, 'I quite understand you not wanting to go into detail about your private life with everyone you meet, and of course, I was *honoured* that you chose to unburden yourself to *me*,' she paused, tugged at her earrings, and continued, 'but people are saying all kinds of things, there's gossip and rumours flying about, and I can't defend you unless I know all the facts.'

'Gossip?'

Sangita sighed and nodded again.

'They were my late husband's parents,' I admitted. 'They were very upset that I inherited his house, which had been in their family longer than I had. We never saw eye to eye, and I'm afraid I didn't want to discuss financial matters with them in the street.'

'There are some very unsavoury things being talked about, I'm sorry you don't get on well with your in-laws but...'

'They begrudge me the chance of starting again,' I said simply, 'I'm sure you don't.'

'Of course not,' she said quickly, 'and it's not like me to pass on these kinds of rumours but if it was only that, I could overlook it.'

'What else is there?' I said.

'Raymond had a visit from Neil the other day. Said you'd been around to see them, said things got a little heated. Why didn't you mention it? I did ask if you were having any problems. Are things escalating?'

I sighed and shook my head wearily. 'It's all exaggeration, Sangita. A tissue of lies. I was invited round, actually, because Neil had heard about Mr Tips's passing and was deeply concerned about me.'

'Really?' Sangita looked confused. 'Raymond said Lucy was most upset. I hate to say this, but it seems to me like we're dealing with something a little more than the local kids playing pranks, doesn't it?'

'Raymond told you all this?'

'Yes. If it was just Lucy getting hysterical I could ignore it. I have been ignoring it. Giving you the benefit of the doubt. But she's seen you poking about in the back garden, and so has Raymond.'

'I was looking for my cat,' I said, sniffing.

'That may be so, but there's lots of other things that don't add up. You opened her mail. You can't deny it. She showed me the envelopes stuffed into the hedge.'

'The postman must have made a mistake. What would I want with her silly catalogues and credit card bills?'

'And screaming after Raymond in the street? Not to mention the little fracas this morning. Just what is going on here?'

'Sangita,' I began warmly, 'you're not going to tell me that one complaint from Raymond, of all people, has changed your mind about me? That suddenly what was Lucy's overactive imagination getting out of hand is all gospel truth? Because of *Raymond*?'

'I've known Raymond longer than I've known you,' she said pointedly, and I felt like an outsider again.

'It was my cat that died,' I said. 'I didn't run him down myself just to have something to upset Lucy with.'

'But you said she did it!'

'I don't know that she didn't.'

'She doesn't drive!'

'She doesn't have a licence,' I said, 'and that's different. I'm sure she's picked up the rudiments from Neil.'

'Annie, I'm shocked at you. You've been through a lot, I know you have. But this? I just can't...' she let her words tail away and her fingers plucked the air. 'I want to hear your side of the story, I really do. But you can't just harass people in the street.'

I paused, remembering what Raymond had said to me about Sangita. It was just possible he had a point, and she didn't have any right at all to set herself up over me, to ask me questions like this.

'To be honest, Sangita, I'm not sure what business my private life is of yours.' She blushed, and started playing with the end of her plait. It annoyed me. Made me want to bat it out of her hands like she was a child.

'I take my role in the community very seriously,' she said, 'and I know people laugh at me for it. I know they do. But what's wrong with wanting to improve where you live? Neil wasn't going to come to me himself, he isn't a member of the Neighbourhood Watch and Raymond isn't either, but the fact that he came to me in spite of that, well, he must be quite concerned. He said, well, Raymond seems to have the idea that you've got some vendetta against Lucy, and Neil just can't see it.'

'Really,' I said disbelievingly.

'You've got to admit, something about all this just doesn't add up. Raymond was still convinced you had a daughter that Liam could play with the next time she came to visit. Did you tell him that?'

'No, I didn't,' I answered truthfully. 'We both know it isn't possible, and why would I go and make a promise that I couldn't keep?'

I was starting to feel like I was at a police station, talking into a tape recorder.

'I know Lucy isn't the easiest person in the world to get on with,' she started again, 'I know you've tried with her. But I just didn't realise how upset she was. She's taken time off work. Raymond seems to think she's genuinely frightened of you now. She thinks you have absolutely no idea what's wrong with taking a dress off the line, rooting through her wheelie bin, pulling the flowers out of her lawn. Did you do those things?'

'That's what Raymond told you? I can't say I'm surprised, I really can't. He would say that, wouldn't he?' I got up to go into the kitchen, wishing Sangita would just accept some tea so I would have something to do with myself. My blood was raging in my temples and for a moment I felt quite annoyed with Raymond: he was obviously bitter and embarrassed that I had rejected his advances, and his wish to get his revenge on me had overshadowed the sense of loyalty he should have had towards Neil.

'Yes. He's worried sick. I know it's hard to tell, but he thinks the world of Neil. Looks up to him almost.'

'Trying to stir trouble for his own benefit, more likely,' I said.

'I'm not quite sure I get what you mean, Annie. Raymond's a very down to earth kind of man.'

'Yes, I'm sure he comes across like that,' I said. 'I don't know him myself, but I know enough to realise he's got motives.'

'Motives?'

'Reasons for wanting me to look bad and lose friends.'

'This is all sounding quite…'

'Look, can I talk to you confidentially?' I said, deciding on impulse to change tack. Things were coming to the end now, I could feel it, and I could afford to act drastically, knowing that in a few days none of this would matter. I didn't have anything to lose. Billy and Ada knew where I lived so at some point Neil and I would be moving on anyway.

'Why of course,' she leaned forward. Neil didn't need Lucy, and he certainly didn't need Raymond either, I would be more than enough and once he'd heard about what Raymond had tried to do to me, he would be so angry that cutting him out of our lives would be the only logical thing to do.

'When I moved in here I made it my first priority to get to know my neighbours. I'm sure you'll agree, it is important for everyone in a community to pull together as friends.'

'Of course,' Sangita said impatiently, 'but – '

I went on, 'Well, that was all I wanted. I never expected it to turn into anything more. But even though we've both tried to fight it, Neil and I have discovered we share a special connection with each other. There's been nothing as tacky as an affair, I can assure you, but Neil, probably out of sheer concern for Lucy and her future happiness, confided his feelings to Raymond and probably asked him for a bit of advice, man to man, so to speak.'

Sangita didn't reply at first, and although I'm sure I was mistaken, I felt her glance at me, a snaky look slither from my feet to my rounded shoulders and back again.

'Are you sure about all this, Annie? Neil and Lucy have been living together for over a year now. We all had our doubts when she first arrived, given her age, but they seem to be making a go of it.'

The fact she didn't believe me at first showed just how successful Neil and I had been at keeping it all locked inside and hidden away from the prying eyes of the world until the time was right.

'Yes, of course I'm sure. What do you take me for? I know it isn't ideal – in fact, Neil and I are both well aware a certain amount of distress is going to occur before we can take this any further. That, no doubt, is exactly why he turned to Raymond. He's a sensitive man and he probably needed a good friend to confide in. He wouldn't want to burden me with his worry, because that's what he's like. So he popped out to chat to someone he believed was a close and loyal friend. Who instantly, probably because of his own desires, he is a single man, remember, went to Lucy. Now they're both in league against me. All I can do is be patient, keep calm and rise above it.'

Sangita paused, then shook her head. I noticed there was a smudge of flour in her eyebrow and knew she'd been baking again.

'You mean *Neil* is the man you've been seeing?' She started to laugh, then looked at me, stopped, and shook her head again: 'Neil who lives next door to you with Lucy, Neil? Are you sure?'

'Yes,' I said.

It was a while before Sangita spoke, and I sat patiently, tracing the pattern on the armchair protectors with my eyes.

'We've met before,' I said, 'a good while before I decided to move here. He helped me once and I've never forgotten it. I was in trouble and who knows what would have happened to me if he hadn't stepped in.'

'And so you moved here to be with him?'

'I didn't know he would be my neighbour when I bought the house,' I said, smiling. 'It sounds mad, doesn't it? I just wanted to live somewhere nice and quiet where I could meet some new friends, get myself together and maybe, in the future, meet someone new. And then when I saw who I'd moved in next to, I realised it must have been meant to be. A sign.'

Sangita frowned.

'Like you being the one to help Barry in the library,' I explained. 'Sometimes there's more to a coincidence than meets the eye.'

'And Neil...'

'He's very shy,' I said, 'and like many men, he's not all that comfortable discussing his feelings. He manages to get the message across in his own way. He's gone out of his way to help me a few times since I've been living here. Things developed from there,' I said, 'and we have a lot to look forward to. That's why all these little rumours,' I waved them away with a flick of my hand, 'don't tend to bother me that much. What Neil and I have found is rare and people are bound to be jealous.'

Sangita had remained silent while I was speaking, worrying at a little mark on the front of her sari with her fingernail. When I stopped talking, she looked at me frowning and shook her head. She wasn't rude to me, or unkind, but I could tell that our friendship was never going to be the same again and it saddened me, even though if I'd been asked to make the choice, I would have been happy to sacrifice it in a second.

'You know I'm not Lucy's greatest fan, Annie, and of course, they aren't actually married, but, well, surely you can't think pursuing Neil is…?'

I shrugged. 'These things never run smoothly, in my experience. And we all deserve a bit of happiness, don't we? I've tried to behave with dignity, but with Raymond and Lucy stooping to spreading rumours, trying to make me out to be some kind of violent lunatic …' I laughed the way people do when they aren't really amused but want to underline the pathetic ridiculousness of something.

'They've hurt me, they really have. With Mr Tips gone – you saw the state I was in. To be honest, I'm shocked you'd want to question me on it.'

'Annie, I don't know what to say,' she stood up. 'I was planning to see Lucy this afternoon, to talk to her in person. Try to mediate a little. She's been talking about going to the police and having you charged with harassment. When she came to me that first time I thought she was being ridiculous, but the poor thing, she probably doesn't know what to do with herself or where else to turn.'

I interrupted her. 'Why don't you go around now,' I said, talking quickly because I'd had a stroke of inspiration, 'she's in, I heard her hairdryer this morning. Take her out for a coffee. Try to cheer her up a bit and get to the bottom of it all.' I shrugged and opened my fingers wide, 'I don't mind you talking to her. I know I've got nothing to hide, and she's going to need a lot of support. I only wish I could be the one to give it to her, but she's taken against me right from the very beginning.'

Sangita stood up and frowned. 'I'll do that,' she said, curtly. 'I'll go and see her right now. Talk to her in private. She should know what's going on. We may not have much in common, Lucy and I, but I can't condone this, this, *arrangement* you've made with Neil. It isn't fair.' She rolled every single 'r' in that sentence, as I remember, heading for the door as she was saying it.

'I don't know who to believe,' she went on, her hand on her hip. I think she was really enjoying herself. 'Losing someone is hard, and we're all lucky enough not to be able to realise just how hard it is. But I don't know what to think.'

'Talk to Lucy then,' I said nonchalantly. 'Go and see her now.'

Sangita left without saying much of a goodbye, and I hadn't even made my way back into the sitting room before I heard her rap urgently on Neil's front door. Far from being angry, I was relieved she was out of my way and I prided myself on my quick thinking in engineering Lucy's absence from the house.

There was a time not so far in the past when a situation like that would have quite flummoxed me, and under pressure, I would have become flustered. Despite the passing of Mr Tips, an exhausting night and a worrying couple of days, I'd handled everything perfectly and this was evidence that I'd obviously come quite some way. I knew Neil would be pleased about my development and, of course, at the opportunity I had created for us. It couldn't really have gone any better.

I spent a few minutes doing a little light housework while I waited for Sangita and Lucy to leave. I even got out a rag and started to clean the front windows. As I worked at the finger marks on the glass I kept an eye on the path. Sangita must have been in the house five minutes or so, maybe less, and when she emerged it was with Lucy.

They were both wearing their coats and carrying shiny leather handbags. Without the slightest glance in my direction (I would have been clearly visible standing with my net curtains gathered around me like a veil) they went down the path and walked in the direction of town.

Their heads were bowed together in conversation, and I could tell by her fluttering hands and flexing eyebrows that Lucy was already getting herself worked up. Sangita was nodding so much she looked like a very serious version of the amusing dashboard ornament shaped like a dog Will had bought for his car. They disappeared around the corner and I smiled, abandoned the damp rag and vinegar bottle on the windowsill, and went into the kitchen to wash my hands.

20

Now I may be many things, but I am not stupid. When I knocked on Neil's front door that afternoon I was not expecting him to welcome me with open arms. I am a realist, and I did accept that he would be disappointed to hear I had unburdened myself on Sangita, and that before he had completed his preparations, Lucy would be aware of our plans. The thought that Sangita would be, even as I knocked, informing Lucy of the changes ahead spurred me on and obliterated any nervousness I may have felt about approaching him uninvited. I was confident that I could use what little time we had alone with each other to explain my motivations, and that he would understand them. Such were my thoughts – so imagine my frustration and confusion when, after ten minutes of repeated hammering on both door and windows, he did not arrive to let me in!

Neil is not a vindictive man, nor does he play games with people. Perhaps he had taken a tumble down the stairs. Maybe he was lying behind the very door on which I pounded, weakly raising his hand to the letter box, and yet unable to make a sound to call for help. He could have tripped with his feet hopelessly tangled in the strap of an abandoned handbag. He could have slipped in a puddle of rose-scented bathwater and dashed his head on the basin. A knife might have fallen from its rack. People are so delicate, so easily damaged: the possibilities raced through my mind like motorway traffic.

Before I had time to think about it, I went back into my own house, put the brass wheelbarrow from the windowsill into my pocket, and used the method I have already described with the wheelie bin to gain entry into his back garden.

I was hoping the back door would be open, but when I tried the handle I found it locked. I wasted no time in doing my duty, and used the wheelbarrow to break the window in the back door. The glass fell onto the kitchen floor with a noise like the patter of dropped coins and I held my breath but no one came. I wrapped the sleeve of my cardigan around my hand and poked it through the jagged hole in the pane to push back the snib. My throat felt like it was slowly being filled with sand and my damp fingers slid clumsily about on the door handle. After several attempts, I opened it and stepped inside on legs that almost refused to bear my weight.

I cried out for him once and receiving no answer, moved on quickly, leaving the wheelbarrow on the kitchen table and pacing through the whole of the downstairs calling his name in a most distressed manner. The kitchen smelled like burned toast, and there was a pan soaking in the sink. (Scrambled egg, if I remember correctly: evidently it isn't just me who finds it a trial to get the pans sparkling after a cooked breakfast!)

I quickly ascertained Neil was not downstairs and if he had been taken ill he had managed to climb into his own bed. Obviously, that's where my footsteps took me next. My thoughts at the time were completely centred on him and his possible state of health, although I must admit, fluttering at the periphery of my concern was a mild curiosity. The unfortunate event of Neil's injury had forced me to act in the way I did and it was an unexpected bonus to see the upstairs of his house, his private space, as it were, and especially his bedroom. People are more themselves in their private spaces than they are when they are out in the world and a glimpse into Neil's personal space was going to intensify our knowing of each other in a way that maybe nothing else would.

But as I said, these concerns were minor. Side effects and nothing more. Any observant and attentive neighbour would have acted as I did (*someone* must have forced entry into my father's last abode), never mind an important friend on whom, it can be assumed, special privileges had been bestowed. I saw my hand running along the banister, my feet on the steps, and held my breath to listen for any muffled groans of pain or cries for assistance. Nothing.

The first room I entered, the largest bedroom and the equivalent of my own, didn't have a bed in it at all. I was shocked. For so long I had imagined us lying close together, divided only by a ruler's length of brick, paper and emulsion. I glanced around it only briefly, enough to see a large table, a sofa and a computer. Obviously an office. More importantly, Neil was not in it. I went into the second bedroom quickly, pushed open the door and called his name.

I'd expected something more masculine, but the room was done out in pinks and purples, the walls painted lilac and stencilled haphazardly with white leaves. It reeked of hairspray. My voice bounced around the silver light fittings and no one replied. The master bedroom, and Neil was not in it. I stood for a moment, puzzled. It only took a second's thought for it all to become clear to me, and I began to feel foolish. Neil must have gone out while Sangita and I were talking – my usually observant eye had been distracted, even as I had been praising myself on my quick thinking.

There was a pair of candles in frosted glass holders on the windowsill, and I stared at them, blushing. What a fix! While it was true that there was no one present to witness my impulsiveness and mock me for my mistaken conclusions, the evidence of the broken pane in the door would have to be explained sooner or later. I looked around again, just to make sure. The bed was larger than mine, a king-size perhaps, and the duvet was pulled back neatly. It was white, covered in lilac swirls and marred here and there by Lucy's stray and curling hairs. The sight of it sickened me a little, and I brushed them away, wiping my palm against my leg afterwards. Who could tell what suffering and misery this neatly made bed had been the site of?

It struck me as I plumped the pillows that Neil would return home first. It may not have been the most traditional gesture to pass between putative companions, but surely the broken window would be proof of my deep-rooted investment in his well-being? Someone who did not care would not have done what I did. Very possibly, Neil was finding Lucy's continued influence more and more distressing, and had fled the building for some much needed space and solitude. How happy he would be to find me here waiting for him when he returned!

There was a dressing table under the window and I went and sat at it. I needed a few seconds to compose myself but the mirrors were unnecessarily large, and reflected both sides of my head as well as my face. It didn't help and only served to make me think about Lucy twiddling with her fringe or scraping at her skin before bed. Can you believe she had three hair brushes? Three! There was a glass pot full of bobbles, a whole drawer full of make-up, and another one crammed with bottles of perfume. The scents clashed, urine-coloured and poisonous, and it was as if Lucy herself was in the room wafting her fragrance about and advising me against frosted eye make-up.

In the perfume drawer, stuffed right in at the back, I found something nasty and sexual. It was both unnatural and an insult to Neil, but if I was the sort of person who wondered about such things, the existence of it amongst her possessions would not have surprised me. I unfolded my handkerchief and picked it up, shuddering. The correct course of action was indisputable, so I made a hammock out of my hankie, held the thing at arm's length and took it into the bathroom. It was so pink it was almost neon and shot through with flecks of silver glitter. If I'd been able to stomach cupping my hands around it and bringing it to my face I'm sure I would have seen it was designed to glow in the dark – perhaps as an aid to the myopic. Otherwise, it was a lifelike replica of what it was intended to represent. The fact that Lucy felt she had need of it should have been a comfort, but my bile was rising and I wanted to get rid of the thing.

I'd planned to flush it down the lavatory because that's where it belonged but its length prevented me. I flushed several times, each time averting my eyes as I waited for the cistern to refill, but it was no good. The thing had wedged itself into the U-bend and glared garishly at me from where it protruded out of the water. It seemed to shimmer, wet and smug, so I turned my back and slammed the lid on it in justifiable disgust.

The first rule of battle is to know your enemy: that's how I was thinking of it then. Lucy had completely taken over Neil's home, poor man. A man's house should be a haven for him, and even a newcomer like me could see that the sanctuary of his own bedroom had been completely cluttered with her detritus. No wonder he had fled. I needed to do something about it. At that very moment Lucy would be sipping frothy coffee with Sangita, trying on dresses, or loitering at perfume counters, testing lipsticks and giggling dumbly. In all probability she was spending his money on more things to stuff into his house. The lines were shifting, and it would have been foolish of me not to take advantage of the circumstances life had dropped into my lap.

There were two wardrobes in the bedroom: one fitted into each of the alcoves either side of the bed. I opened one to a row of shirts and trousers, three pairs of trainers neatly lined up along the bottom, and a stack of magazines about computer games on the shelf at the top. There was nothing personal on the shelves, not even hidden away at the back, but Neil was a private man and wouldn't leave the keys to his personality lying in a cupboard for Lucy to find.

When I walked around the bed and opened Lucy's wardrobe a pile of fluffy sweaters and chiffon scarves tumbled down on me. It was as if Lucy herself was batting at my head and shoulders, not just the contents of her overstuffed wardrobe, and I brushed the trailing sleeves aside and let them fall to the floor. The inside of the doors were covered in articles she'd snipped from magazines about good grooming. The overexposed face of a blonde, overfed child stared back at me from a row of curling photographs. Some unfortunate relative of hers, no doubt. I knelt to count her shoes, jumbled up together in a Perspex box at the bottom of the wardrobe and over-flowing into a crooked row under her side of the bed.

When my mother died, my father went into the shed and brought out a sheaf of flattened cardboard boxes, which he proceeded to reassemble with a roll of brown tape bought especially for the purpose. When he'd done that, he collected every last scrap of her clothing, all the photographs and magazines, her cookery books, knitting patterns, sewing machine and her collection of owl ornaments and packed them away. Some of the boxes had been in the shed for too long and were sticky with cobwebs or speckled with blue and grey tidemarks of mould. They smelled old, like damp towels.

I watched my father load the boxes into the Land Rover, at that point not knowing that she'd gone, and only thinking that she was going to be in hospital a very long time before getting better. My father was kindly taking her everything she would need to make a home from home, never mind the privation the absence of these things would cause to those who were waiting for her to get better and come back.

Of course I never saw my mother, or any of her things again and while I do not know what my father did with them I have to admit that removing evidence of her from the house was probably the wisest course of action available to him in the circumstances. I say this because the following weeks were difficult ones, but who knows how much more difficult they would have been if every time I opened a cupboard or bent to remove something from the washing machine, I was faced with the remains of a person who was not there any more? Better to have a gap, and get used to it being there, than lull yourself into comfort with the relics and reminders of someone who was certainly never going to need twenty-nine clay owls (twelve of them hand-made by myself) ever again.

I looked inside Lucy's wardrobe, and knew instantly what I had to do in order to free Neil from her influence once and for all. I'd been selfish, thinking that it was I who needed rescuing. Now I'd seen the faults of my reasoning I could very easily rescue Neil, knowing that he would thank me for it, just as I had come to, if not thank, then at least accept that my father had known best. I had once made a fresh start, and now that Neil was in need of one, who better to provide the firm helping hand than someone who knew just what was required?

The woollen things were the hardest to destroy, but once I'd taken my cardigan off, found a pair of kitchen scissors and got into a rhythm, I managed to work my way through the entire contents of the wardrobe, including the shoes, in no time at all. The pile of tattered fabric on the bed pleased me enormously. I spent a lot of time running my fingers through the frayed strips and scraps of leather, smelling fabric softener and stale perfume and wondering if I should leave it where it was, or throw the whole lot out of the window to flutter down onto the lawn in a cascade of broken colours. Leave it where it is, I told myself, and decide later: you've a lot to get through.

The dressing table was easy. I broke the mirrors against the windowsill, and cracked the thin wooden frames in my hands. I didn't even get a splinter. Next, I emptied the lotions and perfumes onto the growing pile on the bed and cut all the bobbles in half. I even snipped the bristles out of the hair brushes! Down the side of the table there was a pile of books – mainly gardening books adapted from television programmes, something on *feng shui* and a few large books on interior design. I ripped all the pages out and let them flutter where they liked.

Under the bed, there were more shoes, a cardboard box and a

stack of magazines. I dealt with the shoes, snipping straps and removing buckles and laces as appropriate, then, my arms aching, sat down on the floor and looked into the box. It was rubbish. Old baby clothes, photographs, school exercise books and a pink diary with a gold clasp and a picture of a horse on the front. The pages inside were pink too, and filled with loopy childish handwriting. She was a little hoarder, and materialism is one of the top five personality flaws so I felt nothing but satisfaction as I got rid of the lot. I tore the faded baby clothes down the seams and snipped out the appliquéd bears and bumblebees with my scissors. A stack of letters went the same way, and the eighties Christmas Polaroids that were difficult to tear were cut into four and the pieces dropped into the lavatory until the heap of them obscured what was already there.

Finally, I moved onto the glossies. I sat on the floor with my back against the bed and flicked through them. The magazines had titles like *Your Home and Garden, Beautiful Living* and *Modern Housekeeping*. I glanced at the pictures of new sofas and bookshelves and potted plants, and ripped out the pages one by one. Because it was easier on the wrists and killed two birds with just the one stone, I obliterated some of the text with her lipsticks.

The magazines at the bottom of the pile were newer than the ones on the top, and the subject matter changed as I worked further down. Lucy had hidden those secret, telling publications under a stack of more innocuous ones so that Neil would remain unaware of the intricacy of her planning. Would you believe that each copy of *Bride Magazine, You and Your Wedding,* and *Something New* cost, on average, four pounds, and that she had bought each of these monthly publications since the previous autumn? When you tot up what that amounts to, you can very easily see why Neil was always so tired and preoccupied with his work.

Perhaps it was the stinging fog of perfume that filled the room, or a symptom of my physical exertion, but as I stared at the shining pages, the pictures of skinny girls in white dresses modelling the best way to have a 'fairy tale' this or a 'once in a lifetime' that started to blur and I had to move away and wipe my eyes. I screwed each picture up into a tight ball and carried them in my skirt to the bathroom. There was hardly room for all of them in the pan, and I had to poke at it all with the lavatory brush. When I flushed, the water gurgled out onto the floor, sounding like a stomach. It pleased me to use Lucy's dressing gown to soak it up and save it making a damp patch on the ceiling downstairs.

I was tired, of course I was. I'd much rather have gone home and had a cup of tea, perhaps opened a packet of bourbons and watched an afternoon soap. I'd probably been in that bedroom for two hours, and hadn't even started downstairs yet. The thing is, I'd decided already that Neil needed help, that I was the person to help him, and for his own good all traces of the woman had to be removed from his home. How else would he have room to think? How else would he have room for me? It didn't matter that my neck was aching, my backside going numb. I had a duty, and I was determined to see it through for his sake, no matter what temporary discomfort it caused me. The more thorough I was, the swifter and more complete Neil's recovery would be.

I thought I'd got all of the magazines, but when I returned for one last check under the bed I saw I had missed the last one. Right at the very bottom of the pile and pressed into an oblong dint in the carpet with the weight of what had lain on top of it was the worst thing of all. *Mother and Baby Monthly*.

Mother and Baby Monthly! After what she'd said in my very kitchen – no children, no children, my foot! I giggled, I was so shocked, which is a strange thing to say, but it truly was the most telling evidence of her perfidy I had seen yet and the sight of it quite unhinged me. Indeed you could say it destroyed my ability to think rationally. Clearly, I'd arrived just in time: Lucy was planning to trap Neil using the most old-fashioned of methods. If she was allowed the time to be successful the consequences would be disastrous for us all.

I pulled it out and flicked through the pages. The titles of the articles were laughable. 'Hassle Free Conception', 'Quick Snacks for Sore Backs', 'Positions for Pregnancy', – it was disgusting. I'd only just got started, my cheeks still hot with indignation, when I heard the click of the front door opening and stopped. I looked around at the mess and held my breath. Neil, back to his newly cleansed bedroom? I imagined his gratitude and relief, straightened my skirt and made for the door.

My foot was on the top step when I heard the voices, and I paused, then stepped back. It was Lucy, and she wasn't alone, but talking to someone.

'...something fishy about her from the beginning. Neil won't have it – he thinks it's all in my head. I reckon he just can't be bothered with a confrontation...'

I leaned over the banister so I could hear her better. In the scale of things, gossiping is much worse than eavesdropping, and as she was spouting forth about me, you could say I had a right to listen in and prepare myself for her next move.

'Men, they never want to face up to the truth, do they?' the second voice floated back to me, Sangita – they were back from shopping already! They were standing chatting in the hall while they removed their coats. The time had got away from me.

'I've told him to have a word – to stick up for me a bit, but I don't think he will, you know. We're even arguing about it now, about *her*, for Christ's sake!' Lucy laughed, as if the very idea that I could be important enough to cause conflict between her and Neil was hysterical.

Well the joke was on her because, clearly, she was wrong.

'... tell him what I know, the whole lot,' Sangita chipped in.

Why had I never noticed that self-congratulatory tone in her voice before? To listen to her talk, you'd think she was Lucy's best friend and not mine. I'm obviously one of those people who assume that everyone deals with the world as straightforwardly and honestly as I do, and in doing so, I'd underestimated Sangita. The promise of gossip had lured her away from me and I was sorrowful, but resigned.

'He trusts Raymond. He'll listen to me,' she went on, 'and once we get him on side, we'll go to Charlie and get him involved. He'll be able to find out what she's been in jail for,' she added.

'Probably shop-lifting,' Lucy said, 'nicking cream cakes from supermarkets. Shoving fairy cakes down her top to feed her imaginary friends.'

They laughed and Sangita said something I didn't catch.

'...in-laws can't stand her! You should have heard the shouting,' Lucy said.

'I wish I had, but you can report it to Charlie. He'll sort it out and have a strong word with her, at the very least. I can act in an advisory capacity, of course, and as your community representative... sure there's something he can charge her with.'

'Yes,' Lucy said calmly. 'It's a shame it's gone this far, but she hasn't left us with any choice. I almost feel sorry for her...'

'... too forgiving...'

'... really thinks they're going to run away together?'

Lucy cackled suddenly. I could hear her sucking at the air with her horsy nostrils, panting out laughter like a dog.

Sangita giggled, 'I couldn't keep my face straight,' she said, 'she's got it all worked out. Still, with a figure like hers, she might as well have a good daydream.'

'... good of you to come back with me,' Lucy said, and their voices grew nearer: out of the hallway now, and into the living room.

'I don't want to get into another row with Neil about it. You know when I told him about the letters in the hedge he looked at me like I'd gone mad. You girls sort this out yourselves, he said, like it was nothing to do with him. He really thinks I'm making it all up.'

There was more rustling – the sound of carrier bags – I twiddled the scissors around in my hands nervously and waited.

'He'll believe you now,' Sangita said, 'where is he? I'll talk to him. He'll listen. He's hardly going to back her up, is he? When it comes down to it, he *loves* you.'

'Neil?' Lucy's voice bounced up the stairs, dangerously loud. 'Neeeeeil!'

No answer. Well he wasn't there and I was hardly going to step down the stairs in his place, was I?

'I don't think he's here, San,' she said, apologetically.

'Boys will be boys,' Sangita replied. 'You'll have to keep a tighter leash on him – him and that Raymond.'

'They're terrible, aren't they? You'll come round tomorrow though? Shall I ring you?'

Their voices evaporated: Lucy was taking Sangita to the door and seeing her out. When I heard it slam and Lucy's footsteps approach the foot of the stairs, I tiptoed back into Neil's bedroom to wait. Perhaps a chat on my own with her would be sufficient for my purposes. I leaned against the wall and waited, watching my move-ment flicker across the scythe-shaped fragments of mirror on the carpet.

It wasn't long before I heard her come bounding up the stairs, humming to herself contentedly. She went straight into the bath-room and the door hadn't settled on its hinges before I heard her breathe in, and then let it all out again in a little sob.

I braced myself as she rushed into the bedroom but she didn't see me because of my position behind the door. I wondered if I should step forward, but all the things on the bed had already claimed her attention. Like I said, she was a shameless materialist. She swept her hands over the crumpled paper, picked up a fragment of frayed silk and then found one of the bumblebees. She frowned, as if she wasn't quite sure what it was, then put her hand over her mouth.

Silent for a few seconds, looking at that bee, then a screeching noise, like air escaping from a balloon. She talked to herself a bit, although I couldn't make sense of what she was saying. She put both her hands over her face like she was starting a game of peek-a-boo. Tears slid between her fingers and her knees were shaking so much I thought she would fall over. This went on for several seconds, during which time I stood awkwardly, not quite sure what to do with myself.

In the end I cleared my throat – she jerked her hands away from her face and snapped her head backwards. She squeaked again as she turned, but to be fair, I had probably startled her.

'And you're *still* here?' she said, shivering all over in some kind of hysterical seizure. 'What have I ever done to you?' she wiped her eyes and pulled her shoulders back. 'This is what you wanted to see?' Her mascara had run – looked like spiders on her cheeks. I kept quite still.

'That's it,' she said, 'I'm calling the police. Get out!'

She turned her back on me and hurried down the stairs. I fol-lowed her as quickly as I could but by the time I entered the front room she was already holding the phone in her palm, a tiny silver pellet with a round green screen like a bubble.

'Don't you dare!' I said, and poked her in the side. My main aim was to make her drop the telephone, settle down and listen to me.

I had even planned to offer her the use of my own suitcases, such was my determination to be fair-minded and human in what was a stressful situation for all of us.

'Oh!' she said, rather comically too, to my mind. The little poke had its desired effect. She dropped the phone and it clattered to the floor. We both watched it slide over the boards and rest under the coffee table. I went over to it and stamped it, hurting my ankle slightly as I did so.

'Police, my foot!' I said, and advanced on her. She shrank back a little, her eyes and mouth still round with shock.

'Close your mouth,' I said, 'you'll catch a fly.'

Lucy didn't say anything, just hunched over her hands, then crumpled over and knelt on the floor.

'There are some changes afoot, missy. There was plenty of time for you to see which way the wind was blowing. Your stubbornness has left me with no choice but to act.'

Lucy scrabbled at the floor with her fingernails in her attempt to get back on her feet and I saw the edge of one of the boards catch and ruin her manicure.

'Bride magazines! Babies! Ornamental bamboo for your new conservatory! Are you mad? Haven't you been listening to Neil at all? What makes you think that you deserve any of those nice things?'

Lucy still didn't say anything, so I prodded her with my foot. She leaned over, put one of her hands on the floor, then lay down completely.

'Just like you,' I said, 'just like you! Get up!'

'Annie,' she said softly, 'I can't.'

I leaned over her, intending to give her another prod, but then I saw the wet smeared on the floor and I realised she'd hurt herself as she fell. A scrape to her knee, or a loose nail to her thigh. Something minor, no doubt, but I could see she was going to make a meal out of it. I paused, wondering what to do next.

'I'll help you up,' I said, and I did. I lifted her up under the arms and hauled her over to the couch – didn't even think about the mess it was making of my own outfit. No point giving her an excuse to get hysterical. She lay down, her hands clamped against the tear in her blouse.

'You need to get a doctor for me,' she gasped. 'An ambulance. Please, Annie.'

'Nonsense,' I said, recovering. She nearly had me for a minute! 'You've just taken a spill. I'll get you a wet flannel and you'll be fine.'

I went into the kitchen and wet a tea towel at the sink then left it on the draining board while I made myself and her a cup of tea. The kitchen was clean and well appointed, and it didn't take me long to find everything that I needed, although from the sounds of Lucy's whining you'd have thought I'd been in there for hours.

'Shoes like that,' I said firmly, handing her the flannel and pointing towards one of her heels. It was lying on its side under the coffee table. 'No wonder you toppled. They aren't safe. You want to get yourself some sensible pumps, like mine. Maybe it's time for *you* to update your *look*!'

I laughed but she just closed her eyes and I noticed she was quite ashen.

'You're not going to have any tea?' I said. 'I put sugar in it.'

She opened her eyes but didn't answer.

'Fine,' I said. 'I think you'll find me a little harder to manipulate than Neil, young lady. You lie there and feel sorry for yourself all you like. I'm going to drink my tea.'

Lucy lay there looking at the ceiling for a few minutes longer. When she closed her eyes I kept watching her. I sipped my tea warily, standing over her and waiting for a trick of some kind. She was sweating, and her hair stuck to her forehead in damp straggly ribbons which made her look much younger than she did when she was in heels and skirts and make-up. After a few more minutes, I pushed the coffee table closer to her so she could reach her tea, and went into the kitchen to fetch her a biscuit.

Neil didn't come back for another half hour, which in some respects was good because it gave me time to think.

21

Will had gone into the bedroom that day and left me standing alone in the bathroom. I'd contemplated the reddened flannel lying in the sink, his bathwater draining down the plug hole. Waited, watching those tumbling squares on the linoleum. I could have stood there for hours but I heard him cough next door and before I knew what I was doing my feet had moved and I was going in after him.

He was lying down on the bed with his eyes closed and it looked like he was asleep, except water was coming out from under his eyelashes and running into his ears. Something to do with the way the dark green of his dressing gown jarred against the yellow and orange sunflowers on the quilt cover made my head throb. I wiped the back of my hand across my nose to see if it was still bleeding, but it had stopped. When I coughed, my ribs hurt.

I shuffled and when Will didn't say anything I went and lay next to him.

'I can't sleep in here anymore,' he said eventually, the loudness of his voice in the quiet room startling me.

'I can't be in this bed. Not after Grace. I came in here just now because I felt so tired I just wanted to close my eyes and sleep so I wouldn't have to think about it for an hour. But as soon as I lay down...' he stopped, and I felt his shoulders judder against my breasts.

'I know it's silly, me being on the couch these past two months. I can't face lying down so close to where it happened,' he spoke quickly and without emphasis, as if he was reading the words from a piece of paper. 'I don't think it's going to get better than this,' he said, and I could feel his ribs move under my hands as he sighed and sank further into the duvet.

He hadn't slept with me for a good while, it was true. I hadn't missed it: it was nice to be able to read late into the night and have the whole bed to myself, but fitting our knees together like that, feeling his narrow hip resting against my stomach; it was oddly comforting. Our bed clearly didn't hold the same resonance for me as it did for him.

He'd woken first and I'd only opened my eyes to the sound of him screaming. I'd been thick-headed with sleep, surfacing from a vivid, zigzagging dream about a bouncy castle and croaked at him to shut up. I screwed my eyes closed again and reached behind me to prod him, but he wasn't there and then I was awake properly, eyes opening to see him kneeling up at the end of the bed holding the baby, her limp limbs trailing over his forearm. He was shaking her, and because he was forgetting to put her neck into the crook of his elbow, her head was lolling backwards and forwards. He screamed until his voice cracked. I didn't know what he was saying until I had a minute to think about it afterwards. Something about her being old, which was ridiculous: she was just three months, couldn't even sit up on her own yet. When I understood, it made me feel sick. He was saying she was cold.

Will moved around to face me, his knees bumped mine and it felt strange, to be lying down in bed with him in the middle of the day. He touched my nose with his thumb, brushed it against my bruised lips, smiled and started to cry again. His breath smelled like coffee.

'Let's get a new bed,' he said desperately, as if it was up to me and I was going to say no. 'Shall we? The best there is?' He laughed, a high-pitched hooting noise that scared me. 'A four-poster one if you like, with pink and white princess curtains for you!'

'If you like,' I said. I'd asked him for a four-poster with pink and white curtains when I was eighteen and had seen a picture of one in a glossy magazine. He'd laughed, rubbed my hair and told me there wasn't anything wrong with the one we had.

'You still want to? Then I can come and sleep with you again?' He was excited, his words tripping over each other. Normally he formed sentences like slow-moving trains, each word a carriage attached to the next, all puffing orderly out of his mouth. Now the clasps holding them together had broken and they were racing, each going its own way until he was babbling, almost stammering.

'Let's go out shopping tomorrow and get a new one. And some

clothes or treats or something for you. We can go to Thorntons and you can get whatever you like. You still like new dresses, don't you? And if we get the pink and white we'll need new curtains. Blinds. Frilly nets. Whatever you like. We need cheering up!'

I didn't respond. I'd been thinking about the day when we first met, in particular, him going out into the car park to give my father what-for. If I could pinpoint it, I'd say that was what had sold me on the idea of seeing him again. I'd imagined it would always be like that, him taking charge in life and protecting me from all the mess and confusion that seemed to hover around other people. With Will, I'd thought, it would be easier. I could stay inside, behind glass, and he'd take care of all the distressing, confusing elements, just as he'd done when my father wanted us to leave and I'd wanted to stay and have my photograph taken.

'Do you remember that party in Grange-over-Sands?' I asked.

Will smiled, 'When we met?'

'Yes.'

'I think about it a lot,' he said, reaching under the duvet for my hand. 'I still think of how lucky we were to bump into each other. Of course I remember.'

'What did you say to my father, when you went out into the car park?' I asked, withdrawing my hand. 'You never would tell me.'

'He was in a right temper, wasn't he?' Will said, as if he was talking about a child or a dog: a thing whose temper might be loud or amusing, but never held the possibility of harm.

'I don't quite remember,' he said, 'I was thinking of you watching me through the window and it was making me self-conscious.'

'You must have said something or he wouldn't have just driven away without me.'

Will reached for my hand again, couldn't find it, and rested his fingers on my thigh. He stroked, and it was curiously asexual, even though he hadn't tried to touch me at all since a good while before Grace was born.

'It was him who did most of the talking, really. I think he thought I was your teacher. He told me to tell you he was going home, and,' he paused, 'why do you want to know?'

'I'm just curious.'

'It's not very nice.'

'I don't expect it to be, he isn't a very nice person.'

'He said you wouldn't leave until the buffet was cleared away and he had better things to do than sit and watch you humiliate yourself in front of potential employers,' Will said slowly, stroking my thigh all the while.

'Humiliate?'

'Feed your face, stuff yourself to the gills. Something like that.' Will smiled, 'No wonder you didn't want to go home with him.'

'He didn't ask you to take me home?'

'No,' he shook his head, 'I couldn't get a word in edgeways.'

'But you did take me home?'

'I didn't have any choice, did I?' Will said. 'But I'm ever so glad I did, aren't you?'

I probably asked him about that because I thought the answer would hurt me, and the raw slice of it across the lard of my subdued mood would bring me to my senses and sharpen me up enough to think. It did hurt, but not in the way that I expected. Far from shaking me clear, I felt myself sinking back into the quicksand of a marriage that began because neither of us had any other choice.

'We shouldn't dwell on the past,' he said, 'any of it. We'll have a good time, we'll get some really nice things and forget about all of this.'

I could almost see him with a table and brush, eagerly pasting over the cracks.

'You've got a doctor's appointment,' I said.

'This is more important. Those pills don't make a bit of difference. I need to move on and I can, we both can. We can put this behind us if we're together,' he gently touched my face again, pushed my hair away from my mouth so he could see me better. 'You need to forget all about this. Both of us do.' Whether he meant the bruises, or how I'd got them, I couldn't tell.

'And there's no reason,' his voice wavered, 'I mean, you're still young enough, there isn't any reason why we couldn't try again, is there?'

'For another baby?' I couldn't keep the contempt out of my voice.

'Well,' he smiled damply, 'let's just get tomorrow done with. A new bed. We deserve it! All new pillows and sheets too. Whatever colour you like!' He was starting to sound hysterical again, pleading, and I didn't like it.

'I can't understand why you want to go through the bother of finding and buying a new bed, as well as everything else. I asked for it years ago. *This mattress, Annie,*' I said, mimicking him *'is guaranteed for twenty years and what's more, it's specially designed so people of varying sizes can lie down on it side by side!'*

He flinched but I carried on. 'It's too late for that now,' I said, 'a bed and a bag of sweets, is that it?'

'Don't be like that,' he said quietly, 'I'm trying. Things are different now.'

'A twenty-year mattress. It isn't much of a wedding present. Other girls get diamond earrings! Trips to islands in the sun! A bed!' We rolled apart from each other, the mattress creaking slightly. I looked at the cobwebs on the ceiling, the mouldy patch near the tasselled lamp shade that looked like a gun.

'Do you remember that conversation we had about sleeping with the baby when you were expecting, Annie?' Will asked. 'You were complaining about the mattress then. I should have listened, shouldn't I?'

'It never worked, did it?' I said, the atmosphere cooling again, us slipping back into conversation. 'People of varying sizes, my foot. You were always waking up in the middle of the night gasping for breath because I'd rolled over on you.'

We laughed. Well, Will did. I giggled a little and because it hurt, I took a deep breath and had to stop.

'The health visitor warned you about it,' I said, 'she said it wasn't safe. And you said you didn't get cot death in cultures where the babies aren't left to sleep on their own in cots.'

'I know what I said, Annie. I know.'

'*They don't have a word for it in Africa, or in India, did you know that? Much safer with mother!*' It was getting easier to do his voice, the self-righteous, slow way of talking that he had, the way he was always quoting from books no one had heard of.

He put his face against the pillow.

'I know!' he said. 'What are you trying to say? That it's my fault? Don't you think I don't know that already? My fault!'

He raised his fists and started hitting himself on the forehead like it belonged to someone else. 'My fault! My fault! My fault!'

I think he was expecting me to restrain him, but I moved back slightly and held my breath until he stopped. He had never been that volatile, not in the past.

'I didn't want her in with us,' I said, 'it was you, you insisted. It was all right for you,' I said bitterly, remembering, 'you were fast asleep and oblivious, it was me who was wide awake while she was sucking at me for hours on end.'

He was still out of breath, his forehead red from where he'd punched it.

'I remember what I said to you,' he said, 'I go over it in my head every day. Every night, for hours. It's why I don't sleep. Co-sleeping is best for baby; I was like a broken record, wasn't I?'

I nodded, 'And I never said anything about cot death or smothering. It was you, you did. Whoever heard of someone smothering a baby *in their sleep*?'

Will turned and I was expecting him to touch my hair again, or put his hand around the back of my neck. It was funny. I didn't think I had missed sleeping with him, but being in the warm, just lying there like that chatting. It reminded me of what it was like sometimes; Sunday mornings, bank holidays. He'd bring up coffee and read the papers while I worked my way through a stack of glossies he'd brought back from the surgery, running my fingers over the shiny pages and coveting, while underneath the duvet we tapped our bare feet together. He didn't touch me now, he just frowned, and studied me.

'What did you say?'

'When?'

'Just now?'

'You said it. Whoever heard of smothering a baby in their sleep?'

My face felt hot and cold. 'You never stopped saying it. You wouldn't be told. It was you, you reading those blinking Sears books.'

'In their sleep,' he murmured, looking away from me and edging backwards so no part of our bodies touched. I knew he was doing it, I could see it a mile off because I'd spent years edging away in the night like that myself, my flesh cringing backwards from him while he slept, breathing shallowly so my stomach wouldn't touch his back.

'And you never slept,' he said. 'Never – that's what you said. You said you couldn't. Apparently she fed for six hours on the trot and the only time you ever slept was during the day if you put her in the cot.'

'She should have been in the cot,' I insisted quietly. 'It was your idea for her to be in with us, not mine. You can't blame me.'

Will looked at me sharply and I leaned away from him to see my bloodied face reflected in his swimming eyes.

'I don't want a new bed,' I said, 'there isn't any need. And I don't want to get a new baby either.' I felt angry at what had happened to me that afternoon, angry that even after everything he still wanted to carry on and try to recreate what I'd been so pleased to escape from.

Will sat up and his gown fell open. I looked away from the black hair on his white, flabby chest. He looked at me carefully again and then wiped his hands across his face as if to clean away whatever it was he was seeing.

'Now come on, you're not yourself. No one would be, in the circumstances. Why don't you pop some clean clothes on and we'll get you off to the hospital? That eye is going to need some stitches.'

He was right. It had started to bleed again and my hair was sticky. There were smudges of blood on the pillow and a bright smear across the back of his hand. I looked at it, almost hypnotised by the slash of colour and took a deep breath.

'I am not going to the bloody hospital,' I said, 'I am not going shopping. I am not going to your parents' this weekend, I am not going to another one of those dances, I am not going to have my glands checked, my aura massaged, my metabolic system palpitated. I'm not going to a Farmers' Market, to Weight Watchers, to a Coping with SIDS meeting. I am not,' I said slowly, 'going with you anywhere, ever again in my life.'

I spoke quietly but he reacted as if I'd shouted. It would have been my tone and the uncharacteristic profanity that shocked him. I'd always been so compliant.

His mouth opened and closed a few more times but he didn't say anything and the only sounds I could hear were his lips popping like a goldfish and my own breathing, fast and heavy like I'd been running. He was half sitting, half lying, and I regarded his confused, fussing face. We'd got so familiar with each other over the years we'd spent rubbing along in each other's company that he just didn't see me anymore. It went both ways: when he was at work I had trouble remembering what he looked like. Only the things that are strange to us stick in the memory, and I'd become strange to him, doing something unexpected again after such a long time of being predictable.

'There's no need for all that, Annie, you just need a nap. We can go to the hospital later.' He made a show of examining my face. 'There's nothing life-threatening. It can wait a few hours until you're feeling better.'

His words were like warm water, sloshing around my throat and rising. Slowly, I moved my hand and let it fall on the heavy glass snow globe on the bedside table. He followed the movement of my arm and was looking at my hand as I raised it and allowed the globe to roll over my palm and slip from my fingers. It connected easily with his head, and rolled over his body onto the pillows.

He shouted and pushed himself backwards up the bed, his bare feet scrambling over the duvet, the cord of his dressing gown coming loose and winding around a stringy thigh. The globe had caught him just over the eyebrow and right away he was bleeding, the blood appearing like a dark red curtain sliding down his face. It caught on his top lip, and as he moved his mouth open and closed it ran either side of it like a moustache. It must have hurt and I regretted that.

'Annie!' he said, as if I was a toddler that had just knocked over a glass of milk. 'What's come over you? Are you concussed?'

I couldn't leave it at that. He'd be convincing the both of us it was an accident; making me call someone to take him to the hospital and telling me in a couple of weeks we'd be laughing about it. He wasn't even that badly hurt; we'd probably still have to go shopping. 'You're that clumsy,' I imagined him saying ruefully, once we were both back at home with matching bandages, stitches and gauze and mugs of fair-trade hot chocolate. Sitting cosy in identical armchairs with his and hers slippers, preparing for an early night in our nice new bed.

Two paracetamol each to help with the headaches and nothing more said about it. The thought was intolerable.

The globe had rolled down his chest and was resting between the pillows. Busy trying to stop the bleeding with the edge of the duvet, he didn't see as I picked it up again, moaning at the pain in my ribs as I heaved myself out of the bed and lifted the ball over my head. His blood was on the curved glass, retreating into beads on the shiny surface like rain on a car bonnet. I felt it sliding under my fingers. His gown had fallen completely open and as he turned away I saw his backside, the bony protrusion of a hip, shrunken testicles dangling.

I leaned backwards and groaned as I heaved the globe onto his skull. It shattered, spraying both of us with water and tiny polystyrene balls, as numerous as confetti. By the time the paramedics arrived he'd stopped breathing.

The next few hours were fairly frantic and I'd been quickly swept along on a tide of other people's expectations. Domestic violence is a growing problem and every police officer in Lancashire has received special training in recognising the signs and dealing with its victims sensitively and compassionately.

'It is no longer a private affair,' one officer told me, sternly, and then, after looking both ways down the corridor we were standing in, said, 'you deserve a pat on the back if you ask me. Look at the state of you.'

I touched my face gently and asked for a glass of water and a tissue, both of which he provided. As I wiped my nose, a polystyrene ball fell from my hair onto the floor and rolled along the shiny wood. It was caught by a draught, someone further along opening a door perhaps, and I followed it with my eyes as it bumped along, veering in response to some imperfections in the surface and finally getting wedged into a crack between the edges of the pale laminate. I lost interest in it and looked back up to the policeman. They really do wear radios all the time, even inside the police station, and it fizzed and chattered at his belt. He took my arm gently and guided me along.

'Can't be seen to condone it, of course. You'll have to go to court.

Bail you if I could, but stick it out, love; tell the truth and you'll be home before you know it.'

'Will I?' I said quietly.

'Anyone would have snapped. And you're only young. My little sister got mixed up with someone once. He made a mistake. A big mistake. I was the only copper that got involved, and let's just say the slimy little fucker won't be using his fists on a woman again. You got no brothers to help you out? Your dad not about? No? Well you didn't have any choice then, did you? Shall I call your mum, sweetheart?'

He said I could use the phone myself if I wanted to. Call anyone I wanted, for free! There wasn't anyone, so I just called Will's surgery and left a message for the new receptionist to pass on, letting everyone know he wouldn't be back.

'Don't cry love, really,' he said, when I'd finished on the telephone. 'The doctor'll be here soon. She'll give you something to help you sleep a bit. Be over before you know it.' He patted me on the shoulder again.

Looking back it seems almost underhand, the way I let them make their assumptions about the origins of my injuries. For a long time I was quite at a loss to explain it to myself. Now I know that I was no doubt suffering from concussion after Cliff's antics, and probably more than a touch of shock. In case you didn't know, both of these are medical, clinical conditions that can have dire effects on a person's awareness and understanding. You can look *that* up in any public library.

The next ten months passed by in a blur, full of practical and legal matters I paid little attention to. I waited in offices, sat in court with my best clothes on, was asked to give renditions of what had happened, hear others who had known Will and me do the same. I kept quiet and looked at my hands. My hands: fat and harmless, scuffed pink nail polish, a grey curve of dirt under each fingernail and my wedding ring, which I would never be able to take off, half absorbed and sinking into the flesh.

The time passed very quickly because I was looking forward to going home so much. The wait had its frustrations, of course it did. It occurred to me more than once that I'd just swapped one kind of prison for another. But my black days were just that, days, and they passed. The rest of the time there was the constant sympathy, the pats on the back from the other women, the assurances from my solicitor that when it was all over I could go and do whatever I liked.

On the last day the solicitor practised with me what I was going to say and how I was going to say it. He advised me not to hold back if I felt like crying as I told my story. In the courtroom he set up a projector and showed everyone pictures of my injuries. The men and women whose job it was to decide what was best to do in these matters gasped. I looked at my own face, five times larger than life. I didn't look my best: my chin was bloody and I was wearing a shocked, slightly sleepy expression that the swelling had pressed onto my features. It was quite exciting, almost like being on television.

That, I thought, as I sat in my best clothes on the hard chair and looked at the screen with the rest of them, was the face of someone who had suffered, had been physically and emotionally injured, someone who deserved a bit of compassion, a bit of human understanding. Accidents happen, and people should be allowed to recover from them and start a new life. I like to think if I had been in their position, and one of them had been in my shoes, I would have shown the same empathy and decency and let them go home too.

After it was done, the solicitor offered to call me a taxi to take me to the home of a family member or friend. I thought of the house in Cumbria, but it had been years since I last saw my father, and I had no wish to return there, whatever the circumstances. Now I know that he was already gone, and had died in the small flat he'd moved to after he'd sold my mother's cottage. Died sitting in front of a Calor gas heater that had started to smoke and alerted the downstairs neighbours. It was something to do with his liver, and I didn't even know he drank. So there was no cottage to go back to, even if I'd tried.

The solicitor gave me a leaflet that contained the number of a home where I could stay, for free, with other women who had suffered at the hands of their husbands, but the thought of an unfamiliar bed and strange food made me feel tired and weak, and I realised how much I wanted to go back home. Against his advice, I got on a train, waited for a bus, got into a taxi and eventually went back to my house. The light and noise and the largeness of outside frightened me and I had trouble with the trams. By the time I found myself outside my own front door it was dark, I was hungry, tired and hoping I would be able to discover which drawer Will kept all the takeaway menus in.

I must admit, as well as everything I have already mentioned, I did feel a slight sense of trepidation as I turned the key in the lock. You must understand, the last time I'd seen the place the stairwell had been jammed with the fluorescent uniforms of paramedics and police officers, but as soon as I got into the hallway I knew that the whole place was empty and quiet, the sheets on the bed slightly rumpled, but cold.

Mr Tips scraping at the back door, emaciated and flea-ridden but overjoyed to see me, woke me in the morning and together we made plans for moving to a new house. Two busy months later we were gone, off in a taxi with a whole new life laid out in front of us.

22

For the second time that afternoon I heard a key in the front door, but this time, sitting comfortably with Lucy on the settee, I knew I had nothing to fear for it could only be Neil.

He hesitated in the hallway for a second and then the door opened and he came in.

'You've been a while,' I said, 'I've been waiting. Still, boys will be boys. Shall I make you something to eat?'

'What the fuck?' Neil said, once he saw the mess Lucy had made on the floor, on the couch and over my new dress. He sounded like he was in a film: it's just the sort of thing a person would say, given the situation. I suppose that is why he said it. He came over to me and I could not prevent him from laying a hand on Lucy's chest and putting his face close to hers.

'She had a fall...' I began, but Neil elbowed me aside.

'Fall!' he said, and headed towards the house telephone. I'd prepared myself for just such an eventuality, and went back to Lucy.

'Neil,' I said, and he turned to me, his hand on the receiver, 'you'd better not do that. You're not yourself. Just listen to me and we can sort out this mess,' I gestured towards her chest with my scissors, 'in a few minutes.' Neil looked at me, at Lucy, and at my hand.

'She needs the hospital!' he said, and picked up the telephone.

'It won't work...' I said, but Neil was already punching at the buttons in a panic. I waited until he held the receiver up and saw for himself that, for reasons of strategy, I had snipped the cord.

I sat down next to Lucy and patted at her calves.

'I know you're worried, Neil,' I said, 'I would be too. She's taken a fall, but she's got a tea towel over the worst bit, and,' I swallowed, 'I didn't even know the scissors were in my hand!'

'Oh God,' Neil said, coming over to touch her face again, 'what have you done to her? What have you done to her hair?'

Her face looked huge, partly because it was so slack and pale, and partly because her hair was gone and the brown fronds and tendrils that usually framed her face were lying in a heap in front of the couch. She was breathing, there was nothing to worry about: you could see her nostrils flaring slightly from time to time, and if you licked your wrist and held it over her face you could feel the gasps, shallow, irregular little pants. Still, I will admit that the absence of hair made the situation look direr than it actually was.

'It'll grow back,' I said gently, 'she was really hot. It helped cool her down, she's barely sweating at all now, and I was hardly going to take her clothes off, was I? Best thing for her, I think.' I kicked at the clumps on the floor. 'Good job you've got a hard floor,' I said, chuckling, 'you'd never get it out of a carpet, not even with one of those special bagless Hoovers.'

The thing about her being too hot wasn't entirely true, I'll admit it to you now, just as I planned to admit it to Neil later, once he'd come to his senses and things had settled down between us. Lucy was very easily the sort of person who could blind a man with the obvious force of her physical appeal. My own charms were more subtle, and to assist the transition, it seemed only reasonable to take Lucy down a peg or two. I'd had the scissors in my hand anyway, and it wasn't as if it hurt her. She was fast asleep, or at least pretending to be, through the whole operation. Split ends!

'Annie, she's really ill. You can see that, can't you? Will you let me get my mobile from the car?'

'I prefer a carpet myself. You've got a lovely front room, but it will be so much nicer when we get some carpet down. Something with a pattern, to hide any spills. I can help you choose. You'll need something to cover up that mark anyway. And the couch will have to go.'

'Come away from her, Annie. Give me those scissors and let me help her,' Neil pleaded. 'She's dying!'

'Nonsense, Neil. She's trying to manipulate you. Didn't you ever do the same thing to your mother when you wanted to stay off school? The fact that she's so good at it is exactly why I've been forced to take the action that I have.'

Neil walked towards me and I held up my scissors until he backed away again. Cruel to be kind.

'Sit down,' I said firmly, 'I'll keep that tea towel on there, like that,'

I pressed hard, and Lucy shifted slightly and moaned, 'no point making a mess of your shirt. I'm covered anyway.'

Neil sat down, hammered on his knees with his fists and then stood up again.

'How long has she been like that?' he asked, rubbing his hands over his face as if he was washing.

'Long enough for us to have a good chat. I know you were finding broaching the topic with her difficult, but I've done it now. It'll be a load off your mind.'

'Annie –'

'I know, Neil, but one of us had to do it. It wasn't fair to keep stringing her along,' I laughed. 'She had a baby magazine up there, under the bed. Did you know that?'

'No,' Neil replied, the muscles in his jaw loosening.

'Well, there you go. It wasn't fair to let her carry on planning.'

'Annie, the hospital, please.'

'Blood always looks worse than it is,' I said, 'and what you were thinking when you let her choose an oatmeal-coloured living-room suite is beyond me.'

I looked again at the mess Lucy had made, the ooze on the sofa cushions, dry and itchy on my wrists and greasy on my palms where I held the tea towel. The dark, offally smell of it filled the room but I knew if I stood to open the window I'd risk losing my advantage, and it was clear Neil needed just a few more minutes to widen his perspective.

'What happened to her?'

'You must have expected she'd be disappointed with us,' I said, 'the transition, it's going to be harder on her than it is for anyone else. But she's young,' I said, and looked at the jagged ends of her hair and the stubbly part where her fringe had been, 'and reasonably pretty. It won't take her too long to find someone else.'

'Annie, let me get another towel for her. Something bigger for you to press on.'

'Did she read the book I gave her?' I inquired. 'I thought it might come in handy, given the circumstances.' I paused. 'Only I didn't find it when I was clearing out her things.'

'I'm going to get a towel,' Neil said, but didn't move. He rubbed his chin again, and I heard the crackle of stubble against his palm in the stillness of the room. 'It'll be tidier if I get something else,' he said slowly, 'you don't want to spoil that nice new dress, do you?'

'Now you're starting to talk sensibly,' I said, pulling away the sodden rag and letting it drop heavily onto the floor. 'Off you go.'

I heard him go upstairs, and when he came back he was holding a pink towel over his arm like a wine waiter and he was crying.

'What have you done all that for?' he said. 'Her mother brought her home from the hospital in that babygro. Shit, Annie.' He handed me the towel and I applied it to her abdomen.

'Let me call someone. Please. I won't say anything to anyone – we'll say she fell down, and...'

'It's just like you,' I said, smiling, 'you're such a knight in shining armour. Do you remember when you helped me and I was in a state like this?'

Neil shook his head, but his eyes were on Lucy.

'At that bus stop,' I prompted, but he didn't respond. 'Well, my face was all mashed up. The police had to take photographs because it was past description. You wouldn't have recognised me.'

'What if I call Barry!' Neil said, alight with inspiration. He was already heading towards the door, 'Barry might be in. Barry'll get here quicker. No flashing lights. Shall I do that, Annie?'

His hand was on the door handle before I answered him by moving the scissors closer to Lucy. I didn't like myself for doing it, but he'd left me with no other choice. I knew I wasn't really going to hurt her, it isn't in my nature, but while he doubted it I had a way to keep him with me until the poison of her spell worked its way out of his system. I've never had the experience myself, but I have watched certain documentaries, and to me, it was like trying to prevent someone who is addicted to drugs from taking more of them. At that moment, as from the second I gained entry to his house, his emotional welfare was my top priority.

'Best not,' I said, 'not for a bit anyway. We've got plans to make. Living arrangements, packing and so on.'

'Barry'll have a bag in his house. He'll know what to do. You know Barry, Annie, he'll understand.'

I shook my head firmly and Neil very slowly removed his hand from the door. 'Perhaps we can contact Barry after we've come to an agreement about the packing. And not before.'

'Packing?'

'I've started on Lucy's,' I said, 'as you've seen. Pity she didn't read that book, but I think I've had time to fill her in on everything she'll need to know for the coming months. You needn't worry about her. I've made her well aware of the alternatives.'

'Alternatives?' Neil said.

'Internet matchmaking, speed dating, and so on. It's hardly our concern, is it? I just wanted to make sure I had all the angles covered. Don't want you worrying, do we? Now. Packing. We can get mine done very quickly, I don't have much. We have to think about moving.' I smiled, because I was giving him something to look forward to.

'Press on it a bit more, you're letting it go,' Neil said.

'I realise you're very settled in this house, but I'm afraid we can't stay. My parents-in-law – they know where I live now,' I began.

'Right,' Neil said, never taking his eyes from Lucy.

'You may as well know that my husband is dead – I'm quite unattached, so there's nothing to worry about there. The only blasts from the past you'll get from me could come from Billy and Ada – which is why I think it's better that we move sooner rather than later.'

'Billy and Ada?' Neil looked at me at last, 'What the hell are you talking about?'

'They're his parents,' I said briskly. 'I can explain all this later. Just a couple of old dears who haven't heard of the concept of self-defence. Thankfully, they're in the minority.'

'Self-defence?' Neil said, and started fiddling with the remains of Lucy's telephone. 'Your husband? Your little girl?'

'Had to,' I said briskly, 'but it doesn't matter now. We've got a future to plan.'

Neil let the broken phone slide out of his hands to the floor. The screen was cracked and the sleek silver casing split open to expose a jumble of coloured wires. We both stared at it for a few moments and then Neil looked at me, and pulled his chair closer.

'Yes, but we couldn't have much of a future together if we had to explain what happened to Lucy...' he said quietly.

'There are ways around most things,' I said.

'But it would be so much easier for us to –' he paused and gulped, as if he was going to be sick, 'we could drive her to the hospital ourselves. Us two in the front, together, and Lucy in the back. Then she'd get better and there wouldn't be any –' he swallowed again, 'consequences for you.'

I sighed, and shook my head.

'You're still under her thumb,' I said wearily, 'after all I've done for you. She's not important at all, you just don't realise it, because she's, she's done something to your mind.'

'No,' Neil said urgently, shaking his head, 'she hasn't, Annie. She really hasn't. I just don't want you to get in trouble – that's all I can think about.'

I didn't say anything and Neil stood up again, 'I can't just sit here,' he said loudly, pacing, 'I can't sit here while she's lying there bleeding to death.'

As if she knew she was being talked about, Lucy's eyes opened and she moaned again. Neil darted over and knelt beside her but I encouraged him away.

'Look at her hair,' I urged, 'you can't want her now. Not really.'

Neil kicked the leg of the coffee table very hard just then. Lucy's untouched mug of tea sloshed onto the glass surface, the driftwood rattled and the remote control jumped onto the floor.

'I don't care about her fucking hair!'

'Calm yourself!' I brandished the scissors until I could see that he'd taken a few deep breaths. 'You're going to feel better in a few minutes. Trust me on this, you will.'

'We haven't got a few minutes!' Neil said urgently. I saw he was thinking about making a grab for the scissors and I shook my head. I rested the points of them very gently in the notch between Lucy's collarbones.

'Sit down now, Neil. Help yourself to that biscuit, if you like. Lucy didn't feel up to it, silly girl, but as I told her, the sugar will help with the shock.' He sat, and held the biscuit between his finger and thumb, but despite my nods of encouragement, he didn't eat.

'So what are we going to do?' he asked, crumbling it into fragments. 'Just sit here, until it's too late?'

'Neil,' I sighed, 'relax. I realise we haven't been alone together much before, but that is something we're both going to have to get used to. There is a process of adjustment we could start right now by sitting nicely and having a conversation.' I bit my bottom lip and frowned, 'I thought you would be grateful!'

Neil pulled his chair closer and the legs scraped the floor. He leaned forward and looked into my face.

'What you've done – it's finished now. You don't need to do any more. I'm here. Now it's my job to look after everything.'

He did have a point. He was the man, after all. I had been forced to take the lead in establishing our relationship but it would have been highly inappropriate for me to continue holding the reins once he was in his right mind and in a fit state to take them himself. I giggled and nearly relinquished the scissors to his open hand.

'At last, you're seeing sense,' I said. 'You just can't imagine what all this means to me,' I said, as he came closer. 'I've had some very difficult experiences, and you don't know it yourself but it was you helping me at that blinking bus stop that made me see there was someone else out there waiting for me. It gave me the courage to end things with my husband, and...'

'Put those down, so I can hold your hand,' Neil interrupted. I blushed, and looked away.

'Us being together like this, after all the waiting and subterfuge, those messages in the rubbish bins, the code with the landing lights, it's like coming out from under a cloud. For both of us. I'm not going to be on my own and you're finally out from under her. I didn't think I'd ever get you free,' I laughed. It all seemed so simple. 'Neither of us is ever going to feel bad ever again.'

I looked up at him through damp eyelashes. He wasn't looking at me, and I wondered if I had gone too far. Some men are notoriously commitment-shy and I didn't want to place another burden on his back when one had so recently been lifted.

'But listen to me, going on,' I said, 'you needn't think I've got it all planned out. I'm quite willing to take the lead from you. Perhaps you'd like us to keep to our own houses and just go on a series of dates to begin with? I'll need to meet your family of course, although I'm sorry to say I don't have any of my own to reciprocate. It should make deciding who to invite for Christmas easier, though!' Neil didn't join me in my rueful laughter. 'Listen to me! Just tell me to shut up any time you like. I won't take offence.' I took a breath. 'You tell me, how do you see our relationship progressing?'

Because of my reading, I'd had the whole speech planned out for weeks, and I felt confident in being so frank because to conduct oneself in such a manner is modern, assertive and cannot fail to give the right impression. Having said that, I'd spent so long planning my words and practising my inflections that I'd given little thought to how Neil himself would respond. He merely edged himself between my knees and the coffee table and let his hand fall onto my head.

It had been months since anyone had touched me. Longer than that. There were Sangita's little pats on the arms while we had our chats, and of course the ministrations of Jessica while I was at the salon, but those weren't real touches. His palm rested against my scalp for a few seconds and then he moved his fingers through my hair. The feel of it sent a river of goose pimples down the back of my neck and they unrolled down my spine like a row of falling dominoes. I think it is hard to explain how much human beings need gentleness. As much as they need food and water, at least. I'd hardly noticed I had been lacking it until he touched me and my whole skin started singing.

'You are lovely,' Neil said. He was so shy his hand was shaking and his voice came out quite constricted and expressionless. I could hardly blame him. My own hands were trembling nineteen to the dozen. I'd let Lucy's pink towel slip to the floor and bowed my head into my lap so that to an outsider it must have looked like he was the Pope giving me a blessing.

'That's very nice of you to say so,' I began, but because he'd whispered, and I'd forgot myself and used my ordinary voice, it damaged the atmosphere a bit.

'Lovely,' Neil said again, so that was all right. He moved his hand to the back of my neck, and I kept my face turned downwards, looking at the stains on my new dress and the tacky mess of my hands. It didn't seem to matter to him at all.

'Steady progress is the best progress,' I said, suddenly terrified. It had been so long. 'Will always used to say that. Nice and gradual.

Tortoise and the hare. I don't think I'm quite ready for anything...'
I babbled, but the sensations running over my scalp, down my back
and through my thighs, right into my stomach and the very heart of
me, made me fall silent.

Even when I think of that moment now, I get an old thrill of it in
my chest: just a relic, but it's there all the same. It's enough to make
me close my eyes and feel quite dizzy, and something tells me it will
never fade completely. Neil continued to rub his fingertips along my
scalp and no matter that Lucy was lying right next to me, or my
natural shy nature, my past experience with men had not deserted
me and I lifted my hands to the buttons on the front of my dress.

My fingers were sticky and clogged with clinging strands of
Lucy's hair and the scissors which I still grasped got in the way, but
I slipped the buttons through their holes as far down as my waist. It
gaped open and I lifted my arm and pushed it back over my shoulders. I felt it whisper down my back and fall onto Lucy's feet. The
material gathered around my stomach and I kept my face lowered to
hide the burning in my cheeks. While I've done it before and I know
very well what men expect and what is required of a woman, the
experience has never made it any easier on the nerves. The air in the
room hit my skin and Neil didn't move his hand, or say anything. I
shrugged my shoulders a little in case he hadn't noticed, everything
jiggled in my best under-things and I heard him inhale quickly.

'Neil?' I said quietly, after a few more moments had passed. I was
getting a little cold and looked down at myself. My chest was puckered with goose pimples and smeared with blood. After all my efforts
to prepare myself, it had come to this, and I was quite stricken. At
least the best underwear is red, I thought, at least there's that.

'Neil, is it all right?' I asked, my voice rasping. My fingers knotted
themselves backwards and forwards through the loops in the scissor
handles.

'It's...' he began, and moved his hand around my neck to tilt my
face back. I caught the strange, crumpled expression on his face for
half a second before I leaned forward to him and closed my eyes,
thinking dimly, as if I was very far away from myself, that it would
be awful if the tea had made my breath smell bad.

At this point it is appropriate to refer you to something pertinent I read only this morning, which proves how well I am doing in my efforts to improve despite my difficult circumstances. The book is called *The Dating Game: How To Make Him Play For Keeps,* written by a very articulate American lady who explains how single women should behave to guard against being exploited and then cast aside by the men with whom they become romantically engaged. She speaks for the interests of the modern and independent woman, giving practical tips on the dignified and successful pursuit of a companion.

The book is remarkable. It even specifies such useful details as the best interval to leave before returning his phone call, and what to wear to give the impression that you are available, but not easily won.

Despite last year's efforts to educate myself, I hadn't come across that particular title. If I do feel any regret, it is that I didn't have a well-meaning friend to recommend it to me. I wish I'd read that book; it would have allowed me to see the warning signs and helped me notice what sort of man Neil was. I let myself trust too easily and there's no crime in that. Clearly, I have more time to read these days. I am quite certain, that if I'd had *The Dating Game* with me during that time I would have handled the situation more skilfully, and will do, should it arise again.

The blow came out of nowhere. There is a gap in my memory here. The concussion, of course, but the emotional toll of the cruellest of deceptions couldn't have helped. When I opened my eyes, I was lying on the floor with my dress tangled around my thighs. The indignity of the position was exacerbated by the fact that when I tried to get up the pain in my head and the general disadvantages of my size prevented me, and I tumbled back down, hurting my thigh on the shattered remains of Lucy's telephone.

I blinked and felt blood hot in my hair. My head felt like it was glowing and whether that was from the memory of Neil's touch or the effect of my unexpected injury I couldn't tell. I looked about for my scissors because even then I had not given up hope, but I couldn't find them. The knotted piece of driftwood from the table was lying beside me – he'd snatched it up as I closed my eyes and leaned into his arms. He'd hit me!

Neil was crouching in front of the settee stroking Lucy's face and imploring her to open her eyes. He didn't pay attention to me at all, but the fact that she was lying there as good as gold and I was the one wailing must have let him know which one of us was the more badly injured. She'd only fallen, for goodness' sake! I'd given her a little poke and she'd tumbled onto the floor! It was her own fault: those stupid shoes and bird-like, insubstantial limbs.

Neil must have got his mobile phone from the car while I was unconscious. I was still struggling on the floor trying to get each button into its corresponding hole when we both heard sirens.

'Thank God,' he said, and stood up to unlock the door without even looking at me.

When the officers and paramedics came in it was almost merciful – I didn't have to lie there incapacitated, forced to watch him stroke Lucy's horrible stubbly head for one second longer. The déjà vu was so strong, so peculiarly persistent, that I just lay there and watched. I made no attempt to draw their attention to my own injuries. I merely observed those fluorescent uniforms barging their way into the house and listened to the hushed chatter from neighbours outside. The intermittent blue light fell through the curtains onto my face, blocked now and then by the backs of the people who were fussing over Lucy. They carried her away and Neil followed, pointing back at me with his thumb.

'It was her, she did it,' he said, and finally, someone lent me a hand, hoisted me upright and pressed a gauze pad to my head. I looked at the new face, a woman with round chapped cheeks and blue mascara on her eyelashes.

'You'll need to come to hospital too,' she said, peeling back the gauze and parting my hair with her gloved fingers. I could smell the latex, sharp and powdery.

'Stitches, nothing life-threatening. You hurt anywhere else?'

'No,' I said, because what could she have done for that dragging feeling in my stomach, the stinging behind my eyelids and the lump in my throat.

'Just Casualty then,' she said, 'maybe overnight for observation.'

'Will I ride in the ambulance?' I said hopefully, and tried to catch Neil's eye but he was hurrying after Lucy's feet as they vanished through the door. I heard the doors slam and the engine start.

'You'll come with us,' someone said. I turned and saw the dark-blue uniforms of the police, and they linked their arms through mine, one on each side, and guided me out. Sangita was standing on the pavement, her hair unravelled from her plait and tumbling over her shoulders. I couldn't see her face because of it, but she was bending down low and holding someone's hands between hers, nodding, nodding, offering tea and sympathy, understanding and friendship and solidarity. It was Ada, and Billy was standing slightly to one side as they patted each other.

She looked up as I passed her, stared past me and beamed at the policeman to my left. I tried to grab the edges of the dress and pull them together to cover myself, but they grasped my forearms so tightly their fingers nearly disappeared into my flesh.

'I'll make sure the house is left secure,' she said, not even glancing at me, but looking between the black hats and sounding like one of the prefects at school, 'I'm the Neighbourhood...'

'Yes, we know,' he said, and pulled me on.

'A witness too,' she said, 'you'll need some statements from me and the other neighbours,' she was breathless, her eyes glittering. 'I'll organise Raymond and Doctor Choudhry, that's my husband the oncologist, to come to the station at their earliest conveniences.' She smiled, and her fingers went into her hair. 'I also,' she lowered her voice, 'have Mr and Mrs Fairhurst senior right here, who have some very important information for you.'

We were nearly in the car and she trotted after us breathlessly, leaving Billy and Ada sitting on my garden wall like crumpled heaps of laundry. A hand guided my head down and in. The car smelled powerfully new, and I knew I was going to be travel sick if they put the lights on and went fast.

'Shall I contact Charlie to keep him abreast of events, or will you?' she called plaintively, as the front doors closed and the policemen reached for their seatbelts.

'Buckle up please, Mrs Fairhurst,' he said over his shoulder and rolled the window down an inch.

'Leave it all to us, Mrs Choudhry. You go back home now, eh? Nothing more to see.'

They were still laughing at her as the car rolled out of the cul-de-sac and onto the main road. I hardly heard them because I was twisting in my seat to look out of the back window as the last glimpse of my house disappeared around the corner.

Epilogue

Dear Neil,

I thought it would be only polite, given the circumstances of our last meeting, for me to take a few minutes to pen you a letter and let you know how I am. You'll be pleased to know that my head injury has healed nicely and my doctor has assured me there will be no long-term effects. I can only imagine how this would prey on your mind, so allow yourself to be reassured on the matter of my physical health.

I wonder if you have a new neighbour yet? It would be foolish to suspect not: I know the house was sold months ago. I wish you well with new friendships – in all sincerity. My own living arrangements leave much to be desired, but as I keep reminding myself, they are only temporary. There's one window and most of it is frosted and shot through with a metal grid. I can't see a thing out of it, which adds insult to injury because when I came here I very specifically asked for a view. Whoever was in charge of allocating the rooms certainly had a sense of humour, because through the slits at the top of the window there is a view of sorts. Three inches' worth! Not to worry.

If you will allow me to speak personally to you, and at the risk of causing some disappointment, I will come to the main thrust of this letter. Neil, I do believe there was potential for us, but the task of sustaining our relationship through our separation is fraught with difficulty and the end result is uncertain. I don't like to gamble: long-distance relationships are well known to be beset by problems, and no one wants to commit themselves to a man in his absence only to find out later that he is an emotional cripple and totally incapable of any real intimacy. Please find it in your heart to understand.

They tell me that Lucy is quite recovered from her accident, and furthermore, is expecting a child. This confirms a suspicion that in my heart of hearts I had all along. Tell me, Neil: did you always prefer an unchallenging woman? I feel I can be as frank as this with you, given that I have not decided whether I will post this letter yet. One of the books I have been reading (*Weekend Fixes for a Broken Heart* – I can forward you the ISBN if you feel it would be useful for your own recovery) suggests that letters such as this one can assist one's progression, providing both catharsis and closure. It recommends that the letter itself should not be posted, but kept amongst one's most precious things for later rereading in moments of weakness. If you are reading this you will know if I have decided to follow that advice and let the page lie with my account of the events of last year or not. Whatever the case, and whatever your answer to my question, let's both of us behave nicely. To demonstrate that I have released you from our commitment with no hard feelings, I enclose a letter to Lucy too. You may read it if you wish, but I assure you it contains nothing more than friendly advice gleaned from my own experiences of motherhood.

I will move onto more pleasant subjects. I have no doubt your thoughts will be focused on what the future holds for you, and in this I feel we have something in common. I think of what is to come constantly. I will need somewhere welcoming to settle before too long, I hope, and planning my new life takes up an increasing amount of my time, which, I am told, is a positive sign. The property pages come with the daily newspapers and when I get hold of them I always make sure I take a good look.

I've been told off more than once for defacing the papers before the next person can get a read of them, but the photographs I take for my records keep me centred on my ambitions and are an aid to restless thoughts.

My thoughts are generally untroubled. There is occasional sleeplessness, of course, which is hardly surprising given the standard of the accommodation. I often spend whole nights listening to the creak and bang of doors, the echoes of footsteps on polished floors and the distant sounds of cat-calls and laughter. There is, I have been informed, medication available that would assist with this insomnia, but so far I have declined it. They did not insist, although it was intimated that if matters do not improve, the choice may be taken out of my hands. I prefer to rely on my inner recourses and have said as much. There is no need to worry about me!

There is only one thing that I can be said to lack: I crave fresh air and outside. An hour's drive from where I used to live there is a green hill. In springtime, as my husband informed me on our last visit there, the grass is punctuated with thousands of tiny yellow and white flowers. The view is stunning, and if they haven't marred it by mobile phone masts or wind turbines, will remain so for many years to come. Perhaps you know it? Although I didn't take much interest at the time, I think he was correct in insisting that it be the place where the small white container we collected from the crematorium should be relieved of its contents. It looked like a little salt pot, and he popped the top open and sprinkled powder all over the grass before we went home. The wind was blowing, it was very cold, and I asked to go and sit in the car – I suppose it goes without saying that now I'd be content with a bracing wind or even torrential rain, just to feel the grass under my feet and see those yellow buds beginning to bloom. I think the flowers will be appearing there now and I would like to see them. You can get tired of grey – even the food here is dust-coloured. Perhaps if you ever find yourself in the vicinity you could visit them for me and let me know how they are.

I have just reread this little letter and it does sound melancholy, doesn't it? Perhaps I should have postponed beginning it until after lunch. When I am fatigued, as I am this morning, it does become more of an effort to keep my spirits high. I believe anyone in my shoes would experience mild pangs of downheartedness on a very occasional basis. Nostalgia has become a habitual comfort: some of my fondest memories are of you and the happy times we shared, and for this I thank you. Remembering your kindnesses to me has got me through many a wakeful night. Sometimes when the morning comes I am as refreshed as if I had slept.

Admittedly, my recollections do not always sustain me like this. Curiously, one or two memories of my husband play on my mind in my more morose moments. I will share them with you so you know what I mean – you were always a friend I could confide in.

Once, when we'd been waiting at a pedestrian crossing, I'd grown impatient and had stepped out onto the road before the green man had flashed. Will had snapped out his arm like a barrier, moving so quickly I bumped into his elbow. A car passed in front of us, whooshing along where I would have stepped and sucking the air behind it as it went. I saw a glimpse of us both reflected in the windows. Will was looking at me out of the corner of his eye and reaching into my coat pocket so he could hold my hand. He had fine hair that blew upward with the draught of the car zipping past. The closed, pale look he had about him after our daughter went made him look like a stranger. He reminded me of a ghost, or a startled baby. Our reflection was only there a second, less than that, and then the car was gone, my fingers were clammily tucked into his dry hand, and we'd crossed. I don't even remember where we were going. I remember our reflection sometimes at night.

Or I remember the time he came home from work with a packet of yellow primrose seeds. They'd come with a gardening magazine someone had left in the waiting room and when he saw them he'd thought of me because a few days before I'd complained that our garden was a bit dull, and why couldn't we have some flowers like next door did? I'd forgotten about the conversation entirely, but he hadn't. Still, seeds or not, I never planted them. Just didn't get around to it. When I was packing up the house I found them between a couple of cook books in the kitchen, rattled them about in the packet for a moment and then chucked them away.

I believe these memories demonstrate the spectacular lack of closeness that we had during our marriage, and perhaps that is why it saddens me to think of them. I did do my best. I always do. I don't like to dwell on things, but even when I'm busy doing something else, the episodes crowd at the edges of my thinking, clamouring for attention like neglected children. I am beginning to wonder if they have some relevance I have not yet been able to decipher.

Yours in friendship,

Annie Fairhurst
(Your former neighbour)

THE END

Acknowledgments

For giving an early draft careful and critical attention: Richard Hirst and Kirk Houghton. For going above and beyond the call of duty: the staff and students at the Manchester University Centre for New Writing. For making it happen: Daniela de Groote, Angeline Rother-mundt and Anthony Goff. For practical support which meant the difference between writing and not writing: Elizabeth Harper and Ben Ashworth. For being in my corner: Jenny Diski, Jane Gallagher, Anne Fine and Rob Jones. For not reading this book and providing splendid and unexpected distractions: Duncan McGowan and Baby Skye.